SEPTEMBER THOMAS

Of Dragons and Defiance

A Three Kingdoms Novel

First edition

ISBN: 978-1-7342545-5-6

Editing by Fiona McLaren
Cover art by Rebecca Frank
Illustration by Natalia Junqueira

This book was professionally typeset on Reedsy.
Find out more at reedsy.com

To the strongest woman I know.
Mom.

Contents

Preface   iv

The Gods & Goddesses of Idilea   v

Lexicon & Pronunciation Guide   vi

1 The Blood Moon   1

2 A Strange Sense of Calm   18

3 Lives Stolen   47

4 Nothing Left   56

5 In the Name of Research   64

6 Stick to the Forests   74

7 Someone You Can Trust   91

8 An Admirable Goal   107

9 Duty Calls   123

10 Low Gain   140

11 Alone   153

12 Imprisonment or Death   163

13 Violent Mood   170

14 No Time   186

15 Call it Even   199

16 Potential   208

17 Choose to Live   218

18 Proper Introductions   225

19 Opportunity   233

20 I Knew It   244

21 Watch His Back   251

22	Forget You Ever Heard It	260
23	Your Kingdom Dies Today	267
24	Defend Yourself	273
25	So It Shall Be	280
26	How Fascinating	285
27	Hate-filled Glare	292
28	Risk	308
29	Valuable Assets	317
30	Restore Hope	326
31	Ghost of the Goddess	333
32	See the Way Out	341
33	Trapdoor	350
34	Matters of the Heart	363
35	Anything Could Happen	372
36	How to Breathe	383
37	Red Clouds	403
38	Destroy Your Legacy	421
39	Castle Werentra	427
40	Owl Girl	438
41	Interesting Company	442
42	Good Reason	451
43	True Renegades	460
44	Quite the Ruckus	470
45	It Wasn't a Dream	478
46	Pretty Perfect	485
47	Master of Masks	491
48	Too Easy	497
49	We are the Requiem	506
50	Not Drakken	517
51	The Dark Prince	525
52	Champion	531

53 Do You Trust Me?   538
54 By My Side   545
Author's Note   560
About the Author   562
Also by September Thomas   563

Preface

Three kingdoms on the brink of destruction.
Three princes facing down ruinous fates.
These are their stories…
And those of the women who guided the way to glory.

The Gods & Goddesses of Idilea

Qet - God of the Sky/Light, Wisdom, Justice

Zos - Goddess of Death/Darkness, Vengeance

Ner - God of the Forge, Fire

Lo - Goddess of the Harvest, Home, Healing

Vey - God of Beauty, Precious Metals & Gems, Fortune

Cas - Goddess of Strength, War

Fen - God of the Hunt, Travelers/Messengers

Lexicon & Pronunciation Guide

Seasons

    Fret (fret) - Frost/Winter (January to March)

    Rapt (rapt) - Rain/Spring (April to June)

    Sient (sigh-ent) - Sunshine/Summer (July to September)

    Etret (eht-ret) - Dying/Winter (October to December)

Additional words

    Akren (ak-ren) - Sinners forced to travel the mortal plane as ghosts

    Aurora (ah-ror-ah) - Kingdom of bear shifters

    Eritris (er-ih-tris) - Kingdom of insect hybrids

    Fior (fee-ohr) - Kingdom of wolf shifters

    Idilea (ih-day-lee-uh) - Kingdom of dragon shifters

    Puntataras (pun-ta-tar-as) - Idilean curse word

    Rezar (reh-zar) - Hell

    Strovara (stroh-vara) - Heaven

    Travetry (trav-et-ry) - Fiorian slur for the people of Idilea

    Whipple (whippel) - Tree with healing & hallucinogenic properties

1

The Blood Moon

Three ghostly fuzzballs peered up, downy feathers fluffed, massive yellow eyes fixed ravenously on my thumb and forefinger pinched above their nest. The tiniest owlet succumbed to his impatience and shrieked, clicking his triangle beak in frustration. Suppressing a smile, I dropped the strips of uncooked pigeon. The birds launched into a flurry of flapping wings and clicking talons, shrieking as they fought over the biggest pieces. The tiny warrior who'd stolen my heart snatched up the largest chunk, gulping it down while glaring at his siblings.

"That settles it," I said, resting my wrists on the chilled surface of the boulder and rocking back on my heels. "You've earned a name, Little Prince. What do you think, Q?" I directed my question at the brooding mother with feathers as pure white as the snow dusting the rocks around her nest, freshly fallen this morning. She clicked her beak and burrowed deeper into her home of silver pine sticks and rounded pebbles.

With a shake of my head, I drew a notebook from my satchel, its pages soft with use, and scribbled notes in the margins. The chicks were aging well. At fourteen days since hatching, the owlets were too young for me to take proper measurements like height and weight, but tracking details about their habits and behaviors could help Papa and me monitor abnormalities down the line.

I grinned when my young prince's eyes lowered to half-mast, breaths puffing in hazy clouds. He cooed and snuggled against the bodies of his siblings, absorbing their warmth as they settled in for a nap. I flexed my fingers, joints aching. Even my soft, fur-lined gloves couldn't ward away the relentless bite of fret, a contrary time of the calendar when snarling blizzards were as likely in the forecast as snow melt.

Sniffing, I swiped moisture from my nose and drew the hood of my cloak over my head. It didn't take long for the downy insides to heat, melting the frost that had settled in my long hair. If Papa were here, he would have tugged my hood up himself, asking for the thousandth time why I couldn't remember something so trivial. He always tried to sound so fierce, like one of the frost bears that sometimes blundered through our village, but couldn't hold the façade for long; he was more likely to sweep me into a hug that smelled of sunshine and sweat than he was to yell.

"Be good for your mama," I whispered to the slumbering owlets, their slight breaths ruffling the feathers around their faces. My pencil caught on the edge of my bag as I shoved it and my notebook into the folds of the canvas. "I'll be back in three days. Promise."

The hem of my cloak ruffled around my knees as I hopped from the pile of rocks, oiled boots sinking into the spray of dried pine needles and ankle-deep snow. The reddish hue of the sky peeked through the barren branches of the trees.

As a child, Papa used to feed me haunting stories about the blood moon. Tales of ghosts and nightvisions so profound, I quivered beneath the quilt when I went to bed. One of those stories stood out to me now, here in the quiet of our Owl Wood.

"Remember, Telleree—" Papa was the only person who called me by my full name—*"keep your guard high when blood fills the sky. Danger lurks when you can hear the rotting of the fallen branches in the spaces between your breaths."*

I inhaled deeply, the familiar scents of sticky sap and late-season frost filling my lungs, and locked the air in my chest, ears straining. Branches crackling with ice brushed together. Q's feathers rustled as she checked on her brood. In the distance, a log in the fire popped and snapped as Tuva prepared eveningmeal.

Shoving my hands in my pockets, I shook my head at the folly. A blood moon was just a moon. A story to keep children quiet while the adults hurried to finish their work before the sun's beams dissolved and scattered into stars.

Q's throaty warning call brought me back to myself, back stiffening. Out of sight in the thicket of trees and brush, boots punched fresh holes in the drifts. I dropped my hand to my hip, seeking the knife I strapped there to cut away branches that grew too close to the nests. Q trilled again, three chips this time. All clear. I released the handle when my best and oldest friend emerged from between two birches, panting and sweeping fistfuls of coppery hair out of her eyes.

"Thank Fen I found you here," she gasped. "I hurried, hoping you hadn't left yet." Viv leaned against a tree, her figure slight against the scraggly trunk, trying to peer around me. "How are the little ones?"

I shook my head when she took a step forward. "You can't see them yet. Q's still too protective and her mate is due back anytime. I'd rather not stitch you up again."

Viv's low grumble of disapproval made me grin, though she hunkered back beneath the shady branches. It was impressive she'd volunteered to trek all the way out here. She'd already put in a full day of hunting and tracking, having returned at the same moment

I'd set out to check on the nests an hour ago.

As self-proclaimed keepers of these woods nestled atop Spear Ridge, the twelve families that made up our village divvied up the daily chores and responsibilities. Some tasks rotated, like cooking and mending clothing, but most of us specialized in something. Viv and the Vettel twins were our best hunters. Viv's mother was our blacksmith—one of the best in the land, I was told. Papa and I worked the rich soil carefully cultivated inside the greenhouse. Others helped with the livestock, carpentry, and anything else that needed to be done.

My favorite task—and one that belonged solely to Papa and me—was checking the nests. They spanned outward from our village, providing homes to all kinds of birds: swallows, rushes, ground thrush, even a few fat pigeons. But it was the owls that captivated me. The majestic creatures consumed some of my earliest memories; their citrus eyes and sleek feathers were always just beyond the reach of my pudgy toddler fingers.

The birds were far from domesticated, yet they made their nests in our forests and tolerated our presence. I knew their language as well as I knew my own; the rustle of a wing or click of a beak meant as much to me as a strained laugh or a shouted name. The owls numbered among the few friends I had, living here on the far edge of Idilea, tucked away in the northern mountains marking our border with Aurora. Our village, lovingly dubbed Solas, was as seemingly isolated as the moon herself.

"The chicks are fabulous, though." I answered Viv's question while tucking myself against her side, much like the snoozing siblings not far away. I looped my arm through hers and escorted her onto the path, making her snicker, the heft of her woolen cloak not enough to absorb the vibrations of her body. "Remember the tiny one?"

"The prince?"

He did act quite kingly. "He nearly clawed out his sister's eyes to steal her food."

Viv gasped, slapping her hand to her chest. "How ruthless."

"He's my favorite."

"Stop for a moment." Viv adjusted the collar of my cloak. "This is bothering me. One second." At her direction, I spun in a circle, rolling my eyes as she straightened the wave of feathers I'd sewn into the leather. It was my pride and joy, the cloak that matched Papa's. Every feather we stitched into place told a story about a bird, a setting, a memory.

Viv drew a long line down the flat of my braid and, apparently having not found anything to fix about it, tugged me back around. The light cast by the moon sparkled off the white needles of the pines, making her brown eyes shimmer. She pressed a stray feather into my hands. "You always love the runt of the litter, Tell."

"That isn't always—"

A hoot preceded the shadow swooping through the trees. The owl, no bigger than my clenched fist, ignored the forearm I extended, leather bracer firmly in place, and landed on my shoulder instead. She leaned against my neck, nuzzling the curve of my jaw in greeting. I narrowed my eyes at Viv's broad grin and stroked the screech owl's back, humming softly in conjunction with the bird's happy sounds.

"You were saying?" Viv pressed.

"Pip is a special case," I conceded. "You know that."

She and I shared an unbreakable bond, one forged through stress, perseverance, and love. Three years ago, I'd found the owlet knocked from her nest by her overly energetic brothers and sisters. It wasn't clear how long she'd crouched on the ground, weary and drenched in icy rain, but the way Pip had glared up at me that morning relayed she wasn't anywhere near ready to give up. I'd tucked her into the pocket of my cloak and took her home to set her broken wing.

Through the mercy of Zos, she'd not only survived but thrived, and now she rarely left my side, preferring my arms to the limbs offered by the forest.

"You know, Pip would come with you. If you left. So would some of the others. Maybe." Viv tripped over her words, fumbling to find the sentences that normally flowed from her like water from the mouth of the Oft.

I bristled and stepped away, recognizing the tones of the impending argument. "My responsibilities lie with Solas."

"You have a *place* here, but you have a *responsibility* to live your life the way it deserves to be lived." Viv slashed out with one arm impatiently, cheeks stained splotchy red. "I get it. It's safe here. Sheltered. But we've hidden away for seventeen years now. Haven't you considered what more is out there? What greater purpose you serve? Your knowledge of owls alone could help Idilea—"

"You have no idea what Idilea needs," I snapped. The night that had wrapped around me so gently earlier had sprouted edges as sharp as the azure crystals we used to dig up from the caves as children. "You know why our families fled the capital, the lengths they went to making sure we survived." My lips curled. "You want to turn your back on that? When they need us most?"

Viv flinched and lowered her head, hand partially obscuring her face. For all her bravado, her desire to leave constantly warred with her guilt.

Our parents were not old in terms of passing time, but the mountains and the trials that came with them had a way of aging people in other ways. Papa, Viv's mother, and the people they'd run away with had built this sanctuary, navigating the tough terrain, finding ways to barter for supplies in Stavanger at the base of the mountain, protecting us children all the while. They had gone through so much these past two decades, and it was time for us to step up and pay them back for their efforts.

Square is square, as Papa always said. It was good to balance our debts.

I softened my tone. "We have homes. Family. Plenty of food and companionship. You have your mother's forge and all the forest to hunt in. I have Papa, my owls—the greenhouse." I plucked at the strap of the bag draped across my chest, the cracked leather slippery under my touch. "I'm happy here. Why can't you accept that?"

"I do." Viv shoved her gloved hands in her pockets, her shoulders rising. "But I can't help wonder what's next. The life they've created for us is good, but what if there's more out there? We can't live in fear of the wolven forever."

Yes, we certainly could. I shuddered, the warmth of my fleece-lined shirt and pants doing nothing against the chill radiating from my core.

I had no desire to encounter the soldiers who'd invaded our country, murdered our king and queen, and now held our people hostage. Aside from their amber eyes, the wolven from Fior, which bordered our country to the south, looked like typical humans in one form. But when they shifted, they transformed into creatures straight from nightvisions: massive wolves both taller and broader than most draft horses, long legs ending with sharp claws and jagged muzzles packed with teeth meant for tearing.

The thought of meeting one was bad, but dozens, maybe even hundreds, roamed these lands now, scouring Idilea for slaves to work in the mines.

Viv and the multitude of daggers she'd crafted and mastered might be capable of holding her own against the beasts. But me? Not so much.

My friend launched herself forward, startling Pip into flight, and threw her arms around me in a hug so fierce my lungs seized. I coughed into her hair, embracing her back. Viv pressed her face into my neck. Something wet ran down my skin.

"I'm sorry," she whispered. "I didn't mean to upset you."

As I squeezed her, the chill gripping my insides melted away. "I'm not upset. I just can't see the future like you do. But maybe… maybe we can talk about it again. Later."

That was the last thing I wanted, but I couldn't bear seeing her in pain.

"I'd like that." She drew a shaky breath and swiped at her eyes when she pulled away. In the distance, a bell clanged. Dinner would be ready soon. My stomach grumbled as I remembered the magnificent antlers of the stag Viv and the boys had dragged in. The things Tuva could do with venison…

"Ner's nails," Viv cursed, referencing the God of the Forge, "I lost track of time. Os will have my hide."

"Papa sent you?" I asked mildly, beckoning to Pip, who'd tucked herself into a cradle of silver pine branches.

"He asked that you check on the great horned owls before you headed back."

I ran my knuckles over my chin, frowning. He had stopped by their nest last evening. Typically, we only checked on those owls once every seven days. Not only was their nest the most remote, but as the largest of our charges, they required little outside assistance.

"Why?" I asked, mostly for myself. Instinctively, my gaze darted to the skies. A pine blocked my view of the moon. "And on tonight of all nights…"

"He said it was a feeling?" Her queried response settled me somewhat. Papa and his feelings. Sometimes they were spot on, others—not so much. But if he had his concerns, arguing never did any good. I patted my bag. With four nests left to visit, there was no way would I be on time for eveningmeal, but Tuva would keep something warm over the fire for me.

"I better get going if I don't want to be out till dawn." I took a few steps back, waving at Viv. "As sure as the dark meets the light…"

"We will meet again." Viv finished the saying we'd laughingly adopted as children when we'd overheard old man Petr practicing his rough poetry before propositioning Widow Olsen. Back then, we'd hidden our giggles behind our hands, scrambling into the woods to hide our rampant laughter. Now—a smile tugged at my lips and Viv burst out laughing at my expression. "Hurry, Tell."

* * *

I tugged my scarf tighter over my mouth and nose. The cold that came with living in the mountains rarely bothered me, but cloudless nights like these were special cases. The darkness of the skies and the sharp pinpricks of its stars were the clearest, but the cold was also its sharpest, as if the snow-capped peaks exhaled the last of their warmth in appreciation of the utter beauty.

Feathers fluffed against my cheek, and I squeezed Pip through the hood. She preferred to cuddle like this, stealing warmth from my body at every opportunity.

"Almost there," I whispered, the sound of my voice shattering the stillness like a rock through a rim of ice on the lake. I swiped at my nose with the back of one gloved hand. I'd left the barn owls holed up safely in their shelter not long ago, and only the great horned owls remained.

Of all the birds under our watch, the great horned owls remained the wildest—roosting a substantial hike from the alcove of our village. They also lived nearest the Spear, the tallest peak in the kingdom, and air whistled out of my lungs as the incline increased. A branch buried in a drift tripped me up and I stumbled into the

9

clearing, landing on my knees, legs buried in snow.

I ripped my hood from my head and peered up. Pip cooed softly, and I pressed a finger to my lips, locking in a breath. There, directly overhead, scrawled among the stars was the bright point of Zos' spear, the goddess of darkness suspended in the skies, forever pointing travelers north, a beacon of hope in a sea of black.

Beautiful.

Standing, I stroked Pip's back again and whistled sharply, a signal to the great horned owls letting them know a friend approached. They had a nasty habit of dive-bombing intruders. A few beats passed, and I frowned, stomach knotting.

Nothing.

I should have heard something: an answering hoot or the soft chitters of the newly hatched chicks—a symphony as recognizable to me as the white scars on my fingers, battle wounds that came with offering food to creatures with sharp beaks.

Instead, I encountered silence so absolute I could get lost in it.

Chilled fingers skated up my spine as I scanned the clearing, rubbing the ink tattooed on the underside of my wrist for comfort. Across the clearing, branches of a half-dead emberwood groaned, its trunk angled sideways as a result of the relentless winds. It was that tree the owls claimed as their own.

Pip took flight. My heart slammed against the backs of my ribs. Something was very wrong here. I rushed across the clearing, my exposed skin burning in the red of the moon. At the base of the tree lay a dark bundle, something that looked like a clump of leaves.

My breath caught in my throat. I pushed harder, thighs burning as I fought through the thigh-deep drifts. I wanted to scream, but my voice had frozen. I collapsed beside the pile, a sob breaking my revere as I pulled the limp body of the male into my lap, a shriek catching in my throat when I realized his wings were ripped from

10

his body. Dark smudges on the snow I'd mistaken for shadows were smears of blood.

What of the owlets?

Cradling the body of the owl in my arms, I mounted the stones I'd stacked around the tree to give me a boost toward the nest and peered inside, horror writhing in my stomach. A bloody mass of gray fluff and splintered bones littered the bowl of twigs and string. Nausea churned and I wrenched away from the carnage, nearly falling from the ledge.

What would have done this?

Our owls had fallen prey to predators before, but they never left destruction like this. The carcass of the male, while broken, still had meat on it. I couldn't imagine hunger being a factor.

No, this seemed intentional, as if I were meant to find the bodies of my beloved birds like this: torn and ripped almost beyond recognition.

But what sort of animal was capable of such a thing?

Pip hooted, paused for three beats, and hooted again, wings flapping hard as she lifted from my shoulder.

I froze, recognizing her warning call.

We weren't alone.

Carefully, I lowered the body of the male owl into the nest with his dead hatchlings, promising to return to say my prayers. Pip screeched again. Whatever was out there, whatever had massacred my owls… it lingered on the edge of the clearing. Through my teeth, I whistled acknowledgment and palmed the knife at my hip.

I had to get back. I had to warn Papa, Viv—our friends.

Shadows to the left of the clearing shifted. From between two trees, a wolf emerged. I trembled. I'd never seen a wolf this big, bigger than the rabid black bear Kit had killed two springs ago, its mouth foaming with disease. Legs slender as saplings flexed as the creature rolled back on its haunches, pale yellow eyes flashing. A grumble sounded from its barrel of a chest and its jaw dropped open, revealing a maw of long, pointed teeth. Its tongue lolled, catching a downy gray feather stuck to its black lips. Blood flecked its mangy muzzle.

A wolven.

We'd hidden for nearly twenty years...

And now the Fiorian invaders had found us.

I prayed to Zos the soldier was alone and had stumbled upon me first. If it found Solas...

In a flurry of feathers, Pip launched herself from the trees, understanding my desires perfectly, wings flapping furiously as she arrowed toward home. "Warn them," I shouted after her, boots slipping on the icy rocks as I retreated. "Save them and don't look back."

I didn't say I would be fine. Those odds stretched spectacularly thin.

"You'll regret that." The wolven's jaw didn't move, yet its gruff, masculine voice infiltrated the clearing like the vermin it was. Was it speaking to me telepathically? I'd heard rumors of the foreign magic, but had never encountered it before. *"But it matters not. It's already too late for the rest of your... kind."* He stretched, tendons popping and snapping. *"I'm cleaning up the scraps."*

"You'll have to catch me first."

I whirled, launching myself up the pebbled trail nestled between some trees. The beast snarled, but I didn't dare look back. These trails were as treacherous as they came, but if I could make it to the caves that wormed their way through the depths of the Spear in a myriad of confusing arteries and knotted dead-ends, I stood a chance of escaping.

My lungs heaved as I snapped around rocks and trunks, the leather of my gloves helping me secure my slippery grip on the boulders. I scrambled to run faster, climb higher. The wolven with his four legs and lowered center of gravity kept pace, but barely. I knew this terrain. I understood these trails. I would use whatever advantage I had.

I swiped rock and dirt from the edge of an alcove cut into a cliff, listening to it clatter down the rocks below me, and scrambled higher still. Good. Maybe the wolven would trip on them. Overhead, the blood moon mocked me and I tripped, skidding across a flat sheet of rock slick with ice and snagged some dangling emberwood branches to keep myself upright, narrowly avoiding falling off the edge of a sharp drop-off.

I couldn't hear my pursuer anymore. Had I lost him?

A pine tree with its westward limbs missing appeared up ahead, isolated in an outcropping of stone. My heart skipped and skittered as precariously as I ran. Almost there. Just a twist to the right and I would—

My head snapped one way and my body wrenched the other as something snagged my cloak. Air exploded from my lungs when I landed on my back. I flung my arm out, bracer catching the claws slashing for my face. The wolven's claws skittered across the leather and dug into my cloak—which the beast clenched tight in its mouth. Coughing, gagging, I slapped at the ties strangling my throat, dirt and snow flying as I scrambled for purchase. The ripe scent of fresh earth filled my nose.

"Did you think you would escape?" The words boomed in my head. Yellow eyes burned into my own. The wolven's claws sank deep into the fabric, shredding the delicate feathers. I swallowed the whine threatening to tear me in two. Feathers that symbolized hope and life and joy. *"As fun as you made this chase, you knew it was futile. Travetry like yourself will always lose."*

13

The foreign word scraped against my mind, but I recognized the slur.

My nails finally found purchase in the knot around my neck. With one tiny morsel of remorse, I ripped it apart. With nothing to hold it in place any longer, the cloak wrenched backward, and with it went the wolven, caught off guard and ill-situated on the rock. I sprinted the opposite direction, thoughts soaring, trying to remember where the cavern opened. Blood pounding in my ears, I swung wide around a tree as nails skidded across the sheer path of rock in front of me and stopped.

I'd gone the wrong way.

Intentional or not, the wolven was herding me up the mountain. The incline of the Spear was nearly vertical until it leveled out at the top, producing a narrow ledge barely twenty paces long that jutted over the valley like a drooping end of a pointed hat. To slip and fall meant a drop of tens of thousands of feet to the valley.

Cursing the monster who'd chased me here, I climbed, shaking off the icy cold burning my bare skin. I could hear the wolven below, paws scrambling over the rock as he hurled himself after me. I imagined his hot breath against the back of my neck and moved faster, gloves tearing, skin shredding, leaving bloody stains behind.

Almost there.

With a last burst of energy, I launched myself over the flattened top of the cliff, dodging the snap of teeth that narrowly missed the toe of my boot. Black speckles dotted the edges of my vision and my limbs trembled with exhaustion, but I couldn't lie there. Not unless I wanted to die. With a grunt, I pushed myself to my feet, cradling my bloodied hands to my chest, and surged down the only path forward, dizzy with the realization that a slip would cost me everything.

At the point of the Spear, I stopped, wheezing, peering over the edge, chest swirling with apprehension. Below, way down below, the trees didn't look like trees. The darkened forests stretched outward in rolling shadowy waves, vast and dark as I imagined the ocean might look. I gulped. Directly below clustered a mass of stones dubbed the Dragon's Jaw. Vicious, six-foot-long spears of rock with tips sharpened by the blasting winds of Bayer's Canyon reached upward like fingers.

A fall from the Spear spelled instant death: by tree, by stone, or by terror.

My teeth chattered, and I banded my arms more tightly around myself, regretting the loss of my cloak, trying to figure a way out of this and coming up frightfully empty.

Despite knowing what was in store for me below, falling from here was preferable to having my larynx ripped out or my heart pulled from my chest. Even worse, the Fiorian soldier might take me in as a slave for the mines.

Steel-like claws scraped against stone, freezing my breath in my lungs. I turned, bracing the ball of my back foot on the edge of the ledge, heel hanging out over nothing. Several yards away, chest heaving, the shifter sized me up.

"*It seems you've run out of space.*" One triangle ear split by a ropy scar twitched. "*Will you surrender peacefully? Or do I need to drag you down from there—by the throat?*"

In the distance, a screech owl shrieked in outrage. Pip. Had she managed to warn anyone?

The wolven's ears twitched again, and it spun, eyes narrowing. A blurry mass of dark fur flung itself up the side of the cliff and tackled the beast who had chased me. The wolven yelped, claws scrambling for purchase, but it was too late. He plunged over the edge with nothing more than a whisper of a whimper.

My stomach hollowed as the second, bigger wolven prowled closer.

A long scar parted the fur down the length of its nose, nicking the inside corner of its golden eyes.

What in the bloody name of Zos was happening right now?

He shook himself, tufts of hair standing on end, and shifted, bones twisting and cracking as the beast transformed from monster to man—one wearing the uniform of someone high-ranking in the wolven army if the golden laurels gracing his forest green tunic signified anything. He didn't spare a glance for his fallen comrade. His focus fixed on me, and he took a hesitant step forward, hand outstretched.

"Would you step away from the edge?" he asked, not unkindly. The ropy scar tugged at the corner of his lips, fixing them in a semi-permanent scowl. "No offense, but you're one powerful gust away from blowing right over."

Yeah, like that was going to happen. I scooted back the remaining half-inch available to me, slippery pebbles shifting beneath my toes. I couldn't decipher this shifter's angle. One moment I was being chased by the wolven who'd no doubt murdered my birds and the next moment another soldier had seemingly saved me?

No way would this end well.

"What do you want with me?" I asked.

Keeping his hand extended, his arm solid as the heft of the mountain, he tried again. "Do you live up here? In the mountains?"

"As if I'd tell you." The wind snagged the hair hanging loose around my face.

His dark brow lifted, and I swore that somewhere in the stubble flecking his cheeks and chin, his lips twitched in something that might have been a grin. Or a grimace. "Would you please come away from the edge so we can talk properly?"

Unfortunately, he made the mistake of stepping closer. In my skittish state, I tried to edge backward and found nothing. One moment I was balanced on the cliff, not in the best spot, but in a firmer place than he believed me to be, and the next, my leg plunged into open air. Arms flailing like a newborn chick, I tried to grab onto the rocks I'd clung to earlier, anything to save me from falling, but the pads of my fingers whispered over the surface, slipping right through the reaching grasp of the soldier who'd surged forward in a desperate attempt to stop me, to save me.

But he wasn't fast enough.

A heartbeat later, I plunged into the vast abyss of nothingness.

2

A Strange Sense of Calm

Falling out of trees, losing my footing scaling cliffs, and swinging on ropes over crevices in the caves were nothing like this sensation. Those other times, my stomach had simultaneously swooshed and clenched, energy zipping through me in jagged, raw bursts. My eyes had closed, muscles tensed, bracing for whatever came next...

But this was different.

My stomach still hollowed and my blood sang, but a strange sense of calm wrapped its arms around me. I didn't know when I would hit the ground, but when I did, that was it.

I hoped it wouldn't hurt.

The wolven lunged forward. For one pristine moment, I hung there, back parallel with the earth below, the rounded body of the moon filling my vision, the reddish hue of its rough surface mocking me.

I had ignored Papa's warning.

Then the world sped up. Gravity wrenched me downward with a mighty yank as the soldier knelt at the edge of the Spear, pale eyes burning into me as I plummeted. I blinked, and the wolven was gone; I couldn't tell if he had left, or if I had dropped too far out of sight.

I drew a breath, a long shuddering thing, marveling at my lack of fear. The wind howled in my ears, the bitter chill of the wind clawed at my body, but my mind was intact, my heart thudding rapidly in my chest.

Had Pip alerted Viv and my father? Given the presence of two wolven, it wasn't hard to believe more of them were out there, destroying the serenity of our mountains. Besides, it was common knowledge our invaders preferred traveling in packs.

The knot in my scarf ripped apart. With a mighty tug, it unfurled from around my neck, a ribbon of crimson that snapped into the sky and drifted toward the cliff. I'd spun during my descent, and the mountain passed by along my right side, the layers of rocks and trees and trails winding up its side bizarrely easy to see despite the speed at which I plummeted.

Why wasn't I more afraid?

Though I didn't feel like I was dying, this was the end. The Dragon's Jaws were bared below, and if I miraculously missed the rocks, I would still be flattened upon impact. There was no way out, yet the adrenaline rush I associated with terror remained muted, a mere hum in what should have been a roar.

Words came to me. I tasted them on my lips, their sounds ripped away before they met my ears. But I didn't need to hear them to feel their strength, to gather their comfort close. It was a prayer I'd recited every night since we'd run from Aeros, fleeing the smoke and flame and death.

Goddess of death, your protection, I ask.

Wrap me in your glory.

Shelter me in your despair.

Thieves and sinners...

19

The weary and the lost.
We seek your sanctuary three:
The dark, the depth, the verity.
Your child of deceit implores you now.
Oh, Zos. Oh, let it be.

A dark figure blotted out the moon, the scarlet shimmer barely visible through its bat-like wings. I squinted. Its squarish head swiveled on a long golden neck and a reptilian tail streamed behind it.

My breath caught in my chest.

It couldn't be.

A hallucination.

That's what this was.

Because no way would a drakken—

I crashed into something that most definitely was not the ground. Something roared, a burst of anger and pain that sent shockwaves through my body. The collision sent me spinning, arms flailing, legs kicking, scrambling for purchase as I flipped over and over. Flashes of the forest rushed up beneath me.

I reached for the drakken, its wings flapping desperately. This one's head was jagged, like the long point of a spear, tapered ears angled sharply backward. Its neck lashed wildly, the talons at the ends of its wings flashing silver as it struggled to gain purchase. The shifter released another shriek of pain, sooty scales glittering in the night sky.

My brain stuttered.

One wing was bent at an odd angle, and part of me registered that was what had broken my fall. But its descent was still slowing. And that meant survival. Zos had granted my prayer.

I snagged the pack strapped tightly to the drakken's leg, its three-inch long talons tearing deep grooves into my forearm, but I forced myself to hold on. We spun wildly, the pointed spears of the rocks rushing closer. I fought against the awful sense of vertigo threatening to suck me under.

The drakken's scaly neck bent, trying to get a good look at the parasite clinging to its body. The bag shifted in my grip, and I wrapped my form around the drakken's leg, even as its scales cut through my clothes, shredding my skin.

The pain meant I was still alive.

And I desperately wanted to live.

"You need to focus," I yelled. Holy feathers, the ground was coming up fast. I could make out individual spears of stone below. "We must avoid those rocks."

My voice seemed to steady the drakken, and I forced my taut muscles to loosen, peering up at the creature. Eyes black as the raging river at night regarded me with violent intelligence, and blackened lips peeled back from a row of sharpened, steely teeth. For a moment, one heady, awful moment, I thought it might stop fighting and kill us both out of spite.

Then, with a shuddering croak, the drakken threw its wings wide. The leathery panels caught the air, and we both shrieked as our momentum sharply slowed, threatening to send us into a tailspin. But the drakken refused to be bested in its element and angled its wings in a fashion that reminded me of owls banking to land.

Not really flying, but controlling the fall.

I was sure I'd left my heart somewhere on the spear because I couldn't feel it slamming in my chest. Frigid wind cut across my face as I squinted down, stomach roiling in protest. The angle was good, but we were still approaching the ground far too quickly.

The outlines of the rocks sharpened.

We were going to crash.

I squeezed my eyes shut, arms and legs clamping tightly around the drakken's meaty thigh, throwing my faith into its abilities, and screamed when we crashed through the foliage. Somehow, we'd missed the rocks but had hit the forest instead.

Losing my grip, I went tumbling, branches snapping beneath my weight. I curled inward, wrapping my arms around my knees, too scared to do anything but protect my most vital organs. My shoulder smashed into the ground first and agony exploded down my back. The rest of my body crumbled, unfolding so I sprawled flat, blinking back tears shimmering on the edges of my vision. I couldn't tell where one bruise ended and another began. A scream flailed in my chest, desperate for release, but my voice was gone, stolen by the cold and the wind.

Breath shuddering through my rib cage, I bit down on the side of my hand, coppery blood filling my mouth as I tried to redirect the pain firing from my nerves. It worked a little. I'd just survived an impossible fall, hadn't I? I could handle a few bruises and what felt like a dislocated shoulder.

My brain stupidly whispered reminders about the bloody gashes on my arms and legs from the drakken's talons—*where had the drakken gone, anyway?*—the cheekbone I'd nearly shattered when the wolven had dragged me down in the forest, the ribs I'd surely broken when I'd smacked into that first bough...

I bit down harder, shutting out the thoughts, pushing them into a tiny corner in the back of my mind. I needed to focus. Gradually, the icy flames of agony diminished, drawing tight around the one point where I focused it. Only when I was confident I wouldn't collapse or pass out did I open my eyes.

"I'm alive," I croaked, a sliver of hope fluttering in my breast. Tears slipped down my cheeks and I swiped at them before reaching upward, marveling at the stars flickering between the gaps in my fingers, swallowing back the joy and relief clogging my throat.

"Merciful gods, I'm alive."

I'd almost died.

Zos save me. I'd *accepted* my death.

Yet here I was: conscious, battered, breathing.

Yes, the drakken was still out there somewhere. Assuming it also survived the fall.

But I was wholly, beautifully, unmistakably *alive*.

Soft strands of brittle grass rasped against my cheeks and I nuzzled into the earth, digging my fingers into the weeds, seeking the smooth, round pebbles concealed beneath the long strands. Compared to the Spear, it felt almost balmy at the base of the mountain. To think mere minutes ago I'd crunched through several feet of snow at the highest peak of the Copper Mountains, yet here in the valley it snowed inconsistently, resulting in large patches of dry ground.

Red-tinted aspen branches scratched together in the soft breeze. I sat up, ears straining past the hollow rasps, seeking the familiar rustle of feathers, the contented hoots of owls, but finding none. Not even the thrashing of a drakken—who I realized was actually a shifter—in the nearby forest.

The quiet buzzes in the grass came from brown-shelled insects the size of my palm.

I'd survived.

But my family, my friends, my owls, my home...

I pressed the bloody heels of my hands to my eyes, suppressing the moisture gathering there. No. I wouldn't think like that. Pip had gotten away. So had some of the other owls. I'd faintly heard them when the second wolven had appeared. In addition, our village was strong, and we were a paranoid bunch. We had taken precautions. We trained for the worst. They wouldn't fall easily.

Viv wouldn't fall easily.

With a groan I felt in the depths of my soul, I braced against a log and levered myself upright. The adrenaline was fading, and with its retreat emerged every aching bone, every bruised limb, every slivered cut. Gritting my teeth, I tugged back my sleeve, searching out the worst of my injuries.

The drakken could wait. The need to not bleed out was far stronger.

A trio of gashes ran from my elbow to my wrist, nicking the edge of my tattoo. Blood seeped from it and a half dozen other nicks. I reached for my pack, quietly surprised to find it still wrapped around my body. The strap must have caught under my arm.

I dug out a mound of white bandages, faintly registering that despite the deep bruises, my shoulder was, in fact, not dislocated. After applying a powder that would slow the bleeding and numb the pain, I made quick work of wrapping my wounds. If my luck held, I might stave off infection long enough to properly treat the deepest injuries. The bite mark on my hand had already stopped bleeding, and the scratches on my legs weren't bad at all.

Grounded in the knowledge I was alive and most of my blood still flowed through my veins, my attention shifted to my unwilling savior.

Paranoia settled into my bones. I surveyed the forest, eyeing the shifting shadows of the trees and bushes, spine tingling with trepidation, imagining every movement to be the twitch of a tail, a jerk of a scaly maw. My gut twisted, and I pressed my forearm tightly to my ribs, forcing myself upright with a groan. If they weren't broken, they were most definitely bruised.

"I strongly suggest you stay where you are."

My hands rose at the husky warning. Carefully, fingers splayed wide on either side of my head, I turned. A man with a riot of honey-colored curls stood on a boulder, a bow about half his height strung, an arrow notched. The laces of his thigh-high boots spilled down

24

the sides of the rock, and he'd roughly shoved half of his white shirt into his pants, the other half bunched over his hip. A full quiver rested on an azure cloak bundled at his heels.

"If you are thinking about running, I will, again, strongly suggest you think otherwise." The stranger wet his lips, peering down the length of his arrow. He couldn't be much older than my twenty-one years. "I can and will shoot this arrow between your ribs. If you test me, I will not hesitate to show you proof."

Oh, I believed him. The way he stood and the lack of tension in his limbs spoke volumes about his experience. It reminded me of Viv and how lethal she became with weapons in her hands.

"I hear you," I murmured, thankful the trembling of my stomach didn't translate to my voice.

Beyond the man, the splintered trunk of an asp tree speared the skies, the broken ends rough as if something heavy had crashed into it. The rest of the tree lay at its base, the earth dark with chunks of sticks and churned dirt. A line of muddy footprints led from the man into the forests beyond.

This man must have been the golden drakken I'd glimpsed flying across the moon. Maybe a partner to the black drakken who'd inadvertently saved my life.

Idilea used to be full of drakken until the invasion. Now, the sight of one, let alone *two,* was an outright oddity. It was too dangerous for shifters to reveal their true selves anymore. All it meant was a one-way trip to the mines where their thick hides held up better against the sweltering heat.

Branches cracked somewhere to my left, but my captor paid it no heed, his eyes fixed on me, arms like stones as they bent the bow to his command. The footsteps grew closer and a second figure emerged from the depths of a prickly briarbrush, jaw hard as he tugged his cloak up his arms, over his dark tunic.

25

"Why's she still alive?" he asked, venom in his voice.

The new man was darkness incarnate. Straight, dark hair hung loosely around his triangular face. His nose cut a thin, straight line toward his jaw, which ended in a point. A scar nicked the underside of his chin, which he rubbed absently. His narrowed eyes reminded me of those of an adder.

"Curiosity," the one with the bow volleyed back, answering the other's question.

The dark one gripped his shoulder and rotated it tersely. "I don't know why I bothered asking." He rooted through the pack at his feet. I sucked in a breath, recognizing the canvas' greenish color. "Will you kill her when you're through with your analysis?"

"Undetermined." The golden man lowered his weapon marginally. "How badly broken are you, anyway?"

My muscles ached, but when I lowered my arms slightly, the bow came right back up, arrow as lethally angled as before. Biting back a gasp, I held still.

The second man grunted. "How do you think I feel?"

"Like that time you raced horses with Ollie and nearly got trampled?"

The darker man tsked, pulled a sword of all things from the bag, and held it up. He moved stiffly, shoulder cocked at an uncomfortable angle. I took a step back, forgetting about the weapon aimed at me, heart skittering as I processed this sudden turn of events.

The addition of the blade was bad enough without wondering what foreign magic had been worked on his bag, which was smaller than my own. Too small for such a long weapon.

"Did I say you could move?" the golden man taunted, though he lowered his bow anyway, eyeing his friend, who swung his sword experimentally. The line of tension across his forehead disappeared.

I dropped my hands with relief when he draped the weapon over his shoulder. With his friend armed, he must have decided I wasn't much of a threat after all. Or, more likely, he knew a million ways to kill me without it.

Brusquely, he tucked in the rest of his shirt, hefted his cloak over his bulky shoulders, and slid down the boulder to join the newcomer on the ground. "Who are you?"

"Does that matter?" I asked, massaging the pinpricks of pain shooting down my arm, and bit down on the inside of my cheek. My fading adrenaline opened me up to the hurt of my bruises and cracked ribs, but I needed to think smarter if I wanted to live. Snark would get me nowhere.

The darker man chuckled and tugged the belt of a scabbard around his hips, his sword sheathed. "She has a point, Lukas."

Side by side, the unnamed man was the shorter, slenderer of the two, though the darkness he radiated reminded me of the blurred fog sometimes depicted around Zos in various paintings. The man with the bow, Lukas, was prettier, with rounded cheeks and tumbling hair that brushed his shoulders. It wouldn't surprise me to learn his parents had prayed at the feet of Vey, the god of beauty.

"Let's try this one instead," the dark one rasped, recapturing my attention. "What business did you have falling?" He spun his injured arm in a slow circle again, muscles in his jaw popping. "If you were keen on dying, the least you could have done was avoid crashing into me."

I snorted and hid my dull knife in the palm of my hand, gripping it tightly while rooting through my bag. It wasn't much in terms of self-defense, but it would have to do. "It wasn't intentional."

"Oh?" Lukas implored, batting the darker one's hands away from his shoulder, probing the muscles himself. "It's not dislocated," he muttered and pulled a roll of bandages from his pack. "Let me wrap it before you injure it further."

I tried to remember what little I'd read about shifter anatomy. The arm the second man held so gingerly must have been the wing I'd hit tumbling from the Spear. I wondered how much damage I'd inflicted, and rocked back on my heels, digging deeper into my bag to keep from pointing out that whatever the golden man was doing wouldn't help much.

"Then why were you... descending?" Amusement edged the dark one's tone as he continued the line of questioning.

I barely heard him. Taking inventory of my pack, the coil of panic I'd successfully shoved down earlier now wriggled in my stomach. My notebook. A pencil. Some stray feathers. A travel medical kit. An extra set of fur-lined gloves. Several sticks of chewing sap. I blew out a slow breath and bound my satchel closed again. I always lugged around basic supplies, never knowing what I might need in the woods, but they wouldn't get me far in the valley.

I eyed the curve of the Spear, calculating my odds of a quick return to Solas—assuming the village still stood. If the men hadn't appeared, I would already be on my way back, injured arms, cracked ribs, and all. The head of the hidden trail that led to the Owl Wood wasn't far, but it would still take most of the night and a fair chunk of the morning to make it to the top. Maybe ten or twelve hours? The lack of rope and grappling hooks would make climbing a chore, and I didn't even want to think about my missing cloak.

"Oi, girl." The shorter man's voice pried me away from the task at hand. "You still with us?"

I blinked. "Rude much?"

Lukas chuckled. "She sees right through you, doesn't she, Soren?"

Soren scowled. He'd pulled his cloak over his shoulder and cradled his arm in a makeshift sling. "You should have died on the way down."

He really was something else. I looped my bag over my head and worked my way around the men. "I didn't fall intentionally, and I certainly didn't mean to crash into you, but I did, and here we are. That's all you need to know."

Soren's arm shot out, blocking me from proceeding, glaring. How did he move so quickly? Was that a shifter thing? "You know we have to kill you, don't you?"

I swallowed hard at the sharp sheen of silver glinting in my periphery. Great. He'd drawn his sword. My finger-length blade definitely wouldn't hold up against that monster, even if I got the drop on him and shoved the knife into his throat... which I didn't have the guts to do. With regret thick in my throat, I dropped the knife into the cushion of my pocket, squared my shoulders, and glared right back. "Why's that?"

"Yes, why exactly is that?" Lukas echoed. I couldn't tell if he was mocking me. He sounded closer than he had before. Shivers shuddered down my spine. Qet's curse. I was failing at this whole survival thing, letting him out of sight.

Soren's eyes narrowed further, the ebony of his irises expanding until only a hint of the whites remained. "Because you've seen what we are and you know our names. That's a lot of information, and since we don't know you, that makes you a liability." He stepped closer, the heat of his body washing over me, making me itch uncomfortably. "Is that a good enough reason for you?"

Soren reminded me of the hunting burrhounds we kept leashed on the outskirts of the village, and I imagined him snapping his teeth in my face to further his point. The image would have made me smile if I wasn't losing the precarious grip on the panic bubbling in my belly. I needed to get to the Owl Wood as soon as I could. Getting through these drakken was just the first step.

I extended my arm, making a concerted effort to not let him see it shake. Soren followed the movement, one brow lifting.

"My name is Telleree. Telleree Falk," I said. "I have very little respect for authority, am good at gardening and healing, and prefer to stay up at night than rise early in the day."

Soren tilted his head; he'd lowered his sword, and the point dragged in the dirt. The puzzlement on his face was enough for my calm demeanor to crack. My lips curled upward. I wasn't very good at keeping a straight face on the best of days, and when I lied, my expression almost always gave me away.

"What am I supposed to do with that?" Soren sounded genuinely perplexed.

He still hadn't taken my hand—hadn't moved to sheath his sword, either—and I was about to lower it when the other man darted forward, his grip warm and firm around mine as he pumped my arm.

"Ms. Falk, it is delightful meeting you, odd as it might be." I was getting used to the formality of his speech. I tugged on my hand, but he only tightened his grip. "Please forgive my companion for his manners. He gets angry when he is hungry, you understand?" He winked. "I'm Lukas, and I believe you have already met Soren. Now that we are no longer strangers—" he shot the incredulous drakken a look—"I am happy to announce we will not be killing you."

"Yet," Soren shot out.

"I don't want to kill her."

Soren responded with something that sounded a little like, "Agree to disagree." But metal sang as he returned his sword to its sheath. Lukas again ignored my tug on our hands and brushed a soft kiss to the back of my knuckles.

My cheeks heated, and I finally extracted my hand, shoving it deep in my pocket, fingers shaking. It was beyond time for me to make my exit. "While it was wonderful meeting both of you, please believe me when I say I won't tell a soul about who—or what—you are. It doesn't matter to me; knowing you are drakken has very little bearing on my life." Cue the rambling. "Besides, there's a limited number of people who I would entrust with that kind of information, and all of them have even less to gain with it than I do." I hooked my fingers around the strap of the bag pressed firmly against my chest. "But I really do need to get going."

Soren held back whatever biting comment I could see brewing behind his eyes and stepped aside. Lukas cocked his head, the gesture reminding me of Pip. "Where are you headed?"

"Somewhere you don't need to be." Not understanding whatever game Lukas was playing, I shoved some hair behind my ears and glanced back at the moon. It had almost reached its apex. I'd wasted too much time. Taking a guess about what they wanted, I pointed away from the mountain range toward the northernmost trade town in the kingdom. "Stavanger is straight west of here, maybe two days' journey by foot." I licked my lips. "But I'm sure you can cut that time by flying."

The sentence felt awkward. To think I'd imagined all drakken were locked up by now, yet here I was, speaking with two of them.

The men glanced at one another.

"I promise I'm not lying to you. Spear Ridge is treacherous enough without giving you false directions." I gripped my bag more tightly and darted around Soren, nodding at Lukas. "May Fen guide your way," I added, invoking the goodwill of the god of travelers and messengers. The drakken exchanged another hooded glance.

Technically, it was blasphemy, invoking the names of our dragon deities.

Technically, I didn't care given the present company.

The knot of tightness twined in my chest eased the farther I got from the men without hearing signs of pursuit. This felt familiar. Me. Alone. In the woods. At night. If I'd had my cloak and Pip on my shoulder, I could have imagined myself back in the Owl Wood in the middle of a routine check of the nests.

I dipped beneath a branch, fist braced against my chest as if to keep my heart from slipping out from between my ribs. But this wasn't normal. The forests of the Dragon's Jaw were darker, the air thicker. Even the snow sprinkled in perpetual patches of shade was finer.

It wasn't a change I appreciated.

Thankful for the thrum of blood hot in my veins, I pushed harder. I needed to maintain this pace, with my right shoulder to the wall of the cliff, and I'd reach the trailhead in no time. Besides, moving warded away the chill that grew with the incline, something that worried me. How exactly would I survive the climb without my cloak? I wasn't sure it was possible, but it wasn't like I had a choice in the matter.

While I walked, thoughts spun dizzyingly through my mind. I'd encountered two wolven, but were there more? And why had the second soldier tossed his ally over the edge of the cliff? Just to talk to me? It didn't make sense.

I picked my way around the remnants of a recent landslide.

Not only had I encountered wolven, but drakken, too. Were the two connected? It certainly wasn't outside the realm of possibility. Wolven working beneath the banner of the grand duke and his overbearing authority hunted the drakken who remained hidden in our midst—and despite their bickering about killing me, Lukas and Soren hadn't hidden their forms while they soared through the skies. Curious.

Gnawing on a hangnail, I checked my position in relation to the stars and sped up. Maybe the wolven had thought I was with the drakken. If that were the case, maybe they didn't know about the village. Hope soared on owl's silent wings in my breast. It was possible everyone was alright.

Even if they had approached, whether by chance or by purpose, the owls and burrhounds would have alerted my family to the danger. That would have given our hunters time to prepare, and I'd never seen anyone best Viv in a fight before.

A sudden chill nipped at my nose and I reached for my woolen scarf before remembering the wind had already snatched it away.

"Feathers," I cursed, my voice shattering the eerie silence. I glanced over my shoulder. Sure, it was a blood moon, but where were all the animals? Even at night, the trees and underbrush normally rustled with nocturnal birds and animals hunting for prey or swayed with the wind shaking shards of ice free from their needles and branches.

Instead, all was quiet, as if these woods knew something I didn't.

The hairs on the base of my neck prickled. Wolven?

My hand fisted in my pocket around the knife. I didn't like how much I was coming to rely upon the steel; I'd never been particularly skilled at wielding it. I ducked behind a tree, forcing my breathing to remain even. Think. What would help me the most now? Viv had once taught me a well-aimed thrust at someone's eye could prove lethal—granted, I had to get close to my assailant first. I dragged a hand down my face. That logic also discounted a wolven's gnashing teeth and sharpened claws, both of which would bring me down long before I launched an adequate defense.

I could run, but the last thing I wanted was to lead my pursuer to the trail, plus, four legs were more powerful than two, and while I was in good shape thanks to hiking and foraging, it was laughable to think I would outrun a wolven.

Blinking down at a spray of wintermoss, I considered my last option. Hiding.

If I'd learned anything from the owls, it was the value of good cover.

Moving quickly, I darted into some dense brush that would hopefully discourage anyone from following, and scrambled up the trunk of a brokenbirch, the bark scraping roughly against the exposed skin of my cheeks and wrists, favoring speed over comfort. Once I settled upon a branch high enough off the ground to provide some distance while still bearing my weight, I peered through the five-pointed leaves that clung to the trees, even though fret was almost over.

I adored brokenbirches. Not only were they among the largest of the trees that grew in our forests, making them ideal for climbing, but they often clumped together. Sure enough, a thick limb of a nearby tree intersected the branch I stood on nicely, and I crossed over, hopping from tree to tree until I found one with plenty of cover. No sooner had I settled against the trunk, when I heard the crunching of feet through the grass.

I shoved my gloved hand against my face, muffling my breathing, and crouched low, attempting to become one with the bark. Leaves bunched around me, obscuring my shape from the ground.

Two figures prowled into view, heads bent to the ground. The closer they got, the deeper my frown arched. Seriously? They'd followed me?

"Where did she go?" Soren grumbled, kicking a spill of rocks, sending pebbles flying. "And why are you so interested in her, anyway?"

Lukas chuckled. "Isn't the better question why *you* are so interested in her?"

Soren clicked his tongue and ignored him. "What if she ran? How will you catch her? Flying is out of the question."

"She didn't run." Lukas tugged aside some branches of a holly bush, avoiding the thorns that clustered around its dew-drop shaped berries. My heart smashed against my ribs when he traced a smudged footprint in the dirt, following my trail to the tree I'd climbed. He picked up a chunk of bark I'd kicked loose and tossed it in the air a few times. "She hid. Something spooked her."

Zos save me. They were going to track me down. My eyes darted around, seeking the fastest escape route.

"Found you."

My skin iced over. I'd been so focused on Lukas that I'd lost track of Soren. The shifter stood beneath me now, eerie black eyes fixed on my face. He beckoned with one finger, a taunt, summoning me like a docile dog. I rose to the challenge.

"Why are you following me?" I straddled the branch, legs swinging. "I told you how to get to Stavanger. That's not where I'm going."

Lukas emerged from the thicket, careful to keep the bow strapped to his back from catching on dangling dead vines. He flicked a few waxy red berries into the air, nimbly catching them in his palm. "Soren isn't convinced you won't tell anyone about us."

Anxiety frothed in my stomach as I peered up the side of the cliff. I'd been a fool to think they would let me leave. But how could I prove myself to them without wasting time? The sun would set again before I made it to the top at this rate. "I told you. I don't care what you are. It wouldn't do me any good to tell anyone about you."

And it wouldn't. Spreading that kind of information would only shine a bright light on me and my family. We escaped intrigue during our trade trips to Stavanger by being as nondescript as possible. Spouting off nonsense about rogue drakken was a sure way to bring the wolven right to our forest.

"You also mentioned the people you could tell would not benefit from that information, either." Soren followed my gaze up the mountain, the wind ruffling his hair. Owl pellets. He knew where I was going. I dropped to the ground, bent knees absorbing the worst of the impact, though my many bruises screamed. "Let's say I trusted your word to not say anything, which I don't." He leveled a glare at me—his default setting, it appeared. "Then I would be forced to trust their words, too, and I don't like leaving that to chance."

This was wasting precious time. I threw my arms in the air, frustration overcoming the fear saturating my thoughts. "You want their word, too? Fine. I'll level with you." I stepped up to the drakken, his nostrils flaring as I shoved into his space. Though I was the smallest member of my clan, he and I stood about the same height. "I'm heading up the mountain. That's where my family is, alright?" I loathed giving up this kind of information, especially to someone who trusted me as little as I trusted him. "You and your friend have wings. How about one of you fly me to the top and you'll get their word faster than a burr gorges itself on a honeytree."

I swore Soren's lips twitched in humor. "A honeytree? That's pretty fast." He leaned down. "And that would be a no. Flying isn't an option for me, currently. Remember that time you smashed into my wing?" His brow arched.

Our noses practically touched. "And Lukas?"

The golden shifter spoke for himself, voice tinged with humor. "There is no way I am leaving Soren here alone. No offense, but while I might not want you dead, I am nowhere close to trusting you."

Soren and I barely blinked. His smirk was a lethal warning, like the crest of a silverfin's back jutting from the lake. "Even if I could fly, my wings aren't equipped with super-strength, if you catch my drift."

My cheeks heated. "Are you calling me heavy?"

An arm shoved between us, Lukas inserting himself directly into our conversation. "Enough." He lightly shoved Soren back, scoffing. I got the feeling he fought with Soren on a regular basis and was getting a real kick out of seeing him at odds with someone else.

"I believe my friend is so tactlessly trying to relay that he is tired and would greatly appreciate if you would escort us to your humble abode. We would appreciate the opportunity to confirm your claims ourselves."

"Lukas—"

Lukas snarled at Soren, a sudden predatory shift that had me flinching back. The rumble started low in his chest and hissed through his teeth, pupils expanding as he coiled away from me. "You insisted on this. Remember?"

An icy burst of wind rattled the trees, branches knocking together. I thought I smelled smoke, but when I inhaled again, it was gone. Soren rolled his eyes, bracing his hand on the pommel of his sword in a manner that spoke of casual violence. "If you let me speak, I was going to say I didn't like the idea of a girl wandering the woods by herself. Archer can wait."

I didn't understand the dynamics between them. In the clearing, I'd felt like Lukas was the one running the show; however, I now got the impression that Soren was truly the one in charge.

The darker drakken peered up the mountain. "Will you take us with you? Or will we need to trail you? Either way, these woods reek of wolven and I'm not leaving you alone until I know where you're going and what you're up to."

I pulled my arms across my chest, pads of my fingers scraping across the scars cut into my leather bracers, fixating on the newest, deepest slashes, remembering how I'd gotten them. It could come in handy having a pair of drakken by my side, especially if wolven were nearby. If there was one truth Idileans knew, it was where one soldier emerged, a group of them wasn't far behind.

The image of the second wolven, the one who'd offered me his hand, brushed my thoughts. He hadn't seemed intent on killing me… but I didn't understand his motives. Maybe his were worse than the ones I'd been taught to associate with the people of Fior. Maybe he was just trying a new tactic to coax me into slave labor of a different kind.

The copper in my spine hardened, my mind clearing. Better safe than sorry.

"Alright." I held up a finger. "But if you fall behind or cost me any more time, I will not stop."

Soren released his weapon. "Lead the way."

* * *

"I think. It is time. You skipped a meal. Or two," Lukas puffed. He crouched on a log that stood taller than I did, his back to me, boots braced, muscles straining, dragging Soren up the other side.

I crossed my arms, restraining a shiver at the steadily dropping temperatures, hip cocked, admiring the blond drakken's determination. For all his energy now, I wondered when it would flag. He'd brushed off my hesitant offer of assistance four logs and two sheer rock cliffs ago, and despite my threat to move on, the entertainment of watching the larger man struggle to help his friend without jarring his arm proved too much to pass up.

Soren landed with a crash on top of Lukas. Both men were red in the face, sweat dripping off their chins, panting. Something wicked flashed across Soren's face, and he pushed himself upright, cradling his arm carefully. "You're blaming me? Clearly, you're slacking on your upper strength training."

"Shut up, you oaf." Lukas shoved his friend off him, and Soren slipped down the side of the log with ease that belied the effort it had taken getting him over it.

Soren swept sweat-soaked hair out of his face, rogue humor dancing across his lips. "Lead on. I can't wait to see what challenge you throw at poor Lukas next."

Only an idiot would miss the pain he concealed in that crooked smile. The azure light of early dawn accentuated the shadowy exhaustion clinging to his eyes and limbs, the arch of his back as he hunched over. It was no wonder either, considering Lukas hadn't wrapped his injury correctly.

"Are you sure you don't want me to wrap up your wound?" I asked, motioning to my own bandages. My body still screamed with pain, but I was determined to get home, to see what was left of my life. But regardless of my own pain, I hated to see another suffering. "Your sling doesn't cradle your arm properly."

Lukas dropped beside Soren and strode onward, cloak catching on the brambles. "You focus on getting us wherever we are going. I will monitor Soren's progress." He waved a hand dismissively. "He is fine—"

"Actually." Soren snatched Lukas' hand out of the air in a move so quick I barely saw it. A tremor ran through me, my breath quickening as fear ignited once more. For all their clumsy comradery, these were still drakken capable of killing me with one swipe of a taloned hand.

"I wouldn't mind seeing what she can do." Soren eyed me. "You really think you can help?"

At the edge of the path, a snowshoe hare crouched, black button nose quivering. Its ears twitched twice before it slunk behind some densely packed foliage. I sighed, forcing the fear down where it belonged. Why was I doing this again? Why was I offering to help a stranger? Wasn't I in a hurry?

Because you're a good person. I could almost hear Viv chastising me. She was always the first to jump on me when I talked down about myself, when I doubted my instincts. No doubt in my mind, she wouldn't hesitate to help these men, drakken or not.

"Yes," I said. "I owe you for saving me from certain death, anyway."

"Works for me." Soren batted Lukas away. "Go make yourself useful somewhere else."

"Fine, but if you harm him, I will return the favor tenfold." His bow may have been strapped to his back, but I was under no illusions it wouldn't take longer than a few seconds for him to have an arrow pointed at my head.

I opened the flap of my bag, heart clenching when I remembered Pip wasn't nestled inside like she preferred to when she slept.

"But what if hurting him helps him?" I asked.

Lukas tsked.

"You shouldn't bait him," Soren warned, hissing through his teeth when I untied Lukas' awkward attempt at a sling. "He's very defensive when it comes to me."

Obviously.

Working quickly, I unspooled the linen wrapped tightly around his shoulder and arm, taking stock of the blue and purple bruises blooming on his skin. "I need you to remove your shirt," I ordered.

Soren's dark eyes flashed. "And if I said no?"

"Then I can't fix you."

The shadow that clung to him deepened. "What if I'm too damaged to be fixed?"

I clenched my teeth, molars grinding together. I definitely wasn't touching that. "I assure you I can heal your injury, but I need to see your musculoskeletal frame, so I know what I'm working with."

It was the truth. While I spent most of my time puttering around the woods and digging in the garden, my greatest skills were in the medical tent. From birds to burrs to boys, I'd tended to all of them. My fascination with how bodies worked drove my desire to learn more.

This man here presented a unique challenge. I'd never had a

chance to examine a shifter before, and I practically vibrated with eagerness at the opportunity, wondering what muscles and scars and bones he hid beneath his clothing.

A thrush trilled and snow crunched. Lukas leaned against a tree. Soren huffed and shrugged off first his cloak, then his shirt, wincing when his bare flesh was exposed to the brittle elements. I took his clothes and slung them over a branch, keeping them dry.

"I'll be quick," I promised absently, circling him, my professional side warring with my personal one for the first time since I could remember. Clearing my throat, I told myself the burn prickling my cheeks and chest was from the cold.

The boys I'd grown up with had honed their bodies for hunting and fishing, surviving the elements. Soren was another story. His powerful frame relayed a story of hard work and dedication, his wiry limbs spoke of quick maneuvering and quiet patience, his long and twisting scars were evidence of sword fights and battlefields. He was no boy.

"Like what you see?" Lukas mocked.

"Quite."

I muffled a smile when I caught Lukas' scowl in my periphery. I finally stopped circling and reached out, hesitating before making contact with Soren's skin. "May I touch you?"

It took him a moment to nod, as if he'd woken from a trance, bracing for my touch. Though he'd been expecting it, he still jumped when I traced a trio of muscles that connected his arm to his shoulder, applying as little pressure as possible.

"I've seen people use weapons and hone their skills around them, but I've never seen anyone sculpt their body like it's a weapon before." I traced the line of a tendon, fascinated with how it curved around his back and joined with a web of muscles that seemed distinctly inhuman. "Fortunately for you, this helps immensely."

"How so?"

"It helps me see everything more clearly." I circled his elbow, imagining how the bones and muscles and ligaments came together. As I'd thought, shifter bodies were more complex than human ones: built with more stuff inside them than I was used to seeing. Vaguely, I wondered if his bones were lighter, too, to better allow for flight.

"Show me where it hurts the most."

Lukas stepped away from the tree, a notebook in his hands, when Soren lightly touched a cluster of muscles in his shoulder. I nodded, pulling my lower lip between my teeth, realigning my thoughts.

"How could you tell I didn't wrap him up properly before?" Lukas pressed a pencil to the pages, his animosity to my work clearly forgotten. His protective nature fascinated me, seeing how it waxed and waned with his open curiosity.

I explained how he hadn't addressed the muscles truly affected by the crash. "Soren, would you show me where it hurts in your other form?"

Even as a child, I'd wondered how shifters worked, whether they were like two beings in one body, or if they were merely a person who possessed two forms. Maybe I would finally get my answer.

Silence settled, delicate as freshly fallen snow. Lukas cocked his head, waiting to see what Soren did. He thought for a minute and a loud crackling sound emanated from his form. I stuttered back a few steps, transfixed, as the shifter's body snapped and flexed and transitioned into his second form. A few moments later the drakken I'd crashed into peered down at me.

"Zos protect me," I breathed in astonishment, struggling to regain my mental balance.

The beast cocked his head, the harsh angles of his scaly face shimmering in the moonlight. Right. I had a job to do. Releasing a long breath, I indicated for him to turn around. Soren did as I asked.

Shoving aside questions about how a human could pack all these extra muscles and bones into their body, I examined his injured wing. Lukas trailed me as I lightly handled the extended limb, and when my curiosity was sated, I told Soren to transition back to his human form.

That process took even less time.

Part of me realized the magic allowing the drakken to shift into impossible forms also allowed them to remain fully clothed, for which I was supremely grateful, but I was too caught up in my medical analysis to give it much thought. Something to chew on later.

"That's good." I approached to see his human back at a better angle, thinking of the owls I'd treated back home. I could visualize the injury on his drakken form and realized he needed a splint. The sling didn't support the right muscles.

A hand closed around mine.

"I'm not a fan of how you're looking at me right now," Soren grumbled. "Like I'm something to be dissected. Can you help me or not?"

I peered at him, fighting every instinct to jerk my hand back. "I can."

His eyes narrowed. "Before I let you treat me, I need you to answer something for me."

"What's that?"

"If you weren't trying to die or magically sprout your own pair of wings, why were you falling from that cliff?"

My throat went tight, and I closed my eyes. In the blackness behind my eyelids, a bloodied owl chirped a warning. White fangs flashed. A man reached for me. My foot slipped and my back met nothing but clear, empty air. Soren tugged me closer. The heat radiating from his body warmed my soul. When I opened my eyes again, his face consumed my vision. Fear flickered, and I struggled to search for Lukas, wondering where he'd gone.

"Don't worry about Lukas," Soren said, as if he'd read my mind. "He's more bark than bite. It's me you need to worry about. I'm the one who could rip your throat out at a moment's notice without feeling a moment of remorse. Now answer me and I'll trust you to finish your work."

I squared my shoulders. "I didn't jump. No one pushed me. I wasn't under any magical delusions." I swallowed. "I was chased until I ran out of ground."

I scented smoke on Soren's breath, subtle but sooty. I'd never seen a more intense look on anyone before, even Papa, when he spoke of those dark days spent fleeing the capital.

"Wolven." Soren's hatred was putrid. He released me. "I understand."

Though he'd spoken only three words, something about his tone settled me, grounded me. "Good. Now let me fix you."

He grunted, but released my arm, and I got to work, losing myself in the rhythm of healing an injury. Soren watched without further complaint, and Lukas also remained surprisingly silent, helping me find the materials I needed from the forest and my bag, taking notes all the while. When I finished, I rubbed Soren's elbow consolingly and stepped back. Lukas quickly took my place, the drakken's shirt in hand, peering at my work.

"Does it hurt?" he asked Soren.

The darker man shook his head and shrugged on his shirt. Though he'd been shirtless for at least an hour, he gave no sign of discomfort, and I recalled the near-boiling temperature of his blood surging beneath my fingers. "It feels awkward. I'll need to be careful moving around. But I don't feel any pain."

"You have never worked on shifters before?" Lukas asked me.

I kept my head bowed, putting away my medical kit with practiced efficiency. I'd mentioned the deficiency in my education during my analysis. Now that my attention had shattered, the cold spilled in, dipping icy fingers into the holes and openings of my clothes. I shivered and blew out a puff of cloudy air. "Call it a hunch."

Lukas shook his head, blond hair falling into his eyes, and muttered something that sounded like, "Hunch, my ass," but I couldn't be sure, and I didn't wait to find out more. We'd taken enough of the early dawn light dawdling here, and I had places to be. Before I proceeded up the path, Soren snagged my elbow again. I opened my mouth to snap at him to stop grabbing me, when I realized he offered his cloak. "You need this more than me."

I didn't disagree and soundlessly pulled the heavy material over my shoulders, keenly aware of his scent wrapping around me—clean like river water and pine needles. We didn't speak again as we continued onward, the men trailing my steps closely, eyes boring into my back.

The dull grays and blues of the pre-dawn light gave way to bloody reds and glistening oranges that marked the impending day. We only stopped to drink; the men shared one canteen, insisting I take the other for myself. The higher we went, with the silverpines and evergreens packed together more densely than they had in the valley, the greater my anxiety spiked. As we neared the crest, a scent stung my nose, one that didn't blend with the snow and cold. Fear clenched tight in my gut.

"Smoke," Lukas whispered so quietly I wasn't sure I meant to hear.

Finding new resolve, I pushed faster, harder, practically running up the partially obscured trail, knowing the crest was close. At the top, it was only a quick sprint through the trees, the shifters on my heels. The smell grew thick, choking, the air so hazy I buried my nose in my arm to breathe. The crackling snow gave way to slush, and I almost slipped, catching myself on the white bark of a whisperelm.

Lukas gasped, drawing even with me.

Soren went lethally quiet.

Jaw clenched, heart in my throat, ribs straining with stress as I stared out over the ruined wasteland of what had once been my home.

3

Lives Stolen

Solas had burned through the night, the thick waves of black smoke obscured by the angle of the mountain peaks. The Fiorian soldiers must have found my village not long after chasing me over the edge of the Spear. Of our three dozen cabins, only four still stood; fire had reduced the rest to little more than blackened boards and chunks of ash. Tongues of flame flickered among the rubble, the heat of the coals almost unbearable.

On coltish legs, I forced myself forward, finding the path that led through the center of the homes and buildings. Lukas called out a warning, but I barely heard it. I needed to know what had happened to Papa. To Viv.

The pale, smooth stones of the path usually covered in a film of frost this time of year were cracked and dry, the edges crumbling beneath my boots. A puff of smoke blew in my face and I coughed, pulling my shirt over my nose to protect my lungs. There wasn't anything I could do about my eyes, tears dripping from them in long, slow streams.

I passed the greenhouse first. The wide sheets of glass Papa and I had painstakingly carried up the mountain one by one were shattered, the skeletal metal frame dark with soot and char. The plants I'd breathed life into despite the inhospitable conditions were mangled and ruined, crushed beneath the boots of whoever had stomped them into the dirt. Beyond it, our cottage. Or what used to be my home, anyway. A loud crack split the skies, and what remained of the crumbling roof collapsed into the pile of coals, their hue matching that of the sun blazing at my back.

I didn't need to pick through the remains to know what had come of my belongings. My collection of seeds and medical supplies, Papa's carvings, the worn and yellowed letters written by my mother—all gone. I couldn't swallow past the arrowhead in my throat, its edges as jagged as the pain ripping through my insides.

Viv's house next door fared the same. And Petr's beyond that.

But where was everyone? They should have been here.

A wave of scorching heat rushed over me as another cottage crumbled into dust, but I couldn't stop shaking, the chill striking me through to the marrow. Across the street, much of the smithy had survived the onslaught with its metal-worked walls and doors, but I didn't enter. Something else caught my eye, and I hesitated beside an iron bench outside, one that Viv and I frequently lounged on while waiting for her mother to wrap up work over the years, gossiping and dreaming. I refused to allow myself to fall into the memories. Instead, I tugged on a leather strap caught on the spokes that comprised the back of the bench, revealing a pouch.

Tears flowing freely, I cradled a bag in my arms, peering at the shimmering knives resting in its belly. Viv's knives. She must have tossed them aside or tried to hide them. From what I could see inside the smithy, the wolven had stolen the weapons hanging from hooks and resting in their racks, but these had escaped notice.

With a whimper, I smashed them against my chest, swiping my soot-streaked hand over my cheek. If her knives were here, where was she? Viv had crafted these with her own two hands and trained with them endlessly. If she'd had a say in the matter, she would never have left them behind.

Footsteps crunched behind me, crushing remnants of stone and wood underfoot. A figure emerged from the haze, and though I'd only just met him, I recognized Soren's stature, the way he held himself as if preparing for a fight.

"Telleree, I need you to brace yourself," he ordered, eyes snapping like coals in his carefully blank face. A shard of lightning-like pain lanced through my stomach at the sound of my name on his lips and dreaded what would follow. "Your people… they didn't make it. Lukas and I found bodies in the center of your town, many of them." His hands closed around my shaking shoulders, though he kept a measure of distance between us. "You don't have to see them, but if you do want to, Lukas and I will stand with you."

What he'd seen must have been horrible, if he'd exchanged his glare for something that felt a lot like sympathy. My throat clicked, and it took a few attempts to swallow down the smoke coating it, resenting the anguish sinking its claws into me.

"I need to know what happened to them. I need to know—" My voice cracked, cleaved in two. Rather than finish my thought, I peered over his shoulder into the hazy blur of smoke. The drakken stepped aside to follow me past what remained of the cottages and the bigger building that had once served as Solas' kitchen and dining space. The long tables I'd spent what felt like eons scrubbing after every meal, now leaned sideways, fire-chewed and charred. In the open space out front where we'd enjoyed our meals, chattering about the day's trials and accomplishments, lay a pile of bodies.

A shrill sound escaped my throat, for though they'd burned, the wolven hadn't paid them as much heed as they had the village, and I recognized their faces. Lukas stood off to the side, bow propped on his boots, face lined with pity. His gloves were black, cheeks smeared with blood and soot. He must have straightened them for me, knowing I needed to see their faces like this.

"I need to—I need to get closer," I choked out. After giving me one of those long, considering looks, Soren shifted to Lukas' side, keeping vigil over the remains of people they'd never known. I shoved Viv's knives into my bag, not wanting to risk dropping them as I approached the first body. Helvig, the aged butler who'd discovered a new calling in carpentry; Petr, our butcher; Tuva and her husband, Eof. People I'd spoken to every day of my life. Gone. Their gazes empty, souls departed.

Around and around I went, an uneasiness settling on my shoulders. Despite the number of bodies here, some were missing. Maybe a dozen? I couldn't find the Vettel twins and their father. Viv or her mother.

Then I recognized Papa.

I dropped to my knees beside the last body, a sob caught in the hollow of my chest, an ugly sound that refused to come out. His face was bruised, his nose broken, his throat a gory mess of muscle and tendon ripped wide open. Choking sobs cracked from my open mouth. Blood stained his fingers, slivers of skin that wasn't his caught beneath his nails. He'd fought his attackers, but it hadn't been enough. And now he was here. Cradled in my lap, his clear blue eyes open and unseeing. Beneath him, his cloak was shredded, the feathers he'd so carefully looked after reduced to splinters.

With a shaking hand, I touched his arm, insides weeping at the lack of give in his muscles, the chill of his skin.

Papa was gone.

Never again would he sing while wrapping twine around the wheat. Never again would his booming laugh rise above the conversation at dinner. Never again would he point out the saplings breaking through the stiff earth at the start of rapt, trace the slender veins of a frostmaple leaf, ask me to identify the warbling call of a red-breasted screech owl in the dead of night.

The owls.

Tears dripped from my cheeks, catching on the wrinkles fanning from the corners of his eyes, and I closed them, my heart shriveling into a lifeless husk behind my ribs. There wasn't anything more I could do for him, but that didn't mean my work was done.

"I'll be right back," I mumbled, stumbling over myself as I shot to my feet, knees watery. If I stayed here any longer, I would crack and break into a million pieces. If I allowed myself to collapse into grief, I would never have the strength to find out if any of our precious animals had survived the slaughter. "I need to check on something."

Lukas called my name.

But it was too late. I charged into the forest, barely feeling the boards giving beneath my boots as I raced through their charred and rotting remains. Moments later, dappled shadows spilled across my borrowed cloak, the perpetual night that was the density of the Owl Wood engulfing me in its embrace. And still I sprinted, barely feeling my breath in my lungs, leaping over logs and darting around trees, racing against what felt like time itself.

Then I found the first nest. It belonged to a pair of saw-whet owls who'd only just settled down. Blood pounded in my ears as I approached the pine inside which they'd made their home. I'd barely gone three paces when I stumbled across the first spill of fuzzy feathers. The wing torn from a tiny body.

A sob ripped from me now, like it hadn't been able to before.

Head spinning, breath see-sawing in and out of my lungs, I returned to the main trail, intent on finding the next nest. Over and over again, I found the same thing. Scattered feathers. Bloodied limbs. Bodies with hollow bones partially buried in the spray of fresh snow that fallen across this haunted land.

Snowy, gray, barn, screech, young, old—all birds Papa and I had raised and loved and cared for. Their lives stolen by vicious, snapping teeth and flaying claws.

It was when I was on the brink of collapse that I emerged into the clearing. The one favored by the great horned owls of my childhood. The place where this nightvision had begun. My footprints, messy and dark, scarred the ground. I followed the path of broken branches, wetting my lips, releasing the call I'd whistled repeatedly, hoping in vain one of my owls would answer back.

Still nothing.

"Zos, I beg of you. Please spare her your mercy." Teeth chattering, I pleaded with my goddess, the one who craved the dark and abhorred the light. The goddess Papa had urged me to find strength in my heart to follow, knowing now in our most violent of days the bloody-toothed deity would offer the greatest comfort. I whistled sharply, the questioning call of a screech owl.

Pip didn't answer.

My mangled chest cracked in two, but still I trudged on, following the path I'd taken before, refusing to give up on the last vestiges of hope. Again and again, I uttered that same broken call, only stopping to pick up my cloak where the wolven had abandoned it. My fingers poked through a trio of slashes near the hem and plucked at the splinters of feather shafts. An easy fix, unlike the pulpy mass that remained of my heart.

Quietly, I unhooked Soren's cloak and replaced it with mine, allowing the familiarity of its weight to comfort me. I draped the heavy fabric over my bag and continued toward the cliff that led to the Spear. When I finally reached it, I couldn't feel my fingers or toes anymore, as if part of my soul had departed my body and trailed behind like a ghostly remnant. As I climbed, I recoiled from the bloody stains, recalling the awful sounds of claws beneath me, the whisper of hot breath against the back of my neck.

It wasn't until I reached the tip of the Spear that I stopped, staring down at the rest of the world. The clusters of trees, bright green in the morning sunshine; the shadowed valleys and broad slopes of unbroken snow; and finally, the sharp teeth of the jagged rocks below.

I clutched my cloak around me, brown and white feathers pressed against my nose, their musky scent comforting in a way only I understood, and sat, legs folded beneath me.

Tears stung like nettles in the corners of my eyes and I allowed them to come in ragged, choking bursts, unleashing the torment battering my insides like a blizzard.

Less than a day ago, I'd waved and called out to my father as he chopped wood, his shirt dark with sweat. He'd swiped the back of his hand over his glistening forehead and smiled, his heart in his eyes but no breath left in his lungs to tell me to be safe while I checked on the birds. That was my last memory of him, content with this isolated home he had created here at the Idilean border.

Now he was gone, his throat ripped out, his blood soaked into the snow beneath his body.

So many others who called our village home were also gone, souls headed to the great strovara.

And I alone remained.

"Why?" I begged into my cloak. Then repeated it, louder, surging to my feet as I shouted the demand, my voice echoing off the walls of the mountains. No answer came.

I wasn't going to get one.

The soldiers prowled our lands, killing and enslaving, quashing signs of resistance as they worked our people to death in the mines, digging up and exporting our precious gemstones for their own selfish greed. For years they'd never so much as looked at these mountains, once considered a death sentence for anyone who trekked them. They had no reason to seek us out unless...

Awareness surged with an icy gust that snarled my dark hair around my face.

Unless someone had told them we were here.

I held perfectly still, the tracks of tears frozen on my face.

We had returned from our latest trip to Stavanger a mere two weeks ago, our packs and carts weighted down with necessary supplies to help us usher in the new season: bundles of vegetable seeds, long rolls of summer wool, raw materials to help Viv's mother with her blacksmithing. I remembered the signs posted on the walls outside of the stores and taverns, signs screaming in black ink to report suspicious activity to the Fiorian commanders.

Rewards would be given for promising information.

My chin trembled. I didn't recall seeing any wolven patrolling the markets that day, and as much as I wanted to hope our own people wouldn't have turned us in, they had no reason to protect us, to spare us when we'd already escaped the worst of the atrocity.

Wind whistled around the rocks and I stepped to the edge, peering at the landscape I loved so dearly, woods I'd mapped in my heart. Despite my earlier fall, I felt no fear about the risk I took again, standing so close. My family was dead. My things burned. My village ransacked. There wasn't much to salvage from the ruins, especially not enough to survive on up here.

I needed a plan. Staying here wasn't an option. Without supplies and shelter, I wouldn't last long, and despite my devotion to the goddess of death and darkness, I wasn't keen on meeting her in the afterlife anytime soon.

Steel gripped my spine, wrapping me in purpose.

Viv and at least a dozen of my people were still missing, likely in the clutches of the Fiorian soldiers. I didn't know exactly where they were headed, but I could find out. I could track them down, maybe even find out who had betrayed us.

Dry leaves recently uncovered by the melting frost blew past, mere streaks of orange and amber. I recalled the gleam of Viv's hair as my best friend turned to smile at me before heading back to Solas, the bite of bitterness in her eyes when she slanted a look at the nest, her love for the owls warring with her distaste for how they rooted me to these lands.

My hands clenched into fists at my sides.

I wouldn't leave her to the wolven. Any of them. The people of Fior had taken so much from us. I wouldn't allow them to take what remained. I would find out where they were going and I would free them—no matter what it took or what it cost me in the end. My family was all I had. If there was still a chance that Viv lived and breathed, I would find her.

The low warble sounded behind me. A tiny shadow darted from the depths of the wood, wings pumping furiously. Relief choked me. I reached out my arm, leather bracer extended. As always, Pip ignored the offer and landed on my shoulder, her pine-cone sized body trembling against my neck.

Hope bloomed, dark and dusty in the charred ashes of my soul.

Papa was gone, my home destroyed...

But Pip and Viv lived.

And I had a purpose.

I could live up to that.

4

Nothing Left

Pip flew beside me on silent wings as we headed back to Solas. The going was slow, but I didn't mind the pace, finding time to reflect and murmur small prayers as I collected the remains of the owls at each of the nests along the way, bundling them in the ball of my cloak at my side.

I didn't understand why the wolven targeted them. The question burrowed deep into my mind and festered there, like an infected wound.

These woods housed all kinds of wildlife, including an array of thrush, pheasants, and other fowl, yet I only found mangled bodies of owls. The wolven had specifically and singularly selected them, going so far as to shift into their human forms to climb trees to knock their nests to the ground—and the snarling muzzles that waited there.

It didn't make sense.

Owls and wolves rarely hunted the same prey. They bore no territorial disputes. On top of that, owls were relatively peaceful birds, attacking only when they felt threatened. It was entirely possible a few had swooped to attack the wolven when they encroached on their territory, but going after the nests was an entirely different thing. If they were after my family, stopping to take out the nests would have hindered their progress.

Again, I considered the shifter on the Spear, his quiet demeanor. He'd asked if I lived around here, if I called the mountains my home. Maybe he knew the truth and was baiting me, wondering if I would lead him to Solas, making the massacre easier. Those golden laurels on his shoulders meant something. He wasn't an ordinary soldier.

The sense of contrition I'd perceived from him earlier vanished with a snap, and I vowed to put him out of my mind. The odds of us ever meeting again were slim, anyway.

Finally, limbs heavy with grief and exhaustion, I reached the nest closest to Solas. I didn't want to trudge down the path I'd trampled earlier that night, to see what remained of Viv's favorite snowy owls. But I had to see this through. Numbness settled in my bones when I passed the first bit of gray fuzz, but I didn't stop until I reached the cradle of rocks. Bloody fuzz and splintered bones were all that remained of the beautiful owlets I'd teased with pigeon.

Even my little prince wasn't spared from the slaughter, his big eyes closed to the world forever.

My hands shook when I reached for their tiny bodies, nestling them among the rest of the remains of my birds. My eyes burned with tears that wouldn't come, and I barely felt the chill nipping at my exposed skin when I returned to the path.

At the edge of the village, I whistled for Pip. She landed on my bracer, yellow eyes wide and feathers fluffed. I opened the mouth of my bag against my hip and motioned for her to hop inside, whispering, "Stay out of sight."

While I counted on the drakken to help me get to Stavanger in one piece, I didn't trust them and definitely didn't intend to reveal more about myself than I already had. Let them wonder about my reasons for bringing the bodies of these owls back with me. They didn't need to understand my motives, only believe I didn't pose enough of a threat to them to take me out.

With a trill of discontent, Pip ducked into the depths of the satchel, wrapped her claws around the metal casing of my medical supplies, and promptly closed her eyes, lulled by the dark and the warmth. She'd hidden there many times before, seeking refuge from the brutal winds of the peaks and valleys. I would be careful to not squash her.

I'd been gone long enough for the crackling coals of Solas to blacken, yet the stench of death lingered. Without complaint, I worked my way around the single remaining wall of what had once been Petr's home.

Most of the cottages were equally damaged, but the one belonging to our resident weaver was relatively untouched. Blinking back the burn of a memory of laughing with Flora when I'd miserably messed up what was meant to be violet dye, I ducked inside. Though smoke-damaged, her place was as meticulously organized as always, and I easily found a scarf to replace the one I'd lost. After a beat, I also snagged two sets of gloves, a hat, a change of clothing that looked to be about my size, and a blanket thin enough to stuff into my satchel.

A shadow appeared in the doorway and I gasped, hand pressed tight to my breast, when I found Soren leaning against the frame, arms folded across his narrow chest. He had rolled his sleeves to his elbows, and his forearms and hands were dark with dried blood and soot. The shifter waited for me to scoop up the owls, expression dark with curiosity, then angled his head toward the center of camp. I followed, taking care to not get too close. He'd left his sword somewhere, but his imposing presence reassured me in a way I hadn't expected.

Lukas dipped out of the doorway to a house at the edge of our communal area. He'd also removed his cloak and shoved up his sleeves, his white shirt wet with sweat, clinging to the muscles of his back and chest. He swiped an arm across his forehead, smearing the ash that had settled in his pores, and pursed his lips in a pitying sort of smile when he spotted me.

"There you are." He didn't acknowledge my armful of dead birds. Instead, he thumbed at the cottage over his shoulder, two of its walls heavily charred by flames. "That is the last of the houses. Soren and I checked them again, making sure we hadn't missed anyone."

That was kind. They didn't know me and hadn't needed to do that. My throat locked when I tried to express my thanks, and I settled for nodding stiffly instead. I stepped around him and entered the communal area, limbs trembling with exhaustion.

They were here. Most of the people I'd known for my entire life. The shifters had laid their bodies in long rows, branching outward from a roaring fire pit like spokes on a wagon wheel. Beneath their bodies, they'd tucked bits of dried brush and tinder. The arms of each body were folded across their chests, hands resting on the balls of their shoulders, eyes and noses covered with long bits of fabric cut from their clothing.

Just when I thought I didn't have any left in me, tears stung my eyes.

The drakken had arranged a traditional Idilean funeral pyre.

I knelt at the end of one of those rows and removed the bodies of my owls from the makeshift pouch, carefully arranging them beside Tuva. The former castle cook had often joked owl meat was too stringy and tough to chew, which was why she didn't bother with them, but I knew she just had a soft spot for the birds.

From each of the owls, I took a feather and bound them together with a bit of string, like a spray of flowers. That bundle joined the other supplies in my bag. I would stitch them into my cloak in memory of their sacrifice.

"I'd like to check the bodies again," I murmured, notepad in hand, and flipped to a fresh page. These were people who had sacrificed so much in the name of survival. The world deserved to know their names one day, and I needed to know who was among the missing. Lukas sat on the stoop of the porch he'd exited, elbows braced on his thighs. Soren also didn't object, his dark gaze sweeping across the town in search of danger. A muscle flicked in his jaw.

The soft scratching of lead against paper settled my nerves, and the names flowed onto the page easily. I would give them a funeral pyre now, but a memory board would have to come later. I tugged my scarf over my nose to mute the stench, periodically shooting glances at my new companions, a hint of trepidation wheedling its way under the numbness of my soul.

Though the question had arisen earlier, I now gave it true examination: Who were these men and why were they here? They'd gone out of their way to arrange an Idilean funeral for the members of my village, a tradition that was among the first eradicated when Fior overtook our country. That and eliminating our gods from memory.

I'd heard stories of wolven soldiers pillaging our seven revered temples, massacring the priests and priestesses who protected them. They'd instilled their own dual deities: representatives of the sun and the moon who demanded the dead be buried rather than burned. Their religion insisted the earth protected the souls of the departed while the gods weighed their sins. The idea of burial churned the stomachs of all but the least devoted Idileans. According to our teachings, the earth trapped spirits. By burning them in the open, we allowed our departed to escape their earthly bounds and begin their mission to reach strovara and reside among the gods.

However, to defy Fiorian order meant death by public execution. My hand jerked, the pencil dragging a thick, black line across the page. Isolated as we were, my family and I never adhered to the harsh policies ordered by the Grand Duke of Fior. We only adopted demure statures when we traded in Stavanger.

These drakken would surely have hailed from more populated areas. The richness of their clothing and differences in accents implied as much. We in the north talked like our mouths were filled with metal, our sentences quick and the consonants jagged as the Copper Mountains. Soren and Lukas rounded their vowels, speaking more from the backs of their throats.

I'd invoked the name of Fen earlier, and surely, they'd heard me muttering to Zos on the climb to the top of the mountain, yet they'd said nothing. Perhaps that had led them to create the pyre...

Or they hadn't considered the Fiorian funeral rites at all. They were drakken. Real, *free* drakken. Not just shifters mingling in their first forms, hiding among the masses, avoiding the attention of wolven soldiers on the prowl. No, these men dared to transform. To retake the skies. To snub their noses at those who'd told them they would never feel the weight of their wings again.

I closed the notebook around my pencil and stuffed it back in my bag, my hand grazing the warmth of Pip's body as she snoozed.

As I'd noted earlier, Viveca was not here. Neither were ten others.

I knelt beside Papa's body, thankful for the numbness shielding my raw emotions. Without it, I wouldn't be able to handle this weight. My hands shook as I traced the bruises on his face and the scars on the backs of his hands. With effort, I worked his cloak out from beneath him, the feathers crumpled and smashed. I smoothed them out and laid it across his chest, the sun catching on the hundreds of shades of brown and black and white, turning it radiant.

I pressed my lips to his forehead, tears trickling down my cheeks.

"May Zos guide your way, Papa. Someday I'll see you in strovara, but Viv and the others need me now." I choked back a sob. "It's not the path you dreamed of for me, but you always told me the gods acted with purpose. There has to be a reason for this, and I need to find out what that is."

Someone had left a torch burning beside the roaring fire pit and I grabbed it, joining my new companions at the edge of the pyre. I didn't brush away my tears. There was no shame in grief.

"Is there anything else you need?" Soren asked. He'd reattached his sword to the belt around his hips and unrolled his sleeves, but the cloak I'd returned hung over his arms across his chest, defying the bite of the mountain air. "From the cabins?"

Oh. Right. I handed the torch to Lukas. "I'll be quick."

As I went through the cottages, I tamped down the greasy slick of guilt that came with rummaging through the belongings of others. They were dead and would not need the medical supplies I added to my emergency kit or the coins they'd saved up. I told myself they would want me to succeed in my newfound mission rather than let their things go to waste. But it still felt wrong, and I ducked in and out of the homes quickly, only lingering at the mouth of the smithy.

Viv's collection of knives rested against my hand, against my pouch, and I wasn't sure where her rapier might be, but would I need anything else? The wolven had snatched the obvious weapons, and I ran my fingertips over a row of hammers forged in various sizes. This was Viv's domain. I didn't understand how these tools worked, nor did I like the feel of steel against my hands. On top of that, my satchel hung heavily against my neck and I couldn't risk it weighing me down too much. I left without taking anything and returned to the pyre.

Soren and Lukas stopped whispering as soon as I turned the corner, expressions blank. Lukas pulled back the torch before I could take it.

"What is your plan?" His voice held the weight of authority I'd heard when I'd first met him. "Your home is destroyed. Your family is dead." I tried not to flinch at the harshness of his words. "There is nothing left for you here. Where are you going next?"

"The Fiorian soldiers took several members of my family captive, including someone very dear to me." It was Soren's gaze I sought out next. "I will find them and free them, no matter if I have to go deep into the mines or swim across the sea to do so. They are my responsibility, and by the grace of Zos, I will do right by them."

Soren's eyes flared hot with approval. "So be it."

"We will help however we can," Lukas agreed, allowing me to take the torch at last.

Blood whooshed in my ears and my stomach prickled uneasily with the thought of the unknown that faced me in the future, and I dipped my head in acknowledgment. I wasn't sure what help they might offer, but I would take whatever I could get, because once I left these mountains, I would be in uncharted territory.

With a silent prayer to my goddess of darkness and all her brothers and sisters, I touched the flame to the kindling upon which my owls lay, steeling my soul as the fire ignited, devouring what remained of my past.

5

In the Name of Research

Lukas insisted his stamina was too low to fly Soren and me down the mountain. The drakken were slightly larger than draft horses, barely big enough for one person to climb on their back, let alone two, and that meant two trips. He also steadfastly refused to leave Soren's side, so that option wouldn't have worked, anyway.

That left hiking.

Fortunately, I knew a faster trail down the mountain than the one we'd taken up. Even better, it connected with the road to Stavanger. In theory, the wolven could have taken their captives east to the Exeter Mines and the port city along the coast, but after some arguing, Soren and Lukas dismissed the notion, insisting it made more sense for the wolven to head south to Stavanger, reconnect with the rest of their group, and gather supplies for the next leg of their trip. Having very little to do with the outside world, I trusted their insight.

Before we left, we stopped by the river to refill our waterskins and flasks. Willowweed and embersmoke herbs grew in abundance around the edge of the water, so I collected as much as I could and ground them into a thick paste. Once finished, I ordered Soren to spread some of the mixture on his tongue. Once he complied, I followed. The mixture aided with healing and offered relief from the pain of the injuries we'd endured in our fall. My muscles still protested, but it wasn't an all-consuming ache.

All three of us also cleaned our wounds and treated them with the last of the paste to ward off infection. Lukas offered to stitch up the worst of my scratches, for which I was grateful. I'd stitched myself up before, but something about watching the needle glide in and out of my own flesh made my stomach turn. Once we were as ready as we ever would be, we returned to the trailhead.

Though the landscape looked the same going down as it had going up, the atmosphere between us had drastically changed. I, again, took the lead, choosing the route with the most trees to provide extra cover. Their trunks also gave the men something to hold on to as they navigated the difficult terrain. The world felt grayer, darker, blunted somehow. The scarlet of the briarberries didn't shimmer so brightly, the branches that scraped my face and neck didn't burn quite as much. I only spoke up to offer direction or point out a hindrance, occasionally making sure the men who trailed me like raccoon kits hadn't fallen too far behind.

Soren moved more easily than he had before, though an air of pensiveness trailed behind him. Lukas also spoke less, his attention shifted outward as he glided around the trees and scaled boulders. Every now and again, he called for us to wait while he shoved a rock in his bag or plucked a leaf from a tree. Sometimes he whipped out a notepad and sketched a cluster of fauna that interested him or an animal he'd spotted in the distance. Once, I caught him drawing a scale image of the curl of the Spear high over our heads.

The frequent interruptions didn't bother me. I was no stranger to exercise, but never had I done this much of it at once, let alone with bruises littering my entire body, and these woods weren't exactly welcoming.

"We'll reach the base of the Ridge soon," I offered when Lukas pulled out his pad for the fiftieth time, trying to capture the sleek lines of a thistleferret we'd startled out of its den, black whiskers twitching against its snowy fur. "The incline drops off, and it will be easier to move when we get there."

Soren rubbed the scar on his chin. "Shelter?"

A man of few words, that one. "Some. Do you remember when I yelled at you to avoid those rocks when you were trying to land?"

"You mean, when you wrapped yourself around my leg so hard, I nearly lost feeling in it?" He dipped under a low-hanging bough. "Yes, I remember it quite vividly."

"Semantics." I waved my hand. "Those are the rocks we're about to walk through. They're taller and wider than they look from up high, so they should provide some protection from the elements."

"We will stop there to rest." Lukas bobbled a pinecone in his bare hands, heedless of the inch-long spikes shooting from its seeds. "I know you want to get back as soon as possible, Soren, but we're practically dead on our feet. Recharging is as vital as speed, you know."

That plan sounded marvelous. Much longer and my knees would give out from exhaustion. The medication was also wearing off, and I needed to make more. Then there was Pip to consider. I needed some seclusion to release her from the confines of my bag. I only had a few treats with me, and she needed to hunt to keep up her energy.

Soren propped his hand on the clear, square stone topping the pommel of his sword. "You aren't exactly helping with the speed thing, you know."

Lukas grinned, a real, true grin that lit up his pretty features.

"Anything in the name of research."

Soren tsked and motioned me forward. I took stock of where we were and resumed walking, encouraging the men to avoid the leaves of the poison oak wrapped around the trunks of the aspens on our left; their venom could soak through cloth and hair, burning the skin underneath and searing it away like acid.

My skin itched. It felt strange taking the lead.

Normally, Eof led the way to Stavanger, his steadfast attitude coming in remarkably handy when the pressures of extended travel settled in. While he led, I trailed at the back of our group, giggling with Viv as we darted off the trail to explore clusters of boulders or poke at the insects sunning themselves on the rocks, hurrying back when we could barely hear the caravan anymore.

Here, at the front of the line, a sense of responsibility settled on my shoulders. I understood, now, a little of the weight our parents bore every single day.

The sun had disappeared behind the tallest of the Ridge's peaks when we finally stopped. We still had an hour or two before the light fully faded, but in the shadow of dusk it wouldn't take long for the cold to settle in, even here in the valley. I'd already spent one night chilled to the bone and had no desire to repeat that experience. I took the opportunity to separate myself from the drakken, murmuring an excuse of gathering firewood. Neither paid me much attention as they quibbled over which twelve-foot-tall rock offered the best protection for our campsite.

When their arguing was but a buzz in the background, I opened my bag and whistled. Pip darted out, landing on my outstretched arm, carrot-colored eyes wide and expectant. I shook off my glove and stroked her head, appreciating the silk of her feathers.

"Did any of the other owls escape?" Of the birds I'd found, five were missing.

She issued a low warbling noise. Affirmative.

Tension knotting the muscles between my shoulder blades relaxed. A few of them were still out there, and with any luck, they were following us, too shy to emerge. I scanned the bushy furs and the imposing heights of the oaks, ingrained instincts helping me pinpoint the likely areas where one might be roosting, but didn't see anything obvious. Not surprising, if somewhat disheartening.

Pip tittered, and I smiled, rubbing her head again.

"You need to stay out of sight, alright? Something weird is going with those drakken. I don't know what their motives are, but we need each other right now, and that's about as far as my trust in them goes. I'd rather they not know about you or any of the others." I nuzzled her tiny head with my nose. A shadow passed overhead, and we both blinked up at the spotted hawk swooping low in search of prey. Pip clicked her concerns. "And keep yourself safe, too. You're smarter than those hawks, but no daring decisions."

The screech owl released a warm, liquid, throbbing sound from deep in her throat, vibrating her whole body. Her understanding resonated deep inside me, releasing a silvery sensation in my chest. It was a feeling I thought I'd abandoned along with the charred remains of my home.

With one more peep, she took flight and settled in overhead, nearly disappearing into a bundle of dead leaves caught in the crook of a tree. Not wanting the men to get suspicious of my absence, I hurried to gather wood and returned to the cluster of rocks where they had laid out their blankets.

Lukas poked at some kindling he'd already ignited. "Soren's checking the perimeter. He will be back in a moment."

He took the sticks, and I pulled my blanket from my pack, spreading it out on the shale common here at the base of the mountains. Papa used to tell stories about the long veins of copper that tangled deep within the soil and the many small mining communities that had once dug for that valuable ore—most of them shuttered in the wake of the Fiorian takeover. For some reason, the wolven preferred gemstones over metal.

"Would you mind answering a few questions about this terrain?" Lukas sat beside the fire, leaving about six feet of space between us. I wasn't sure where his bow had gone, but I remained alert to the dagger strapped to his thigh. He'd used both the smooth and the serrated sides of the blade to cut things from trees to shove into his bag. The drakken slapped a piece of yellowed parchment on the ground and unfolded it, revealing a map of Idilea.

Against my better instincts, I leaned in. I knew the basics of how our country looked, but I'd never seen anything so detailed before.

"It isn't often we get up to these parts, and I am filling in some of the blank spaces up here." He tapped the triangles labeled 'Copper Mountains.' "Since you live here, I thought you could contribute."

I wet my lips. I couldn't see the harm in sharing what I knew. It wasn't like I needed to protect the secrecy of our village any longer. When I nodded my acceptance, he unearthed a pen from a fold in his sleeve. Ink purpled the tips of his fingers.

I tapped my nail on a spot along the inside of the border with Aurora. "That's my village. We never put up a sign, but we call it Solas." Our sanctuary. My pulse thundered, and I forced myself to breathe evenly, driving the anxiety away. "These forests, the ones along the top of Spear Ridge—" I traced the line of peaks that formed the highest points in our country—"they're the Owl Wood."

Lukas' pen stuttered, a motion so slight I wouldn't have noticed if I weren't so keenly aware of the stranger's proximity to me. "Fascinating. Everyone we have met so far said no one could live at those altitudes, but somehow, you all managed."

Rather than answer the implied question, I took a sip of water from my flask, one Viv's mother had crafted for me upon my sixteenth birthday, and returned to the map. Lukas followed my lead, and we settled into an easy rhythm: I pointed out trails and peaks, circling canyons and the openings to long-abandoned mine shafts, and Lukas asked questions, an endless stream of them as he added the tiniest details to the page.

Soon, the forests of my home, a world I knew so well, came to life right before my eyes, and the lingering tightness in my chest released.

This mattered.

We mattered.

Solas was gone, but I could ensure it would never be forgotten.

"This looks great." Lukas laced his fingers together as he stretched the stiffness from his hands. "You know this area well."

I smiled against my knees, which I'd drawn up to my chest. The fire threw off so much heat, I was tempted to remove my cloak. "I guess so. I've lived here most of my life."

"About that." I jerked at Soren's voice, finding him sitting on a boulder at Lukas' back. He'd propped one foot on the rock and hooked his fingers over his knee. "How long is 'most of your life?' You look to be around our age, so you must have been a child when you arrived here." His mouth flattened, and I fought to keep my spine from stiffening. "And why would you all choose to hide in such seclusion? Does your dark goddess protect you?" His voice dripped with cynicism.

A log snapped and sparks popped in the fire. I held Soren's gaze. The warm lull of my brief partnership with Lukas leeched from my skin like warmth in the snow. My ears rang. These questions would have arisen at some point, but I wasn't ready to answer them. Didn't know if I ever would be. My distrust compounded my concerns.

"That's a good question." I leaned back on the heels of my hands, errant needles prickling me. "In fact, I've got one for you, too. In an area so isolated, what were a pair of *drakken* doing flying around while Fiorian soldiers prowled the woods?" I emphasized the word drakken with a glance at the leather band on his wrist that he fiddled with frequently. I had no doubts that his drakkentorre, which allowed him to shift, was tucked beneath it, firmly pressed to his pulse.

Soren's face hardened, not that his expression changed much anyway, but he stopped fidgeting and tucked his arm against his calf.

According to the myths Papa had recited, ancient dragons used to roam these lands, fearsome beasts larger than castles, capable of breathing fire and acid. When human immigrants moved northward and discovered Idilea, they also encountered these glorious creatures. Many dragons dismissed the humans, and either hid or fled to more remote areas. However, seven dragons saw the potential in humankind and stayed.

They learned human ways and sought to understand our race. After many decades of our alliance, the leader of the dragons embraced his love for humans and wished for them to embrace the skies alongside them. He gifted the humans his tears, granting them rare abilities of fire and flight, dubbing those people his children, his drakken.

That dragon later became known as Qet, our god of wisdom and light.

His six siblings took places of honor and revere beside him.

Since that day, those touched by the dragon's blessing could transform into the glorified creatures, but they could only do so when in contact with drakkentorre—the hardened remnants of his tears that pooled in caverns and ran through one of our mines. Our leaders decreed the plentiful gems be spread throughout the nation, left in bowls in the marketplaces and in temples for all citizens to scoop up and test their abilities. No one truly understood *who* could shift, only that there was a possibility everyone could. The only thing we did know was that the ability was discovered during childhood, never over the age of ten, and those with the power could use their abilities immediately.

The king made it clear the stones held no value outside of their ability to grant shifters their abilities. It was also widely recognized that bigger stones didn't make bigger or grander dragons, nor did beautifully cut stones amplify the elegance of one's scales. Based on that understanding and the faith we held in our gods and goddesses, there was no point in hoarding or stealing them. And so they remained, glistening chunks of rock scattered throughout every town and city, a trial that everyone tried, waiting to see if they, too, could sprout wings and scales.

Until the Fiorian invasion.

It only took three days for their army to obliterate ours. They seized the stones from the surviving drakken they captured and blew up the drakkentorre mine. Anyone found in possession of the stones was deemed a criminal and thrown into the mines to slave away.

However, just like my family had hidden in the mountains to avoid detection, it appeared some shifters still existed outside the wolven notice.

"Are you threatening me?" Soren rasped in response to my rhetorical question.

"No more than you're threatening me," I quipped, clenching my fists to hide my trembling. "Merely observing."

Soren didn't so much as blink. After a few beats, his jaw flexed, and he slid down the boulder. A few stomps and he dropped to his blanket, his back to me as he pulled it around himself.

"I guess that means I am taking first watch," Lukas said. He tucked his map into a green pouch, the fabric treated with wax to help it shed water, and removed something from another pouch, this one lighter in color. He tapped the material against his palm, picking over his thoughts.

"I do not know much about you, Tell, but you've got some serious iron in that spine of yours." He tossed me a stick of what I now realized was jerky. He continued, faintly distracted, as he scanned the dark terrain. "I admire iron. It's a malleable metal, but prone to shattering when worked too much. I worry you might face a similar fate if you are not careful around him. Soren will respect you for challenging him, but push too hard and he will snap back."

With a quick nod of dismissal, he scaled the rock Soren had claimed earlier, ready to take his watch for the night. I blinked at the spot where he'd sat beside the fire, his pack carefully assembled, its ties pulled taut.

Why had he warned me?

I hadn't gotten the impression Lukas liked me, beyond being an asset to his research. But maybe more was going on here, more I didn't understand. Could it be he wanted me to succeed in this new and foreign world?

Sighing, I tugged my blanket tight around me. Pip trilled softly from the trees nearby, a comforting sound that I hoped the others would dismiss as typical forest wildlife.

I didn't understand these drakken, but the fact they hadn't killed me yet gave me hope. Maybe, just maybe, we could come to some kind of understanding before it came time to part ways.

Until then, I counted on Pip to watch out and alert me to any danger.

6

Stick to the Forests

The gray owl dubbed Grim for his morose hoots found Pip during the night. His hauntingly hollow call roused me as Soren shook Lukas awake, and I opened my eyes, head pillowed in my arms, wondering if I'd heard correctly. When the sound came again, I sat upright, blanket tumbling off my shoulders, ignoring the look Soren shot at me across the crumbling ashes of the fire. Sure enough, there the gray was, tucked in among the limbs of a silverpine.

My eyes burned, and I pressed the heels of my palms against them, fighting back a fresh wave of grief. Grim had been my father's favorite. Papa never said it in so many words, but he doted on the bird. That the gray had survived… it felt like my father was here. Pushing me onward.

While bundling up my blanket, I wondered which of the owls might seek us out next. The snowy and barn owls were shyer, but welcomed our treats and attention, however, the burrowing owl named Fritz was another trip entirely. That bird possessed too much attitude for his own good.

While the men pulled their supplies together, I walked through the woods in search of the creek, intent on checking on Pip and cleaning up. It felt good to scrub the blood and soot from my face and arms, but I decided against changing clothes for now. It wasn't worth the risk of exposure, even with two owls keeping watch.

After Pip snuggled deep into my bag for a much-needed snooze, I filled my flask and returned to the clearing. Lukas tossed me a hunk of jerky. I wolfed it down as I double-checked my bag, hoping it would quell the tightness in my stomach. Had the wolven left any of our food, I would have taken it in a heartbeat, but as with the weapons, they'd stolen that, too.

"Let's go," Soren ordered, waving me over while Lukas unfolded the map. The drakken tapped the main road arrowing south to Stavanger. "I want to avoid that route in case scouts are looking for stragglers who might have escaped notice at your village." I immediately regretted the venison I'd scarfed down, swallowing hard to keep my nausea at bay. Lukas frowned at Soren, who paid him no heed. "We'll stick to the forests. It will add time, but it's better than being out in the open." He shot me a look. "Unless you think the gods can keep us safe."

I bristled. His smirk deepened when I grabbed for my wrist, concealed beneath my shirt. It was the second remark he'd made about my beliefs, and this one came out as a challenge. "Zos will protect us if she deems it necessary, but given our skill sets, the odds favor her leaving our fates in our hands for now."

That wiped the irritating sneer from his face.

Yes, I believed the gods guided our actions, but I also believed they gave us room for error, opportunity to carve through our mistakes. Zos had guided the survivors of Aeros to our secluded home, where we'd resided peacefully. The wolven had eventually come for us, but I didn't blame the gods. I blamed our invaders and their brutal intentions. Gods and goddesses had far more important things to do than monitor humans and guide their paths all day long.

As for Soren's plan, the owls would alert me if problems arose. It also mirrored one I would have used had I made it this far on my own.

"I agree it's safer to stay off the main roads," I said, hoisting my pack onto my back. I'd added a second strap to it last night, one tucked away in the depths of its pockets.

Soren's frown deepened.

Lukas shrugged and rolled up the map, returning it to a pouch primly labeled 'maps.' I wondered if the other packs in his satchel were marked with similar calligraphy.

Soren took the lead and set a brutal pace. Not liking how it felt being sandwiched between the men, I asked Lukas to go ahead of me and took up a much more comfortable spot at the rear. It also gave me an opportunity to watch the drakken and observe their interactions.

As they had on the way up the mountain, they made no effort to hide the strength of their friendship. The dynamics of it fascinated me. Of the two, Lukas was more bookish. The academic. The commander with a head for strategy and a sponge-like brain ready to consume information. Soren was all lean muscle and quiet violence. He was the warrior you wanted at your back in an attack, the captain who spoke with his sword first.

It made sense for them to work together, the two sides of comradery. An ache in my chest deepened. They reminded me of my friendship with Viv, how we could read what the other was thinking with just a glance. With everything inside me, I hoped she was alright, prayed the wolven hadn't hurt her or what remained of my family.

Grim hooted another all-clear as I trudged through a tangle of ivy. It didn't escape me that Soren moved more stiffly today, and

I wondered if his injury had flared up. I'd mixed another blend of medicinal paste this morning with what remained of the herbs I'd salvaged, but he'd dismissed my offer of help with a cutting glance. Oh well. It left more for me later.

I wondered if he was on edge because of what I'd said last night or if was he irritated in general. Maybe he really was in a hurry to get where he was going.

Whatever the reason, I wished he would slow down. Despite my morning treatment, the aches in my back and legs had compounded during the night, sleep making the pain more pronounced. Moving helped, but I still felt like a horse pulling a carriage had trampled over me. Hooves, wheels, and all.

The sun climbed higher, and despite the hours that passed, we had yet to see anyone on the road. Not exactly unusual. Much of it was overgrown, remnants of when a small town used to exist up this way. It had been abandoned decades ago, left to rot when the cold this far north became too much for most to readily bear. I anticipated seeing more traffic when we hit the fields and farms on the outskirts of Stavanger.

The monotony of our march and the relative warmth of the hills lulled me into a sense of peace. It was easy not to think too much when so much of my attention was focused on not tripping over tree roots and avoiding poisonous plants. The light sheen of sweat coating my arms and face felt good, proof of our productivity. We were getting somewhere.

Even Soren loosened up a bit, his gait less stilted, though his hand hovered near the pommel of his sword. Lukas drifted midway between us, pad of paper in hand, his unstrung bow buckled into a brace on his bag, occasionally looking over his shoulder to make sure I was still there, always ready with a smile or a quick word about a difficult patch of terrain.

I sank so deep into that sense of calm and contentment, I almost missed the throbbing notes of the gray's warning.

My foot snagged on a vine and I nearly fell, catching myself on an aspen to stay upright, heart crashing into my ribs. Three. No. Four. Four outsiders coming in fast. Two on four legs. Two on two. Wolven. Some shifted, others not. They'd be on us in minutes.

I surged forward, not caring about the leaves and branches I broke along the way. They'd found our trail; it didn't matter how much noise we made now. Lukas turned before I barreled into him.

"Soldiers are coming." I motioned behind us, arm wrapped around my middle, gasping. Soren must have heard me, because his sword snaked out a moment later. "Four of them. They're right behind us."

Lukas didn't bother asking how I knew what I did. His bow appeared in his hands as if by magic, and he rooted through his pockets, seeking the string he'd tucked away. While he got his arrows set, Soren slunk toward us, nearly silent in the underbrush. "Let them come."

I didn't know what to do. Like everyone in Solas, I had some exposure to defensive techniques, but I was more apt to trip over my own feet than I was to pose a serious threat. Viv had always been the one who stood her ground in a fight, whereas my best recourse was to run, relying on my cleverness to get me out of my messes—like I had when coming face-to-face with the wolven on the Spear.

Unfortunately, running here wasn't an option, especially with two drakken so obviously ready to face the attackers head-on. My hand fisted around the knife in my pocket. I could use it, but its blade was dull. I cursed myself for putting off sharpening it for so long.

As if sensing my inner turmoil, Soren stepped between me and the threat. "Stay back," he warned. "Leave this to us, and whatever you do, don't get in the way."

Lukas whipped up his bow, bag at his feet and the quiver draped over his shoulder. He tilted his head, listening to something beyond my range of hearing. "She's right. Four of them are coming in fast. Maybe five. They are in both forms."

"Good." Soren set his stance, danger etched into his sinuous limbs. "It's been too long since one of them faced me like the dogs they are."

Several figures exploded from the brush.

The first wolven died before its front feet touched the ground, an arrow protruding from its eye and exiting out the back of its mangy head. Another arrow was already in Lukas' hand when Soren charged, engaging the soldiers still in their human forms. The flashing silver of his blade never stilled, parrying the attacks of his enemy as if engaged in a choreographed dance. Viv could learn a thing or two from the drakken.

I pressed my back against a tree, the bark smooth beneath my palms. The taller of the soldiers, one with a bleeding gash across his face, snarled an insult at Soren. I didn't catch the move that slit the soldier's throat, but my stomach roiled when blood gushed down the front of the man's shirt, his eyes bright with fear and death.

"Filthy *travetry*," the remaining soldier yelled, sword swinging furiously as he engaged Soren, who seemed almost bored. He'd shifted his weapon to his left hand. If I hadn't bandaged the drakken's shoulder myself, I never would have guessed he had an injury.

"Watch yourself, Tell," Lukas shouted, knocking into me as an arrow soared over my shoulder, nicking my neck. I landed on the grass with a grunt, rolling into a protective ball as Lukas stood in front of me, two arrows notched in his bow. His expression was flinty when he released them at the same time. Someone shrieked and Lukas shook his head. "Fuck, he's quick."

He pulled me upright as the second of Soren's soldiers fell, a bloody hole cut in his chest. One of the soldier's arms had been hacked off at the elbow. Soren flicked blood off his sword as he stood over the bodies of his challengers, splotches of red staining the side of his neck.

"One more?" he asked Lukas, who spun in a slow circle, feet padding lightly on the slender green shoots of grass, finding his way to the center of the clearing.

"Pretty sure." The golden shifter swiped at his ear with his shoulder, dislodging a fly buzzing there. "Maybe two. I am having a hard time getting a read on—"

A hoot, louder than one I'd ever heard before, sounded from the left and a shrieking soldier stumbled into the clearing. His arms were thrown over his head, trying in vain to protect himself as a Grim dove, wingspan wide as my own arched back. His talons raked bloody grooves across the man's scalp. The soldier tried to bat away the swooping, screaming bird when Lukas' arrow found his throat.

Satisfied with the kill, Grim chortled and, with one massive beat of his wings, disappeared into the foliage once more. Soren frowned, following his trajectory, blood dripping from the point of his sword. Relief pounded through my veins, quick as whitewater rapids, and I started forward when a hand wrapped around my neck, squeezing my throat, dragging me roughly backward. I glimpsed alarm on Soren's face before I slammed against a body that radiated far too much heat. I gagged on the stench of rotten meat, struggling against the arm that locked itself around my chest, trapping my arms at my sides.

Foolish. Foolish of me to let my guard down.

"Enough," my captor hissed. Adrenaline pounded harder, and I thrashed, struggling to loosen my captor's grip, but he adjusted to my flailing body easily. I stilled when something very, very sharp pressed against the pulse at my throat. My heart thundered faster, recognizing the imminent danger.

The soldier's face appeared over my shoulder, a rough patch on his unshaven cheek scraping against my own. I quivered at the elongated nose and fangs curling from his partially shifted features, realizing those were claws digging into my side in addition to the knife at my neck. My head felt light. I didn't dare swallow. If I did, I was likely to slit my neck.

Soren took a step, and the knife pressed down. Wetness trickled down my skin. The drakken halted, head cocked.

"Not a step more or she dies, boy." The man's breath reeked of blood.

"What is it you want?" Lukas asked, foot braced on the chest of a dead soldier. He'd lowered his bow. "If you want the girl, you can have her. She is just a straggler we picked up on the trail."

Blood roared in my ears, heart flailing so hard I thought it might crack my ribs. Lukas couldn't be serious. I'd escorted them down that bloody mountain, had offered my help to heal them, and this was how they repaid me? Black speckles danced across my vision. I needed to calm myself, to breathe, but I couldn't. The soldier was taking too long. I was going to die. Or be enslaved.

Barely a day into my promise to save my family and I'd already failed.

Soren dropped his sword and lifted his hands. "Take her and forget about us and what we did to your friends. No harm, no foul. And you get fresh blood for your mines."

"Yeah?" The wolven huffed. "I'll forget all about—"

His body jolted, voice disintegrating into a wet gurgle. Lukas dove forward, snagging the soldier's arm and pulling it away from my throat as he dropped to the grass. I clung to the drakken, arm thrown around his middle, trying to force air into my lungs. I was alive. But how?

Lukas' hand pressed against the small of my back as I turned to my captor. A dagger protruded from his eye socket, blood streaming onto the green and gold of his tunic.

"Tell? Are you hurt?" Lukas shook me as if wasn't the first time he'd asked the question. He tried to twist me around, but I resisted, staring at the body of the wolven as Soren wrenched the dagger from the corpse with an awful squelching sound. I flinched. He wiped the blood on the soldier's uniform and stuck it into a sheath concealed under the wide sleeve of his cloak.

My thoughts went fuzzy. A wolven had nearly killed me—again.

The very creatures I'd hidden from for most of my life had almost ended it twice in two short days. Only sheer luck had saved me. It wasn't like I'd done much except run and hide.

Soren stepped between the soldier and me, his face filling my vision. A streak of drying blood brushed across his cheekbone and his hair stuck out at odd angles, damp with sweat. He smelled of copper and death. His expression was as hostile as ever, but his eyes were the warm nutty brown I'd glimpsed on the way up the mountain and not their standard burning black.

"Snap out of it," he ordered woodenly. "You aren't dead or your goddess would have greeted you by now."

When I didn't react to his insult, he snapped his fingers in my face. The effect was instantaneous. I crashed back into myself with the force of the Capulatian River breaking through the ice jams that clogged its shores this time of year. I jerked against Lukas' hold, coughing and choking as I bent over, dropping to my knees, feeling for the cuts around my neck. They were shallow, the injuries already clotted. When I didn't feel quite like dying, I rasped, "Thank Zos."

Apparently convinced I wasn't a threat to myself or anyone else, Soren moved away, leaving Lukas to examine my injuries. His lips pinched white as he stroked the longest one. "Why don't you clean up? There is a river on the other side of those trees." He tilted his head to the right. "You do not want that getting infected."

I forced myself upright, but when I went to follow his instructions, I spotted Soren crouched beside one of the bodies, checking his pockets. I halted, bile swirling in my gut, not dissimilar to the black flies already swarming around the open, bloody wounds. Lukas and Soren had killed them. Six wolven—dead. They'd made it look easy. While part of me marveled at their skill, a bigger part throbbed, struggling to process the seemingly endless trail of death I was walking.

Lukas stepped between me and the carnage, and I refocused on the tangled ties of his cloak. He shoved something into my hands. I recognized the straps of my bag. "Close your eyes. Walk about thirty paces to your right and you will be there. Do not look down, do not hesitate. Soren and I will find you when we finish cleaning up here."

Obediently, I followed his instructions to the syllable, careful to keep my path straight, only opening my lids when the babbling of the river rushing around rocks and through water dragon weeds met my ears. Smooth, bluish gray stones lined the shore. I crouched, breathing still short and raspy, gripping the bandages over my tattoo. My head buzzed distantly.

What was happening to me?

One moment everything was as it should be: I had my home, my owls, Papa's warm embrace, and Viv's quick laughter. The next moment, everything I loved and owned was gone. Up in smoke.

Trembling, I smoothed some hair back from my face. The water ran slowly enough for me to see my reflection on the surface. Purple smudges of exhaustion limned my eyes, circles that had never been there before. My face seemed thinner; my blue eyes darker. I dipped my hand into the water, dissolving the image, and splashed it on my skin, patting the moisture in for good measure.

A shudder worked its way down my spine as my fingers found

the cuts on my neck again. So close I'd come to death, and how fortunate I was to have escaped. Unlike Papa. My birds. The family we'd embraced not out of blood but by choice. They were gone, but I was here, along with Pip and Grim—

And I couldn't help but wonder about Viv.

I hunched forward, bones of my knees digging painfully into the river rock. If she were here, she would order me to get a grip, tell me this panic attack was nothing more than that. A bodily reaction to shock and change. I could almost feel her hand on my back, holding my hair away from my face, encouraging me to find my center and embrace the calm.

Slowly, painstakingly slowly, I floated back into myself. I breathed in deeply, released it out through my nose. Once. Twice. Three times. My pulse evened. My stomach settled. The vertigo faded.

I was here for her. I'd trudged back down that mountain for her, and I would do whatever I could to save her from whatever fate she faced at the hands of Fior. She was tough. She would get through whatever challenges the wolven presented her with. And she was counting on me…

Or she would be if she knew I was alive.

It wouldn't surprise me if the wolven told her they'd chased me over the Spear.

Lukas and Soren were talking somewhere behind me, but I didn't bother listening in on their conversation. Deftly, I pulled a bottle of ointment, gauze, and a second, smaller roll of bandages from my bag. I uncapped the bottle, breathing in the spicy burn of fireflowers, a scent that reminded me of long days grinding herbs and mixing poultices, and applied a few drops to my palms, working it into the injuries around my neck. Isabella and I found this concoction worked wonders for cleansing and reducing the risk of infection.

As I wrapped up my injuries, the movements familiar, I evaluated my situation from a fresh perspective. I needed to know where I stood now to understand where I needed to go next—and like it or not, the drakken were part of this journey. Not trusting them with everything about my past was one thing, but it was another to not reassess my situation as it developed.

Given some perspective, I knew Soren probably could have kicked me off during our freefall by the Spear. The cuts inflicted by his talons along my arms and legs were deep, but when he'd stopped panicking, he'd allowed me to cling to him. He had listened to my shouted advice and had done his best to avoid crashing into the worst part of the valley.

He and Lukas could also have killed me when they'd found me at the base of the clearing. Both were clearly capable, and I was an obvious threat. However, Lukas had argued on my behalf, and both men had followed me to Solas under the guise of safety.

I cut the bandage with my knife, tucked the end into the wrapping, then peered into the water again. My injuries itched under the dressing, but that meant they were healing. In a day or two, I would be able to safely remove the bandages. The ointments I'd applied would hopefully prevent scarring. When the drakken found me, I would need to help Soren. The cut on his arm looked deep, and I wanted to re-set his shoulder.

It was true. Though injured and clearly eager to get to their original destination, they'd followed me up the hazardous trails of Spear Ridge. When we'd found the burned-out husk of Solas, they hadn't left me to my own devices. Rather, they'd honored the old ways and helped me set the pyre to send off my family to the otherlife.

They could have abandoned me then, having fulfilled their obligation to getting me somewhere I knew and used to feel safe. Instead, they'd asked me about my intentions and offered to help. I still didn't know exactly what that help might be, but they certainly hadn't needed to go out of their way to aid a stranger.

Over and over again, they'd assisted me, giving me space, allowing me to process everything at my own pace. They didn't know anything about me and I'd made it clear I wasn't about to answer any of their questions, yet they welcomed me into their camp.

And they'd just saved me again now.

The river whisked away the cleansing herbs I rubbed over my hands and arms.

When I'd hesitated after warning them about the danger, Soren had recognized my weakness and accounted for it, putting himself in front of me. It wasn't a necessary step. He owed me nothing. Yet he had all the same.

"Steadier?" Soren asked. I hadn't heard him approach, but I was getting used to that about him.

"Yeah."

"Good." He knelt, shrugged off his cloak, and splashed water on his face. Unlike me, he didn't stop to stare at his reflection in quiet introspection. Instead, he blotted the water streaming down his nose and chin with his sleeve. Before he rose, I snagged the edge of his shirt. He stilled, the shadows around his orbital bones darker in the shade of the woods.

"Thank you," I said. They weren't words I spoke out of respectful obligation. Gratitude rose in my chest, nearly choking me, making my words tight, my voice small. I bowed my head in subjugation. "For saving me, I mean. Back there. For not letting that wolven kill me."

The drakken was quiet for so long I risked a glance.

"What makes you think I killed them to save you?"

It should have stung, how simply he brushed aside the notion of protecting me, but I felt… relief. An avalanche of it.

"Maybe I just like killing things," he added after a beat.

I fiddled with the ties of my leather armbands, then sought out his piercing gaze. "Your motives are your own. It doesn't change the outcome."

His eyes narrowed.

Not prepared to hear his counter, I held up a roll of bandages. "May I treat your wound? I'd also like to re-set your arm. I believe the bindings shifted during the night. You move like you're in pain."

Soren opened his mouth, most likely to reject my offer, when Lukas dropped beside him. "Don't you dare say no. Let her clean your cut. You know how disgusting wolven blades are." He shot Soren a look when his friend glowered. "I know. You are tough and all that, blah, blah. But you don't have time to deal with an infection right now." Soren flinched when Lukas rapped on his shoulder. "And if that heals wrong, you might never fly again. How will you lord over everyone if you can't threaten to attack them from above?"

The laugh that burst from me surprised me as much as it did the men. Soren wouldn't have looked more shocked if I'd shot him with Lukas' bow, and Lukas stared like I'd punched him.

I shook my head, shoulders shaking. "Sorry. You two are something else, you know?"

Lukas chuckled and rinsed off his face. Soren waited a beat, but shrugged off his shirt with a grumble. He flinched when the chilled tips of my fingers brushed the angry red slash across his biceps, but stilled when I washed away the blood and applied fireflower ointment to the injury.

When I'd treated him on the mountain, I'd fixated on his musculoskeletal structure, marveling at the similarities he shared with my birds. But here, with a fresh injury, I saw him in a different light. He was almost too slender for the amount of power he wielded with his fists and sword. Where Lukas' arms bulged with muscle, Soren's biceps and triceps were ropey, nearly hard as bone.

I worked in silence, keenly aware of his attention and the scratching of Lucas' pen. Soren understood the questions asked through my fingers when I unwound the bandages, probing his muscles for areas of pain. The splint had shifted, but the fix wasn't a difficult one, and before long, Soren slipped his shirt and cloak back over his head.

Attention broken, the sounds of the forest filtered back in: thrush pecking for wyrms in the grass beneath the pines, the wind hushing through the skeletal oak branches, the slurping of the river as it frothed around obstructions in its winding path. Lukas lounged nearby, notebook on his chest, eyes closed as the midday sun shone warmly upon his face.

An air of expectancy tinged the air as I repacked my bag.

I knew which question was coming, but Soren wouldn't need to ask it. Even if he did, I felt he would make some sarcastic statement about how he didn't want me to bullshit them about my goddess rising from rezar to personally warn me about the threat.

I drew a deep breath, cooling the apprehension bubbling in my belly. He hadn't said anything yet, no need to get worked up about it. Besides, Lukas' warning nipped at me. They had saved my life more than once. Intentionally or not. I needed to offer something in return.

"I communicate with the owls," I said, keeping my head bent over the tightly coiled bandage. The back of my neck burned beneath their gazes. Zos help me, this better be the right decision. "That's how I knew the wolven were coming. Two of the owls who escaped slaughter are following us. I raised them." I scratched my arm, risking a glance up. "They're keeping watch and alerted me."

My stomach snared, curling into a tight ball under Soren's scrutiny. What would he do? I'd protected those birds and my secrets my entire life, yet here I was offering them up, piece by piece.

"How did they alert you?" Lukas asked, genuinely curious.

It was easier to face him than Soren. "Their calls. I grew up around them. There's a reason those woods are called The Owl Wood." I picked at a loose thread on my trousers. "I understand their calls and the messages they're conveying. It's more than just warnings or sounds of comfort." I struggled to find the words. "It's like I hear the messages out of their patterns. Things like numbers, whether someone approaching is human or animal, even emotion. They're smarter than most people give them credit for." I grinned. "They understand a lot."

Lukas squeezed the notebook in his lap. "And they understand you?"

"Every word."

"Are they here? Now?" Lukas looked around. I wanted to laugh. He would never spot the owls that way. They were masters of camouflage.

I tucked my kit into my pack and tied the flap shut. "Not exactly. They're scouting. You'll recognize the gray. He chased that soldier out of hiding." The memory of the bloodied talons and the screams of Grim's victim flashed across my vision. Goosebumps rippled across the skin. "The other is getting some rest."

Head light with my confession, still not sure whether they believed me, I picked up my bag to hook it over my shoulders, but Soren stopped me. He fingered a sable feather on my cloak. I'd caught him staring at the material on more than one occasion, a furrow between his brows. He pulled back with a nod as if he'd interpreted the secrets woven in with the browns and grays and whites.

"You should turn this inside out before we get on the road." He plucked at another feather, one I'd collected after setting the wing of a barred owl several years ago, and smoothed it down, long fingers gentle. "Associations with owls are dangerous. Flaunting that relationship is even worse. I wouldn't want you to get hurt."

Stunned by his quiet sincerity, I hesitated a moment too long, and his eyes shuttered, closing off the glimpse I'd seen of the man who hid behind violence and anger. Lukas helped him to his feet, avoiding my searching look. The hair on the back of my neck rose at the solemn set of his face, the jerkiness of his movements.

What was I missing here?

How could associations with owls be dangerous?

Something more was going on here, something I'd missed and didn't understand.

Something very important.

7

Someone You Can Trust

I never felt comfortable around strangers.

Unfortunately for me, the streets of Stavanger were full of them. A sea of merchants and citizens of all shapes and sizes squeezed together on the narrow roads, eager to purchase necessary equipment, sell their wares, or simply take in the little entertainment this thumping heartbeat of the north had to offer.

Saliva pooled in my mouth and my stomach rumbled, enticed by the dueling aromas of sweet stickybuns left over from breakfast and the rolls stuffed with meats and cheeses fresh out of the oven. The worn heels of my boots clacked uncomfortably on the cobblestones, a marked difference to the earth and leaves and grass I was used to. The grooved coins I'd swiped from Solas dug patterns into my palms and I squeezed them in my pocket, counting the indents in the tin as I shoved between two farmers discussing the lack of rain.

I wiped my mouth on my sleeve, convinced I'd started drooling, and forced my eyes away from the stalls lining both sides of the street just in time to catch the back of Soren's dark cloak slipping through the crowd. Food would have to wait. Besides, Lukas had doled out the last of their jerky earlier today, and I needed to think about my next steps before I spent any coin.

I dodged around a group of people chattering over woolen scarves, sticking close to the drakken as best I could. Overhead, a woman sang a sweet harmony, perched on an apartment balcony overlooking the organized chaos. This city had always carried a special aura: one of intrigue and mystery and chance. Like I was a breath away from an entirely new life. A new beginning.

That sense of expectancy thrilled Viv, her green eyes alighting whenever we passed through the gates, a bounce entering her step that didn't exist in Solas. She lived in the village, but the city and all its people were her home.

Unlike my best friend, I regarded the sensation with careful consideration and a hefty dose of distrust. I squinted into a darkened alley crunched between the two-story buildings where those without homes often stayed, bundled up in ragged tents and bedrolls with ill-mended holes, faces skeletal as they waited for vendors to throw out their scraps.

Change wasn't always for the better.

For as devout and numerous as his followers had been, Vey was a fickle god of fortune, known for doling out poverty far more freely than he handed out riches.

A hand wrapped around my wrist and I bit back a scream when I recognized the bottle green of Lukas' cloak. "Keep up," he shouted over the din of the merchants shouting their wares and women haggling over vegetables and wheat. "Wouldn't want you getting lost in this mess, now, do we?"

A dimple punctured his cheek when he flashed a grin and I couldn't help but rise to his eagerness, allowing him to drag me along in search of Soren. He wasn't difficult to find.

The drakken had a way of commanding attention, even when he clearly craved the opposite. He dressed no differently than most here, but the black of his cloak seemed darker, the leather of his boots shinier. The way he moved was stealthier, like an asp preparing to strike, especially with his hand braced on the pommel of his sword. Once, he glanced back, seeking us out, and the sharpness of his features, so similar to the triangular face of the drakken who'd roared at me as we careened to the ground, struck me as strangely regal.

We followed him to an alcove between two vendors selling woolen scarves and fur-lined coats. I flinched at the clap of a gong, and Soren glanced at the massive clock fixed over a large building I recognized as the court of justice. The clock sounded again, marking two past noon, and Soren shook his head. I'd never seen him so anxious, shifting on his feet, attention jumpy.

"We're late," he said.

Late for what, I had no idea. I'd relayed my need to find a specific merchant while in town, but the men had been cagey about their plans.

Lukas sagged against the wall, fingering the clasps of his bag to ensure they hadn't been tampered with. "Archer will not care."

"Archer doesn't worry me."

Both men glanced at me, and I held up my hands defensively. "It's not my fault the soldiers attacked us." Soren's blank assessment drilled into me. I lasted all of three counts. "Alright, it might have been partially my fault with the fall and all," I acquiesced. Again, I held back the information about the bearish soldier. His disconcerting offer complicated things in my head. "But you can't blame a girl for her survival instincts."

"No, I suppose we can't," Soren said drolly.

Lukas shoved his hands in his pockets. He'd lost his gloves in the woods at some point. "Why don't you go on ahead, Soren? Do what you need to do to clear the thing we need cleared. I will wait with

Tell."

I squeezed the coins again, fighting the urge to roll my eyes. If they didn't want me listening in, all they had to do was walk a few feet away where the noise from the crowd would drown them out. Soren considered the suggestion. "Fine. I'll send Tik when we're ready." He rooted around in his pockets and emerged with a handful of silver. Lukas scowled, but accepted the coins as I stared. I'd never seen so many vetter. Of the change in my pocket, only one was a two-vetter coin.

Soren flicked his thumb at me. "Get her some food and you some gloves. Try not to lose them this time, would you?"

How had he known I was hungry? He'd been ahead of me the entire time and I'd been too far away for him to hear the moaning of my stomach. Was I really that transparent?

I opened my mouth to argue they keep their money. I could look after myself now the immediate threat of the wolven had passed, except Lukas pinned me with a long-suffering look. "Before you go thinking this is charity, it is not. It is payment for getting us out of the mountains and helping me fill in the map. If that is not enough for your pride to swallow, you can pay it off somehow down the line. But take what we are offering before I force it down your throat."

I snorted.

Soren had disappeared.

Lukas flipped a coin high in the air, the metal tumbling end over end, then snagged it with one carefully timed motion. The sunlight caught in his hair, highlighting the honey in his locks. "Well, what will it be? Stickybuns or stuffed rolls?"

Yes, I truly was that transparent.

* * *

Stomach achingly full for the first time in days, I tightened my scarf, taking extra care to fully cover my bandages. I'd removed the bracers when I'd turned my cloak inside out, thankful for Soren's reminder. Papa and I never wore our feathers into town, opting to leave them behind in an effort to not attract extra attention. Now I wondered if there was more behind that decision, if my father had *known* about whatever dangers we faced given our relationship with owls.

Lukas brushed my elbow as he returned from disposing of our garbage. Though he grinned, he seemed distracted, his attention fixed on the clock. He didn't hide his concern about leaving Soren well. I wondered if they parted ways like this much—if ever.

"Do we need to find Soren?" I asked. Devouring the caramel-coated stickybun had kept most of my questions out of my mouth, but it was killing me now, not asking where he had gone or if it had anything to do with my request for their help. For all the kindness they'd shown me and as much as I wanted to trust them, they were still extremely mysterious. I didn't want to believe they had lied to or misled me.

Lukas patted his pocket where one of his newly acquired gloves peeked out of the folds and hummed somewhat distantly. "What? No. Sorry, I have a few things on my mind."

"Oh, I see." I tightened my grip on my bag where it hung against my hip. I'd changed the straps again on the outside of the town walls, preferring to have it by my side for security reasons. "If there's somewhere you need to go, don't let me hold you up. Like I mentioned earlier, there's someone I'd like to see. I don't want to trouble you after all you've already done for me."

"No, that is not—" He put a hand on my upper back and pushed down hard, bowing my shoulders, dragging his gloves out of his pocket as if showing me something with the stitching along the sides. One of them dropped into the dirt, but he didn't move to pick it up.

Around us, the roar of the crowd and thunder of the merchants died down.

"Do not look at the road," Lukas murmured, angling our bodies away from the street. "Soldiers are patrolling and they will not hesitate to arrest you for the most minor of offenses."

I'd glimpsed the men in their green cloaks and dark brown tunics patrolling the marketplace before, but mostly at a distance. The older members of Solas had issued similar warnings, urging us as children to keep our heads down and avoid them. Fiorian soldiers mounted on sleek horses that looked nothing like the shaggy mountain ponies we favored were notorious for dragging people into jail cells for everything from suspected theft to looking at them wrong.

It made me sick, the unbending control Fior had over our nation.

From the corner of my eye, I watched them hesitate at the mouth of the street. Four soldiers rode on horseback in diamond formation, backs straight beneath their armor, the leather and metal treated against the heat of dragonfire. They loosely grasped their reins, leering at those around them. It felt like someone had stuffed my mouth with wool and I had trouble swallowing. I wanted to look more closely, to see if any bore a long scar down their nose like the one who'd shoved my attacker over the cliff had. But I didn't dare.

Lukas' hand pressed more firmly between my shoulder blades, the touch drawing me back into the present. That's right. We didn't have time for hasty gestures. I had time. Besides, there were hundreds, maybe even a thousand wolven infiltrating this northern territory. And if that shifter indeed held the status I assumed he did, the odds of running across him at random felt slim. He was more likely to be surrounded by a troop of soldiers or escorted in a carriage than be part of a routine patrol.

I knelt and picked up the glove Lukas had dropped, shaking my head as if exasperated at his antics. As I did so, I noticed an image scrawled in black paint at the base of the alleyway wall. A symbol the size of my hand. It reminded me of the rune representing Zos—a vee with a slash between the uplifted bars that didn't quite reach the edges and dashes that ran perpendicular midway through each of the V brackets—however, it was sloppily done. This vee looked more like a valley cut deeply between two peaks, with little dashes running parallel on either side of the point. A slash between the uplifted curves could almost be mistaken for a head.

It looked almost like an owl spreading its wings.

I snagged the glove and rose, blotting the moisture left by the slush before presenting it to him. "Be more careful next time," I chided. "Gloves don't grow on trees."

"Can you imagine if they did?" Laughter danced in his voice as Lukas pulled the glove on and wiggled his fingers experimentally. The black leather creaked. "A grove of random trees with huge branches and gloves sprouting from the ends like leaves?"

The volume of the marketplace had returned to normal. The wolven must have passed. I sent a silent prayer to Zos, thanking her for the lack of activity. Someone would have surely fought or screamed if they'd chosen to make any arrests.

"Who is it you want to talk to?" Lukas asked.

I toyed with the edges of my hood, watching a girl who looked to be about half my age twirl in the street, woolen dress flaring around her ankles, plaited hair flying as she grasped a signboard advertising wild honey over her head. A boy with cheeks stained red approached her timidly, darting glances over his shoulder.

"I doubt you know him," I hedged. "We're acquaintances."

When I grew bored with bartering over goods with my father, I'd often sought the company of Flora, our resident weaver and seamstress, enjoying the opportunity to touch new materials and goggle over the latest fashions. I pictured her favorite shop keep thumbing his bristly mustache as he poured over our wool, declaring it yet another batch of some of the finest in the land. Flora had once said she enjoyed working with him because he gave us fair deals on fabrics and accessories we couldn't easily produce at home.

"His store isn't far from here, actually." I pointed over my shoulder. "Lighton's. It's in the textiles district the next block over."

Lukas nodded thoughtfully. "I recognize the name. A woman next door sells the pens I prefer." He fumbled around in his pockets and offered a lopsided grin. "Let's go. It appears I lost my last writing instrument with that pair of gloves."

This time, he allowed me to lead as we wove through the clusters of people packing the marketplace. He stuck close, occasionally tapping one of my shoulders, indicating which way to turn as he kept an eye out for wolven soldiers prowling through the masses on foot. I wondered if the southern marketplaces were as busy as this one. While I loved the activity it offered, I often found it exhausting.

Something occurred to me as we walked. "The soldiers here and the ones in the woods—they spoke out loud."

"Sure." Lukas dodged an arguing couple.

"But the wolven I encountered on Spear Ridge, the one who chased me, I heard him in my mind." I risked a glance back. "Is it true they speak telepathically when in their second form?"

The drakken scratched his cheek. "Absolutely. They can project their thoughts to anyone they wish. I tried to track down the magic that fuels their conversation once, mostly to see if humans or drakken could replicate it, but I would need access to the palace archives to truly conduct my research." He shrugged. "Maybe someday I'll get my answers."

Interesting. I stewed on his comments for a beat.

"So, what's up with this fellow we are seeing?" Lukas interjected, the question just loud enough to be heard over the giggling of some girls clustered around a stall. I liked how he asked. We. Not you. Like we were a unit.

I muttered an apology when I clipped a bearded man with my elbow. "I think he knows how the soldiers found my family."

Lukas moved to my side and felt his attention sharpen. "Why do you think that?"

Always the open-ended questions with him.

During our last visit, I'd bounced between Petr selling our extra meat and loading fabric into the back of Flora's cart. When Soren, Lukas, and I picked our way through the forests, I'd remembered feeling like something was wrong during our last visit. The shop keep had held himself like a tightly strung bow, and he kept his questions clipped, the ruddy red of his temper riding high in his cheeks. The transaction took about half the normal time, thanks to the lack of conversation. I'd mentioned his curious behavior to Flora when we'd left, but she'd brushed it aside, assuring me everyone had their bad days. Now I wished I'd said something more.

"Call it a gut feeling," I replied. The contentment brought by the sweetness of the stickybun had faded, and I struggled to keep my expression neutral as my mood soured.

We were careful when we came to market. Always. Keeping our heads down and our errands straightforward, never making unreasonable demands or acting out of turn. Sure, anyone could have turned us in, told the Fiorian soldiers we didn't fit in as well as we should have, but the owner of Lighton's had *known* something.

Thinking over it now, disgusted with my naivety, I recognized the signs of guilt.

Still, the shock that reverberated through me when we stopped outside his shop hit me like a thunderbolt. Lukas snagged my hand and squeezed. I fumbled for words while staring at the space over the door. It gleamed off-white where the sign had hung, the letters visible in the faded paint around it. The windows were shuttered and nails pinned a board across the door. Abandoned.

"If you're searching for Bran, dear, he packed up and left a few weeks back," a woman called, voice high and rough with age. "Strangest thing, too. I've never seen him close for so much as a day in my twenty years running this here stand, yet overnight, he loaded up his wagon and left."

I blinked, finding the woman sitting behind a broad table across the street. A sign leaning against one of its legs proudly boasted of her craftsmanship in all things writing and calligraphy. Lukas' vendor, I assumed.

"How long ago?" How those words slipped past my numb lips, I would never know.

She jabbed a gnarled finger in her ear, shoving back wispy, white hair that spiraled out from beneath her floral-patterned shawl. "Oh, let's see. Not last week. Maybe the week before? I remember yelling at these brats running around. They knocked my table over, spilled half my ink." She examined the greenish wax caught in her nail and shook her head. "Youth these days."

My skin burned under icy streaks of sweat. Two weeks. The last time we'd visited. I remembered those children, watching them scurry all over the place, nicking apples and carrots from beneath the noses of less-attentive shop keeps.

Two weeks ago, I'd kept my nose down and my shoulders bowed, following every order to stay out of sight. Though I hadn't fully understood the threat, I hadn't cared. I was happy. My family had been alive. For all of their instincts, no one had guessed someone we treated well, who knew little about us outside of the exchange of goods, would betray us.

I supposed it was possible the man had packed up and left because of a family emergency…

But that didn't feel right.

The timeline fit too conveniently with the events that had ripped my life apart.

"I thought I recognized you, boyo," the woman said, unoffended by my lack of response. "How many of my utensils did you lose this time?"

"Only two, I will have you know," Lukas replied cheerily. Coins clinked as he shifted them from hand to hand. "If you would, I need four—no five—pens, a notebook, and maybe a few refillable cartridges if you've got them handy. I know you mentioned those children spilling your ink."

"Nonsense. I always keep my special supply tucked away for those customers I like best." The crone coughed wetly. "That'll be eight vetter."

With effort, I pulled myself together and turned away from the building. It hurt too much to look at it, even if it was just wood and nails and not the inner-city sanctuary that brought Flora so much peace. I squeezed my scarf, the wool soft and warm beneath my fingers. Only she could transform the rough and itchy threads in such a way, making fabric so soft it rivaled rabbit's fur. Flora, who now resided in the lands of the gods. I brushed the underside of my wrist. Maybe she watched over me now.

Lukas tucked his newest acquisitions into labeled pouches in his bag. For someone so organized, it amazed me how easily he seemed to lose things, and how unbothered he was by that fact. I didn't own much, but I couldn't imagine misplacing items and shrugging it off so easily.

"Are you alright?" he asked, straightening.

I unlocked my arms from around my chest. "I will be. It's a setback, but I'll figure something out."

A cart rattled down the street, wheels as tall as I was clattering over the cobblestones. Two dull-eyed donkeys pulled it along, their reins loose in the grip of the yawning farmer seated behind them. A woman scuttled alongside, shouting about fresh coffee and sweet treats while waving at the bins stacked in the back. It must have been a popular cart, because several people hurried over, rattling off their orders before the cart stopped. In the confusion, the farmer dropped the reins and one of the jennies veered sideways.

I jumped out of the way, my hip knocking into the woman's table with a painful jolt. Lukas jumped the other direction with a sharp cry, shouting something about getting control of the situation. As I tried to make sense of what had happened, a gnarled hand curled around my wrist and yanked me down. I collapsed against the table, twisting against the uncomfortable hold, and met the now-fiery eyes of the crone.

"Hush now, child. I have but a few moments." Her gaze skewed to the farmer who'd hopped from his seat and was yelling at Lukas in the middle of the street. "I know who you are; I know why your people hide. Never have I cared and never would I sell you out."

Ugliness twisted in my gut, something filled with poison and barbed with spikes. "Who—"

"Never mind that now. All you need to know is I'm someone you can trust." She reached into her shawl and produced a chain. At the end of it gleamed an opalescent gem no larger than the first knuckle on my thumb. Drakkentorre. My breath caught in my throat. A shifter hiding in plain sight. Her wrinkly jowls shook as she acknowledged my surprise. "There. I know your secret and you know mine. Square is square."

The tension in my stomach squeezed harder, recognizing Papa's turn of phrase. Who was this woman? She squeezed my wrist again, the bones grinding painfully together. I whimpered.

"Information is power, child, and if you're here seeking it, that means something has happened to your people?"

Oh, what the rezar. My gut wasn't telling me this was a bad idea. "They killed most of my village and I believe they took the rest captive. I'm all that remains."

The crone nestled back in her hood, shawl obscuring her crackled features, absorbing the blow. A donkey brayed and wheels scraped across stone as the farmer and his daughter sorted out the mess they'd made of the marketplace.

"Very well. Information is also money, you should know." She peered at me with eyes so clear I could see myself in them, the astonished puzzlement obvious on my face. "As Fior sinks its claws deeper into our nation, into the fabric of our society, the desperation mounts. For many, that means giving in." She pointed a gnarled finger at a piece of paper tacked to the wall, one proclaiming in big, bold, black letters that information regarding rebels would be heavily rewarded. "People would sell out their own mothers if it meant a sack of vetter and a favor from the soldiers. My fears match yours, child. We both know what happened 'cross the street."

She reached into the folds of her coat, rooting around until she produced another pen. This one shorter than the ones she'd sold to Lukas. She pushed it into my hand, folding my fingers around it.

"Worry not, child. There are others who resist, those who, when push comes to shove, throw everything they have in to shoving. They call themselves the Requiem, and they are gaining power and influence. You've likely seen evidence of their presence already." She cupped the back of my head, drawing me in so close our foreheads nearly touched. Distantly, a warning bell chimed in my head.

"In these darkest of times, there is no right or wrong—only one choice or another. It's not up to me to influence you. But consider the company you keep, rely on your instincts. You're blessed with good ones if Mia passed anything on to you."

My ears roared at the mention of my mother. I'd read her letters, talked about her with Papa, thought about her often, but never had I heard her name spoken outside the Owl Wood. I squinted into the blackness of the woman's shawl, trying to decipher the clues tucked in among her worn features. Perhaps she was from the—

"Those drakken you follow, they walk a treacherous path. One rife with good intentions on one side and destruction on the other." The woman nodded to the pen I'd jammed into my bag. "If you find yourself in a tough spot, show *them* that. It's all I can do to help you now. May Zos light your way."

My heel caught on a paving stone when she shoved me back, burying her face in her fist as she hacked up a lung. Lukas popped up not a second later, steadying me before skirting the table to crouch beside her, round face open with concern. "What is wrong? Can I get you anything?"

"Just choked on some dust, boyo," the crone managed between coughs. She was good. Really good. If I hadn't been present, I never would have guessed her capable of the intensity she'd emitted. She first patted her shawl to her lips, then Lukas' shoulder. I imagined I could feel the added weight of the pen she'd given me, wondering what she had meant and if I could trust her. "Nothing to worry yourself over."

Lukas rubbed the back of one wrinkled hand and stood. "Good. Wouldn't want anything bad happening to my favorite supplier."

A woman in a periwinkle-colored dress stepped up to the table, woven basket clutched tightly in both hands, and the crone fixed her attention on her newest customer, dismissing us as if we'd never been.

Lukas cleared his throat, tugging me away from the stall. "Sorry about that, getting separated and all. The donkeys must have spotted a snake or something."

"It's fine."

Movement behind him caught my attention. A boy with smudged cheeks and dusty blond hair leaned against the wall of an alley, tossing a green apple up and down. His eyes caught mine and skirted toward Lukas. I nudged the drakken with my elbow. "Friend of yours?"

Lukas pretended to scratch his nose, surreptitiously glancing back as the clock sounded again. Three gongs this time. The urchin tilted his head and melted into the shadows, his message apparently conveyed. Feathers, this felt like a scene from one of Viv's books, the kinds written about other worlds full of crooks and cutthroats and thieves. The cloak and dagger mayhem she eagerly devoured, inventing new fantasies in her head, since the reality in which we lived wasn't enough to satisfy her cravings for adventure.

"Let's go," Lukas said. The joy he'd exuded so eagerly earlier had hardened to stone. "Soren is expecting us."

I rocked back on my heels. I knew what I'd said, but I tired of people leading me around, of feeling like everyone was in on a secret that I was on the cusp of grasping. "Are you taking me to the people you mentioned? The ones who will help me find my family?"

He tugged on the tip of a glove. "They are. And they are not. Be prepared to get half of what you desire. Nothing more."

With a sweep of his cloak, he left me to interpret that cryptic message.

I closed my eyes, remembering the warmth of Papa's hands closing around mine, his callouses grating as he offered his unwavering support. I could picture the sorrow that filled Viv's face when I'd lashed out at her before, telling her under no uncertain terms that I didn't want change in my life, even for her.

My spine locked. That may have been true then, but this was now. "Lukas, wait up." Legs aching, I jogged to catch up.

I didn't know who to trust, but I had faith in myself, in Zos. She and my gut never guided me wrong before, and I wasn't about to start doubting either. No matter how difficult the road ahead, I needed to find my family who still lived. If that meant following these strange drakken with their violent tendencies and shadowy associates for a few hours more, I would do it.

Information is power.

The crone was right about that. Whatever I was about to learn, whatever halfway point I reached, somehow, someway, it would lead me closer to them.

8

An Admirable Goal

Given the way the drakken had acted upon entering the city, I'd expected to find myself knocking on some basement door or slinking through the side alley entrance of a shady business that sold bat wings and love elixirs. Something far less conventional than—

"A tavern?"

Lukas grinned and mounted the four steps to the doorway of the three-story establishment. Laughter spilled from a crack in the window beside it, the air buzzing with energy. "Not just any tavern. Snowmelt is the most popular place in the entire city. You will love it." The door opened at his back and a young woman with rosy cheeks clattered down the stairs, twirling her amber scarf around her neck, eyes glassy and unfocused. The drakken caught the edge of the door before it closed. "No need to dawdle."

There seemed to be plenty of reason to dawdle to me, but I couldn't hide my eagerness to find the source of the laughter, and stepped into the brightly lit space. My hands flew to my breast, thumb stroking the symbol on my wrist, sparks igniting me from the inside, incapable of hiding my amazement.

I'd never seen an establishment this large. The main room was open, with maybe fifty tables of all shapes and sizes scattered throughout. About half of them were full. Booths with bright red cushions lined up neatly along two parallel walls strung with paintings of waterfalls and forest clearings, offering varying degrees of privacy with their long backs and high bench arms. Two or three dozen lamps hung from the high ceiling in shallow brass bowls, the glow of the candles warm and inviting.

I tugged at the ties of my cloak. The fire roaring in the stone fireplace that took up a quarter of the wall opposite a long, shiny bar threw off so much heat I wondered how the people sitting closest to it hadn't melted. Cloaks and coats were draped across chairs, their occupants eating and drinking merrily, many with their sleeves rolled up. A woman in a sunshine yellow dress that ended at her knees spun past, eyes alight with laughter at a patron's joke, maneuvering her full tray around Lukas, who already had his cloak off and draped over his arm. She stopped at a table in front of a staircase situated to the left of the fire and started distributing drinks.

Apparently satisfied, I'd had enough time to peruse the humble atmosphere that was Snowmelt Tavern, Lukas started toward the bar, flicking his fingers for me to follow. I followed his order without argument, eyes wide as the plates filled with piping hot food. Seven men sat at the bar, mugs of light-colored ale in their hands, talking among themselves. They didn't look like people who would typically interact with one another—their attire ranging from low to upper-class.

A merchant with a double chin wearing a well-cut jacket that cleverly disguised the hefty paunch of his gut lifted his cup at Lukas. The golden drakken squeezed his shoulder and murmured something I couldn't hear that made the man laugh uproariously.

"Oh, Luk, as surprised as I am to see you here, I'm glad you're the same as ever." He wiped moisture from the corners of his eyes. His kind gaze landed on me. "And who might this beautiful blossom be?"

"Server in training," Lukas replied, lifting his chin when another patron called his name farther down the bar. "Ash says he needed more staff, and you know me: I live to serve."

I ducked my head, staring at the floor and fighting to keep the burn creeping up my neck from hitting my cheeks, keenly hoping the merchant would move on to something new. I wished I'd taken my cloak off when I'd had the chance; I felt horribly out of place with it on.

The man grunted, glugged some beer. "Shy thing, ain't she? Rory, another glass." I nearly wept with relief when he shook his glass at the woman leaning against the wall of taps, carelessly swiping a rag over a plate. She met his gaze, dropped her rag, swooped her arm low, middle three fingers pressed tightly together, and hooked it back up in the shape of a J before picking up her rag again. "I'm busy."

The patrons at the bar gasped into their mugs, nervously glancing over their shoulders, but a few whooped and hollered in celebration. I blinked, trying to mask my confusion over her gesture.

"It's an old insult," Lukas whispered, leaning close. "She basically told him he 'swooped too low,' or acted out of turn." He lifted a shoulder at my blank look. "Drakken used it a lot in the military, but common folk picked it up pretty quickly."

Respect for the woman's bold behavior bloomed in my chest as I, too, glanced around the room, reassuring myself there weren't any soldiers among the crowd. Such gestures were a death sentence if witnessed by the wrong person. Drakken and the old ways were forbidden subjects following the invasion.

Lukas nudged me with his elbow. "Come on, let's slip out while they are distracted."

An entrance wide enough to fit four people across separated the end of the bar and the wall. Women in skirts that ended mid-thigh and men in tunics fitted tightly to their chests darted in and out, following a choreographed dance I couldn't follow, trading trays that hung empty at their sides for full ones laden with plates of meats and vegetables coated in dark, spicy sauces that made my mouth water.

Lukas drew me close as he followed a server through the opening and into the kitchen. Men and women wearing navy-colored uniforms with stained black aprons hustled around tables of various lengths, some chopping herbs with knife strokes so quick I could barely follow them while others monitored pots bubbling on stovetops and inside large fire pits. They barely noticed as we hustled past, busy listening to orders shouted by a twig of a woman with a white kerchief wrapped around her hair.

We slipped through yet another door at the back of the kitchens and entered a landing at the base of a dark staircase, this one narrower than the one in the main dining area. Lukas bounced right up, taking the steps two at a time, forcing me to run to keep up with his jovial pace. The staircase let out into a hallway lined with doors. Candles burned in sconces between them, creating a cheery glow. He stopped beside a room at the end of the hall, one with a coiled snake carved in wood overhead, his hand on the bronze doorknob, waiting for me to catch up.

"How do you have so much stamina?" I gasped, bending at the knees, panting. Between the aching muscles, the hike down the mountain, the lack of sleep, and the sensory overload, I was nearing the end of my mental and physical ropes. "Aren't you exhausted?"

His smirk deepened, exposing his dimple. "It is called practice.

Practice until you drop, then force yourself upright and keep going." He paused, eyeing me critically. "Maybe you should take a moment to straighten up. You will want to be prepared."

That wasn't ominous or anything. Silently cursing the men who'd led me to this place, I shook out my hair and ran my fingers through it to work out the most egregious of tangles. Then I tugged off my cloak and draped it over my arm, situating it so the feathers remained concealed. My face was sweaty, but there wasn't anything I could do about that or about the state of my clothing choked with travel dirt and day-old sweat. This would have to be presentable.

"Good enough," Lukas agreed and swung the door wide. In my haste to enter, my foot caught on the doorjamb and I stumbled into the room, immediately drawing the attention of three people standing around a wide table. I straightened, allowing Lukas to guide me farther inside so he could close the door.

Like a hawk seeking its target, I found Soren swathed in shadows first. His lips twitched in something that might have been a smirk. Beside him stood a woman about a decade older than me, with mousy hair and rather ordinary features. My throat worked in something that might have been a greeting, but it stifled when she drew a dagger from her thigh sheath and pressed its point into the desk.

"And hello to you," admonished the third person in the room, his voice soft like warm sugar. Deceptively warm. A prickle of fear sparked at the base of my spine, senses sharpening and body stiffening with keen awareness. "Though I suppose Lukas is technically in charge of the introductions."

Lukas snorted. "It is not like you don't know who I am, and Soren told you who she is or she would not be here right now."

"But it's the propriety of it all," the man protested and leaned back on a desk, tattooed ferns wrapping around his wrists and winding up his forearms. His royal blue tunic shimmered in the flickering flame of the many candles, as if someone had painstakingly threaded silver into the weave. He cocked his head and ran a hand over his trimmed gray beard. Silver notes shot through it and his combed back hair. His eyes were extraordinarily pale, so pale I couldn't make out their color.

"Genetic defect," the man offered, reaching for a chipped mug on the desk.

I finally found my voice, the blockage in my throat clearing enough for me to speak. "Pardon?"

"She speaks." He took a sip of whatever he was drinking, face contorting with disgust. I recognized that look. Isabella used to make it when she poured dragon's breath into her tea to keep herself awake when mixing remedies and poultices that required days of precise attention.

"You were staring," the man continued. "Not that I blame you; one doesn't look this good without garnering attention." He paused. "I'm used to it by now."

The woman with the dagger snorted. "Get over yourself, Archer. We all know you preen like a friggin' goldfinch before the mirror every day." She pointed her blade at him. "Someday someone will do us a favor and mar those pretty features of yours."

"We can only hope," Archer said dryly. He took another sip of his concoction and made another face. "Qet's teeth, this vile tea is cold." He held it out. "Someone hide this before I'm tempted to drink from it again."

"I'll get right on that." Soren settled into one of two chairs bracketing a modest window. Someone had pulled the shades shut.

"That's my cue to leave." The nameless woman rolled the top page of whatever they'd been looking at into a tight scroll and tucked it under her arm. A sketch on the corner of the page, a series of interconnected lines, snagged my attention. It felt familiar, but I couldn't remember where I'd seen it. "It's been a ball, children. The next time we meet, let's actually get some work done, heh?"

Her attention swung to me, an earnest plea in her fathomless eyes. "Newbie, don't let them get t'ya. They are jus' boys after all. Nothin' more, nothin' less." She tapped my arm with the document as she passed by, slipping quietly through the door.

I shifted on my feet, more confused now than I had been when I'd entered. Was that advice supposed to help me? And if so, why would she offer it to a stranger?

"I resent that," Lukas called after her, unconcerned as he circled around Archer and pulled a smudged glass from beneath the counter of a table along the back wall. Decanters in a variety of shapes and sizes filled with colorful liquids and powders littered its surface. He held up a purple jug for inspection.

"So, girl, let's talk." Archer took another sip of his drink and swore again. "Soren ran me through your circumstance, but I'd rather hear it from you."

I couldn't hold it back any longer. Relaying information I'd learned backward and forward was second nature to me. "Before we delve into that, may I offer you some advice?"

Archer's brow rose, which I took as a positive sign.

"If you have it, asp syrup will cut the bitterness of the dragon's breath." I nodded at the mug he'd lifted to his mouth again. "It won't dampen the effects, but it'll be more palatable."

The mug lowered. "I never said anything about dragon's breath."

A challenge. Though Viv was more competitive than me, I never could back down from a challenge. I locked my hands behind my back, squaring my shoulders. "It's a logical assumption. Dragon's breath is the most acute of the herbs designed to help with wakefulness—which you're using to counter those bags beneath your eyes."

Soren snorted, and Archer set the mug down slowly, considering me. I released a breath, feeling like myself for the first time since I'd encountered the wolven.

"For all its positive effects, its downside is the intense bitterness it develops when it goes cold. We grew a lot of it back home since it's a winter herb, and it was a favorite of our healer, but she used to make that face all the time when she let it sit too long." I shrugged. "She always kept asp syrup on hand to counter it."

Archer tugged on a silver piercing in his left ear. "And what of the alcohol content in the syrup?"

Fair question. Bartenders prized asp syrup for its sweetness and its natural properties that mimicked alcohol. "The potency of the dragon's breath nullifies it. It's a chemical reaction between the herbs."

Bottles clinked together and Lukas produced a bottle of pale liquid flecked with bits of reddish crystals. He held it up to a candle and swirled it around. "I wonder what that chemical agent is," he muttered. "Bloodvine has similar qualities of dragon's breath, but isn't anywhere near as fast-acting." He held up a bag of gray powder. "I wonder if it would have the same impact."

"This isn't a trick to poison me?" Archer asked. What a strange question. Did he often face such threats? I hugged my cloak tighter against my chest, trying to not feel the intensity that he exuded, a more brash form than the presence emitted by Soren, though both made me feel like I was in the presence of people far more important than they made themselves out to be.

"I don't know who you are," I replied. "I have no reason to poison you."

Soren snorted again from his corner of the room, elbow resting on the arm of his chair, chin propped in his open palm.

Archer's grin turned coy. "You know, I almost believe you." He leaned backward across the table, tunic stretching across his stomach, revealing deep ridges of muscle. Lukas took his mug with a hoot of delight and uncorked the syrup. "I'm in the mood for some fun. Let's try this theory of yours—"

"It's not a theory."

Silvery eyes met mine again. "I'll try this *concoction* of yours. Either it kills me or it doesn't. If it kills me, I applaud you for succeeding where dozens of others failed. If it doesn't, I might be willing to talk about your... concerning situation."

Everything inside me stilled, the thoughts that constantly bounced around in my brain falling eerily silent. Here it was, my opportunity to find the answers I so desperately sought.

Archer accepted his cup from Lukas, saluted me, and drank deeply, the angle revealing the letters Z-E-N inked on his three middle fingers. A chair creaked as Soren leaned forward and Lukas bounced on the balls of his feet, notebook in hand, pen flying across the page. Several seconds passed, and even though I knew Archer would be fine, I couldn't help the nerves that danced in my belly.

"Are you dead yet?" Soren finally asked, popping the tension.

Archer licked his lips. "If this is death, it tastes pretty grand." The mug thunked hollowly on the table, rustling some parchment as he set it down. I blinked. Holy Zos, he'd chugged the whole thing. I'd expected a sip, but he'd gone straight for the jugular without so much as a flinch.

Who were these people?

In two steps, Archer was in front of me, hand extended. I accepted it. "Archer Skojare. Wanderer extraordinaire." His hand was too hot against mine. "If your aim is to kill me, I'd prefer you know my name when I expire. Helps with the whole guilt trip thing." He winked, the intensity about him falling away. I settled back into my skin again.

"I don't know. Killing you seemed easy if all it took was mixing a few liquids you had at your disposal." I managed a half smile. "Telleree Falk of the Owl Wood. Tell to my friends."

Archer pressed a coy kiss to my knuckles and moved to a cot on the side of the room across from Soren and Lukas—who had taken up the last remaining chair. The older man sat on the crumpled sheet and leaned back on his hands.

"Well, Telleree, let's hold off on the friends thing until we know each other better." His smile dropped away and unease swirled in my belly when I found myself looking into the face of a hardened soldier, a cold-blooded killer. Which of his faces was the mask? "Speaking of this 'Owl Wood,' I hear you've lost something dear to you. Tell me more."

Needing a moment to pull my thoughts together, I dropped my bag beside the door and carefully folded my cloak on top. I stroked the stitches pulling together the three long rips torn by the wolven's claws, drawing strength from the memories of all I'd endured until this moment.

Still crouched over my bag, I began. "There is a belief that only stragglers and vagabonds wander the mountains to the north. No one has shown interest in building towns at the base of the Spear Ridge peaks since a fire thirty years ago burned Aagarten to the ground." I stood, remembering the shell of the town we'd passed on our way to Stavanger. I tugged on the edges of my sleeves and approached the table, not really seeing the documents scattered across it.

"It's miserably cold, the wildlife is formidable, the land nearly impossible to tame—and that's before considering that you still have the mountains to deal with." I would have grinned were it not for the sorrow clamping around me like a vice. "But that's where we lived.

At the top of the highest mountains, tucked back in the darkest of woods. We wove the thickest clothing and learned to make seals capable of keeping the cold out of our homes; we recorded the habits of the wildlife and honed the skills of our hunters; we built a greenhouse and cultivated the land. None of it was easy, but we made it work."

I fluttered my fingers through the orange flame topping the pillar of a candle, remembering how Viv and I used to play a game, seeing who could leave their fingertips in the longest. Stupid games, but wonderful memories. Tears burned in the back of my throat. The trials we'd experienced hadn't been easy, Zos knew none of it came easily, but it was worth it for the solidarity that formed between us, the meals that tasted heartier after a hard day's work, even staring up at the blackest of skies, realizing how tiny we were in relation to it all.

"Three nights ago, I was almost done with my evening chores when the woods got too quiet, too still. Something was wrong. The forest felt off. And then—"

My vocal cords tightened, remembering the tiny body on the ground, the flashing golden eyes that followed. I wasn't ready to talk about any of this yet, the grief cutting low and slow. Silently, I thanked the men scattered around me, attentions fixed and focused, for giving me a moment. It took some swallowing, but I finally forced the lump of coal in my throat back down.

"A wolven jumped out of the woods. I've seen them in their human form, but never like that. I get it now, why people ran. Why they were so hard to fight." The world around me went blurry, the memory of that evening playing out in front of my eyes. I described the chase, how the soldier sprinted at my heels, nearly bringing me down, the confrontation at the top of the Spear, the fall and crashing into the drakken. How I'd felt finding my family dead. My home burned.

Life as I'd always known it irrevocably and irreplaceably destroyed.

It was Soren who handed me a handkerchief, the softness of the gesture running counter to the hardness of his eyes. I dabbed my streaming eyes and brushed away the moisture on my cheeks, twisting the square of black fabric so tightly the threads threatened to pop.

Archer perched on the edge of his cot, elbows resting on his thighs, head propped in his hands, thumbs supporting his chin. I wondered how many stories like mine he'd heard, wondered if his story sounded similar. The nastiness of the wolven was a well-established fact. Since the invasion, we Idileans didn't live to live anymore, we lived to survive.

"How many people resided in Solas?" Archer asked.

I scratched my wrist. "Fifty-two."

"And how many are missing?"

"Eleven."

He dragged his fingers over the length of his collarbone. When his eyes met mine, they were as fierce as the actions Soren and Lukas had taken to protect us earlier today. In them I saw outrage. Pure, unfiltered outrage.

"What were you doing there?" he asked.

"Pardon?"

"Spear Ridge. You describe the conditions well, and no one, to my knowledge, knew a village of that size was established up there. And I know many people." He stated it like an accusation, like we should have spread word about our haven at the edge of the world. "Given the challenges you faced, why were you up there in the first place?"

Ah.

I'd thought about this, about what I would say in this moment. Weighed the secrets sloshing around in my head, their contents threatening to spill. However, the facts remained, no matter how much help they offered or how I'd forced myself to put my trust in Soren and Lukas, their motives and the motives of whatever operation they ran remained a mystery.

"Papa and his friends sought solidarity," I said, back straight and voice strong. I wouldn't lie, but I wouldn't give them much. "They saw what Fior was doing and wanted nothing of it. They didn't want to raise their children in a world of fear and pain, so they hid us away, taking care of us in the best way they knew how."

"An admirable goal." Archer ran a finger down his nose and over his lips. "When did they make this decision? To live in the Spear Ridge?"

My lungs constricted, and my heart pattered faster. Dizziness spun. Did he suspect who we were? What we really were doing up there? Why we were hiding like rabbits in a warren? No. Not possible. When the wolven had overtaken Aeros, nearly everyone had fallen to their fangs and claws. We were among the few fortunate enough to escape with our lives.

That said, I couldn't resist offering a nugget, desperate to know if anyone else out there might understand. Anyone who might connect with my memories of that day. "Seventeen years ago."

Someone inhaled sharply at my back. They understood the significance of that date. It was impossible not to, really. Especially if these were members of the so-called Requiem the old woman had suggested they were.

Archer approached, his steps deliberate, giving me time to retreat if I chose, but I held my ground, refusing to allow him to intimidate me. He stopped a breath away, my head tipped so far back I wondered when it would crick, and bent, his nose stopping so close to mine I would have had a hard time slipping a feather between us, his silvery gaze fiery and liquid all at once. I scarcely breathed. I felt those eyes track across my face, brush my very soul as he read every expression, noted the condition of my homespun clothing, and finally caught on the silver ring I wore on my middle finger.

"What were you running from?" he asked.

My nails bit deeply into my palms. "The situation that was our reality."

"And what was your reality?"

"That we would die if they found us."

His face betrayed nothing. "Soren says you revere the old gods."

My jaw firmed, molars grinding together. What was their deal with the gods? "I do. I say my prayers to Zos. When the light has gone, you can only counter darkness with darkness."

Archer's eyes curved upward, crinkling at the edges. Approval? "You might be surprised to learn you're not the first to hold that particular belief, though it is a peculiar way of looking at the state of the world." He cupped my chin, and I shivered. "Soren also says you shelter owls and can talk to them. You wear their feathers."

These questions were not what I expected, and I had a hard time untangling the relevance. "I do."

"That's a unique hobby. Something you learned from your father?"

"Something I learned for myself."

His eyes went flinty. "Is that really all you have to say? You want my help and then refuse to answer my questions?"

"I haven't lied." I rose on my toes and Archer adjusted accordingly. "I have no intentions of lying, either. But you haven't earned the right to all my secrets, and those are mine to share when I'm ready and not a moment sooner. Either you believe me and see my plea for the earnest request that it is, or you don't." I stopped, swallowed hard, closed my eyes. "In the name of Zos, I ask you to help me get what remains of my family back.

"You have seen my experience with herbs. I have a vast background of medical knowledge, which Lukas and Soren can attest to." My eyes skirted across their faces, pleading. "When I have my family back, I can use those skills to help you with... whatever it is you're doing. If you want." I closed my eyes fiercely. "Please."

"I see."

I knew now which face he wore as a mask. Though Archer was more approachable from the offset, clearly aware of the power a smile and some light banter held, it was obvious he and Soren were cut from the same cloth. Whatever they'd seen, whatever they'd endured—it shaped who they were now. I only hoped a thread of kindness was as tightly woven into their beings as the threat of violence.

The older man stepped back so suddenly I swayed, as if an invisible string bound us together. He glided to the bar, snagged another glass from beneath the table, and poured a fingerful of amber liquid into it. But he didn't drink. And he didn't turn around. His knuckles had gone white where he gripped the edge of the counter.

Soren and Lukas rose, and their gazes bounced between the two of us: Lukas with keen interest and Soren with curiosity.

"I need time to think this over," Archer said. He threw back the contents of the glass, the column of his neck exposed as he swallowed. "What you ask is neither simple nor straightforward, and your resistance to giving me the information I need to know muddies the situation significantly."

Now that my temper had cooled, the first cracks branched through my resolve. Should I have said who I was? Who my father was? No. I couldn't. I'd promised. I'd said what I was comfortable saying. Nothing more. Nothing less.

"I'll meet with you again tomorrow, Telleree." Only a true master could tuck his emotions behind a wall as smoothly as Archer did. "We've set aside a room for you to use this evening. Lukas will show you where it is."

With one last hard look, he strode past me and opened the door. Before he slammed it shut behind him, his eyes caught on my cloak, on the feathers I hadn't quite tucked away, lips twisting in something that might have been grief.

9

Duty Calls

Steam wafted from the bowl of soup, and I swirled my spoon through the large chunks of potatoes, carrots, and celery entrenched in the thickened light brown liquid, hoping it would cool faster. My stomach released an ungodly gurgle. Good enough. I brought a spoonful to my mouth, blew on it, and moaned as I chewed. Food this flavorful ought to be illegal.

A tall tankard of beer so dark I couldn't see through it joined the fist-sized roll beside my bowl. The barkeep with all the attitude from earlier, Hatti, beamed, leaning against her hands braced on the lip of the counter. "Toldja you'd like it."

"Like it?" I shoved another bite into my mouth, eyes closing as I savored the velvety texture of the broth, the symphony of herbs and spices that melded with the fresh vegetables. "I could eat this all day, every day."

Between the food and the softness of the bed in the room gifted to me for the night, I was willing to stake my bets on this being the best tavern on the entire continent.

"I'll pass your compliments along to Robbie. He's manning the soup station tonight," Hatti said, tapping her long nails on the gleaming counter top. Eveningmeal had just begun and only half of the tables were full, but people were trickling inside, stomping freshly fallen snow off their boots and shaking it from their cloaks.

I'd snagged a quick nap in the room Lukas escorted me to after the meeting with Archer, but found myself too restless to stay isolated for long. The nerves of making my request refused to settle. Despite my offer, I wasn't sure it was enough. I imagined they got a lot of requests like mine, and I wasn't sure my expertise would sway them toward my mission.

Besides, we were always in motion in Solas, and the idea of doing nothing when I had so much work ahead of me made me itchy. I'd stowed my cloak and leather bracers under my bed—too paranoid to leave them in the open after Lukas' warnings and Archer's strange expression—and followed my nose downstairs.

Hatti had taken immediate pity on me, placing an order without asking me a word.

I reached for the steaming roll, glancing at her pink hair again. She'd woven it into a pair of braids that started at the edge of her hairline, trailed over her head, and were tied together in two tails in the back. Viv loved her hair, but hated wearing it down because it got into her eyes when hunting, smithing, and practicing. She compromised by cutting it short, but this style would suit her perfectly.

"Does it take you long? To do your hair?" I clarified at Hatti's quizzical expression. "I have a friend who would love to mimic it, but she's also wildly impatient."

Hatti patted one length of her braid, laughing. "It took a bit to learn at first, but I don't think about it anymore. I could probably pull this together in my sleep if I wanted." She leaned against the counter again, more relaxed than she had been earlier. "If you bring your friend here, I wouldn't mind showing her a few tricks to make it work properly."

"She would like that." I blew on another spoonful of soup and brought it to my lips, though the food I'd already consumed had hardened into a rock in my stomach at the reminder Viv was missing. That I didn't know when I might see her again.

"Are you from around here?" Hatti asked. "I feel like I've seen you around before, but I can't remember where."

I chewed, grateful for the excuse it gave me to think. I probably shouldn't be here, like this, making conversation in the middle of an open area. Not with soldiers crawling everywhere. Soren probably would have told me to stay in my rooms and get something brought up, but after living my entire life surrounded by people, I couldn't fathom a world where I was on my own. Even Pip was stuck in the woods with Grim, waiting for me to return.

I swallowed. "We live not far from here but only stop by every now and again. We don't visit the tavern much, but I'm familiar with the market."

A shout from the other end of the bar snagged Hatti's attention. "Duty calls," she murmured. "Things are picking up, but if you need anything, just holler." She pushed the tankard of beer closer to me. "And try the stout. It's sweet and bitter, but I think it'll be a good match for you." She winked. "It's my favorite."

I tugged the glass closer, eyeing the bubbles with apprehension. I hadn't ordered the drink, but after chatting for a few minutes earlier, Hatti had insisted on pouring a glass, saying Snowmelt prided itself on its brews. My knowledge of beer began and ended with the ingredients used to make it, so I'd asked her to pour me whatever she thought was best.

The fresh scent of melting snow washed over me as I ran the last of my roll around the inside of the bowl. "These seats taken?" a gruff voice asked. I shook my head stiffly, and two men dragged stools out from under the counter beside me.

A man about Papa's age shook big, white flakes from his dark hair, patting down the wet spikes with a grumble. "The last of the snow finally melts, only for a new wave to fall again. We'll probably get six inches with the way it's coming down."

The room had filled considerably. I curled into myself, peering into the glass, heart squeezing uncomfortably tight in my chest. I should return to my rooms if I didn't wish to be recognized. As Hatti had demonstrated, my family had clearly made more of an impression than we'd realized.

"Got that right." The man's companion tossed his brimmed hat on the counter and sat on his folded cloak beside me. "Business is bad enough with those soldiers prowling around. If it doesn't stop snowing before dawn, the crowds will be halved in early market."

"If not more." The man who'd spoken first raised two fingers, signaling Hatti. His shirt was the same shade as the brush that grew in the shade cast by evergreen trees and appeared to be of fine quality, cut to fit his lean shoulders perfectly. He tipped his stool back on two legs, casting a cursory gaze around the room, and continued, "But it's the soldiers who are the real problem. It's bad enough with them patrolling the crowds and stirring up trouble without them dragging prisoners right through the center of town."

The second man hissed between his teeth. "Keep your voice down, Knarl."

A chill swept over me, settling like ice on my skin. Prisoners? I sank deeper onto my stool, abandoning all thoughts of leaving. So, the soldiers *had* come to Stavanger after all. If they'd gone straight for one of the mines, my plan would have grown a million times more complicated.

"I know, I know," Knarl mumbled. "It's telling though, isn't it? They're bound to the Llyn Mines—the worst of them all—but you saw how many humans they had with them. Only three drakken among the lot. You know what that means, right?"

The second man ran his fingers through his bristly gray beard. His hooked nose was too large for his face. "I counted four in gold shackles, but I get your point. They're running out of shifter blood. If they want those gems, they're going to start burning through the rest of us next."

The men fell silent when Hatti stepped up to take their order.

I brought the mug to my lips but didn't drink, the spicy, chocolaty scent making my stomach churn. I wasn't familiar with the transport of prisoners, but I did know Fior subdued the drakken population largely by taking them by surprise in their initial attack in the capital—Aeros. Their golden armor was wrought with a spell that protected against drakken flames and acids. Those they didn't kill they took as prisoners, seizing the drakkentorre from our shifters by force. Without the ability to transform, the shifters still boasted tougher skin and stronger muscles than most humans, and toiled away in the mines for the rest of their lives.

That said, our drakken population had never been particularly large to begin with. Roughly a quarter of our citizens were gifted with the ability to shift, and only about a third of those ever continued on with their education, learning to use their heightened abilities and second forms to their fullest extent. Many remained within the towns, using their skills to aid in their crafts and careers, rather than join the military or manage the government.

When the wolven had conquered our capital and military, Grand Duke Brandt issued a decree ordering all civilian drakken to surrender immediately. Those who didn't were murdered on the spot. Some turned themselves in. Most didn't—and the grand duke made good on his threats.

Thousands of civilians died at the hands of the soldiers. Some had tried to escape our borders to the south and west, only to be met with the teeth and claws of the invading army. Others attempted to fight back, but they weren't up to the strength or agility of the soldiers who were specially trained to take down our forces. Others attempted to stay in the skies. The wolven knew what they were doing, though, and tracked them, waiting for them to land or crash out of exhaustion.

Less than two months after the attack, anyone with drakken blood left hiding among the general population hunkered down and abandoned shifting altogether. There was no way of singling out those with magic without seeing them shift, so it was up to civilians to turn them in—incentivized by hefty rewards.

"What do you think they did?" Knarl took a hearty glug of amber ale. "The humans? I mean, the red-head looked like she was ready to cut someone—" The greasy oil of guilt pooling in my belly caught fire—"so I could see her causing trouble somewhere. But a few were kids, barely older than my niece."

His companion shrugged, either tiring of the conversation or not interested. "Did they have to do anything? It's not like there's a court system to try them for their crimes." He paused. "How is your sister doing, anyway? Last you said, she'd finally rid herself of that deadbeat and found a man worthy of her time."

"Eh, he's fine. Lazy, but I think that's what she…"

I tuned the men out, trying and failing to mask the grin sweeping across my face. Excitement popped like kernels of corn in my stomach. My family was among those prisoners. I was sure of it. Those with red hair weren't common among Idileans, especially this far north, and Viv always had a mean look about her when she got in a mood, and I bet she was in a frost of a mood now.

After checking on some patrons with rosy cheeks and starbright eyes in the corner of the bar, Hatti wandered over and motioned at my drink, now forgotten on the table. "Not to your liking?" She sounded almost sad.

"It's not that." I tried to come up with an explanation other than I couldn't risk dulling my senses in unknown territory, but came up blank.

Her grin warmed her face. "It's alright. Sometimes the flavor is too bold. I get it, you don't—" She paused at the sounds of shouting outside, and we weren't the only ones turning toward the entrance. The double doors flew open, crashing into the wall with a bang, revealing a trio of shadows standing beyond the reach of the torchlight outside. The lively bustle of conversation filling the warm hall went silent. Even the waitstaff froze in the middle of their rounds.

"Make way, you northern *travetry*." Two Fiorian soldiers in stately emerald uniforms swaggered inside, hands on the hilts of their swords, metallic eyes flashing in the light of the candles bracketing the walls. The one who'd spoken lunged at a server who hadn't moved out of the way fast enough for his liking, teeth snapping together as she tumbled to the ground, scrambling to get away from the danger. "The colonel's coming through, and you don't want to get on his bad side."

Hatti smothered a gasp when the third figure stepped inside. He stood about a head taller than his subordinates, who were already taller than most of us—common for those from Fior. Horror dawned, creeping through me like first frost, and I wound my arms around my middle. I should have left. Staying here was a massive mistake.

I recognized the colonel and the scar that connected with the corner of his lips and hooked under his chin, continuing down into the vee of his shirt. He'd shaved recently, the dark stubble from the Spear gone, making him appear younger than he had before. But it was definitely him. The second wolven. The one with the golden laurels on his shoulders. The shifter who'd offered to help me in the moments before I fell.

The look the colonel cast about the room was dull, uninterested, and he tugged on the clasp of his heavy cloak, tossing it to another soldier who lagged behind.

Shivers quaked through me, threatening to rattle my teeth, and I clenched my arms even tighter. If he recognized me, I was done for. He'd sought me out before, and I had no desire to be dragged into his mess. The only thing bringing me hope was the knowing he likely believed me to be dead and wasn't looking for me. Though I couldn't be sure he hadn't seen the drakken, let alone stuck around to see them save me.

On top of all that, I'd bathed in my room earlier and had donned the fresh tunic and trousers left for me. Gone was the scraggly girl with the torn and bloodied clothing from the mountain. Now I was a nobody, a face in the crowd.

"It smells good in here," one soldier said. People scrambled aside, hopping up from chairs and hiding behind one another, giving the soldiers wide berth as they passed the first rows of tables. "Surprising, given the state of this shoddy town."

A group of women hurried to their feet when the first soldier hopped onto their table, knocking over the candle in the center. It sputtered out as it rattled against his muddy boot. He raised a hand to his forehead as if he were a pirate scanning the Caswich Sea for ships to loot.

"This spot won't do; only the best seat in the house for Colonel Kohl." A flinty grin engulfed his pockmarked face when he paused his perusal of the bar, eyes falling on me. I froze solid as a block of ice. Then the soldier tracked movement beside me, movement I also caught in my periphery. It wasn't me he was after. With her pink hair and cropped blue top, Hatti was easily the most colorful person in the room. "And a place beside the prettiest girl sounds like the best place to me. You agree, Stefan?"

Baldy snorted.

The colonel wasn't paying them any mind, attention fixed on the fire roaring at the back of the room as he tugged on the fingers of his gloves. He didn't seem like the same soldier from the Spear, the one who'd spoken with compassion as he implored me to step away from the edge. If he cared so much about others, why wasn't he stopping these men or calling order to this ugly scenario?

The icy horror that locked me tight melted, giving way to the freshly stoked coals of my anger. My trembling stopped. It wasn't right what they were doing here. They might have all the power, but this display meant to invoke fear wasn't necessary. As if he'd felt my scrutiny, the colonel turned, lips pulled into a frown, square jaw tight. I hastily looked away, self-preservation kicking in at the last moment.

"Out of the way." Baldy jumped off the table he'd so crudely commandeered and veered to the right, toward me. I closed my eyes, molars clenched so tightly they squeaked. This was bad. So very bad. The soldier approached the table in front of my stool. A family of six was seated there, and upon realizing his intent, most of them stood, hastening out of the warpath. Only a girl—maybe sixteen—remained seated, face pale. Her mother grabbed her shoulders, hissing at her to get up, to move, to get out of the way.

She wasn't quick enough.

Baldy yanked the mother away from her child and thrust her toward her family, watching in dismay. An older man hooked his arm around the struggling woman. "No, Lera. You can't."

"But my baby," the woman shrieked. "She's just a child. She's afraid."

"Lera—"

"Don't hurt her," the woman pleaded, sagging against the man's arms. The people closest to them edged away, not wanting to be in the spotlight. Everyone except for a shadow...

I blinked.

Soren?

His sullen stance was unmistakable, arms crossed over his chest, one foot propped on the wall at his back, chin angled down, eyes hidden by the short curtain of his hair.

"Did I stutter, little girl?" The cruel one stood behind the teenager, not six yards from me. He grabbed her chair and spun it around with her still seated in it. It creaked as he leaned his weight against the back, looming over her. Trickled down her cheeks as she stared up at him. "Did you not hear me when I said the colonel was here?"

"N-no, sir," she managed, shaking so hard it amazed me she voiced anything at all.

The violence flooding my veins was foreign, the taste metallic on my tongue. I wanted to scream. To strike the soldiers down where they stood. This was wrong. They'd taken over our nation. Enslaved our people. Sowed fear like seeds. Now berating a girl so scared she couldn't move. I couldn't—

The soldier crowded her further. Inches separated his body from hers. "And yet you sit here? At his table?"

She choked, tears flowing faster, trying to speak, but nothing came. Instead, she bowed her head in supplication, accepting whatever fate she faced.

The soldier grabbed a fistful of her auburn hair, jerking her up to look at him. "You must have a death wish." Claws sprouted from the tips of his fingers, his mouth morphing into the early stages of a hairy muzzle. "I'm more than happy to grant it."

With a snap, he threw the girl on the floor. His boot lashed out, catching her in the ribs, and she screamed, a shrill sound that shook the rafters. The soldier pulled back to kick her again. I didn't remember moving. One moment I was in my seat and the next I was throwing myself between the wolven and the child, dropping to my knees to wrap myself around her in a flimsy excuse for a shield. My side exploded with pain, but I kept my grip tight around the girl. She stared at me, brown eyes glazed with panic.

The soldier let out a surprised sound. "Who dares—"

"How dare you." I released the girl and rushed to my feet. The crowd had faded away, the edges of my vision going black, leaving only me and him. "You beat a child because she's too scared to move? A child who has nothing to do with you? Haven't you done enough? Haven't you—"

The back of his hand cracked across my cheek, stemming the flow of words from my throat. I'd barely processed the sting of his strike when a hand clenched around my throat, squeezing so hard I couldn't breathe.

"You'll die for your insolence." Scalding, garlicky breath washed across my face and I clawed at his hands, struggling to get him off me, wondering if the last thing I would see was the glare of his metallic green eyes. At least I'd done something in my final moments, even if it was in vain.

"Release her."

The fist clenched around my throat tightened, claws shredding the delicate skin, before heeding the order. My knees crashed into the stone floor with a crack, but I barely felt it, too busy hacking in gasps of air, one hand cupped around my aching throat. I was alive. Somehow, I'd survived again.

Gradually, the shock faded from my oxygen-deprived brain and I rocked back, tears and snot smeared across my face, glaring up at my savior. The roaring in my ears had nothing to do with my most recent brush with death and everything to do with the colonel peering down at me, frowning in confusion and something like amazement.

A shudder rippled through me at the recognition that gleamed in his intelligent gaze.

Stupid. I was so very stupid.

Even Zos couldn't save me now.

He leaned in. "Where do I—"

Someone stepped between us, their body blocking my view of the colonel. "Excuse me, sir, but if you're ready to eat, I've got some of our specials ready for you." Hatti. Behind her back, her hands flicked at me to move. To leave. To get out of here.

I barely heard the colonel's brisk reply. Someone snagged my wrist and was pulling me backwards, toward the doors. When I stumbled, struggling to keep up with their hasty movements, the person swung me up in their arms, cradled against their chest, shielding me from the soldiers behind us. Soren. The sharp angles of his face were unmistakable against his cloak, and he clenched his jaw as he shouldered through the door, squeezing me in warning. Though night had fallen, the aggressive heat thrown by his body warmed my blood, and I relaxed against him, trusting him to keep me safe.

The drakken hustled through the streets. Though I could tell he was rushing, he was careful to keep from jostling me too much. I couldn't figure out his mood, and quickly gave up, watching the town pass as my adrenaline faded, the aches from the injuries inflicted by the soldier growing in intensity.

Bastard.

I wished Cas, the goddess of war, would hunt him down with her hounds and cut out his heart, like she'd done to her former lover, Xedris, hundreds of years ago when he'd stolen her golden sundial and precious shield of truth.

Flurries whipped around us, the wind blowing so hard it kicked up the drifts piled along the side of the road and against the buildings. I pressed closer to Soren. The men who'd sat beside me at the bar were right. We probably would get another six inches of snow tonight, if not more.

The drakken was gentle when he finally stopped in an alleyway. He eased me to the ground, allowing me to get my feet beneath me before bracing his hands against the brick wall just over my shoulders, black eyes scrutinizing my face.

"You fool."

I flinched at his insult, spoken so softly it was nearly a whisper.

"You almost died back there, I hope you know." Brick crumbled beneath his fingertips, but I boldly held his gaze. Let him spill his vitriol. It couldn't possibly be as bad as everything I was thinking about myself. He leaned closer, the leather of his glove cool as he cupped my chin, jaw tightening as he brushed my cheek. It felt swollen. "If Hatti hadn't stepped in, you would have met your end. You and that girl you tried to save. Are you truly so desperate to reach the afterlife?"

I rose on my toes, gripping the front of his cloak, the snow piling on my boots and the freezing wall at my back forgotten. "What would you have me do, Soren? Leave her to die? Let that monster beat her until he got the retribution he felt he deserved? Until he killed her?" I shook him, my eyes flickering between his, demanding to know what was going on in his head. "They would have. And they wouldn't have cared. She was scared featherless. That girl saw the wolven and went into shock. She didn't deserve to die because she was scared."

His half smile stopped me from shaking him again. The corners of his eyes crinkled, and his hair skewed sideways over his forehead.

He brushed my cheek again so softly that tears stung the corners of my eyes.

"I didn't say you were wrong. I just pointed out you almost died." He eased back, taking his sweltering body heat with him. "Are all women who grow up in the mountains as fierce as you?"

My mind blanked. Me? Fierce? The boys I'd grown up would laugh their heads off hearing that adjective ascribed to me. Then again, I recalled the flames that had burned my insides, the way I'd jumped in the face of that soldier. I had acted without restraint. My throat worked around a lump, and I pulled my arms around myself, fighting against the shivers racking my body.

With a sigh, Soren removed his cloak and held it out. I took it without hesitation, enjoying the spiciness of his scent engulfing me, like burning leaves and lemonseed. The material was so warm I nearly purred.

"Never mind. I can tell you're about to overthink everything." He took another step back, rubbing the scar on his chin. "I do want to know why Kohl stepped in. Though he's not known for aggression, he's certainly not compassionate. He's one of three colonels in the Fiorian military. Only the general and the grand duke himself rank higher." Darkness edged into his tone. "But when that soldier was choking the shit out of you, he stepped in. I don't get it." He fiddled with the knives sheathed on a strap draped across his black shirt. "Does he know you?"

I toyed with a lock of my hair, smoothing it over my fingers. One strand was longer than the others, throwing off my rhythmic pattern. When I closed my eyes, those silvery eyes bored into mine. Soren said he lacked compassion, yet he'd acted compassionately toward me twice. That had to mean something.

"He tried to save me in the woods." I kept my attention fixed on my hair. Soren leaned in to better hear my whispered admission.

"He pushed the wolven who was chasing me over the edge of the Spear, then tried to pull me back. That was him. I see his face when I close my eyes like it's burned into my lids."

Soren went quiet for so long I risked a glance, my stomach tying itself into knots. Like me, the drakken was connecting the dots. Regardless of his actions toward me, why was one of the highest-ranking members of the Fiorian military tracking a bunch of villagers through the tallest of Idilea's mountains? Surely, he had minions to carry out such tedious tasks. We'd been sold out, but we didn't have any drakken among our meager population. Was camping in the mountains enough reason to necessitate an inquisition?

They were looking for something. They had to be.

The sour taste in my mouth told me they'd found it. They knew we were escapees of Aeros, and they'd come to settle the score. Or at least... some of them had. Kohl's motives remained a mystery.

A group of people hurried past the mouth of the alley, heads bent and hands shoved in their pockets, boots crunching in the snow. I took back my earlier assessment. This storm was a full-force blizzard. I hoped Pip and Grim would be alright in the woods. It wasn't like they hadn't weathered storms before, but they were far from home, away from protection.

I would have to seek them out in the morning, after the worst of the blizzard passed.

"I see," Soren murmured at last.

"You do?"

A tiny grin quirked his lips. "Don't worry, the image you present is still quite blurry."

My heart squeezed.

"Fortunately for you, I don't have time to press you tonight." His hand settled on his sword, his dark clothes melting into the shadows at his back. The blowing snow brought his silhouette into relief. "I think it's time we get you back to the tavern. They'll have given up searching for you by now, and I know a secret way in." He shot me a look and moved toward the main road. "This time, stay in your rooms. Nothing good can come of showing your face downstairs again."

That reminded me. "I hope Hatti is alright. She stepped in so suddenly—"

"Hatti can handle herself."

I balked. He sounded so sure of himself. "And I never paid for my meal. I completely forgot." I shoved my hands in my pockets, finding the grooved edges of the coins settled at the bottom. "I need to—"

"Already taken care of." Soren looked over his shoulder, brow quirked.

"But—"

"She's one of us, Telleree." He shook his head at my distress. "I promise. She will be compensated appropriately. And don't worry yourself over the wolven. If they had attacked her, our people would have stepped in. Like I said, she can handle herself quite well, unlike a certain someone who seems to attract danger like the plague."

I didn't have an answer for that. I'd wondered the same thing myself. Keeping my mouth shut, I followed closely on his heels, head bent against the roaring of the wind. Blizzards were the worst. A few blocks later, the wind blew Soren's mumbled words back at me, words I surely wasn't meant to hear: "What is it about you that makes people so eager to put their lives on their line to help you?"

My fists clenched, but I bit my tongue. Sure, I'd made some of this mess, but I'd tried to stay out of it for most of my life. Until recently, I'd never asked anyone for help of this magnitude.

When we finally stopped at the back of a brick building I recognized as the tavern, Soren turned. "Make sure to get some sleep tonight. That's the best treatment for your injuries. I'll see if I can get some salve."

I waved him off. "I've got some in my bag."

"I'm sure you do." He pulled open a door cleverly concealed in the grout and waved me through the opening. A torch burned in a holder just inside. "Go all the way to the end, take the spiral staircase to the third level, and follow the wall until you feel a groove. That will open three doors down from your room. You'll be safe there."

"But what about you? Will you sleep?" I hesitated. "You took overnight watch, and you fought off those soldiers this morning. Surely, you're exhausted."

His face hardened, the brutality of the expression on his face so intense I wavered. "I have somewhere I need to be." His fist tightened at his side. The same hand that had brushed my cheek so softly. "There's someone I need to see."

10

Low Gain

The window opened with effort. The blizzard had frozen it shut, but after running a candle along the metal edges of the frame, I was able to force it upward, high enough to throw the shutters wide, exposing a wonderful realm of sparkling white. Snow tumbled off the sloped roof and landed with soft thumps on the street below. Drifts half my height angled up the walls of buildings lining the road, and many store owners were already hard at work, taking advantage of the morning light to clear snow from the cobblestones.

I inhaled deeply, appreciating the crisp, clean chill, squinting over the glare of sunshine bouncing off all that white. This, here, felt like home.

Reluctantly, I shoved the window back down, leaving a tiny gap at the bottom so I could hear the commotion outside as people rose to welcome the day, and returned to my bed. I'd risen early, too anxious to get much sleep. After dressing in the freshly laundered clothing dropped off by a servant, I spread my belongings out on the quilt to take inventory.

Considering the haste with which I'd packed and the state of the homes I'd pillaged, I was surprisingly well-stocked. All I needed were a few supplies for my medical kit and a hearty supply of travel food, then I'd be set for whatever new challenge presented itself. Satisfied, I repacked my bag, only hesitating when I reached for Viv's bandolier.

With a sigh, I ran a finger down the sheath of the weapon Viv had dubbed Epic. The leather pouch disguised the masterpiece that was the wavy blade, about as long as my forearm. She'd told me once this make of dagger was ceremonial and her mother had favored them as a memory of the old times, back at the palace. However, Bree didn't believe in weapons lacking functionality, so they'd traded the jewels that normally would have encrusted the handle for quality steel that rippled with blue streaks. Having Viv's daggers with me made it feel like my best friend was that much closer.

I straightened, right fist clenched over my heart, the other poised over the small of my back, bent my head and prayed. It felt good, allowing myself the luxury of my morning habit. I'd skipped the ritual the past few days, feeling skittish around the drakken, but I needed this. I needed to feel the connection with the goddess of darkness to whom I valued most highly.

Of the seven deities, Papa's trade dictated I should offer my prayers to Fen—the god of the hunt, travelers, and messengers. My father had operated the aerie at the castle, managing all kinds of birds, ensuring messages dispatched by those at the capital found their way to destinations across the kingdom. Encouraged by my love of raptors, my father had shared his nightly prayers to Fen with me, teaching me the inner workings of the god he held so dear.

After our world burned and we'd fled to Spear Ridge, that changed. One night, my father interrupted my prayers and pulled me into his lap on my bed. Once situated, he held up the stub of the candle burning beside my blanket. His voice was soft, softer than I'd ever heard it before, and he'd told me: "There is a time for light, Telleree, but now we embrace the dark." He blew out the candle, cradling me closer as the tendrils of smoke swirled around us. "While you must never lose faith in the light, in times like these, you must allow the darkness to guide your way."

He told me embracing the dark didn't mean the same thing it did in the picture books my mother used to read me. It didn't come with a desire to commit atrocities or hurt others, but he wanted me to understand we lived during a time of war, that we didn't have the luxury to view everyone in a positive light. Papa said I would witness horrors and I should be prepared to fight back.

When our eyes adjusted to the dark, he explained we didn't always need light to see in the dark, that the dark created its own kind of light.

He drew the rune of Zos in the dust on the floor.

"That is our lady of darkness and death. To her we will offer our prayers, for we have lost so much, and it is she who has witnessed our suffering, she who will help us get it back." He spoke reverently. "Zos is our goddess of vengeance, and someday she will see our plight absolved."

It had taken time to embrace Papa's mentality. I'd spoken with Bree, with Isabella—and others in my village. Some agreed with his sentiments, others didn't, encouraging me to forge my own path and follow the gods of my choosing. It wasn't until six months later, when I'd uncovered the letters my father had saved from my mother, missives they'd sent to each other in the early months of their courtship, that I embraced all Zos had to offer.

Qet and his love of light and sky and wisdom had a place in our world. I respected his role, especially how he'd created the first drakken and had led our country through centuries of peace and light. But darkness had overrun our lands, and it seemed only natural to fight dark with dark.

Even when a particular cynical, brooding drakken seemed intent on challenging my every thought when it came to my faith.

A knock at the door interrupted my thoughts, and I shoved the daggers into my bag.

"Who is it?" I called, pushing my arms through the sleeves of my inside-out cloak while kicking my bag under the bed. If Kohl's soldiers had found me, I doubted they would have knocked, but I was glad I'd left the window cracked, regardless.

"The tax collector. Time to pay up."

I rolled my eyes, recognizing Lukas' droll voice, and twisted the lock, throwing the door wide in invitation. "As if."

He cleaned up nicely, his golden features better suited for civilization over the rough-and-tumble lifestyle of the woods. A fitted, royal blue tunic draped over his white, long-sleeve shirt that accentuated his muscles, and he'd replaced his scarred trousers for black ones that didn't have holes in the knees. If I wasn't mistaken, he'd also trimmed his wild hair.

"Bold move, Falk, considering you've been living off the grid for the better part of two decades. The amount you owe the government is enormous." He shut the door and frowned. "Why is it freezing in here? Surely you know how to light a fire."

I pointed at the window over my shoulder. "I wanted some fresh air. It's beautiful out there, I'll have you know."

"Beautifully unfit for going outside." He shut the window himself, then blew into his cupped hands. I shook my head at his antics. Under my cloak, I was already sweating. "Archer is ready for you," Lukas continued, then put his hand on my shoulder when I reached for my bag, one strap sticking out from under the bed. "You can leave that here. No one will bother your things. This wing is ours and the room is yours until you leave."

My stomach flipped. "Lead the way."

The little sleep I'd gotten had taken the edge off my exhaustion, making it easier to take mental notes as Lukas guided me through the twisting halls of the inn above the tavern. I hoped Soren hadn't lied about paying Hatti. I wasn't sure I would see her again to thank her for her kindness.

Lukas rapped his knuckles on a door with a wooden crow over it, waited a minute, then shrugged. "Soren must have gotten up while I was eating. That will make this simpler."

I dutifully followed him down the stairs, and we stopped outside a door with a familiar snake insignia.

"One moment, please," I requested, not waiting to see if Lukas would comply before shrugging out of my cloak and turning it around so the feathers faced outward. There was significance to them. I didn't understand what, exactly, but I fully intended to use the shield it offered. That and the pen I clenched tight in my pocket, the gift from the woman in the marketplace.

Lukas opened his mouth, closed it again without saying anything, and rapped on the wood. As he had the day prior, he didn't wait for an answer before opening the door to Archer's room. Someone had cleaned up since last night. The smudged glasses on the bar had disappeared and the parchment was rolled and stacked in a corner. Soren lounged in the chair he'd taken up residence in before, a leg thrown casually over one arm, and beside him, leaning against the window frame, stood Archer. He passed a rolled-up document between his hands.

Soren looked over when we walked in, his gaze sweeping over the feathers decorating my shoulders and arms, before meeting my eyes. A message was written in those depths, but I couldn't decipher it. I didn't particularly care. I'd made my power play—even if was the only one in my arsenal.

"You know what I like about the snow, Telleree?" Archer asked, attention fixed outside.

"There are a great many things to like about the snow. To isolate one would be disingenuous." I wasn't sure what it was about Archer that made me comfortable enough to slip back into the tattered shreds of my old self, but I would take it. "And I don't know you well enough to guess your mind."

Archer's lips quirked. "I thought you'd say something like that. However, I'll give you my assessment: I appreciate the snow's mystery. Not only does it blunt sound, but it disguises things right before our faces. It can wipe out existence at its worst... and in the aftermath, it offers a clean slate."

Poetic.

He dragged a hand down his face. "I'm taking a leap of faith here. A leap that might be ill-advised if I listen to my subordinates, but you've made some friends in rather high places. Friends who tell me you're worthy of my trust." A log shifted in the fire. Sparks flew from the grate. "I hold their opinions paramount, and that's why you're privy to what I'm about to tell you."

Archer pulled the curtain closed. His eyes narrowed when they settled upon my shoulders, but he didn't mention my makeshift armor. For now. He moved to the desk and placed the parchment on its empty surface. "We are the Requiem."

Whatever he'd expected to see on my face, he didn't find. Aside from what the old woman had said, the name didn't ring any bells. A knot of tension in his shoulders relaxed.

"Given your isolation, I'd wondered if you'd heard of our efforts, but I can see now you have not. It's quite a miracle then, then, that you found us at all." He crossed one foot over the other. "We are highly sought after by allies and enemies alike, and we are careful to whom we reveal ourselves. A rebellion won't succeed if moles dig holes in the operation."

The flame that ignited in my breast last night, the one I'd finally banked when I'd gone to bed, flared again, hot with anticipation. A rebellion. The old woman was right. There were people trying to drive the evil that was Fior from our borders.

Archer motioned me forward and unrolled the document, revealing that curious sketch again. Today, the pieces fell into place. I recognized it as the symbol I'd glimpsed in the alleyway when I'd knelt to pick up Lukas' glove.

"This is our sign. It's possible you've seen it before. We use it for official purposes, but the populace has embraced it, too, and scrawls it everywhere. It's a middle finger to Fior, who can't clean them up fast enough." Archer sounded entirely too pleased about that fact. "You see, we've claimed Zos as our patron of vengeance. Qet has a time and place, but as you so eloquently put yesterday, Zos alone can grant us the power and the tools we need."

I schooled my face. I could almost hear my father speaking.

"We didn't always have this symbol. It started off with sketching her rune on the walls, an act of defiance against those who tried to strip us of our gods. They destroyed our temples, took away our drakkentorre, but the grand duke and his minions didn't realize we don't need temples to worship: the gods live in our minds and hearts."

The edges of the pen bit into my palm so hard I knew they would leave a mark. It was bizarre hearing rhetoric I'd been fed my entire life funneled into a cause rather than an excuse to hide. The inferno in my breast blazed hotter.

Archer grinned slightly, trapped in a memory. "An early member of the Requiem had too much to drink one night and drew Zos' symbol on the wall. One of the biggest we'd ever seen. It looked like this." He motioned at the page. "What does it look like to you?"

I wet my lips. "An owl—or maybe a dragon—spreading its wings."
Archer nodded approvingly. "We thought so, too. It felt like
good luck, given how Zos is often depicted with an owl perched on
her shoulder or swooping in from the background, so we adopted
the modification of the rune for our own purposes. Many in our
organization felt Zos herself granted us her blessing."

The hairs on the back of my neck rose. I knew where this was
going.

"And now you understand why you're such a curiosity to us,"
Archer said. "You don't hesitate to invoke Zos' name, you revere
owls—even understand them, you dare to wear their *feathers*, and
no one, absolutely no one, knows who you are or where you came
from. You, like the snow, are a mystery."

I squared my shoulders, the cloak hanging heavily down my back.
"What does this have to do with finding my family?"

He clicked his tongue and wandered to the bar where a pitcher
filled with amber liquid sweated. Ice clinked as he poured a glass,
then offered it to me. "Tea?" I shook my head. He took a thoughtful
sip.

"What happened to your family is not isolated. It's what Brandt
does: he takes, and takes, and takes until there's nothing left to take,
and then he finds a way to dig his needs even deeper." Archer cast a
slow hand around the room. "Everyone in here has been touched by
their violence. My sister was murdered while managing her shop.
Lukas watched his father be taken captive and later executed. And
Soren…" His silvery eyes flickered. "His parents and brother died at
their hands."

Soren ran his hand through his hair, focused on a split in the
floorboards.

"We need support," Archer pushed. "Our ranks are growing every
day, but we need more. We need people who are willing to go all

the way to push those mangy dogs out of our borders once and for all." He rapped the desk with his knuckles. "Telleree, you show signs of being an excellent recruit. I see your rage and I've heard about your actions, like in the tavern when you stepped in front of that child with no thought to your own safety." He paused, gathering his thoughts. Took another sip of tea. "I've considered your offer of working with us as a healer. Soren and Lukas both vouched for your abilities, reiterating you think quickly on your feet. I believe you could be a valuable member of our operation."

Here it was. The push that came with the pull. I'd tossed and turned, wondering if the worth of my healing skills would be enough to gain the information I requested. And now it was laid out in front of me, a buffet of mixed offerings.

Sensing my wavering sentiments, Archer pushed harder. "We are preparing several large-scale attacks on key locations around Idilea. We are closer than ever to pushing the wolven out and freeing those enslaved by their wicked means. Those attacks mean wounded. And we need talented people like yourself on the front lines, patching them up. We may have many under our mark, but they are hardly indispensable. You have an opportunity to save many on our path toward victory."

It sounded impressive, that a group like this might have the ability to do so much. But no matter how much their cause made my heart beat faster, Archer hadn't answered my question. I held up my hand before he could push ahead.

"You're saying all the right things, Archer, but I still need to know: what of my family?" I took two steps closer. "Yes, I loathe the soldiers who destroyed my home, my father, my family. But I still have people out there. People—" *Viv*—"who aren't in the mines yet. They have a chance to escape that fate, and I need to get them back, no matter how slim the odds. If what you say is true, then you can help me and then I'll do everything in my power to give you the support you need in return."

Archer took another sip of his drink, shoulders tense. Lukas had started pacing in my stead, not meeting my eyes. Only Soren seemed unaffected by my outburst, his silence as thoughtful as ever.

"I hear your concerns," Archer said at long last, setting his glass down. "But I can't grant your request."

My heart dropped to my stomach.

I'd known this would be the outcome, but I'd clung to my hope like a child drowning in the middle of the river with no one around to hear her scream.

"I'm sorry, but I'm in charge of this entire operation, and I must think of the bigger picture." Archer sounded genuinely apologetic, and, again, I wondered how often he was presented with similar requests. My heart constricted. Probably all the time. "I understand your frustration and I empathize with the situation you find yourself in. However, I simply don't have enough people to risk on such a low-gain operation."

Blood pounded in my ears.

Low gain.

The dozen people I had left from my old life, my friend and her mother, who I loved with my entire heart, would be sent to the mines where they would likely perish.

And Archer called them low gain.

The head of the Requiem was still talking. "If you join us, I promise you will be involved in the operations that will eventually free them—"

"How long?" I interjected. "How long before these operations are carried out?"

Lukas groaned and pinched the bridge of his nose, eyes screwed up tight. Archer wet his lips. "Several months. As many as three."

Three months. Three entire months my family would be left on their own. Three months where they could die, where they would believe me to be dead. And if they didn't believe I had died, then surely, they'd think I had abandoned them.

"If I could help you, I would," Archer said, stopping Lukas with a hand on his shoulder when he passed. "But even if I had soldiers to spare on your operation, the trail has gone cold."

"But I know where they're going," I shouted. "I heard it last night. The Llyn Mines. To the southeast. There's not—"

"The snow will have covered their tracks." Archer's voice was firm. "Trust me, we intend to free *everyone* in those mines, eventually. But to trace their path in all this snow? It's impossible. Assuming we followed them exactly, we would have to make a move before they passed the outer perimeter of the mine. Once they're inside, there's nothing we can do. Not right now. We aren't ready to attack yet."

I fumbled with my thoughts, then remembered what the old woman had said. About needing an ally in the worst of times. This seemed pretty bad to me. I pulled the pen from my pocket and held it out to Archer. "If my plea isn't good enough, then consider this another drop in my bucket."

Archer couldn't have looked more shocked as he took the pen from my shaking fingers. "Now, where did you get that?"

"It was a gift." I tipped my chin. "From someone who supports my cause."

Archer pulled off the cap and traced the looping silver design that ran the length of the pen. This device meant something, especially given the way Lukas stared at it as if he'd never seen a pen before. With slow deliberation, Archer capped it and returned it to me.

"Who are you really, Telleree?" he murmured, a peculiar look on his face.

"I'm a girl asking for your help."

Archer shared a long look with the drakken before dragging his hand down his beard. "I'm sorry, but I can't. Not right now. I simply don't have the troops."

"But—"

He smiled slightly. "Your plea is noted and will be considered. I can't act now, but I will see what I can do about moving the timeline up."

This wasn't good enough. Not by far. An offer to free my family somewhere down the road was too vague. I couldn't, in good conscious, join them when there was something I could do now. Sure, I wasn't the best fighter, and I hated the feel of steel in my hands, but I was smart. I had my owls. I could track them. I could find them and I would find a way to free them.

I shoved the pen into my pocket, cursing myself for playing a card I didn't understand. Given the way Soren was staring at me darkly, I wasn't sure I should have used it at all. That pen and its secrets... I'd overstepped. And now I needed to get out of here.

I understood why the Requiem couldn't help. Archer's reasoning was one hundred percent sound. But I couldn't accept it. I opened my mouth to tell him as much when I realized what doing so might mean. They'd revealed a lot of information to me. They'd done so with the belief I would join them, recognizing they posed the best option to achieve my goals. Denying them now could come with consequences.

Soren had already shown how willing he was to cut down those who stood between him and his goals. Though I had no intention of revealing what I'd learned to anyone, he could very well kill me next for being a loose thread.

"I need some time to think." My voice sounded small, even to me. I hated that. Seeming weak before people so powerful. More than that, I loathed the pity emanating from Lukas. He'd known this was coming, but he was the empathetic sort. I got the feeling he didn't like it much more than I did, but it wasn't his family on the line.

"May I have a day? To think this over?"

Archer straightened, relief loosening the lines of his body. "Of course. I've thrust a lot at you and it's not an ideal situation to be in, I understand that. However, I hope you'll come to see things our way. I truly think you will be an asset in our efforts."

"Thank you." I ducked my head, taking care to avoid looking at the shadowy corner where Soren sat, and dipped outside. The door had barely snicked shut and my thoughts were already drifting away. I had a lot to do in very little time.

11

Alone

I f they found me in here, I was dead.

Guilt slithered through me, slick as goat grease and equally difficult to blot out. The door closed at my back. I'd taken precautions, knocking first before trying the knob, but that hadn't felt like enough. Unfortunately, my time was running low, and it wasn't my fault Soren left his room unlocked. I pressed my back against the door, observing the pair of double beds bookending the room. I'd assumed Lukas stayed in a room of his own, but it turned out they really did everything together.

I had found most of what I needed in the market. My pockets felt light, but I'd picked up enough necessities to last me for a while. I'd come to thank Soren for helping me last night and see if he could shed more light about Archer's offer, but now that I knew Lukas slept here, too… my timeline moved up a bit. There was one thing I desperately needed that I hadn't been able to afford: a current map of Idilea.

And I knew just the person to borrow from.

The same person whose maps I knew I could trust, unlike most of the outdated scraps of parchment I'd uncovered in the market that mislabeled key parts of the mountain range.

I dismissed the side of the room with small rocks and stray weapons scattered everywhere, the chaos of Soren's existence easy to differentiate from Lukas' organized space. Another quick glance at the door, and I pulled open Lukas' bag, rifling around inside, grinning as I flipped through pouch after marked pouch: pens, paper, correspondence to deliver, medicinal powders, jerky, and more. I hesitated over an envelope marked 'emergency funds,' the weight of the coins was almost too difficult to pass up, but I put it back and flipped to the last envelope.

Finally, the maps.

I sat on the bed, making a mental note to pull the quilt tight when I got back up, and thumbed through the parchment. The maps with the most wear were of the southern region of Idilea. Given their accents, I assumed that was where they were from. I set those aside and flicked past some maps of countries outside our borders.

One document, heavy with markings, stood out to me, and when I unfolded it, I discovered a map of their upcoming plans. Or what I assumed were their plans. I couldn't make heads or tails of what the different colors and crisscrossing lines meant, but the mines were circled heavily with x's, slashes, and o's. A code? Definitely not something meant for my eyes. I pushed it back into place and finally found the document I was looking for.

The eastern part of our country boasted two mines: the Llyn Mines known for their wealth of rubies, and the Exeter Mines farther to the north—prized for the rich emeralds carved from its depths. I studied the path from Stavanger to the southernmost mine. Most of the land between here and there was wooded. A lake, taller than it was wide, pooled in the way, forcing the road to wind around it in both directions to reach the mine. I wouldn't be able to take that road lest I risk notice, but the map would keep me on track.

I opened my cloak and shoved the page into the pocket over my heart.

Forgive me, I begged Lukas, rubbing my tattoo. Though far from the worst of sins, I'd never stolen from anyone before and didn't care for how the theft weighed on my mind now. It wasn't Lukas' fault Archer had denied my request. He'd fulfilled his end of our bargain. Despite that, I needed this or I wouldn't survive on my own, and I didn't want to risk following the directions of maps I couldn't trust. Swallowing hard, I pulled the last few vetter from my pocket and dropped the coins in the bag with the maps before sealing it tight and returning it to its rightful spot.

I couldn't help but look at the bed across the room and the quilt bunched at the foot of the bed. Try as I might, I couldn't figure Soren out. He worked for an organization founded on the beliefs of the old gods, yet he relished in some sort of obscure pleasure in challenging my faith. Did he not believe in the very goddess the Requiem was sworn to follow? Or was it just *me* that triggered his pessimism?

Voices sounded from the hallway. I couldn't make out what they were saying or who they belonged to, but the urgency to move swept through me. To be caught here… I refused to entertain what might happen next. A beat later I was on my feet, the quilt pulled taut, and beside the window. Like the one in my room, the cold had sealed it shut. But after a few seconds of grunting and pulling at the frame, I got it to lift high enough to sneak out of. Once outside, I shoved the window shut and slipped to the edge of the roof, surveying the ground, thankful Soren and Lukas were situated on the second and not the third floor. I took a breath, silently thanked Viv for all the times she'd pushed me out of trees just to teach me how to fall, and dropped into the alley between the tavern and the clothing shop.

The landing knocked the breath from my lungs, but nothing felt broken. I snuck to the edge of the alley. Eveningmeal was approaching, and I hoped to lose myself in the crowds. With one last look at the tavern, I pulled my hood over my head and stepped alongside a stream of hardy merchants heading north out of town, near the area where I'd left Pip and Grim.

As I'd hoped, they paid me no heed, and I slipped through the gates with no one the wiser. Even the soldiers didn't take notice, too busy talking among one another to care about anyone not stirring up trouble. It didn't take long to find my way into the woods, where I called for my owls, mixing spoken words with sharp whistles. The longer it went without an answer, the greater my anxiety mounted. Surely the blizzard hadn't blown them away.

I was two breaths away from climbing a particularly unforgiving silverpine when a sharp hoot sounded from my left. I stilled. A chatter joined the call of the great gray, and I nearly slipped in the snow as a blur darted out of the brush. Pip crashed into my chest with a happy squawk, and I caught her in my arms, cuddling her close. This was the longest we'd been separated since I'd rescued the owlet.

"I missed you so much," I murmured, stroking the brown feathers protruding awkwardly from the top of her head, feeling her body quake in agreement. "I'm glad you're safe."

The gray arrived on silent wings, his wingspan as imposing as always, and landed on the outstretched branch of an oak tree. He regarded me calmly, then fluffed his feathers, shaking away stray dust and snow. What I didn't expect was the barn owl that dropped beside it. His heart-shaped face bobbed when he looked me over. Apparently satisfied with my presence, he preened his rose-gold feathers.

"You guys found Ghost?" I gaped at Pip, bringing the screech owl up to my shoulder. Her beak threaded through my loose hair thoughtfully. "That's incredible. I wasn't sure if he would seek us out." I reached for the newcomer, giving him a chance to pull away if he chose. When he didn't, I stroked the plumage around the starburst of his face.

"Welcome back, Old Man," I said. "Are the three of you ready for an adventure?"

Grim shifted on his branch, and the barn didn't bother looking up from his preening. Pip tittered her agreement and flew to the gray's side, large eyes wide with eagerness.

"Alright. We're going to find Viv and the rest of them. But I need your help."

* * *

If asked to choose between the best tracking dogs in the country and wild owls, I would choose owls every time. I set out eastward, using the setting sun and rising stars as a guide, periodically consulting the map to make sure I was following the correct tracks cutting through the snow. Most roads started going east, then veered north and south. The last thing I needed was to end up on the wrong route.

For some, the two feet of snow the storm had dumped overnight would have posed an issue. However, I'd grown up surrounded by the stuff, and, like we had on our way south, I stuck mostly to the forested areas, preferring to stay out of sight of the few merchants and stragglers who opted for the more run-down route.

It wasn't an easy task navigating the trees without snowshoes, but I forced myself forward, knowing my troubles were nothing compared to those I tracked. Trips and falls I could handle. The true key was not stopping long enough for my sweat to freeze. I was comfortably warm under the light of the moon, but all it took was waiting too long at the wrong moment and I could easily fall victim to hypothermia.

My struggles also gave Grim and Ghost plenty of time to scour the woods for signs of the soldiers and the prisoners they dragged along with them. They had a day and a half head start, but I was moving alone, whereas they had dozens of people to worry about, people who might not be at the pinnacle of health.

As long as I stayed on track, I could catch up. I was sure of it.

Several hours later, when the moon peaked overhead, Ghost emerged from the darkness, his upturned face as luminescent as his name. He hooted twice, and I closed my eyes, sending prayers of gratitude to Zos for blessing me with such loyal, intelligent birds.

They'd found Viv.

And I was catching up.

It took a little steering from the owls and some help from the map to avoid a checkpoint in the region, but I finally felt confident in my direction by the time the sun rose again. My muscles burned, still not healed from the exertion from the mountain climb. I knew I needed to rest. And eat. Probably in reverse order, though.

But staying out of sight and not freezing to death in my sleep were of utmost priority.

I hadn't had the finances to purchase a tent, and neither of the men had left any obvious gear in their rooms. Sleeping in the branches of a tree would work, but exposed me to the increasingly powerful gusts of wind from the north. Not exactly ideal. Snow and dead leaves crunched underfoot as I slogged through the briarbrush, wincing when thorns scraped at my exposed skin.

Grim and Ghost had fallen asleep with the moon and would catch up with us later. That left me and Pip—who had to be on her last wings. Exhaustion edged her tiny voice when she trilled, alerting me to the presence of nearby flurryfoxes. They were heading the opposite direction, most likely seeking food as they prepared for a new delivery of kits, but I didn't want to risk encountering them.

The foxes sometimes grew to the size of medium-size dogs, with sharper teeth and wits to boot.

However, that gave me an idea.

I brought my hand to my brow, shielding it from the sun. "Pip, are there any large evergreens nearby? Something with branches low to the ground?"

The screech owl hooted and darted away. I'd barely made it a dozen steps before she returned, pipping about finding the perfect thing. I followed her voice until I found her perched on the branch of a massive evergreen, talons curled around a knobby branch. I rubbed her head. "Nice job. Give me a few minutes, and I'll have a nice home ready for us."

Flurryfoxes dug burrows deep into the ground. I didn't have time for all that, but they also chose entrances to their hovels near the base of silver pines, enjoying the shelter offered by the low-hanging branches that also obscured them from predators when they emerged, the silvery branches matching their fur perfectly. I hoped to achieve something similar on ground I didn't have to clear using branches that shielded the ground from the snow steadily melting in the light of day.

I crawled beneath the tree and scooped out a hole among the dead needles, building a trench around myself to trap the heat inside and avert prying eyes. Finally satisfied with my work, I ripped a large branch off another evergreen and dragged it under the tree with me. I called to Pip, who ducked into my hood, and crawled into my little hole, dragging the branch over us.

I'd slept in far better conditions, but this was safer than sleeping outside. Even in her slumber, Pip would keep an ear out for danger and alert me immediately. It was also warmer than lingering in the canopy of trees, my muscles relaxing after a few minutes of huddling beneath the bough.

With that thought, it didn't take long for the sharp scent of pine to beckon me to sleep.

* * *

Ghost woke me from a thankfully dreamless sleep. Sheer exhaustion had chased the nightvisions away. He and Pip dozed while I gnawed on hard bread laced with herbs and nuts, the map in my lap as I plotted my next move. Though sleep was necessary to stave off collapse, I hated the itchy feeling between my shoulder blades, the one that demanded I move faster, push harder.

Plan set, I tucked Pip into my hood, crawled out from under the tree, brushed off the broken bits of needles and tree dust, and pushed forward again. To keep my mind sharp, I focused on the landscape, ears popping the farther south I moved into the lowlands.

The forests still spread thickly through this territory out east, but the silverpines gradually disappeared as the deciduous trees mounted. Some I'd only seen in the books we'd kept back home: fireelm and its canopy of star-shaped orange and red leaves; flexible whipple with their long, bowed branches and bark that could be chewed or boiled for pain relief; spruce trees with narrower trunks than their northern cousins and needles that bordered on blue.

A thin layer of snow still crunched underfoot, but it was nowhere near as cold as it was in the mountains. I kept my hood up, using the leather to catch sound in the way animals swiveled their ears, but pulled my scarf down past my mouth, no longer requiring the wool to stave off the bite in the wind.

Every now and again, I pulled Lukas' map from my pocket, careful to not smudge the page with dirt or sweat, and added my own markings, little specks denoting landmarks that caught my eye. Maybe someday I would give it back to him and abate the guilt that clung to my insides like fresh sap.

The longer I walked alone, even with the owls keeping me company with their quiet hoots and warning cries, the greater the silence grew. I missed the shifters and their casual banter. My heart ached thinking about Viv and the way she used to treat every walk through the woods as an excuse to attack invisible enemies with her latest creations. And most of all, I wished Papa were beside me. I remembered the way his voice changed when he pointed out animals tucked away in the brush, how he snacked on fresh berries he'd scooped off the briars, the warmth of his hand on the top of my head when I said or did something that surprised a laugh from him.

There was being alone and comfortable.

And then there was this.

Alone. And not knowing if that would ever change.

Grim and the barn emerged during the night, hooting their encouragements while scouting for predators. The tracks of the wolven soldiers and the people they lugged along with them were easy enough to follow, but now I worried about scouts left behind, monitoring for suspicious activity. Nothing yet, but I couldn't afford to let my guard down.

At one point, when the scent of fresh earth stung my nose for a particularly long period of time, I knelt and poked at the tracks. Wagons had cut deep grooves in the snow and dirt, and when I rubbed it between my fingers, the dirt crumbled easily. The wind hadn't blown the powdery, crystallized snow that lay on top of the drifts into the grooves yet, and the dirt hadn't frozen to the ground.

I was gaining ground.

The promise of making good time spurred fresh energy into my limbs, but the exertion of the past few days was never far, and I had to take several breaks as the dawn sky slowly lightened from black to navy to sherbet cream. I wanted to collapse into sleep for an entire day, to change out of my wet clothes that stank of old sweat, but I didn't dare attempt either. The threat of danger kept dodging my heels and ringing my nerves.

The downward trajectory of the lowlands gave way to rolling hills that appeared mild enough from the crests, but actually proved troublesome both uphill and downhill. Downward, I risked tripping over my own feet, and going up, the air gasped in and out of my lungs so hard I thought I might pass out.

It wasn't until I crested one particularly brutal hill and paused at the top, hand pressed to my brow, shielding against the sun, that I spotted something new on the horizon. Something I almost dismissed as a formation of clouds, but returned to twice more, mouth pursed, squinting.

Not clouds. Smoke. Or steam, maybe.

Whatever it was, it billowed from the ground in great puffs, like I imagined the breaths of a dragon would appear when it prepared to release a burst of flesh-rendering flame. The plumes blossomed and faded into a wispy haze the higher up they went.

My heart thundered in my chest, exhaustion forgotten, anxiety and wonder twisting into a tight cord around my spine.

The Llyn Mines. I'd finally found them.

And disappearing into the woods maybe a half-day's hike away, at the base of more hills: the caravan I sought.

12

Imprisonment or Death

"Now what?" I asked out loud, needing to hear my own voice for the sake of my sanity. I'd followed the wolven this far, but I still didn't have much by means of a plan. I sank into a crouch and pulled out the map. Based on the legend, I wasn't far from the mines. The hills leveled out along the treeline, and the forests dominated the terrain up to the edge of the lake. I needed to catch them before they hit the water. If they used boats to cross, I was done for.

Then there was the issue of what happened when I finally caught up. I'd been so focused on the first half of my mission that I hadn't given much thought to what came next. Head throbbing, I wanted to scream in frustration, but bit back the emotion. There wasn't time to lose my mind. I lowered my pack to the ground, checking its contents.

My weapons were limited. I wasn't well-versed in using Viv's daggers, though I'd had the foresight to switch one of her sharper blades out for the old one in my pocket. I had a length of rope, about twenty feet, flint and steel, bandages, my trusty medical kit and its plethora of powders and elixirs, a meager supply of hard cheese and stale bread, a spare change of clothing...

Wait a moment.

Vaguely, I registered a soft hoot, but didn't pay it much heed as I withdrew the medical kit and a small pouch I'd stuffed full of leaves and acorns and pine needles—items I had hoped to study further when given the time. Swords and bows weren't my forte, but I was far from helpless. I tapped a vial of blue-green poultice. On its own it, the remedy treated stomach aches, but when combined with the powdered shell of black walnut, it created a dangerously acute laxative.

And that didn't come close to the worst I could create.

Healing potions transformed into poisons if not brewed carefully. Sticky saps could be laced with acids that ate through anything. Even needles could cause immense pain when administered carefully.

While good options down the line, my focus snagged on the bark of the whipple. The strips of bark were used as a pain reliever when dried, but when wet and green, it created a powerful hallucinogenic, which was why most of the trees had been cut down more than a century ago when wildfires had swept across our lands. Entire villages succumbed to the effects of the burning whipple, killing thousands either by poisoning or paranoia. Humbled, the trees were chopped down and carted away to the sea for disposal. If I could use something similar now, I could—

"Look who we have here. A straggler."

Every muscle in my body locked tight.

"Never doubt the boss." A second voice joined the first, their words projected straight into my mind, like Lukas had confirmed they could do. Feathers. I hadn't kept an ear out for scouts.

I drew a deep breath and stood, brushing powdery snow from my thighs and knees. Pip darted between the trees, a low, urgent sound vibrating from her throat as two soldiers emerged from the grove to my left, their wolven bodies lean and rangy, black tongues lolling from their jaws, panting their amusement.

The owls had been trying to warn me about the incoming scouting party, and I berated myself for being so foolish. I had been so consumed with my thoughts, I'd tuned them out. It wasn't often I was able to completely forget myself, and I'd managed to do so at the worst possible time.

"Hello there," I said around my heart shoved in my throat. My foot knocked against my kit still scattered on the ground. Double feathers. Even if I fought them off or—let's be honest—escape, I would lose my most valuable tools. "Can I help you?"

The wolves separated, tails swinging lightly. Whispery laughter trickled through my mind. *This mouse is braver than she looks.*

"Shame. I've heard bravery turns the meat tougher."

I shuddered at the image that formed in my thoughts: my body torn to shreds by their jagged teeth, limbs scattered every direction, the snowmelt dark with ruby-red blood.

Stay calm. Think of a way out.

The mangier scout drifted closer, slushy snow splashing under the weight of his paws. His lips pulled higher, revealing blackened gums, icy blue eyes watching me with the keen intelligence of a predator that knew its prey had no chance to escape.

No. I couldn't think like that. I wasn't dead yet, for Zos' sake.

"I live in a village a few miles south." I hooked my finger over my shoulder. The shaking in my voice was hardly fake. "I'm collecting some supplies for our healer. I promise, I mean you no harm."

The wolven with icy eyes snorted. *"We're not stupid, girl."*

"What do you think she knows?" The second wolven asked, swinging his snout toward his companion. I wondered why they included me in their conversation. *"The boss said to not kill the spy, but what's one, tiny human?"*

165

Oh. They wanted me afraid. Threatened.

Mission accomplished.

"I'm not a spy," I countered weakly. My knees shook and I knew how weak I sounded. Those teeth could shred me in a moment. "Please. Just let me go."

"Kill her or don't, it matters not to me," the second one huffed, ignoring my pleas. *"Just get it over with."*

So talking wasn't going to get me anywhere.

The one with the dark brown fur loped around me in a half-circle. A splotch of white rested between his shoulder blades. If I timed myself just right, I could make a rush for the oak. Its limbs hung low enough for me to swing up onto. But I would have to be fast. Faster than I'd ever been in my entire life. And even then, I had no idea if wolven could climb trees—not like they couldn't just morph into their human forms—

A third wolven with black fur emerged from the grove beside the oak. His ears flew back, and he snarled. Whatever he snapped at the wolven circling me wasn't projected into my thoughts, but by the stiffening of their bodies, the fur along their spines bristling, I knew it wasn't anything good.

I blinked away the spots that burst behind my eyelids. My hands trembled inside my pockets and my knees felt watery. The handle of Viv's knife knocked against my knuckles and I feebly wrapped my fingers around it, even though the thought of cutting into another living being made my stomach churn.

"Girl." My attention snapped back to the newcomer, who stood just out of slashing range. *"Drop the weapon in your pocket. If you surrender peacefully, we won't harm you."*

Those words cut through the panicked ramblings swirling like black clouds in my thoughts. They were giving me an option. For some reason, I mattered to whoever gave these wolven orders.

Colonel Kohl's face flashed through my mind, recalling the way he'd stared at me in the tavern. I knew he'd recognized me. And if that was the case, he probably guessed I would follow my family.

But then—what was his true motive? If he had given these scouts their orders to not kill me, then why was he so intent on keeping me alive? What value could I have? Nothing about this made sense. Not him killing one of his own people, not extending a hand to save my life, and certainly not tempering the actions of these soldiers now.

Or perhaps the colonel had nothing to do with this, and they were trying to trick me.

That seemed more likely.

"What will it be, human?" The soldier who appeared to be in charge didn't so much as blink. His posture relaxed, not that he had reason to worry. *"I don't have time for your moral quandaries, but make your choice. Imprisonment or death?"*

"I'm not a threat to you," I insisted, lifting my eyes to the skies, searching out the cloud of hazy steam in the distance, praying for a miracle. Slowly, I removed my hands from my pockets and held my arms over my head. Surrender was better than death. "But I'll come with you."

"I thought so." The wolven took one step forward before a screech like knives scraping across ice ripped through the skies. My hands flew to my ears in a weak attempt at blocking out the noise. The wolven barked, lowering flat to the ground. A rumbling roar erupted next, weighty enough to rattle the ground. I forced my eyes open, blinking back my fear. A black blur streaked past.

The wolven with brown fur leaped, teeth bared, and the blur crashed into it. The soldier went flying, body tumbling snout over tail. Black wings flared wide, revealing a rippling mass of scales and a long neck. Flames erupted from the drakken's mouth, engulfing the wolven where it lay, the scent of burning fur scorching my nostrils.

Another screech. A drakken with scales of glossy gold swooped, wings flaring wide as it crossed in front of the sun, turning the membrane bronze. Its head swung around, tail curling as it sighted the three of us below.

Something like amazement flashed hot in my chest, overtaking the panicked fear. The first time I'd seen these drakken, I'd been in some sort of weird dream state. But here, now, seeing them demonstrate such power—it was like violent poetry in motion.

Ears pressed flat against his skull, the mangy wolven sprinted, rushing for the shade of the oakwoods at the same time Lukas plummeted, wings pulled flat against his body. Legs flying, the wolven dove into the shelter of the trees and the drakken crashed through the foliage. An explosion shook the earth. The wolven howled in pain before the sound was abruptly silenced.

The leader rounded on me, glistening teeth pulled back in a snarl. *"You did this."*

I tripped over my feet as I backpedaled, knife in hand, fumbling to pull the sheath off the blade. Metal glinted. Fangs flashed. The wolven lunged. I threw the knife in front of me, desperation overtaking the awkwardness. Before we collided, Soren crashed into the beast, needle-like teeth buried in his neck. The drakken landed hard, pinning the wolven to the ground with his talons. The soldier's legs kicked, its claws skittering off Soren's slick scales, ugly snarls ripping from his muscular chest. The drakken's bottomless eyes brushed across mine, and he crunched down.

Blood geysered. Heat splashed across my face and hands.

The wolven's head rolled, stopping short of my hip. Chunks of flesh dangled from its neck, muzzle pulled back in a macabre snarl.

I shrieked and batted it away, blood coating my fingers. Soren flung the wolven's body into the woods. His head whipped around, halting me mid-scramble, those fathomless eyes eerily focused. One lip pulled back, an expression so reminiscent of the dark man himself that I stilled. He had saved me. Soren and Lukas had saved me. Again.

13

Violent Mood

"You'll never get the taste of that out of your mouth." Lukas spat on the ground for effect. He'd emerged from the forest wearing a pair of loose pants, a soft white undershirt, a wrinkled blue tunic, and a pair of boots with floppy laces. His cloak puddled at his feet while he organized his bag, berating Soren. "You are absolutely disgusting."

"Nothing like a little blood in your teeth to start off the afternoon," Soren replied. He tucked his gloves under his arm as he scrubbed blood from his hands with a palmful of fresh snow. His silver sword leaned against his knee. "It puts me in a violent mood."

"You're always in a violent mood."

Soren tsked. "And you need to lighten up."

Lukas muttered something about fur and brains as he dragged his cloak over his shoulders and flicked the clasp shut.

A sour taste coated my tongue, and I resumed my work reassembling my scattered medical kit. I squeezed the vial of powder I'd been considering before the wolven had arrived, and a shadow dropped beside me. Soren fiddled with the opening of a pouch I'd kicked away accidentally, gaze fixed on the vial. Something lemony cut through the coppery bite of blood that clung to his heated skin. "You're quiet, even for you."

"Thank you," I murmured, shoving the rest of my gear into my pack without rhyme or reason. Anything to get it out of the snow. "For saving me. I'm not sure I would have escaped otherwise."

Lukas scoffed and clambered onto a boulder, scanning the horizon. "Qet's teeth, you are dense. You would not have escaped because you would have been dead."

Soren didn't disagree with that morbid assessment.

I fiddled with the leather laces wrapped around the sheath of Viv's knife, uncertain of how to proceed. Lukas had always been the ray of light and courtesy against Soren's veil of death and darkness. Now their roles appeared swapped, despite Soren literally ripping a person's head from their shoulders.

"That's not true," I murmured. "They would have taken me prisoner—one way or another."

"How do you know that?" Lukas braced his hands on his hips, glowering down at us.

Again with the aggression. I must have really ticked him off.

"Because they told me." Even if they hadn't, the soldiers never cared about who they pushed into the mines just as long as they had bodies toiling away, carving gemstones from rocks. "I think they threatened death to get me to move along."

I jammed Viv's weapon into my pocket and scanned the field, hands braced on my knees. The drakken had dragged the bodies of the soldiers into the woods, but the melting snow still shimmered bright crimson in spots and most of it was tossed up or thrown around, evidence of the fight.

"That's unusual," Soren said. I still couldn't look him in the face. My pants and boots were soaked and spotted with blood, but there wasn't anything I could do about it. The change of clothing I carried was equally disgusting, even if it was dry. "Typically wolven attack first and ask questions later. What convinced you they'd follow through with their word? You looked like you were about to surrender to me."

I rubbed my eye, which was starting to twitch. "I think the colonel recognized me, back at the tavern. He must have figured out where I was heading. They mentioned having orders to take me into custody."

Lukas and Soren exchanged a glance.

Get in line. I had a mess of questions myself.

Like why the wolven were in the mountains in the first place, Kohl in tow. Had they been looking for my family this entire time? Escaped members of a regime dead and buried? If they had known, why was I any different? Wouldn't they want me dead, too? Or was the colonel searching for something?

I searched the treeline, relaxing marginally when Grim spread his wide, wide wings, perched in the depths of a silverpine. Odds were good Ghost wasn't far away.

Forget the soldiers. My concerns didn't take into account the existence of the two drakken in front of me or their standing within the Requiem. If I cracked and spilled my secrets, it would only be because they'd confessed first. I felt like we stood on the precipice of a very large, very intimidating fall, and what lay at the bottom was anyone's guess.

"May I have my map back?" Lukas asked. His tone had softened. I'd vowed to return it, after all, but when I tried to hand it back to him, he refused to take it until I met his eyes. When I did, I found a strange sort of understanding reflected back at me, as if he connected with my quagmire of concerns.

Soren stretched. "Now that you've got it back, can we head home?" A heavy thread of irony underlined his words. "That's why we're here, isn't it?"

The wind hushed through the trees and the branches bobbled, rattling moisture from the bark. Lukas returned the map to his collection. "No, I believe we are here because you got worried and insisted we follow her, Archer's orders be damned."

"Archer has too much on his plate as it is. He needs to focus on things he's capable of controlling," Soren countered.

Lukas tsked. I doubted Soren took kindly to being controlled.

Soren strapped his sword to his hip. "And you were worried about your map. Admit it."

"I'm not the one who got in a tizzy when they realized Tell hadn't returned to her room," Lukas argued. "And then panicked when they discovered the footprints on the roof."

"Lukas." Soren spoke his name like a warning.

The grin on Lukas' face spread and he danced out of reach. "I believe your exact words were, 'that fool girl is going to get herself killed if we don't—'"

A snowball smashed into Lukas' face, cutting him off with a sputter. His hands flew to his eyes, wiping beads of snow off his skin and lashes. Soren chuckled and dodged the retaliatory throw. I laughed, incapable of holding it back despite the seriousness of our circumstances. This felt like a dream, yet my legs ached and my ribs pounded beneath the bruises, evidence I was very much awake. For some reason, that made me laugh even harder, clutching my sides as I fought to stay on my feet.

What is it about you that begs others to save you?

Soren had asked that in the heart of the blizzard. It had rankled me, though it was starting to feel more like a fact than a rhetorical question. These drakken had been set in my path again, so there had to be some reason for it.

"I think she has cracked."

"If she's cracked, it's because you keep talking out of turn," Soren replied.

"I'm fine," I gasped, taking a deep breath to calm the bubbles frothing in my belly. The shock of almost being taken prisoner must have finally worn off. I wiped the moisture from the corners of my eyes, clearing my throat.

A low whistle sounded moments before a tiny body swooped into my sternum. I cuddled Pip to my chest, stroking her wings, listening to her concerned sputtering, then her report as she buried her beak in the hollow beneath my collarbone. Her worry calmed me. Settled me. My humor winked into starless black.

"We should move." I threw my pack over my shoulder. "They're getting away."

Soren blocked my path. "Didn't we just get you out of danger? You're the last person who should be tracking a bunch of soldiers right now." He gave the pocket where I'd concealed Viv's dagger a hard look. "Seriously."

"Seriously." I planted my hand on his chest and shoved. He stumbled, not expecting the strength I thrust behind the motion. "I didn't come all this way to fail. My family is down there and I will save them, even if I die trying." A shiver tracked up my arms. "Thank you for arriving when you did, but if you're going to hold me back now, you can return to where you came from. It sounds like Archer has plenty of work for you already."

Soren's eyes shaded to black. The danger I'd come to associate with his existence engulfed him like storm clouds overtaking the blue sky.

"There you have it, Sor," Lukas said, amused. "She will die trying. We can't have that now, can we? I mean, you did say she did not know what she was getting into and you had to resolve that, didn't you?"

My stomach curdled. "Is that really how you see me? Weak?"

Yes, I'd underestimated what I was up against, and it was almost embarrassing how many times they'd come to my rescue. I squeezed the vial clutched in my fist. Losing focus had nearly cost me everything, but I learned from my mistakes. It wouldn't happen again, and I had a damn good plan for what to do next.

"No," Soren ground out. A million and one thoughts swirled like stars in his eyes. "Pursuing your dreams, especially those that serve the greater good, is never weak. But refusing to recognize when you're in over your head and turning away help when it's offered *is*." He shouldered his bag, eyes sliding to my hands again, and I realized I'd shoved my sleeves up to my elbows. It wasn't the vial he'd eyed before. It was the tattoo I'd chosen for my skin.

The drakken angled his head when I shoved my sleeve down over the heel of my hand. "Zos huh?" He muttered something under his breath, then spat out, "For as much faith as you put in a being you've never seen, I wish you would extend a fraction of that for the people who've demonstrated nothing but concern for your well-being."

His words were a blow to the chest, one that cracked my ribs.

Before I could craft a reply, Soren spun on his heel and stomped down the hill, right alongside the murky tracks left by the caravan.

"Come now, do not look so glum." Lukas slung his arm over my shoulders, tilting his head after the darker drakken. "You have the support of two highly skilled beings such as ourselves. Do not worry about him. He is just coming to grips with something he has not had to contend with for years." He winked. "Give him a chance and don't squander his offer."

He said it like a threat.

"What is he contending with?" I asked. Soren knelt in the snow at the base of the hill, peering at something in the mud and muck.

"Concern for someone beyond our inner circle."

My mind blanked, off-balance. Why was he telling me this? He was Soren's best friend, his confidant. What was he hoping to gain by sharing such secrets?

"Keep being yourself, but be open to other possibilities, too." Lukas pressed firmly on the small of my back, urging me forward. Together, we sloshed through the mess of melting snow. "Your ideals challenge his. It is a good thing, maybe even a great thing, but only if you do not destroy one another first."

* * *

"So what's your plan?" Soren asked when we reached the treeline, his toes brushing the blurry shadows cast by the trees. "You have a plan, right?"

I tugged on the fingers of my gloves. The adrenaline geysering through my veins had subsided since the fight, and I felt more like my old self. I truly had missed traveling with these two. "I'm still working on it."

Soren's lips thinned. "You charged halfway across the country by yourself to take on a bunch of Fiorian soldiers near one of their strongholds… and don't have a plan?"

"I said I was working on one."

"I am not surprised." Lukas crouched beside a bush of thorns, scrutinizing the shiny skins of the blue berries ensnared in its prickly grasp. "Is that why the soldiers got a jump on you?"

Irritation prickled like the needles of the bush he poked at. "They caught me because I lost focus, not that it's any of your business."

Soren clicked his tongue. "I'd say it's our business since we had to tear—"

"Oh look, they're back," I interrupted, pointing out Pip and Ghost, who settled like dust motes on the wide branch of a tree. The latter's head swiveled, keeping the newcomers directly in his line of sight. I hadn't lied. I had the beginnings of a plan, but with the information gathered by my birds, I could figure out if it would actually work.

Lukas and Soren flinched when a sharp hoot echoed from the trees. Grim. Coming in fast. A grin cracked my lips. About time that owl started acting like his usual self. I ripped off my left glove with my teeth and shoved it into my pocket, set my feet, braced my knees, and lifted my arm. The fresh scars cut into the bracer by Soren's talons stood out boldly against the smaller marks.

Grim hooted again, four-foot wingspan stretched flat as he glided through the trees, a whisper of pale gray against the backdrop of green. A twitch, a flap, and he twisted, feet extended, talons wrapped tight around my arm. I grunted, shifting my weight to keep my balance. Stable again, I rubbed the top of his head. His large, round eyes closed as he leaned into the touch. "Hey, buddy. Did you find anything interesting?"

He glowered, talons tightening, and nipped at my wrist, his sharp beak finding a spot on my skin not already marred by similar pecks by dozens of birds over the years. I swatted him away from the bloody mark.

"Fine, if it's going to be like that." I pulled a treat from my pocket, something I'd picked up from the market, and he snapped it up. Maybe someday things wouldn't be so quid pro quo with the largest of my owl friends.

A muffled gasp had me looking up. Lukas stared wide-eyed at Grim, who re-set his perch on my arm, feathers fluffing as I brought him closer to my body. "That owl is as big as you are, Soren."

"It is not." But Soren's tone didn't hold its usual casual conviction. His eyes flicked from the bird to me and back to the bird, who swiveled his head to keep the darker man in sight, recognizing the danger he presented. "When you said you watched over owls in your woods, I thought you meant owls like the little one over there." He flicked his thumb vaguely in the direction of Pip, who hooted her objections to the adjective. "Are they—is this—"

I stroked the rim of feathers fanning out in wide half moons around Grim's eyes, enjoying knocking the drakken off-kilter for once.

"Great grays are among the tallest of their species. Snowies and great horned owls weigh more, but this guy can still hold his own." He ruffled his slate-colored feathers, preening under the attention. "All owls are naturally quiet predators, but I'd argue Grim is the most silent. He typically warns me when he's approaching, like you heard him just now. But he liked to sneak up on Papa. It's part of the reason we always wear the bracers. We never know when the owls would want to land." I chuckled. "Sometimes I think we're moving trees to them."

Warmth filled my chest watching Grim smooth his beak over the softer feathers along his wings. It always felt like this when I talked about these birds. And my father. Though he'd moved on to the afterlife, having Grim here felt like getting part of him back.

"And you communicate with them?" Lukas drew closer. He'd locked his hands behind his back, but his arms shook slightly, and I could tell he was restraining himself from touching the bird himself. The curiosity must be driving him mad. "As in, you can actually talk to them and they understand what you say, and vice versa?"

"Yes." I pressed a kiss to the side of Grim's head. "You can touch him if you like. He'll probably nip at you, but since I'm here, he won't attack."

A sound gurgled out of Lukas' throat that might have been a scream, and he took the final two steps forward. Like I'd done countless times at Solas, I guided him through how to approach Grim, giving the bird time to adjust to the drakken's presence.

Finally, softly, Lukas' hand landed on the coarse feathers of his back, the tips of his fingers sinking into the downier bits as he stroked. A ball of sunshine exploded in my chest at the joy on his face.

This. This was why I loved my life, loved my owls and my woods. I recognized that expression of wide-eyed wonder because it was the smile I dawned nearly every day of my life.

"He is smaller than I expected," Lukas said, feathers flattening beneath the pressure he applied. "I thought he would have more mass, but he really is a tiny thing beneath all the fluff. Ow." He jerked, rubbing his hand where Grim had nipped him.

I smothered a giggle. "I warned you. Grim's as vain as they get."

"His retorts are sharper than Soren's, that is for sure." With one last look of longing, he fell back beside his friend, who cuffed him on the shoulder.

I extended my arm toward Soren. It was starting to ache. "You want to touch him?"

Amusement flickered across his face. "No. But I wouldn't mind a closer look at the haunted one back there sometime." Ghost. Soren had picked up on the obvious connections people associated between the birds and specters. Viv often called Ghost my Little Friend of Death—both for one of the nicknames of his kind and for their association often depicted with Zos.

"Sure," I told Soren, who tilted his head and rested his hand on his hip, right beside a dagger hanging from a sheath. The sight of the weapon sobered me. We weren't here to talk about owls. We were here to track down my family, to free my best friend.

I poked Grim in the ribs and dodged his peck. "You got your treat and some extra attention. Now tell me: what did you learn?"

The owl glowered balefully, shook his tail feathers, and finally thrummed low in his throat. I paid sharp attention to the messages he relayed. His hoots told only half the message; much of his language relied on non-verbal cues. Things like the changing grip of his talons around my arm, the angle of his body, even the subtle twitching of his wings. I tuned out the men and asked questions, probing for every last bit of vital information.

When he finished his report, I fed him another treat and he let go, wings pumping twice as he soared to join Pip on her branch. A shiver coursed through my belly. Grim had picked up more than I'd expected. He must have gotten closer than instructed. He was lucky the soldiers hadn't seen him, regardless of how thankful I was for his help.

"What did he say?" Soren rasped, arms crossed.

"There are twenty soldiers. More than I anticipated, but it makes sense since they're escorting anywhere between forty and fifty prisoners." Given the number of villages we'd passed along the way, it didn't surprise me they picked up more people as they approached the mines.

"The Fiorian troops are mostly in their human forms now. Grim made it sound like they're getting more relaxed the closer they get to the mines. I doubt they're expecting any attacks this close to base." I glanced back at the crest of the hill where we'd abandoned the bodies of the scouts. "They either haven't noticed their scouting party is missing or they don't care."

"It could also be they were not expecting you to be as close as you were," Lukas reasoned, tapping his pen against the page beside his scribbled notes. I appreciated how he didn't question the information. There was no doubt in my mind that he would pick my brain later, but he accepted the information at face value. "The farther they had to run, the longer it would take to get back." He jotted down something else. "However, that does tighten our timeline. Even the most relaxed officer will realize what has happened sooner or later."

"Can you describe their formation?" Soren asked.

I looked to Grim, who fluttered his affirmation. With his guidance, I accepted Lukas' notepad and drew a rough sketch. When he realized the amount of detail the bird picked up, Soren pushed harder, asking questions about the number of horses they were using, how the prisoners were organized, the materials used to restrain them, and their overall attitude. As fantastic as his analytical abilities were, Grim's understanding flagged toward the end, when we drifted from the technical into the emotional state of the situation.

The drakken didn't seem put out by that, however, brow arched as he considered the page. Leaves crunched as Lukas circled him, peering at the map I'd drawn with keen interest. Wordlessly, he pointed at the ends of the line, then somewhere off to the east, and Soren nodded.

I cleared my throat, reminding them I hadn't vanished. "What are you thinking?"

I had my own ideas, but they required some work, maybe too much work. Part of me hoped they would have a more straightforward approach.

"Twenty is a lot for us to take on," Soren said at long last. "Even with two drakken and the element of surprise, it's a stretch. Especially since it sounds like they're wearing that damnable gold armor. I have one blast left in me, but it'll do nothing but hurt the people they've captured."

"One more blast?" I asked, unfamiliar with the phrase.

Soren nodded. "Drakken are limited in how frequently we breathe fire. We need time to recharge."

Lukas bobbled some berries as if they were physical icons of his inner thoughts, balancing one another out. I'd cautioned him against eating them when he'd snagged a few off a vine earlier, but their skins weren't poisonous. "I would rather not use our second forms if we can help it. It is fine to show off every now and again to boost morale, but this is too close to a Fiorian stronghold." He tossed a berry at the plume of smoke rising over the tops of the trees.

"Can you fight?" Soren asked, with a curious look at me. Predictably, he'd found a tree to lean against.

"Not very well," I reminded him.

Soren's brow dipped and Lukas dragged the tip of his finger across an arrow in his quiver leaning against his leg, producing a drop of blood. He frowned at it and smeared the spot across his skin. "Even if you could hold your own, I don't like the odds of three against twenty. It leaves a lot to chance. If only there were a way to, I don't know, knock out the wolven or something."

Pip hooted, darting to my shoulder. I rubbed her head automatically.

"It won't be three against twenty, though." I tapped the snow beside the train of horses with the toe of my boot. "We're forgetting about the prisoners. Surely some of them can fight—whether it's with skill or out of sheer survival instincts."

"Including this friend of yours?" Soren asked, a bite to his tone I didn't recognize.

I nodded. "There's no one better."

Soren fiddled with some spidery leaves of the whipple danging in his face, thin lips pursed in thought. A shroud of darkness had settled thickly around his shoulders.

"I could scale a tree," Lukas suggested. "Pick off as many as I can with my bow. Soren could rush in from the front. And Tell, if you could cut some prisoners free—"

He rambled, twisting through several strategies, each more dangerous and unpredictable than the last. My hope of a straightforward solution crumbled. We would have to fall back on my plan. The information Grim provided made it a little more feasible, though it wasn't without its share of risks.

"Or we use what the gods have given us," I said when Lukas finally fell silent.

The men waited for me to expand. Zos save me, I was actually going to propose this. Soren didn't react when I snagged the branch dangling in front of his face and ripped off a leaf. "This is a whipple tree, one of a few dozen I spotted from the crest of the hill."

Soren's expression remained carefully blank. I wet my lips and plowed ahead. "When green whipple wood is burned, it produces a powerful hallucinogenic, one that can be deadly during extended exposure." I paused. "Have you heard of the Great Burnings from two hundred years ago?"

A sly grin unfolded across Lukas' face. He got it. His skin was icy when he took the leaf from me, twirling it between his index finger and thumb. "You are mad. Absolutely insane. But I kind of love it." He offered the sprig to Soren. "It reminds me of that time—"

"—in Carthos. When we knocked those guards out," Soren finished for him, eyeing the waxy bit of green in Lukas' palm as if it were a snake lurking in the grass. "I follow."

I wasn't, but whatever it took to win them over worked for me.

Soren dropped the leaf, which spiraled as it floated to the ground. "It might work, though. Dozens of trees produce a lot of smoke."

Lukas tapped his pen at the corner of his mouth. "And the risk? Still within your parameters of what you are comfortable executing?"

The shorter man pondered this, arms crossed, boots half-sunk in sticky mud. From the depths of the forest, a redbird trilled its dewy mating call. The drakken peered at me, then the owls, and finally the notebook Lukas clasped against his breast. A stray whipple branch brushed against his elbow. "Yes. It's less risky than anything else I can think of."

I rubbed my hands together, anticipation of finding and freeing my family bubbling, even as apprehension gripped me in a stranglehold. Me. My ideas, my knowledge, had proved useful. I might not fight particularly well, but I wasn't helpless. "So we're in agreement?"

Lukas scrawled something into his book. "We are, but we still have a few kinks to work out."

"Naturally." I tugged on my thick scarf, the rough fabric pillowy between my fingers. "This material should be sturdy enough to filter out the worst of the particles, keeping us relatively safe." Enlightened, I dove into my bag and pulled out my remaining shirt, which I promptly ripped into several long strips. "And if we wet these and wrap them around our faces beneath the scarves..."

Lukas' grin was brilliant. "The moisture will filter out the smoke. I never would have thought of that."

"It won't take long for the heat to dry them out." Soren held his up to his face. "We'll have maybe a half hour's time—probably less— before we feel the early effects of the drug, which means our clock is ticking. We'll have to act quickly before..."

I recognized my cue and thought back to the musty history books I'd borrowed from Stavanger years ago. "If I recall correctly, it affects the auditory senses first. Whispers, pleas, screams, that kind of thing. Older texts mention priests before the Great Burning would burn whipple at ancient ceremonies as a way to connect with the gods and goddesses, so it should be bearable."

I scratched my arm, nails dipping in and out of the ridges left by too many scars to count. "Vision goes next. People have reported seeing visions, most of them horrible. Others have lost their sight entirely. It's when you go groggy that you're in trouble. Your system starts to shut down, starting with your brain and ending with the respiratory system." I closed my eyes against the bitter reality of what we were about to do. "It's an ugly way to go."

Lukas considered that, tapping the butt of his pen against his palm.

"But we have time. It takes a lot of smoke and extended exposure for the symptoms to get that bad."

"What of the Idileans?" Soren asked. "Our facial coverings will help us, but what about them? No use saving dozens of people if they're all acting crazy or are on the brink of death."

Grim piped up, uttering a low, sleepy hoot from somewhere overhead. His message sent a chill down my spine. My hands went to my hips, searching for him in the bunches of branches. "What do you mean, they saw you?"

The owl hooted again, more loudly. I frowned. I'd misheard the intonation. Not them. Viv. Viv had seen Grim. And if Viv had seen him, it was possible that she would realize I was on her tracks— the gray had never paid her any interest before, choosing to linger around Papa. She also recognized a few of their key warning sounds, ones I'd taught her. Not many, but enough to work with.

I couldn't conceal the grin that stole across my face, the soft chuckle that escaped my lips. It all came together just like that.

Soren straightened. "Here we go."

Lukas motioned for me to continue, scarf still pinched between his fingers.

"Here's what we're going to do…"

14

No Time

I wet my finger, breath locked tight in my chest, tested the direction of the wind, and tipped what liquid remained in my flask over the rag. The fabric still dripped when I tied it over my mouth and nose, pulling my scarf up over the top. Hopefully, it would stay in place.

Downwind and downhill, a single soldier shouted commands. Metal rattled, wagon wheels crunched through debris, and horses whinnied, eager to get into a warm barn with plenty of hay. If their pace held, they would reach the fortress of the Llyn Mines by dusk. Time ran thin.

The fire at my feet crackled when I added three more dry branches, coaxing it higher. If this plan of mine didn't work—I swallowed my apprehension, forcing myself to continue the thought—if this didn't work, a lot of people would die.

"Hang in there, Viv. I'm coming," I whispered, stroking my rune of Zos. Grim had relayed a two hoots, one she should recognize as "alert," and the other for "fire." She should be able to improvise from there. Wildfires were always a concern in the mountains.

Nimbly, I darted down the line of the dozen or so fires I'd set, gradually expanding their range, trying not to freak out about the lack of stones containing them. I'd ordered the owls to stay upwind and far away. The stories never spoke of the smoke affecting animals, but I wasn't taking any chances with their lives. The knife in my pocket had never felt heavier. I was already taking a huge chance with the lives of everyone else.

I flinched, dropping to my knees, when an arrow thunked into the soft bark of the whipple beside my shoulder. A green thread twisted around the shaft. Lukas and Soren were in position. Mouth dry, I ripped the arrow from the tree and shoved it into my bag. A beat later, I plucked the cork from the vial in my hand and sprinkled the powder over the fire, nearly tripping over my feet when it popped, snapped. Exploded. Flames roared up the side of the whipple, scorching the bone-white bark.

"Lo, forgive me." I appealed to the goddess of the land and harvest as I raced down the line of fires, sprinkling powder over each as I passed. The heat was almost unbearable, but I kept my scarf tight around my face even as sweat slicked down the ridge of my spine. "You know me. I love trees, especially the ones I can climb. This may seem irresponsible, but I promise it's for a good cause. If I survive this, I have the feeling it will be the start of something big."

The weight in my chest constricted around my lungs, twined around my ribs. My actions felt more monumental than simply taking steps necessary to free my family. No, this was more.

Much more.

The last fire exploded with a blast, engulfing the whipple in a flurry of red-gold flame. Without wasting a moment, I turned east toward the caravan, jumping and dodging branches as white smoke clung to my heels, driven by a sudden increase in the wind.

Maybe the gods were watching, after all.

I stopped, lungs heaving though I tried to keep from gasping, when a second arrow flew out of nowhere, burying itself into the meat of the tree in front of me. Feathers, Lukas was a good shot. I jerked this one, too, out of the wood, and shoved it heedlessly into my bag. Up ahead, the green of a wolven's cloak flashed as he hustled the prisoners trailing at the end of the line. Any farther and I would have crashed into them.

Haze shrouded the air between me and them, and I closed my watering eyes against the burn of the smoke. I'd tried to pick trees relatively more isolated from the rest, but I knew only the luck of Lo and some influence from Qet would keep the flames from engulfing this entire forest, reducing it to ash like it had two hundred years ago.

Shaking myself from my stupor, my grip on Viv's knife firmed, and I worked my way along the line, searching for a certain head of coppery hair. Grim insisted she was somewhere near the middle, but the line was long. I'd underestimated what fifty-odd prisoners looked like.

I passed a little too close to one scout monitoring the flanks. He coughed wetly into his hand, muttering something about wishing they would hurry up so he could find a warm bed to lie in. Using his distraction to my advantage, I darted around him, keeping an eye on the caravan as the smoke thickened.

To my relief—and unlike the wolven who'd removed most of their outerwear due to the rising temperatures—many of the prisoners had pulled scarves and wraps over their mouths and noses. Some of them even looked wet, and I wondered where they'd gotten the water. Goosebumps trembled down my arms. Viv had gotten my message.

I scrambled up the side of a log and realized I was much closer to the front of the line than I'd thought. Too close. I scanned the line of miserable people, heads hanging low as they walked single file, hands bound by rope in front of their hips. My breath quickened. Had I missed her? Was that possible with her crazy bright hair? Could I really have—

There she was.

My heart stuttered when she turned to look behind her. I couldn't see most of her face, but given the squint of her eyes against the smoke, I imagined her foxish features were tight with concentration and exhaustion.

A soldier stepped between us, his broad back to me as he called to one of his comrades at the front of the line. "Hurry up. Something isn't right—"

A man screamed from the back of the line.

Time to go.

A black blur leaped from the shadows beside me, taking advantage of the distraction of the commanders leading the caravan. Soren's sword slashed faster than I'd seen it move yet, his first victims falling in a splash of gore and mud. I was on his heels, rushing the soldier who'd shouted, shoving him to the ground. His head cracked against a rock and he went silent. I didn't stop to check on him.

Viv's eyes met mine, wild with anticipation of the fight as I skidded to a stop beside her. "You're still alive. I knew you were still alive."

Zos, I'd missed her husky voice.

The prisoners jostled one another, but had stopped their forward progress as Soren slaughtered the Fiorian soldiers at the front— heedless of their shifter states. I gripped Viv's wrists, holding them steady, and the silver of her knife parted the ropes like buttercream. Viv didn't stop to massage her joints, snatching Epic when I offered the handle, the weapon looking far more correct in her hands than they ever would in mine.

"Take out the soldiers," I instructed her hurriedly, wishing like rezar I had time to embrace her, feel her warm and alive against me.

Instead, I moved to the next prisoner, working a smaller Stella blade from her bandolier slung across my chest. "Soren and Lukas can't take them out all on their—"

"Watch out," Viv shouted, lunging forward, eyes fixed over my shoulder. An arrow nicked the side of my neck as it zipped past. Viv pulled me out of the way as someone gurgled and fell. The soldier I'd shoved before: an arrow buried deep in one eye. Gulping in oxygen, I berated myself for not making sure I'd killed him. Or incapacitated him. Foolish.

"Telleree, if you aren't dead, I could use your help right about now," a male voice shouted above the screams of the prisoners. Soren spun out of the smoke, blood splattered across his scarf, and I imagined that twisted, evil grin glued across his face. His sword flashed and more ropes parted, separating prisoners from the caravan, before engaging a wolven who leaped from the smoky grip of the trees. "I'm a bit busy here."

I shook myself from Viv's grip and thrust her forward as three more soldiers stumbled around the side of the wagon, hands pressed to their eyes, screaming as they absorbed whatever awfulness was playing out behind their lids. "Help Soren."

She looked ready to protest, but her gaze flattened and after a quick squeeze to my shoulder, she sprinted forward, knife glinting off the flames licking through the trees.

Flames.

The fire had spread, after all.

I waved my hands in the air, drawing the attention of nearby Idileans. "Keep your faces covered," I yelled, motioning to my own face, then pointing behind me. "Head south. Gather in the large clearing beside the lake. That will get you out of the smoke. Once you're there, wait for us. We have a plan to keep you safe."

Based on the bodies that shifted in a mass around me, at least a few of them believed in my goodwill. I couldn't dally to be sure. The fire was closing in and the soldiers had already killed several, either on purpose or as a result of trying to fight off an invisible enemy.

I didn't allow myself to see much beyond the reaching hands bound by scratchy brown rope, couldn't bear to see if any of the bloodied bodies I stepped over belonged to members of my family. My knife parted the ropes easily as I worked down the line. I repeated my earlier commands as I went, forcing my voice louder so people could hear it over the crackling fire and screams of the soldiers either dying at my friend's blades or caught in the throes of a nightvision.

Against my lips, the fabric was nearly dry, but I couldn't stop to wet it. My head felt fuzzy, but the voices hadn't started yet. Time was on my side. Barely. I steadied the knife in my grip when I approached a woman at the end of the line. Her huge, brown eyes reminded me of the does that accidentally ventured too far north in search of mates.

"You'll be alright," I murmured as I sliced through the ropes, half distracted by a woman's ear-splitting scream from up the line. As such, I wasn't prepared for the prisoner I'd freed to throw herself at me in what I first thought was an embrace and then realized was a panicked attack. She didn't have any weapons, but she reached for my scarf and, to my abject horror, tore it off, rag and all. She wrapped it around her own face as she sprinted into the woods before I could think to follow.

I sucked in a gasp and realized what I'd done when the smoke swirled hot and wild inside my lungs. I lifted my shirt, bringing it to cover my nose. I needed to get out of here. Of the three of us in the rescue party, I'd taken the greatest risk with the smoke. And now I'd inhaled it directly.

If I panicked now, I would die.

When I turned to follow the stragglers, a whimper reached my ears. A girl crouched on the ground, the last in the long line of Idileans waiting to meet their fates. She struggled to pull away from the dead wolven to whom she was shackled, her wrist bloody and raw, bits of white bone visible against the oozing red. I gagged. A bark of a sob ripped from her throat, her ruddy face slick with tears as she pressed a hunk of the soldier's green cloak to her nose.

Talons.

Shaking my head in an effort to clear it, I dropped to my knees beside her—or at least the girl I hoped was the correct one. There were definitely two of them struggling in the mud now. She lifted the hank of rope when I held out my hand and gestured with the knife. It frayed, split, and she ran, following the smattering of blurry of footprints cutting through the snow.

I rocked back on my heels, shirt drawn back up over my nose, rubbing at my temple, trying to remember why the alarm bells clanging through the trees sounded so familiar. Head light, I sagged against a tree, gazing up at the flames flickering through the canopy, raining bits of ash down on my face and shoulders. Another peal of bells sounded, closer than before, and I squinted through the white haze at the figures rushing away from me, arms pumping and legs whirring as they outran some invisible enemy, their bodies little more than black silhouettes.

I coughed into my arm, throat ragged, wishing I still had my scarf. Or my flask. Anything wet would be nice. Blackness touched the edges of my vision. A scream accompanied the fresh peal of warning bells. Invasion. We were under attack. My muscles groaned as I staggered upright. I needed to get out of here. The wolven must have sent backup from the fort like we'd feared.

Wait. Why had they sent backup again? Papa said the wolven rarely crossed into our lands, only lingering long enough to trade. They'd never attacked us before, too intimidated by our prowess in the air, the threat of the drakken who made up our army and navy.

Why would they need backup now?

Hooves pounded. A horse pinwheeled around a pair of trees, head swinging as it struggled to stay upright beneath its master's commands. A dark figure clung to its sweat-soaked back, pressed low against the horseflesh. I flinched when he dropped his arm, anticipating the swing of a sword. Would I feel my head removed from my shoulders? Instead, he gripped my arm and nearly yanked it out of my socket when he dragged me up in front of him.

Wings spotted with muted browns and whites and golds fluttered, kicking up motes of dust and dry bits of sawdust as hundreds of birds took flight, spurred on by a frantic wave of scarred hands. The large glass panels of the aviary that normally protected the flock from the harsh rays of the sun were lifted. Open. Lips pressed against my head through my hair. I rested against them, the warmth of their comfort drawing me in.

"Hang in there, Telleree." I barely registered the familiar voice, couldn't remember why the world rattled beneath my feet. I coughed into the curve of my arm again, frowning at the weight banded around my chest. "You can't die on me yet."

Die? Why would I die?

I leaned into the hand cupping the back of my head and peered into my mother's soulful brown eyes. Wetness trickled down her cheeks as she threaded her fingers through my hair, her thumb clearing a smudge of dirt on my temple I'd gotten while playing with the boys earlier.

The air vibrated with tension, my small chest tightening with emotion I didn't understand. Another unfamiliar peal of bells coursed through the aviary. My mother's grip tightened, and I pressed my nose to her shirt, inhaling the warm sugar perfume she spritzed on every morning. Papa clutched his keys, the metal pieces jangling as he hurried around the perimeter of the room, unlocking cages and shooing birds from their depths. I'd never seen the aviary so empty.

"That's the last of them," he shouted, ducking behind his rickety desk at the end of the hall. He reemerged with a flat, brown box, which he shoved into a satchel. "If we hurry, we can take the hidden passages to our rooms. We'll need—"

"There's no time." My mother's lips moved against my temple. She pulled me harder against her, like she worried she might never hold me again.

My breath shuttered, tears burning my eyes. I hugged her back, palm sliding across the embroidered dragon crest that engulfed the back of her tunic. "Mama? What's wrong?"

She lifted me with her when she stood, my legs instinctively wrapping around her middle. I clutched at her, knee knocking against the sword buckled at her side. Papa's arms came around both of us, eyes rimmed red. Mama tilted her head when another array of bells sang, a fresh wave of tears dripping from her chin. "You hear them. The navy has fallen, Os. It's only the army standing in the way of Fior. I don't know how they did it, but they sped up their timeline by months, nay, a year."

"Mia—"

"Keep quiet for your Papa, Telleree. He needs you to be a big girl now."

I fought her when she lifted me away from her body, my insides thrashing wildly. My father's arms bound around me, hefting me tight against his chest.

Mama cupped my father's cheek, stroking the black stubble he forgot to shave unless reminded. "I'm their captain. If we stand any chance of fending them off, I have to be there."

"But you aren't a drakken," Papa protested, his normally deep voice tight with fear and worry. His arms clutched me more firmly. My heart threatened to spill out of my throat, it pounded so fast. I whimpered, trying to follow Mama's plea, not understanding what was happening. She went to work with the troops all the time, but this felt different. "Let the royals handle it. They can—"

Mama shook her head, the short, dark strands of her hair brushing the sides of her face. "I swore an oath, just like my father did and his father before him. I will lead my troops, no matter how dire the outcome may seem." She brushed the black tattoo on her collarbone, barely visible through the folds of her shirt, a rune I'd drawn alongside my letters over and over again. "Qet has called upon me—like he has all of us. He needs us to secure our borders."

My father's eyes flashed, though his grip on my back gentled. He smelled like sweat and fear and dust that gathered in the nests. "Then I'll help however I can. The birds will—"

"No, you must escape." My mother closed the distance between them, pressing her forehead to his, my body cocooned in their shared warmth. "You must take our little girl, our ray of life and light, and you must escape from here. Do whatever you must to survive; that will give me hope. I need you to do that for me, Os. I need you to swear to me, swear on Qet and Cas and Fen that you'll stay alive. That you'll do whatever it takes to stay alive. For me. And I'll come to you when I can."

Another shattering peal of bells. I couldn't see their faces with my nose smashed against his chest, but my father's voice was choked when he replied. "I will. I'll head north. As far as I can go." He pulled my mother closer. "And you better find us."

They separated, my mother pressing one last kiss to my head. Then she was gone, her back straight and proud as she strode out the door and into the white smoke swirling there.

A shard of awful ice-like glass ripped through me. I screamed, reaching for her, throwing myself against my father's hold. "Mama. No, mama! Wait for me."

The world jittered, rocking beneath me. I surged forward again, reaching for those swirls. If I tried a little harder, pushed a little more, I could break free. I could see her. I could join her. Before—

"Damnit, Telleree," a voice hissed like the buzz of static. "You're gonna knock us off the horse."

A powerful arm banded more tightly around my chest.

I couldn't see. I rubbed the back of my hand against the pits of pain that were my eyes.

When I opened them, I stood alone in the aviary, the cages silent and empty. A growl echoed from the hallway outside, rippling through the smoke. I stumbled backward, drawing my cloak of feathers tight around me like a shield. I searched for a place to hide, to run, but the cages closest to me were closed and locked. The windows overhead shuttered.

Another growl.

A pool of something dark and red puddled around the cobblestones. My back crashed into the row of cages with a rattling clang. A paw big as my head stepped in the pool of liquid too thick to be anything but blood, followed quickly by a long leg thick with wiry black hair. Pale blue eyes blinked and the wolven fully emerged from the mist, muzzle dripping with moisture, lips pulled back in a snarl.

A long, twisting scar slashed across its nose, nicking its eye.

Found you.

I screamed when it lunged.

My elbow crashed into something soft, and someone grunted in my ear. The world thinned and light spilled through the veil.

"Would you knock it—" I didn't wait for the disembodied voice to say anything more. The wolven's teeth sank into the meat of my forearm, the pain like nothing I'd ever felt before—not even when I'd fallen into the bush of poisonous nettles. The scream shredded what remained of my voice.

I was falling. Falling. Falling.

Air burst from my lungs, and I wasn't screaming anymore.

I lay on my back in the courtyard. I'd tripped as people scrambled around us, jostling and shouting as they hurried to and fro. My father dropped low, hollering for someone to wait up.

Mama wasn't with us. Were we meeting her somewhere?

Papa hefted me over his shoulder with a grunt. "Stay close."

I struggled to not fight him despite his uncomfortable grip, and my attention snagged on a pair of boys ducking around the corner of the stables, bodies pressed flat against the wall as they tried to avoid notice. One had hair the color of sunshine and the other glared with an expression so dark it made me shudder. The dark one noticed me bobbing away, my fingers like claws digging into my father's coat. His head canted, his mouth opening as if to call out—when his friend dragged him through the crack of the stable doors.

A woman hunched under the weight of too many bags rushed between me and the stable, her wrinkled hands snarled around the wrists of two crying children. When she passed, the boys had gone.

My father rounded a corner.

I tried to scream, but couldn't. A pair of wolven circled, snapping at our heels, long teeth red with blood. I clawed backward, away from the threat, tripping over myself. Somehow I was back on the ground, alone, abandoned. The wolven lunged again.

Someone yanked on me, and I spun around, the world dipping into black.

"Don't you dare," a woman yelled.

"She's going to hurt herself if we don't snap her out of this."

Something cold and horribly wet crashed over me. I sucked in a frigid gasp. It was so icy it burned. Burned like the wind screaming through the mountains. Like the snake poison devouring my veins last summer. Like the forest burning to the ground around me—the result of a fire I'd set.

Arms came around me, a warm body pressing against me. A person who smelled like oiled leather and sharpened steel. Her face pressed into the nape of my neck, squeezing me as hard as she could, and my arms came up around her, needing her reassurance. Needing her.

Viv.

Heat curled in my stomach, spreading through my veins, part of me settling for the first time since I'd tumbled from the Spear.

I'd know her anywhere.

I blinked through the water trickling down my face, the dry grass and spotty snow of the clearing slowly emerging.

"I'm alright," I murmured, barely recognizing the gravel that was my voice. Viv made a soft sound and pulled me closer. Maybe she needed this embrace as much as I did.

Blinking away more of the blurriness, I shifted so I could press my nose into her hair, and caught sight of Soren, arms banded tight around his chest as he glowered. It should have seemed hostile. Aggressive. But I felt the worry wafting off him in waves. Lukas stepped up beside him, swiping his bare arm over his sweaty forehead, a bucket dangling from his fingertips.

He grinned when he met my eyes. "The water worked."

15

Call it Even

I splashed more water on my face. The shivers caused by the icy tendrils meant I was alive. I wanted to wash out my hair and scrub the bloodstains from my clothes, but I settled for rubbing away the dirt and smoke from my exposed skin. It was too cold, and we had too little time for vanity.

In the distance, dark gray thunderheads roiled over the grove of trees writhing in the reddish-gold flames of the fire I'd set. Leaning back, I braced my hands on my knees. The intensity of the fire didn't sit right with me. It shouldn't have burned that quickly, given the softness of the earth and the green of the trunks.

Downstream, a little girl yelped as her mother rubbed blood from her face. Though the woman's face drooped with exhaustion, she laughed when her child shied away from her touch. Of the sixty or so captives we'd rescued, roughly three-quarters made it to the clearing Soren and I had scouted out. Only five belonged to my family—including Viv and Bree.

Metal clanked and clothing rustled as the saddles of the horses we'd saved were checked over. We hadn't recovered many supplies in our haste to escape, but Soren promised we wouldn't need many where we were going. Thankfully, he and Lukas had a plan for that, because I definitely hadn't thought that far ahead. My goals had focused purely on the rescue.

"I still can't believe you're alive," Viv murmured beside me. Something small and incredibly soft fluttered in my breast. I dried my hands with the hem of my tunic. She'd hugged me at least three times since Lukas had dumped water over my head, and now sat cross-legged, my cloak in her lap, carefully straightening the feathers as was her habit. Pip had settled on her shoulder, nuzzling her throat. "One of the soldiers said they killed the girl they found out in the forest." She brushed a fading yellow bruise on her cheek with the back of her hand. "That's all he said."

I crawled over to her, failing in the fight against my imagination. She would have fought like a frost bear with her captors over the massacre, the burning of our village. I could imagine the fear on her face when she demanded more information about my fate. When I extracted my cloak from her hold, I spotted more long cuts on her hands and arms, which she quickly covered up with her sleeves.

Another time, then.

"To be fair, I should have died," I said instead. "They chased me over the Spear."

Viv snagged my wrist in a death-grip, her eyes red-rimmed from the smoke. "They what?"

I laughed humorlessly and settled beside her, hips touching, tugging my bag into my lap. Pip swooped from Viv's shoulder when I upended it and nipped at my fingers until I held the flap open for her. She settled inside with a quiet hoot. "It's a long story."

"Here, turn a bit while you explain what happened." Viv slipped the strip of leather from my hair. "And hand me the comb you keep in there—yes, that one. Your plait is a mess."

Starlight pulsed through me, hot and welcoming. It was as if no time had passed. If I closed my eyes and shut out the conversations around us, I could almost believe we were back in the Owl Wood, backs against one of the many birches, talking while working our way through a pile of mending, Viv correcting me all the while. She was a stickler for appearances.

But we weren't a hike away from Solas or tucked back in the Copper Mountains.

This wasn't a normal day by any stretch of the word.

With Viv's hands methodically smoothing my hair and my belongings spread out on the grass waiting to be organized, I launched into an abridged version of the last few days, starting with crashing into the drakken that was Soren and ending with the fight to the death with the wolven scouts at the top of the hill. When I finished, Viv cut the thread of the hole she'd mended in my tunic with her teeth and returned the needle to its case. She brushed off her shirt, seeking the men standing in the center of the mass of people, a curious expression on her face.

"So. A boy thinks he can fight better than me, huh?" She plucked Epic from her bandolier, flipped it in the air, and caught it by the hilt on the way back down. "Color me intrigued."

Of course that was her takeaway. My answering grin felt foreign on my face. In many ways, I couldn't believe I was here. Now. Alive—even after I'd sucked in enough poisonous smoke to kill a horse—with my best friend by my side, berry-red bruises not dulling her vibrancy one bit.

When she turned back around, the tightness in my chest squeezed at the intensity burning in her gaze. She squeezed my knee, hand lingering as she leaned in. As if pulled by an invisible string, I mimicked her. Our foreheads touched, and I twined her fingers with mine, savoring her closeness.

"I don't know what I would have done if I had to live in a world where you died." Viv's voice was softer than the rustle of wind through dry grass. "I think part of me did die that day when those soldiers ransacked our village." She squeezed my hand harder, blinking back the wetness filming her eyes. "I'm so sorry. They killed Os and there was nothing I could do to save him. He put up such a fight when they burned everything down, but when that last soldier showed up and told us what had happened to you... he went wild." She choked back a sob. "He was like a man unhinged, trapped in a world where he'd lost everything. They killed him after they broke him." Her voice firmed, the tears drying. "And they will pay for that."

I couldn't breathe.

Tears welled behind my eyes, but didn't fall. I wasn't ready to hear this, to learn about what had happened in Solas. Not yet. Not on the heels of reliving that horrible day when we'd fled Aeros. Everything inside me still felt raw, stringy and bloody like a fresh kill, remembering the misery on my mother's face.

For so long, I'd shoved aside those memories, dwelling on happier days before the attack, remembering her through her letters and vague, blurry childhood memories of the way the laugh lines on her face stretched when she smiled and how she never could get mad at me no matter how badly I behaved.

But now that my memories of that day had surged past that mental block, all I could see was the earnestness in my mother's brown eyes, the way she swallowed her pain when she spoke of her duty to her county. She knew she was walking into her death, that she was saying goodbye to her family, but she held strong—making sure I was cared for before embracing her destiny, and the men and women she'd sworn to fight alongside.

I used to think my father was the strongest person I'd ever known. But my mother—she had him beat.

202

With her free hand, Viv cupped the back of my head, eyes squeezing shut while we absorbed each other's pain. Breathed through the suffering. When I felt stable again, I opened my eyes, staring down at our entwined hands, marveling at the strength of her long fingers against the scarred skin of my own.

"Knowing you were out there, somewhere, is all that kept me going," I managed. My throat felt too tight. "Ask Soren and Lukas. The only reason I'm here now is because of you."

"And me, I hope," a woman chimed in merrily.

Viv released me with a whoop and I leaned back, smiling up at Bree, my best friend's mother and the best blacksmith in all the country. She stood with her muscular arms braced on her wide hips, white-speckled hair tucked in her usual neat bun. I'd greeted her with a hug earlier—along with Petr and the Vettel twins, who'd also survived. Bree had promised to talk with me after helping the drakken get things in order. When people were in need or a big task needed to be completed, Bree had always been the first to volunteer for the effort.

"You know it," I replied.

She pulled me up into another tight embrace. If I imagined hard enough, I could almost smell the metallic residue that used to cling to her clothing. Her lips pressed against the side of my head in a touch that felt so familiar to the last one given to me by my mother that the tears I'd gamely held back trickled down my cheeks.

"Your father would be so proud," she whispered. Then more loudly, as I dried my eyes on the back of my hand, she proclaimed to everyone else around us, "Time to go, you hooligans. Gather round the horses if you want to live."

Zos had truly blessed me with wonderful people in my life.

When I finally collected myself, giving a firm if somewhat watery nod to Bree to indicate I would be alright, I grabbed my bag, careful of the slumbering owl inside, and went in search of Lukas. There had to be something I could do to help.

Naturally, I found him on top of a small boulder, pen and paper in hand, issuing orders in a quiet yet firm voice. Viv stuck to my side like sap and he appraised us both.

I cleared my throat. "Do you know where Soren is?" I owed him a huge apology.

Lukas rolled his eyes. "Don't know why you would want to see that broody bastard, but if you insist, he is somewhere over there," he twirled the end of his pen toward a cluster of boulders not far from the grouping of horses, "probably lurking in some shadows. While you are over there, see if you can get people into the saddles. We need to leave soon."

Sure enough, I found Soren leaning against a boulder, glowering at the world as he monitored the chaos without so much as a helpful word. His deathly stare and the air of mystique wafting from him in waves likely warded off anyone who might have approached. Or maybe it was the black and purple bruises blooming around his swollen eye. I winced and stopped a few yards away, Viv at my side, watchful as ever.

"How's your elbow?" he rasped.

I winced again, rubbing the back of my aching neck. I'd socked him in the face while caught in the throes of the hallucination. "I'm sorry for hurting you. I wasn't myself."

"I know."

"To be fair, you then let me fall from the back of a galloping horse."

"You caught me off guard." He crossed one boot over the other. "And I didn't let the horse trample you, so there's that."

The banter helped me steel myself, prepare for what was to come. I appreciated Soren all the more for it, though it irked me how well he seemed to understand me. "Call it even?"

Soren's mouth tipped upward. "Are you forgetting the bit where I rode into a burning forest to save you?"

"You would have done that for anyone."

Viv huffed, but I didn't dare break eye contact with the drakken to gauge her reaction. Soren's brow rose, his gaze sweeping over me. "If you say so."

Someone shouted in the background. A horse whinnied.

"So we're even?"

"Regarding the black eye? Sure." He stepped forward, hand resting on the pommel of his sword. "But I count three times I've saved your life." Another step forward. I gamely held my ground, not missing a single flick of his lashes, every stretch of his muscles. Soren always moved with an edge of danger, but this was different. "Someday, I may call on you to pay up."

"That's close enough." Steel scraped against steel as Viv stepped between us, Stella daggers in hand. She'd designed the weapons herself, featuring a curved handle, a triangle shaped blade with one straight and one angled edge. The angled side was sharpened to an invisible edge, and the opposite side was blunted and reinforced, giving the weapon extra strength in combat. "I appreciate all you've done helping my friend get to this point, but if you think I trust you around her, you've got another thing coming."

I could kill her.

She'd always been like this, defensive, protective. But this took it to a whole new level.

Soren's eyes narrowed, and I could almost see the walls in his head rebuilding.

"We leave as soon as Lukas is satisfied with his checklist." His gaze flicked back to me as the din of the gathering civilians grew louder. "We plan to push through the night. The soldiers will come after us when the fire dies down and they realize their latest convoy hasn't arrived. Will your owls help if we need them?"

"Of course. Ghost says they're getting some sleep in a grove over the hill. They'll catch up." I scrubbed my hands over my face. As much as I wished I could curl up with my birds and collapse into an exhausted slumber for two full days, I knew I wouldn't be able to sleep. Not out here, in the open, exposed like this, with the memories of the dead pulsing through my thoughts.

We would be much safer once we entered Dowhurst to our south, a coastal city handpicked by Soren and Lukas. It, like all populated areas of Idilea, boasted its share of soldiers, but Lukas swore they had places for the refugees to hide. They would be safe and presented with options about how to move forward with their lives.

That was good enough for me. As glad as I was that we'd saved these people, I wasn't ready to bear the responsibility of caring for so many, especially when I was as low on resources as I was.

"Good." Soren drew up alongside Viv and leaned into her. She stood taller by a good three inches, but he somehow managed to look down on her. Not that it intimidated her. I recognized that sly smirk.

"And you, Vex, was it?"

"Viv." She flashed her teeth. "But *akren* like you may only call me Viveca."

If he resented being compared to the souls whose earthly deeds were so sinful that Zos ordered them to walk these lands as specters, Soren gave no reaction. "The next time you challenge me, be ready to use those needles of yours."

Viv spun her dagger and tossed her short hair back haughtily. "Name the time and place. I'll show you what these *needles* of mine can do." That was Viv. My grin stretched ear to ear. She only got more relaxed when threatened.

Soren glared at her for two more beats and stalked off, his shoulder brushing mine as he passed, black attitude trailing him like a cloud.

"I don't think that improved his mood now, did it?" she asked no one in particular.

Bree took her by the elbow. It didn't surprise me she wasn't far away. She shook her head, though her eyes danced merrily. "No dear, it definitely did not."

I bit back a laugh and hurried toward a group of women trying to decide who would ride the horse first, but my thoughts lingered on the cluster of rocks. I wasn't sure if I was ready to call Soren a friend yet, but it looked like he would get along with my best and oldest friend just fine.

16

Potential

In theory, we could have made it to Dowhurst by dawn... assuming we all possessed wings and weren't hindered by injuries and exhaustion. Soren gave up on his mission to reach the coastal city around the time the sun dipped below the horizon. Anyone able to walk was already dragged down by at least two others who couldn't, and the plodding horses were desperate for food and rest.

"It will not be a comfortable night's rest," Lukas intoned as we threaded our way around the people huddled on the ground, shivering in their scraps of clothing, heads resting on their arms, exhaustion overtaking their fear of recapture. "But it is better than none."

I couldn't agree more. As one of three people here not beaten, starved, and promised a destiny that pointed to an early grave, I needed to make sure everything was set before I so much as thought of sleep. Even Viv had passed out alongside her mother, despite her protests that she would stay up as late as she had to waiting for me.

Turned out the mighty fox was actually a kit.

"Two of the men offered to keep watch, but I would like for

everyone to sleep now since they can," Lukas murmured, adding a few more tally marks to his notebook. "We need to make better time tomorrow. The size of the group is dragging us down."

His unasked question hovered between us like a feather floating to the ground.

"Ghost and Grim are keeping watch. Pip is scouting for other owls." A dark void gaped wide in my chest. "But the wolven have been thorough in their efforts." *To eradicate them.*

Lukas nodded, either unaware of my inner turmoil or choosing to give me space to deal with it, and flicked his pen to the corner of the page, leaving soft trails of grayish ink. The bundles of people were thinning. Only one figure hovered along the edge of camp, his back turned to us. "I assume they helped you get as far as you did without being discovered."

"Owls are smarter than you give them credit for." I'd offered that advice before, and would echo it again until I made believers of everyone who mattered.

"You wound me. I never said I doubted their intelligence." Lukas' eyes flickered. "However, I lack the ability to speak with them as you do. Wasn't aware it was possible, frankly."

Weariness sharpened my temper. I wished he would ask what he wanted to ask instead of dancing around it. When we stopped beside Soren, the man as immovable as rock, I peered into the web of branches cutting across the dimly lit surface of the moon. "I'm not hoarding secrets, Lukas. If you want to learn a few bird calls, all you have to do is ask. Now listen."

I cupped my hand around my mouth, mimicking the call of the Great Horned, finding the right pitch that allowed the soft sound to carry through the trees, but lacking the volume of a shout. It wasn't easy to accomplish, but I had plenty of practice.

A trio of hoots, sharp off the top that dipped into low, hollow beats, answered my question.

"That's the all-clear."

Soren strode over, his silhouette straight and narrow in the dark. I held up my hand to keep the drakken silent, then cupped my hand around my mouth again, the question slightly different this time.

A beat passed. A long screech split the night. A half beat. Then another screech. I dropped my hand. "That's the warning cry."

"Which owl is that?" Soren asked, scanning the crooks of the birches.

"Ghost," I replied. "You don't need to call out to them, though they will respond if you do. Just keep an ear out for those sounds. They'll make the all-clear ones through the night until it's time to go or something happens that requires your attention."

He nodded.

"Interesting." Lukas scribbled in his notebook, nose buried in the pages. "That is a huge help." He paused, remembering something. "I will be right back. I need to check on the horses."

Grim sounded an all-clear, and I stepped closer to Soren, our arms nearly brushing, listening to the crunch of Lukas' boots though the undergrowth fade away. Unlike how I felt around Lukas and the frenetic energy he embodied, Soren's silence was comfortable. I tilted my head back, searching the skies and pinpointing a few of the gods etched in the stars.

Zos was easiest to find.

"Your friend is not what I expected."

Soren's soft voice was a caress, one I felt from my crown to my toes. I folded my arms, but kept my eyes fixed upward. "And what were you expecting?" I wasn't sure why I wanted to know, didn't have the faintest idea who he could have been anticipating, but found myself craving his answer.

"Not her."

I tugged on the fingers of my gloves. "Viv is my best friend, has been most of my life. Her mom, Bree, practically raised me alongside Papa. She might not be my mother," a sharpness lanced my ribs, quick and direct, "but she's cared for me like one. There is no one I consider closer."

"I see."

He said it like a question, only I couldn't fathom what he was asking.

The breeze lifted a curl of my hair, dragging it across my cheek. Soren tracked it when I tucked it behind my ear. I ducked my head, uncomfortable with the singular attention.

"What will happen to the refugees?" I asked.

He hummed, a soft sound that vibrated across my soul. "We will split them into groups to be sheltered by others loyal to the Requiem. They'll be fed, housed, and presented with a decision. Most will return home when it's safer. They might try to pick up the pieces of their old lives or they'll craft new ones while they wait for the threat to pass."

Soren lowered to a crouch and picked up a branch, fiddling with the budding leaves attached to the length. "But some will join our ranks. They'll be angry enough, or intrigued enough, to set aside what they once knew and sign up to support our cause." Tiny green leaves fluttered to the ground. "Those are the ones with a burning desire for change, the ones we need to support, to mold to our cause. The time is almost here to fight back. And soon we'll be ready."

"But not quite," I said.

"But not quite," he echoed.

I shifted my weight. A shadow with wings threaded through the trees, darting faster than Pip ever could. The bat squeaked when it chomped down on its prey, winging out of sight once more.

"Why did you come for me?"

The energy humming between us intensified. It was almost painful, the way it grated. Soren's sleeve brushed mine when he stood again, like a quiet caress. An insane desire twisted up through my belly, one that wanted me to close the minute space we maintained. One that wanted me to pull his face to mine so I could look into his eyes when he answered.

"You didn't have to, especially since you're injured. My problems aren't yours." My thoughts were fragmented, my sentences choppy. The words squeezing against my ribs. "You've already helped me so much: you brought me to Archer, offered me a future—and I turned it away. You could have—*should* have listened to Lukas. But you came, anyway. He said you insisted." I finally caved to the impulse and closed the gap, my hand wrapping around his biceps, tugging him around. "Why? Why did you do that?"

His black eyes were unfathomable pits of darkness, writhing with secrets all his own. "Would your goddess have come for you?" he countered. "Helped you fight those wolven? Free the prisoners?" His grip firmed around my wrist, hard enough to bruise. "Would she have ridden into the fire to pull you from its depths before it devoured you whole?"

He was infuriating. I tugged against him, but he refused to relinquish his hold. "What is your deal, Soren? Why do you hate Zos so much? Your organization was founded on her name and likeness, rooted in her core principles, yet you mock me time and time again for my faith."

"Because what is faith but foolishness?"

His admission doused my anger like a bucket of water on a candle. I couldn't look away. Refused to blink. I'd finally rooted out the rotting core of his beliefs, the wounds he'd allowed to fester. He wasn't alone in his thoughts. Many in Solas had felt the same. Abandoned. Disheartened. Trusting only of the world they could

212

see and touch for themselves.

He allowed me to adjust his grip so his thumb swept over the precious ink embedded in my skin.

"Faith may seem foolish," I said. "It's believing in things you can't see and will never prove. It's a belief in something that you maybe shouldn't, seeking a guiding light in moments of darkness, even when the one you seek is darkness incarnate." He stared at his hand, the spread of black beneath his fingers. "Has it ever occurred to you that Zos brought you to me? That she put you in my path to help me when she could not?"

He shook his head. Not in disagreement, more like he was struggling to wrap his mind around what I was saying. "You and me and Lukas. Viv. We were all brought together for a reason. Now it's up to us to unearth what the master plan is."

"I can't agree with your beliefs," he shot back. "It gives beings who are long-dead credit for happenstances they have no influence over."

I rocked back on the flats of my feet. "And that's alright. My beliefs don't have to be yours, Soren. Never would I push my faith on another, even when they could desperately use the guidance. But I find it strange you believe in nothing, given your cause."

Soren's fingertips swept under my palm in a quiet caress. "I didn't want you to get hurt."

"What?"

He swallowed. "You asked me why I came. It's because I didn't want you to get hurt." He paused, closed his eyes. "I shouldn't care about you, but I understand the pain you feel. How you felt when you saw Solas burned to the ground, your family slaughtered in cold blood. Something inside me wants to see this to the end, to make sure you find the place where you're supposed to be."

I inhaled deeply, absorbing the scent of lemonseed unique to him. Something about Soren seemed lost, as if a part of his soul cried out for comfort he couldn't even feel. Even now, he might not see it, but part of him was open to the gods, to the belief in something more, even if he wasn't willing to admit it. Acknowledgment of the tenuous tie between us was enough.

The tension thrummed so taut between us, I could practically strum it. Soren's face and all its angles seemed sharper, the glow of the moon casting long shadows, twisting his features into something ethereal. A face that felt familiar yet strange at the same time.

I couldn't help but think back to Aeros as my father fled with me over his shoulder and remember that little boy, the one who whipped around the corner of the stables, heels digging into the earth as his friend dragged him along. The one whose dark eyes drilled into mine as Papa focused on getting us out of the city. The child who lifted his hand as if to reach for me.

"And I care about you," I said carefully. "You've rescued me from tough spots too frequently for me to not care about what happens to you now." I could practically taste his relief, understood the grating confusion that swamped his face, engulfed his eyes.

It took effort for me to tug my hand from his and tuck the trembling appendage into my pocket. I wanted to tell him everything, spill my secrets in the shadows, allow him to see me for what I was. Maybe it wasn't a hallucination, a twisting of my mind superimposing Soren's features onto those of that child by the stables. Maybe he was the boy I saw, another survivor of an ugly history.

But maybe he wasn't.

The intensity ground into me so deeply I wanted to scream.

I had to shatter it.

"What were you doing—"

"What happens next?"

We spoke at the same time, but my question was louder, shorter. The emotion on his face smoothed.

"What happens when all these people are relocated? Will you return to the mines?" I swallowed, remembering the columns of smoke and steam rising into the sky. Everyone we saved bore fresh scars, new wounds opened by their captors. Even Viv tried to hide a brutal slash across her arm and the careful way she held her chest indicated she nursed broken ribs.

Anger, potent and pungent as summer mists, swelled until there wasn't any space left inside me. Those signs of abuse were only the start. If these people bore such signs of suffering after less than a week under the control of the soldiers, what were they enduring in the depths of the mines? How many had died removing colorful stones from the core of the world?

My thoughts swirled and clashed together in bright slashes of red and orange and black, a cacophony of sound and aggression unfamiliar to me. Unfamiliar, but oh, so wonderfully welcome.

Gems that came at the cost of lives, each one as sacred as the next.

An entire country cowed by its slavers and whipped into submission. People who didn't have anywhere else to turn, so they went meekly into the mines, turning out wealth they would never realize until their hearts gave out.

People praying for the Requiem to take its stand and save them all.

"Will you return to the Llyn Mines? Will you break them free?" My thoughts cascaded freely now. I allowed an unfamiliar aggression to engulf me. I clutched at Soren, dragging him down to my level like I'd desired to earlier. "What will you do? What will the Requiem do?"

I needed to know. The sun might not rise again, yet I needed to know the answer to this question before all others.

The drakken's face hardened, his jaw protruding, the panels of secrets clapping down behind his eyelids. "I can't tell you what we plan to do next."

If he'd slapped me, I wouldn't have been more surprised. The grass tripped me up as I stumbled away from him, rocks crumbling freely beneath my boots.

"You turned down Archer's offer, remember?" He turned his back. "I agree with him. You have potential as a healer. Your friends also have potential. We could use you and I want nothing more than to find a place where you fit, but you left. Remember?"

His words slashed through me like wolven claws.

I'd never felt so betrayed.

And I had absolutely no right to feel that way.

"It doesn't have to be like this. There's always time to turn back." He stepped into my space again, his heat curling around me like a snake twining its seductive rhythm through the grass. "You'll have four days. Lukas and I will remain in Dowhurst during that time. We have work we need to address there and will give you a place to stay while you get your feet beneath you.

"I can't make this decision for you, Telleree. And I won't." He heaved a full sigh. "It's a big one. One that could and probably will cost you your life. I can tell you we are doing the right thing, that we will liberate this country of the scourge infiltrating it. I could feed you stories of the grandeur you'll accomplish at my side, at the salvation you'll reap when our work is finished, but that would be a lie.

"Everything we're trying to do comes at a cost. A steep one. It will beat you down and break you in ways you never thought possible. You will sharpen your teeth on triumph and weep for the loved ones who sacrificed themselves along the way." His eyes flickered. "And you will dig deep into the depths of your soul to keep yourself going. You will give your all and then some, and maybe—just maybe—it will all be worth it in the end."

He ran his hands through his hair in deep, anguished strokes. "I won't make that decision for you. It's a decision you must make for yourself."

He backed away. "I hope you don't regret the choice you make."

And then he was gone.

Ghost hooted the all-clear.

17

Choose to Live

I startled from sleep with a flinch and a gasp. Before I could process the swaying branches of the whipple, a knee slammed into my side again, crashing into bruises inflicted by the wolven. I curled inward, biting back a shriek as I registered Viv flailing beside me. Her arms and legs lashed out, her face fiercely contorted as she fought an invisible force trapped in her mind.

I shoved away from her slashing fist that would have shattered my nose and threw myself on top of her, knees braced on either side of her rib cage. "Viv, wake up." I shook her shoulders, grunting when her punch caught me in the solar plexus.

Shaking off the pain, struggling to stay on top of her flailing body, I shouted in her ear, "Viveca, wake up! You're going to hurt yourself." The cold edge of a knife pressed against my throat and a hand slapped the side of my head, fingers digging into my hair, holding me immobile. The edge of the blade scraped against my skin when I swallowed. Viv's eyes were open but unfocused, her lips pulled back in a snarl as she glared up at me.

"Viv," I tried again, the words barely louder than the swish of leaves rustling around us. "You will hate yourself if you hurt me."

She blinked, and the hand in my hair squeezed harder, nearly ripping strands straight from my scalp. My eyes watered. A shadow shifted in my periphery, and I caught Lukas' gaze when he stepped around a tree, hand on the pommel of his sword. I narrowed my eyes at him, warning him to stay back. Sure enough, he halted, limbs tense with urgency.

"Viv, please. It's me. Telleree."

The sound of my name froze her. The hand in my hair relaxed, and when she blinked again, she'd regained consciousness. Her emerald eyes flicked to the knife she clutched to my throat and, with a whimper, she jerked back, tossing the knife somewhere out of sight.

"I'm sorry." Her arms flew around me, squeezing me to her as she repeated her apology. Lukas released his sword and stepped away, face alight with approval. Gradually, I relaxed against my best friend. Though I hadn't given thought to it at the time, fear had worked its way into my limbs, locking them tight. I pressed my nose into her hair, breathing in the snowdrop scent of her skin.

Home. She smelled like home.

"I'm alright," I managed when it felt like she might crack my bones. "But I might not be if you don't let up soon."

Her grip loosened, her hand sweeping down my back in a long, slow motion. "I was dreaming of the attack. When the soldiers found us at Solas. I couldn't—wouldn't—" She nudged me back so she could look at me properly. Her eyes glistened with unshed moisture, her agony so close to the edge I wished I could climb into her and absorb it for her. "No. You don't need to know. You don't—"

"Honey, calm down." Bree returned from gathering our minimalist breakfast and grabbed her daughter's hand. Viv clutched it so hard the blood drained from her fingers, and I eased off of her, brushing dirt from my knees and tunic when I stood. I looked away when

Bree wrapped her arms around Viv, pulling her upright into a quiet embrace. It hurt too much to look at them, to see the pain they'd endured and *shared*.

An ugly thought sounded through me.

I should have been there.

Instead, I had tried and failed to lose a soldier in the woods and foolishly fell off a cliff instead.

I should have been there for them. If I'd run faster, if I'd turned left at the fork. If I'd known how to use a sword or a knife, I could have helped them.

"No, I want to know." I nearly choked on the words. Viv snapped around and Bree regarded me thoughtfully, eyes hooded with dark memories.

The pain of the unknown nearly ripped me in two, crying out for me to take back those five words, yet finally relieved to have them out in the open. I'd seen the evidence for myself. I knew what they'd gone through. But at the same time, I didn't.

I needed to know what had happened.

How my father had died.

"Are you sure?" Viv's quiet question nearly broke me.

I hope you don't regret the choice you make, Soren had said.

Then and there, I vowed I wouldn't regret my decisions from here on out. They were mine to make, to bear, to grieve, and to celebrate.

I squeezed my hands in my lap and nodded, wishing Pip would land on my shoulder and offer the tiny comfort of her small body, but my eyes were dry and my voice steady when I replied. "Yes. I need to know what happened."

"I'm still not sure how they found Solas, but I suppose for all the traps we set and the steps we took to protect ourselves, we slipped up somewhere." Bree rubbed the heel of her hand against her eyes, breaking the bleakness of her thoughts. "Anyway, we'd just finished with supper and Viveca and I were working on a new sword for Emry when we heard the howl."

"It was the scream," Viv countered, gaze distant. "Someone screamed. I heard them go quiet, and that's when I knew something was wrong. I ran outside and a soldier grabbed me." She touched her biceps where the creature's teeth had dug into her. "It hurt so bad I dropped my knives. I barely remember grabbing them, let alone where they landed."

"They fell behind the bench." I recalled fishing them out. "They landed out of sight. The soldiers took all our other weapons. I only found yours by chance."

"Thank Qet," she murmured, stroking the length of Steiv, the longest of her knives meant for shattering the blades of swords. The one she'd held to my throat mere moments ago. "I think they hit my head. Things went a little blurry. I remember being thrown on the ground. Mom was beside me." She squeezed Bree's hand.

"The wolven rounded us up like sheep for slaughter," Bree murmured. "They'd already killed so many by the time they got us together. I didn't want to see them lying there on the ground. It shames me now," she dragged the back of her hand across her mouth, her fingers catching the tear tracks streaking down her cheeks, "but I wanted to preserve their memories in my mind. Remember them when they were alive, not ripped open and bleeding."

Bile rose in my throat, and I choked it back down.

Viv squeezed my knee, her gesture too hard to be comforting. "Os was the only one not screaming or crying or simply sitting there with glazed eyes, blanked out. They killed the criers. Cut out their throats." Viv shuddered. "He was calm. He kept asking the soldiers what they wanted. I remembered wondering how he could be so steady in the face of our world being ripped apart, but I think it's because you weren't there. He thought you still had a chance. But then this big one stepped up, an ugly fellow with hair the color of wheat that stuck up in a million directions."

My ears buzzed. Not one of the wolven I'd encountered then.

"He called us criminals convicted of our crimes long ago. He said we'd escaped our fates for far too long and now it was time to perish, to pay. To reconcile for what we'd done." Viv sobbed out a gasp. "It was like he knew who we were, what we were doing up there. But how? No one knew. No one knew," she repeated, head in her hands.

Bree pulled Viv's back against her breast, hands stroking long lines down her spine. "He offered us a choice: to die in the ruins of our home or to keep our lives and follow them down the mountain in shackles." She blinked owlishly. "He said something else, but one of your owls burst from the trees—the big one with the gray feathers." My heart pounded in my chest, a quickening beat that vibrated against my ribs. Bree gazed at me with sympathy. "He was shrieking something, but I couldn't understand—you know that metal speaks to me far better than living things ever did—and Os lost it."

Viv shook her head, tugging on her rusty-red braid. "I recognized the call for fall, but that's it."

"No," I breathed, the word barely louder than the whisper of tall grass stalks rubbing together. My world went hyper-focused. I'd sent Pip to warn them, to relay the message so they could escape, but she must have seen me fall from the Spear and relayed that instead.

Bree scrubbed the heel over her hand over her cheek. "Os couldn't control himself. He threw himself at the wolven, yelling. I'd never seen him like that, so angry, so unafraid."

I wanted to plug my ears. To cover my eyes with my hands. To block out these words.

"I'm sorry, Tell. I'm so sorry."

"They ripped out his throat," I finished, tasting salt on my lips. I wasn't aware of when I'd started crying. "I went back. And they left him like that. On the ground. Torn up and covered in blood."

Viv wrapped her arms around me, pulling me close when the first sob broke through me. We stayed like that for I didn't know how long, long enough for the moon to eclipse the bow of stars Fen gripped in her hands.

When we broke apart, eyes puffy and bloodshot, Viv continued shakily, "I think they would have slaughtered us all, except this soldier came out of the woods and took charge of everyone. He was so serious and it was like he caught them off-guard." She traced an errant design on my knee. "Everyone except for him wore normal, green cloaks, but his had these gold bits on the shoulder, like ivy or vines."

Colonel Kohl. I drew a shaky breath.

"He grabbed the big guy and threw him against a tree, then ordered everyone to stand down. Tell, it was crazy. One minute there was so much chaos and carnage—I thought I was going to die, and the next it was so still." Viv shivered, running her hands over her arms. "Only about a dozen of us were still alive, fighting to survive, and the newcomer ordered us to stand or else we would be executed. I can't describe the look in his eye, but it was almost like he was daring us to choose to live."

The mystery of the wolven commander thickened. Soren had said it earlier, wondering why a soldier of his stature was in the mountains at all. This story confirmed it. The other soldiers clearly hadn't expected him to show up. So why was he there? And why had he saved their lives?

Bree picked up the story, rubbing her wrists, which had yet to form scabs despite the salve I'd applied earlier. "They bound our hands and ordered us down the mountain. We stopped in Stavanger where the guards were changed out, and then they continued eastward. To the mines. And then you and your friends found us."

There was more. Much more they weren't telling me.

But this was enough.

I didn't know how to handle the pain clawing at my insides like a flurryfox caught in a trap. I didn't know where to direct the anger brewing and bubbling viciously within me.

A screech from the trees drew me from my thoughts, and I quickly isolated the snowy blur perched on the bobbing bow of a birch tree, a shard of moonlight turning its feathers to flames. A snowy owl. My chest pinched.

Wordlessly, I pointed. Viv and Bree followed the line of my finger. My best friend gasped, swiping at the tears streaming down her face. "Is it Quinn?"

"No." The markings around her eyes weren't the same. "But it's the first wild one I've seen."

Viv cuffed me lightly on the shoulder. "They really do find you, don't they?"

Pip alighted on the branch alongside the wild bird, preening her feathers. "Maybe."

They'd done it. They'd found another owl.

Despite everything the wolven had done to vanquish them, they still existed. Against the odds, they survived.

Together, the three of us huddled together, watching the birds, welcoming the quiet contentedness of their presence. And it didn't take long for me to realize that the owls had survived...

And so had we.

18

Proper Introductions

U nlike the rag-tag city of Stavanger, Dowhurst needed no walls to keep wild beasts and ill-begotten ghouls from its streets. Fresh snow falling from wispy gray clouds flaked around us, fat and fluffy. This storm wouldn't hold for long.

I drew my hood up, sheltering Pip perched on my shoulder as we shuffled past a pair of guards murmuring near a sign welcoming us to the sprawling coastal city. I'd once heard Dowhurst described as being three times bigger than Stavanger, with four times the population, and I believed it. Aside from a sign planted in the middle of the block, half its letters faded from constant sunshine, I couldn't tell where the city limits started, let alone where they ended.

My head swiveled as we trundled through the bustling streets, wishing I could stop to see and smell and *touch* the wares the merchants had to offer. Everything was so uniform farther north, tucked away in the camouflage of the mountains, but this world was foreign. From the doors painted brilliant colors screaming for attention to flowering plants spilling from pots to twinkling lights strung up on poles, this city shrieked liveliness. This wasn't just a town to own a home in; this was a community that *enjoyed* what life had to offer.

I lifted my head, inhaling deeply, filling my lungs to capacity. I couldn't taste the salt of the sea, but I knew it was there, off in the distance, briny and blue and frothing with life I'd never seen before.

Our group had dwindled the closer we got to Dowhurst, Lukas siphoning off small clusters at a time, ordering them to stop at farms we passed along the way, promising they would find supportive, welcoming families inside. They would get the help they needed for as long as they desired.

Soren's words rang through my head, reminding me that once the refugees were cleaned up, they would face a big decision ahead. One I personally wasn't particularly keen on making.

Tired as they were from the constant walking and lack of sleep, most of the refugees hadn't argued. In some ways, it was rather amazing how easily and blindly they accepted the drakken's assistance. Maybe my presence, as one of their own, calmed them. Or maybe it was because the men were so authoritative, taking charge with none of the cruelty their Fiorian counterparts had to offer.

When I'd questioned their decision to break up the group, Lukas told me we couldn't enter the city with a group of sixty or so people. Even if the wolven here hadn't heard about the incident farther north, the sheer number of bedraggled and beaten people would have drawn suspicion. Now, after embracing the Vettel twins and saying our goodbyes, all that remained were Soren, Lukas, Viv, her mother, and me.

"Oi, how about we speed it up?" Viv sniped. "It's not like we haven't been walking for six days straight or nothing."

Soren rolled his shoulders. "Why don't you lead, since you're an expert on everything."

"Oh no. I leave the leading for the broody, sour-faced one of the group." Viv trailed her fingers through a display of scarves hanging from a rack outside one vendor's stall, her index finger snagging on one colored the exact shade of her hair. "I wouldn't want to disrupt the power dynamic, shortie."

The drakken flipped her a rude gesture over his shoulder.

Bree and I exchanged a look behind Viv's back. Those two had been griping at one another since we'd hit the road this morning. My friend's brush with the terrors lurking in her mind had put her in a ripe old mood, which, apparently, dictated she take it all out on Soren—who caved after a day of ignoring her. Strange for a guy who, until now, had barely seemed interested in talking.

"Alright, enough." Lukas shouldered through a group of girls in stilted shoes tittering over chocolates and wiggled his hand out from a bundle he clutched to his chest. Cinnamon and honey rolled over me as he shoved the sweetroll at Viv. "Eat something. You are annoying the shit out of me, and it is because you are hungry."

He'd barely worked the second roll from his bag when I snatched it away, shoving half of the sticky mess into my mouth with a groan. His lips pursed, and he passed me a second one. "Case in point," he muttered before handing a final treat to the demure Bree.

"But they're sweetrolls," I protested around the mass of dough, words muffled and squished together. Viv giggled and threw her arm around me, the crown of her head resting lightly on mine. Lightning sparked in my chest at the subtle contact, and I nearly choked while trying to swallow.

"If you want, you can have the rest of mine." Viv dangled her sweet in front of me.

Lukas shot a look over his shoulder as a dour-faced Soren eyed the sugar-coated ball he'd been handed with distrust. "No. No sharing. I got plenty for everyone."

Viv snorted a laugh and spun back around, her lips brushing my ear. "An orderly one, isn't he?" The hairs on the back of my neck rose as her breath washed over me. "Wanna bet on how long it will take for me to push him over the edge? I wonder what he's like when he's truly flustered."

I batted her away with a grumble, struggling to understand these strange reactions. Viv wasn't acting any weirder than normal. We'd always been like this: touchy-feely and close. But something had changed. I shoved the second half of the bun into my mouth and chewed mechanically. The dark notes in the caramel combined with the yeastiness of the dough in a way that settled my nerves.

Lukas' plan worked like a charm, and the meal quieted Viv. Either that, or the caramel had glued her teeth shut. Whatever it was, I embraced the momentary quiet of our group, seizing the opportunity to listen in on other people.

Though nearly everyone spoke Common, their accents varied dramatically. It made sense, given this was a port city, even if access to trade was now tightly controlled by the Fiorian navy. Some people pronounced consonants with the quick, jagged edges that Viv and I had grown up with in the northern part of the country. Others preferred the lower, more rounded syllables of the south, like Soren and Lukas. And then there were others: accents that lilted and soared like birds, and some full of growling undertones, as if they were chewing on rocks.

"I want piercings like that." Viv nudged me toward a tall woman with a multitude of silver rings lining the cup of one ear. When she turned to her companion, a pair of violet gems punched in the fold her of nose flashed. "But in copper."

I eyed her face critically. "Yeah, I can see it."

Viv flashed a grin and looped her arm through mine. "I'm not saying you need to get a full face of tattoos—though I'm dying to know which culture those come from because they look super badass—but I wouldn't mind seeing you expand your tattoo on your wrist."

I murmured my agreement. Nearly everyone wore coats or jackets, but it wasn't cold enough to necessitate gloves, and I'd spotted a fair number of hands with delicate artwork weaving around their fingers, across their palms, and disappearing into their sleeves.

It might be fun to immortalize my owls around my hand someday, maybe circling the rune of Zos I had to keep hidden for fear of Fiorian soldiers spotting it.

"What do you think the armbands mean?" I asked Viv, referring to the metallic bands some wore outside their coats circling their biceps. I'd noticed children wore simple, straight bands, but a number of bands worn by adults were twisted in spiraling, looping shapes.

Viv's brows drew together.

"It's a Zeftan tradition," a male voice replied. I jolted, wondering when the man on my right had joined us. He moved so quietly, shifting around people like water around rocks. "Symbolizing marital status, significant achievements, that sort of thing."

He was built like a fishing rod and towered over me and Viv—even taller than Lukas—making his stealth all the more impressive. His hair was black as pitch like mine, but buzzed close to his head, and he'd shaved off his eyebrows, giving him a perpetually surprised expression. His hazel eyes lacked hostility, the shades of gold in their depths shimmering with mirth.

"But we haven't fostered trade with Zefta for..." I counted in my head "... a century." Curiosity nipped at me. "Not since the drought forced the mass exodus from their country. You're saying their descendants carried on the tradition?"

The man motioned at a couple with armbands wider than the widths of my hands, exposing a trio of silver bracelets wrapped tightly around his forearm. "Dowhurst is a proud melting pot, even in these troubled times."

Viv's arm wrapped around my middle, pulling me closer. "Excuse me, but do we know you?"

I hadn't realized I was drifting closer to the stranger, drawn in both by my curiosity as well as the intrigue that wafted around him like perfume.

A corner of his mouth lifted, eyes darting to the head of our group. "Not yet."

Lukas sighed and elbowed Soren.

"Aleksi." Soren stopped abruptly, and I held out my hand to keep from crashing into his back with a muttered curse. "About time you found us."

"Apologies." The man's tone was wry as he ushered us off the main road and down a side street lined with buildings packed so closely together they formed one long wall. Windows stacked four stories high overlooked the street, some cracked to allow the chill of the afternoon air in. "Perhaps send a missive next time, sir."

Sir? So this newcomer was also with the Requiem, and my suspicions were correct. Soren *was* an important figure. I just needed to figure out why.

Soren shoved his hair out of his eyes. "No time. Too busy."

I glanced between the three men. Though irritated, Soren didn't seem especially surprised by the stranger's presence, and Lukas hadn't bothered to reach for his bow, like he had a tendency to do whenever he felt that Soren needed protection. Those outward signs of trust allowed me to relax a little.

"Fortunately, one of my sparrows recognized you." Aleksi rolled back on his heels. My interest piqued. Sparrows? Could he understand the birds, too? "Any farther and you might have tangled with our..." his gaze flickered to me—"most welcome, though heavily-equipped guests."

Soldiers.

Lukas clapped the man on the shoulder. "Good to see you're doing well, as I'm sure Soren was getting around to saying."

Soren tsked.

"My city hasn't burned to the ground yet," Aleksi said, "so that's something."

It was killing me to keep quiet.

Viv had no such qualms. "You gonna introduce us, shortie? Or are we chopped liver to you?"

That touch of a smile quirked Aleksi's mouth again. He eyed Soren. "Shortie?"

"Shut it."

Lukas shouldered his friend out of the way, making the proper introductions, short and nondescript as they were. "Consider them friendlies, though they have not committed yet." Aleksi looked even more intrigued, though he did a good job of keeping his questions hemmed in. "We need a place to crash for a few nights. Do you have anywhere that works?"

Aleksi shuttled his fingers across his full bottom lip, gaze sweeping over the upper stories of the housing establishment distractedly. "Will you be staying with them?"

"Preferably," Lukas said. "And we have business to attend to regarding some sheep, so we would like to be close to central if we can."

We were still speaking Common, but I felt like I only understood a quarter of the words. Viv grumbled under her breath, sharing my sentiment. I hadn't filled her or Bree in on all the Requiem matters yet, but I would need to soon.

"Jester's Hideaway is empty."

Soren fiddled with his sword. "That won't draw suspicion?"

"Safest place I got. Plus, with it being part of the tavern, you'll eat well."

Lukas perked up at the mention of food. I bit back a laugh. His decision to grab those sweetrolls hadn't been an entirely selfless act, no matter how he tried to play it off. "Come on, Soren, it will be fine."

Soren didn't seem convinced, but whatever had him on edge wasn't enough to overpower Lukas' eagerness. "Alright then."

Our newfound friend nodded down the road. "Follow me."

Lukas kept pace with him, rattling off a bunch of nonsensical information. Before I could follow, Soren snagged my wrist.

"Four days," he whispered, dark eyes burning into mine. "Your time runs thin."

19

Opportunity

I barely brought my hands up in time to keep the floor from breaking my nose, but the impact jarred my body, aggravating bruises both new and old. "Do you have to use *all* your strength?" I whimpered.

The floor vibrated against my ear pressed flat to the floor. Tight brown pants showed every curve of Viv's well-muscled legs, and her face appeared in my line of sight when she dropped into a push-up and bopped my nose. "Will a wolven pull his punch if he gets his teeth in you?"

"If his teeth are in me, I don't think he needs to punch me."

"You know what I mean."

Sure. Yeah. "Whatever."

I braced against the smooth, wooden boards of the floor and tried to force myself upright, then gave up with a gasp. Upon learning of my deficiencies when faced with both Colonel Kohl on the Spear and the scouts in the forest, Viv had renewed her mission to teach me self-defense, proclaiming it a "necessity of life."

In my opinion, it was another way for her to avoid facing the reality of what happened to her. The time she spent planning detracted from sleeping, which for her remained plagued with nightvisions.

"You really are terrible at this," she joked, straightening. "How have you hidden this from me for so long?"

"I didn't. Remember when you tried to teach me to use your daggers because you wanted a sparring buddy? Your mom ordered you to give up the next day because she thought you were going to accidentally sever one of my limbs."

Viv laughed. "Oh. Yeah."

I flopped on my back, hands resting on my stomach. She had a point. After three days of repetition, I should be better at this. I truly was the definition of hopeless when it came to defending myself. It didn't matter what I did or how hard I worked, it was like there was a disconnect between my brain and whatever it was that made limbs move. Whenever I watched Viv demonstrate something, I understood what she was doing perfectly, yet when it came to replicating it… I ended up here.

On the floor.

Dead—if we were in real life.

I ran my hands down my ribbed shirt, marveling that it was possible to wear just one layer here comfortably. One layer *without sleeves,* to be exact. I couldn't remember the last time I'd been comfortable in only my undershirt. Even in the warm months of Sient, it was still too chilly in Solas to be outside without a light jacket.

To our delight, Jester's Hideaway lived up to everything Viv and I had worked up in our minds: a small shanty with a rickety porch that opened up to a cozy, well-equipped kitchen and eating area on the bottom level. A narrow set of stairs led up two more stories, revealing four equally sized bedrooms. As was the case with the rest of Dowhurst, the spaces were richly decorated with brightly painted walls, plush fabrics, and delightful little toys—some of which proved to be useful, like the self-lighting candle.

None of those comforts lived up to the heat. The glorious, blissful heat.

The hideaway was tucked in the alley behind Eelshead Tavern, virtually invisible from the street because it was built into the back of the tavern. The bedrooms each came with a fireplace, but fireplaces from the kitchens of the tavern also roared on the other side of the shared wall, throwing off a tremendous amount of heat. I couldn't stop sweating, but I'd never felt more wonderful in my life—bruises aside.

"On your feet." Viv stepped over me, one foot on either side of my waist, riotous curls pulled back in two tails, and offered her hand. "I didn't hit you that hard."

"Yes, you did." I limply reached up, allowing her to snag my wrist.

Viv grunted as she hefted me upright, brushing dust off my shoulders. "No, I didn't. Even your owls are laughing at you."

I glanced at the rod holding up curtains the exact shade of dandelion where three owls perched. Grim had buried his face in the base of his back feathers, but Ghost and the snowy bobbed their heads in delight. Pip trilled gleefully from her spot on the quilt, tawny wings flapping in encouragement.

Viv rounded me, and I recognized her prowling gait for what it was. Before she threw her arms around me in a hold she would want me to break, I flopped on the bed and hustled Pip onto my chest to dissuade my friend from toppling onto me.

"No fair," she pouted. "It was just going to be the one more."

I snorted. "It's always 'one more' with you."

She'd been like this, bubbling over with frenetic energy, since I'd filled Bree and her in on details about the Requiem. No matter what she did, she couldn't hide her interest in the adventure, knowing only one thing held her back.

The guilt hit hard.

That conversation was three days ago.

My time to make a decision, as Soren had so succinctly put, *wore thin.*

"V?"

The five-legged chair at the desk groaned when she dropped into it. "Yes?"

"Will you tell me, honestly, what you think of the Requiem? Would you join?"

Viv hummed low in her throat. "Truthfully?"

I boosted up on my elbows, forearms flat on the quilt on either side of me, needing to read her face during this conversation. "Always."

"There's a lot to consider here, and you're smart to think it over." She stood, flipped the chair backwards, and dropped down again, legs wrapped around the back. The toes of her black boots grazed the floor as she leaned forward.

"I love how we were raised and where we were brought up, but you know I always wanted something bigger, so keep that in mind when I tell you this." She ran her fingers over her lips and twirled a strand of coppery hair around her index finger. Her grip on the chair was hard, the lines of her healing injuries puckered and pink against her skin.

"I resent Fior for what their soldiers did to me, to my mother, to you—for destroying our entire village and everyone in it. I hate that they reduced us to nothing in a matter of minutes and that they've been doing this for the past seventeen years. We've been isolated from the kingdom, sequestered on that mountain peak all this time because of them, because of what they did when they thought they deserved the rights to our land more than we did. And they shouldn't get away with it." She banged her knuckles on the back of the chair, staring distantly at the wall.

"The Requiem offers an opportunity to get even." She spread her fingers wide. "You know me and a fight: even when I'm the underdog, I think I'll win. As much as I don't like that Soren fellow— if everyone who is a part of that organization is as buckled down as he and Lukas are, I'd say they have a pretty good shot at winning this thing."

She paced to the window, where she pulled back the curtain and peered outside. "I'm tired of being on the inside looking out at the world, dreaming of what could someday be. I want to be a part of something bigger, contribute my skills. There's so much good we could do for this world. I know it sounds like a huge risk, but…" The curtain slipped from her fingertips, obscuring the daylight once more. Her eyes were big, full of hope and stars. "Without risk, there's no payoff. And you know as much as I do, there's some very sweet payoff involved here, if we can pull it off."

Dissatisfied, I lay back on the bed, gazing at the cracks in the ceiling. She hadn't said anything I hadn't expected, but I definitely needed to hear it. Viv sighed, and the bed dipped near my feet when she sat. A moment later, she lay beside me, our arms touching.

"But I'm also with you. You're my best friend in the whole of everything." Her hand wound around mine, our fingers calloused in different spots, two sides of the same survival story. "Whatever you decide, I'm with you. I can't imagine my life without you in it—Requiem or not. But I want you to remember that Solas is gone. Everything our parents worked to accomplish is destroyed. There's nothing for us back there."

I squeezed her hand more tightly and Viv squeezed back, pressing closer so our sides smashed together. Her thumb traced the side of mine.

"Ma says she's going to sign up." Viv reached toward the spackled ceiling with the hand not gripping mine. The snowy startled and flew across the room, landing on the dresser bumped up beside the door. "She's been hanging out with a smithy associated with the Requiem, and she's pleased with the work they will ask her to do. Swords, daggers, pitchforks, poleaxes—you name it, she will be able to craft it. And they're weapons that get to be used for good. For freedom. It's what she says she's meant to do, what she was doing before we had to run."

I swallowed hard. Bree's decision didn't surprise me, but the speed at which she made it did.

"But you need to make up your own mind, Tell. Give it some more thought. I know this isn't want you wanted, but maybe our wants aren't chiseled into stone, you know? Maybe they can change." She rolled over, pieces of her hair brushing my cheeks as she leaned over me. "Think about it. And if it's not the Requiem, what would you rather do? How would you spend your time?"

I swallowed the tears gathering in the back of my throat and nodded.

Things were changing.

"Yeah. I will."

And I needed to decide whether I'd change with them.

* * *

My legs swayed beneath me, the bark of the tree catching on the fabric whenever I clenched my knees around the branch to brace against a rogue gust of wind. I rubbed the feathers of the cloak draped over the limb beside me, breathing in the scent of dry pine needles that would always invoke memories of home. At the base of the tree, a six-pronged elk stripped leaves from a briarbush, the thorns no match for the tough skin on the inside of the herbivore's mouth.

Unable to sleep after my conversation with Viv, I'd dressed and grabbed my things. Viv had barely woken, eyes glassy when she rolled over to watch me leave, and I slipped down the stairs, through the vacant kitchen, and into the shadows to the edge of town—thankfully without notice. I'd picked this tree, one inside the forest but with a view of Dowhurst, for a reason. Even this late at night, with the moon past its apex in the sky, bonfires burned and drunken cheers occasionally drifted from the streets.

Pip cooed from her spot on my shoulder, pointing out a raccoon scrambling up the trunk of an oak a few yards over. It chittered, reflective eyes flashing blue-green. With a sigh, I tugged the heavy material of my cloak into my lap, plucking at the feathers, remembering the owls who'd shed them, chest aching as I recalled my father beside me, stooping to pick them up, eyes bright as we worked, eager to return home to add to our plumage.

So many memories sewn in this cloak. So many experiences: like the time I'd gotten stuck in a silverpine and refused to come down until my father climbed up after me; or when I'd busted my hand open helping Bree fashion a sickle and dripped blood over the tawny owl feathers, permanently staining them because I waited too long to scrub it out; the memories of Viv borrowing my cloak, draping it over her shoulders, ends gripped in her hands as she sprinted through the Owl Wood, pretending to fly.

The cloaks my father and I had sewn together in honor of our favorite birds.

My mother's favorite birds.

Nose runny with more than the cold, I dragged my satchel into my lap and flipped up the lip, finding the patch I'd sewn inside the bag. It was old, the embroidery worn and its color fading, but I knew every bump and valley by touch, recognized the shapes it wove even in the relative darkness: A dragon with its wings spread, soaring over the black silhouette of a castle in the background. In the foreground, a pair of swords crossed over a golden crown.

The crest of Idilea.

The image embroidered on the back of my mother's cloak, and the last thing I saw when she left us to fight for our country.

This patch was the only artifact I had of hers, one of only a handful of things my father had snatched from his desk before escaping with me into the chaos that ushered in the collapse of Aeros.

I remembered Petr's booming laugh, the taste of Tuva's thyme and pepper rabbit stew, the crackle of the bonfire we burned every night, even in the heart of Sient when the sun lingered on the horizon far longer than it had any right to.

My thumb swept across the tattoo on my wrist. A prayer and a promise.

"What am I going to do now?" I whispered partially to myself, partially to the ghosts of the past, and partially to the dark goddess. I didn't expect an answer.

I never did.

My father warned me of the fickleness of the gods, how rather than offer their wisdom outright, they guided our decisions through signs and symbols, sometimes so subtle we missed them if we weren't careful. That said, despite my misgivings about leaving home, my favorite stories were those of the gods' chosen ones, the people they revealed themselves to during the hard times and the challenges they presented. Those tales were always woven with danger and intrigue, love and death—but always hope.

I settled back against the trunk, drawing my foot up to brace against the branch. Snow crunched beneath cloven hooves as the elk tired of the prickly thorns and waxy, red berries and ambled toward more supple offerings.

Was it time to move on? Was Viv right and it was time to stop hiding?

Were we meant to have hidden for as long as we did?

I brought my scarf to my nose, inhaling the hint of smoke that clung to the fibers, remembering the fires I'd set. I'd done that. Me. I'd followed my heart, and I had done what I needed to in the name of saving my family and dozens of others. And it wasn't just them. Blue eyes flashed behind my eyelids—the girl I'd stepped in front of when the soldiers at closed in at the inn.

Potential.

That word uttered by Archer resonated deeply within me.

For most of my twenty-one years in this world, I'd lived a sheltered life surrounded by those who loved, respected, and cared for me. I'd raised owls and learned their language. I'd mixed poultices and mastered the healing remedies I encountered in the old books we'd bought. I'd learned the forest and embraced my own mind.

Potential.

Soren and Viv had said it, too, with that faraway gleam in their eyes, as if sighting a world beyond the one laid out before us. A world full of promise and glory. Retribution.

We had fled Aeros. We'd left behind the fighting and the blood, survival front of mind. But the ugliness of Idilea being ripped into and stomped over hadn't ended. I just hadn't seen it. Now I did: in the terror thrumming through that girl, limbs locked in frozen shock; in the bodies of my loved ones drenched in blood and ash; in the hollowness of Viv's gaze when she smoothed her fingers over the cuts and injuries inflicted upon her by those who had no right to touch her.

Of the mines I hadn't glimpsed, where thousands toiled day after day, praying for change.

The cloak bunched in my grip, feathers crinkling. I ran a trembling hand over my face, limbs taut with a plethora of emotions panging

241

all at once.

Solas was gone. My world had changed.

Laughter rose from the street circling the outside of Dowhurst. A couple walked, arm in arm, either uncaring or unseeing of the soldiers watching them from the rooftops. I wasn't like them. I didn't relish the feel of the city. The rush of the bustling streets didn't call to me, and I almost resented the feeling of the walls closing in. Even in Stavanger, a town closest to the climate I loved most, an itchiness lingered between my shoulder blades, an inescapable force.

No. Home wasn't a city or a place.

My home was in the people around me, the memories I replayed inside my head. My home was with my father and the life he'd devoted to keeping his promise to my mother. I choked down a sob. Home was with my mother, kissing me on the head, pain filling her eyes when she left to fulfill her duty to her kingdom.

All my life I'd channeled my father and his love of the peace he'd created.

A peace that didn't truly exist.

The time had come to channel my mother and her devotion to a cause. It was time to find my place in the world as it existed. Viv had asked me to think of my future. Outside of the Requiem, my options were limited. Working on a farm or operating a stall in the market didn't appeal to me.

No.

I had helped people when I could, and I wanted to keep helping.

I wanted to eliminate the misery I saw in their gazes and slay the haunted expressions that followed the soldiers as they shoved their way through the markets.

The time for hiding and training and learning was over.

Like my mother the day those dreaded bells tolled knew she needed to step up, to brace beneath her mantle, take up her sword, and to dive into battle with everything that she had.

Decision made, I pulled my cloak back on and looped my satchel around my neck, dropping to the ground with the ease of a squirrel. Armed with the lessons of my past, I turned back to the city and the future that awaited.

20

I Knew It

Returning to Jester's Hideaway took far longer than I anticipated. By the time I emerged from the woods, most taverns had closed up shop and the streets were woefully empty. That gave the soldiers more room to prowl, making oddities like me stand out more. Slipping through the shadows like I had earlier took more skill to avoid notice.

Once, I stumbled over a lip in the cobblestone and nearly spilled into the well-lit street, but I caught myself just in time, bracing against a building just as a soldier stepped into view down the block. I flattened myself against the wall, barely moving or breathing as he walked past, metallic eyes glinting as he paced, one hand on his broadsword and the other scrubbing the dark stubble on his chin. Only when someone called out and he cut in the direction opposite me did I breathe again, not wasting the opportunity to scurry through the alleys like the rats skittering in the gutters beneath.

The tightness in my chest loosened when I rounded the corner and found myself at the base of the rickety staircase leading to the front door. I jiggled the knob, my breath clinging to my lungs when it stuck, positive I had left it unlocked.

I sagged against the door, sweat cooling on the back of my neck, forehead pressed to my arm, and nearly toppled over when someone inside pulled it open with a jerk. A hand snagged my flailing form, and I toppled into Soren, sans his normal veneer of carefully cultivated boredom or hostility.

"We wondered when you would be back."

"You what?" I extricated myself from his hold and stepped around him, trying to steady my throbbing heart. "And who's 'we?'"

At the kitchen table, Lukas lifted a chipped mug in greeting, grin wobbly and eyes bleary. "You should join us." He kicked at the chair across from him, jolting it away from the table.

Soren brushed my elbow as he slipped around me to get to the counter, sending a small shower of sparks through me. I blamed my nerves for the sensation, wondering how I should break the news of the conclusion I'd reached. The confidence I'd felt in the forest had vanished upon seeing them.

The drakken removed a kettle from the stove, poured steaming liquid into a mug that he pulled from the cabinet, and swiveled to put it at the place setting before reaching for his own glass. Ghost perched on the edge of the table, feathers fluffed as Soren stroked a big hand down his back. Of all my owls, he had taken the greatest liking to the newest members of my entourage.

Hesitantly, I sat and wrapped my chilled fingers around the mug. The tea smelled of elderberry and spring grass. I closed my eyes, allowing the heat to unravel the knot of tension pulsing between my brows. "I wasn't expecting you to be here."

"We have been a bit out of touch, haven't we?" Lukas picked at a piece of wax dried onto the table. He sounded wrung out. "It is why I am not a huge fan of coming here; always too much work, too little time. I could use some sleep, but we leave in the morning.

Annoying."

I followed his thumb to a pair of bags leaning against the wall and lifted my gaze to Soren. The drakken had been so busy I'd scarcely seen them, let alone had a moment to talk with them about my impending decision. Would they have left without saying anything?

The chair creaked when he tilted back on two legs, arms crossed, rocking slightly.

"Has everyone been relocated?" I asked, spinning my mug on the table. Ghost's head swiveled one hundred eighty degrees, eyeing the offensive piece of pottery with distaste.

Lukas nodded. "The paperwork is the worst bit. Such a pain when we are handing out new identities so fresh the ink is still wet. If I had some—"

"I'm coming with you." The words burst from me like a bubble popping. I couldn't hold it in any longer. "Whatever you need, however I can help the Requiem, I'm in."

The corner of Soren's mouth ticked up so subtly, I wouldn't have noticed if I weren't staring at him already. Something sly and satisfied burned in his gaze, as if he'd expected this outcome and merely waited for everyone else to catch up. Soundlessly, he set his chair back down on four legs and reached for his mug, clicking his tongue at Ghost when the bird nipped at him.

Lukas blinked owlishly, eyes clearing marginally. "I must be more tired than I thought, because I swear I heard you say you are joining the Requiem."

"That's the plan."

"Whoa." He carded his hands through his thick hair, skewing his golden curls in all directions. "I did not see that coming."

It surprised me, the sting of disappointment I felt hearing his admission. It wasn't like we'd known each other for long, but I felt close to these two men. They had been by my side for a huge transformative part of my life, and for Lukas to think I would walk away without a look back, I wasn't sure how to process that. What had he thought I would do if I had chosen not to join?

"Why?" Lukas slung his arm over the back of his chair. "Why go this route? I thought for sure Soren scared you off with all his talk of gloom and doom and the brutal reality that we are probably going to die before we see our next birthdays."

He cast a dark look at his friend, who shrugged. "I live for honesty." Lukas groaned.

Floorboards creaked, and the stove ticked as the house settled. I picked up my mug now that the liquid inside wasn't boiling hot, and took a long sip. Wildflowers. It tasted exactly like the smell of spring. I allowed myself a single moment, a beat to find that calm, quiet place within me. "I want to find my purpose in this world."

The window rattled against a sudden gust of wind.

"Papa and my mother lived their lives with purpose. Bree knows what she is meant to do. Even Viv has an idea of where she needs to go and who she's meant to be. But I feel like the last downy seed clinging to the dandelion head, waiting for the right gust to whisk me along." I paused, thinking back to my conversation with my best friend. "I think it's time I take a few risks."

Tentatively, I took another sip of my tea, wetting my suddenly dry throat, and met Soren's eyes. He leaned forward like I was the most important thing in his world in that moment, which drove me to continue with my thought. "I like standing up for people. I'm not good at defending myself or fighting back, but I like being helpful. The Fiorian soldiers and the atrocities they've committed are unacceptable."

I recalled the heady scent of fear that saturated the market in Stavanger when the soldiers passed through. My spine straightened as heat flared in my belly. "The suffering of our people needs to end.

Now that I've seen the pain they've inflicted first-hand, I believe Fior needs to be stopped, and if there's anything I can do to assist with eradicating them from our kingdom, I'll do it."

Lukas twirled his empty cup. "Damn."

Soren rose and reached for the kettle again to refill his friend's mug. He had yet to respond, and it was his answer I craved the most, wondering what this man with his secretive thoughts felt about my conviction. If he thought I still was the foolish, naïve little girl he'd met at the base of a mountain, or if he'd seen the woman I'd become.

Regardless, I wasn't ready to stop. Not yet. Taking this step, moving in this direction, meant stepping out of the shadows and into the light.

Secrets weren't always meant to stay that way.

Going against everything I'd ever been told, I followed my instincts and took a chance.

"My father operated the aviary at Eversturm Keep. My mother served as a captain in the Idilean army." I breathed in deeply. "I was four when the Fiorian soldiers invaded. I remember the city burning, the people screaming when we fled."

I blinked against the memories flitting across my vision, blurring the kitchen and the pair of men in it. These memories didn't hurt as much as they used to, their sharp edges dulled with time.

"My mother left to defend the castle. She fought with my father, insisting it was her duty as captain to do what she could to save the royal family and the kingdom." I flipped my pouch open, revealing the embroidered patch I'd carefully stitched inside its belly. "She left us and told my father to run. She told him to take me and get as far away as he could—to not look back."

I smoothed my thumb over the crest and covered it up again, concealed beneath the flap. Soren's face had gone pale, his lips pinched white as he stared at the bag. He caught my questioning expression and motioned for me to continue.

"Nearly everyone in Solas lived in Aeros and ran during the chaos, fleeing with little else but their loved ones and the clothes on their backs, seeking safety where there wasn't any to be found. We ran, the army following us every step of the way. Some died, others tried to hide in the villages we encountered. I don't know what came of them.

"I just remember my father telling me we needed to keep going, keep pushing farther north. As a child I didn't understand, but now I realize what would have happened if they'd caught us. We were wanted fugitives of the capital. I know why my father and Bree chose Spear Ridge; why they built a home there and hid away, embracing their new lives, only coming down out of sheer necessity. To be caught after all this time, the punishment for their crimes would be unspeakable."

My lips felt numb, and I squeezed my fingers together, not daring to look at the drakken, feeling the weight of their stares on the crown of my head. "I know Fior is still searching for people who escaped the castle that day. I know they still hunt those people, wanting to destroy the last vestiges of a kingdom long gone." It was true. I'd seen the wanted notices too many times to count, most worn and faded with age after being tacked on notice boards and outer walls for all this time.

"If you need information about us, about who escaped, I'll gladly tell you. I imagine it might come in handy if you're looking at retaking this land." I paused. "But I only know of the several dozen of us that hid away in the mountains. I don't even know if any members of the royal family survived, but I know my mother went to protect them.

"Now I intend to follow her example. Maybe not with a sword and shield, but in my own way. I want to serve, to see the next chapter in this story, to find my place in it." I finally smiled, muscles twitching with a strange blend of relief and contrary gratitude. Ghost nuzzled my hand, his plumage soft against my skin. I stroked his head, thankful for my owls, for Viv—for the few things I had left amid all the destruction.

When I finally met Soren's eyes, my breath left me in a punch.

They burned hot and wild and fierce—full of hope and something that might have been fear.

Lukas dragged his hands down the stubble dotting his cheeks and chin.

"I knew it." Soren clenched his fists and stormed around the table. I scrambled to my feet, backpedaling, trying to gauge his mood. "I knew—"

The front door opened with a bang, crashing into the wall. A tall figure shoved inside and slammed it shut against the gust of cold air, thrusting a trio of locks firmly into place. Aleksi pressed his back against the wall, sweat streaking down his face. "They're coming."

21

Watch His Back

"How far out?" Soren demanded. He didn't waste time asking questions like who was coming or how many enemies we needed to worry about, as his eyes darted from Aleksi to the tiny kitchen window to the staircase.

Aleksi shook his head, swiping his sleeve over his forehead. "Three minutes. Maybe less. I barely got word of their intentions before their orders were dispatched."

Soren cursed viciously, practically gliding over the floor to their bags, shouldering them easily. Lukas pinched his nose, eyes closed as he leaned over the table, tea cold and forgotten. "Are the tunnel systems open yet?"

Aleksi shook his head. "Still digging them out after the last earthquake. Even if the paths weren't blocked, I wouldn't recommend them. They're unstable at best."

Lukas' jaw worked. "Our best chance is to cross the rooftops, then. It might buy us enough time to scatter."

"Too late." Viv darted down the stairs, shoes soundless on the hollow boards. Pip flew down behind her. She tossed the pack I'd left upstairs to me and thumbed the bag hooked over her shoulder.

It bulged with the supplies we'd picked up over the past few days. "They're on the roof. None too subtle, either. If they're hoping for a sneak attack. I could give them a few pointers."

My owl landed on my shoulder, tiny body trembling. Ghost rocked from his perch on the chair, head spinning as he listened to noises too quiet for the rest of us to hear. Thankfully, the other owls were in the woods where the wolven would be no match for their intelligence.

Soren peered out the window again. "Is Bree up there?"

"Nope." Viv scraped her fingers through her hair and drew it back into a short, messy tail. "She's with Garth, working on that special shipment you ordered."

Special shipment?

Soren nodded thoughtfully, considering Viv and Aleksi. "Anyone have any idea how many there are? It looks like we'll be fighting our way out of this one."

Viv shook her head. "I counted five, maybe six sets of boots on the roof, but couldn't guess how many are on the ground. I grabbed our stuff and hauled ass down here." I pressed my bag to my thigh. I didn't have much, but what little I did have, I needed.

"My sparrows didn't get that information," Aleksi murmured. Outside, something scraped against the stones, and I leaned across the table, blowing out the trio of half-melted candles, casting us in darkness.

A hand squeezed my shoulder. "Good thinking," Soren murmured. He pressed something into my hand. A dagger. I recognized the shape and feel of the sheath. I gulped. "Use that."

"But I don't—"

"If you travel with me, you travel armed." He paused. "Do not hurt yourself on accident."

Good luck with that. I strapped the sheath to my thigh and whistled for Ghost, who landed nimbly on my bracer. "How many are we dealing with?"

His white plumage bobbed, and he trilled. I opened my palm, and he tapped it twice in the center with his beak.

"Twenty," I whispered. "Twenty of them outside. Give or take one or two."

"He can tell all that from in here?" Lukas asked.

I ran a hand down the bird's back. "If they can hear a mouse scampering through a hole under the snow, they sure as feathers can count the louts fumbling around outside."

"We can handle twenty easily enough. The three of us will confront the ones on the street." Soren's sword sang as he pulled it from his sheath. Viv and Aleksi followed quickly, the former grinning in that bloodthirsty way of hers. Lukas reached for his bow, stringing it up with practiced care. "Lukas, you pick 'em off as they come down the stairs. I don't want to risk sparring with swords in that enclosed space. It leaves too much for chance. Telleree—you watch his back."

Ghost launched himself to the top of the cabinets, the moon of his face practically glowing in the dark, and I drew my dagger. It looked sharp. Really sharp. Though I'd been practicing, the grip felt unnatural against my palm. Bandages and thread and gardening tools were more my thing, but Lukas was relying on me. I wouldn't let him down.

Aleksi braced his hand on the doorknob, his rapier pointed downward as he prepared to rush outside. Viv hovered near his back, a sword of her own in her grip. Bree must have dropped it off when she'd visited earlier. "Ready?"

"Let's go before they beat us to the surprise," Viv muttered sardonically.

Aleksi chuckled and threw the door wide, moving aside with it. My heart leaped to my throat when she charged through the opening with a shout and a clash of metal, Soren close behind. Someone screamed and the coppery scent of blood filled the air. With a grimace, Aleksi ducked through the door and disappeared onto the street. I hurried to Lukas' back, giving him space to pull his bow without getting in his way.

"This alright?" I asked.

"Perfect." He never sounded rattled. Ever. And I didn't want to be there the day he lost his cool. The step I'd avoided earlier near the top of the staircase squeaked under the weight of someone's body. Lukas whispered, barely loud enough to hear over the shrieks outside, "They are coming down, so brace yourself."

Talons. I wiped my sweaty palm on my pant leg. This was it.

I lowered my center of gravity, channeling my best Viv impression as I held the dagger out in front of me, keeping her lessons about posture in mind. Hopefully, she was alright. There was plenty of shouting and screaming, and I couldn't differentiate between those I knew and those I didn't in the cacophony of sound.

Lukas' bow thwanged once, twice, three times. The first two targets dropped soundlessly, but the third groaned out a warning as he collapsed. I didn't dare look, keeping my eyes fixed on the kitchen, darting from the doorway to the window and back again. Adrenaline pounded in my veins, hard and fast as the waterfalls that spilled through the Copper Mountains, making me light-headed, almost dizzy. I adjusted my grip on the dagger, the point bobbing in uncertain circles as I shifted from foot to foot.

A wolven howled, the sound muffled through the walls, and Viv exclaimed with triumph. I tried to get a look through the darkened doorway, wondering how many of our enemy remained, but Lukas shifted at the same time. He grunted, falling to his knees, bow rattling to the floor as he clutched an arrow in his side. His leg twisted around mine, snagging my ankle, and I tumbled to the ground at the same moment Soren shouted a warning.

I rolled to avoid breaking my ankle and my knife dragged right across Lukas' body, drawing a deep line through his coat. The feel of the blade slicing through skin made me gag, which I immediately regretted because, feathers, I'd hurt Lukas. Me. The angle of the impact knocked the weapon from my grasp, where it disappeared beneath the kitchen table.

I reached for the drakken, wondering how deep the wound was, barely registering the shadowed presence thundering down the stairs. What if—

The drakken shook me off, reaching for his sword, and lunged at the figure who swiped at his face. Lukas' momentum knocked me backward, and Ghost launched from his spot on the cabinets, wings flared wide as he dove at someone behind me.

A roar followed as the bird clawed at a wolven's eyes. It must have entered through the door when I'd gotten tangled up with Lukas. The ugly beast bristling with black fur skidded sideways, swiping at the owl, who dragged his talons across its nose, narrowly escaping the soldier's reach with an indignant hoot. The wolven slammed into the sink, speckles of blood flecking the counter top, and snarled when it caught sight of me.

It was going to kill me unless I did something.

I fumbled on the ground, searching for the knife, but came up empty, my arms shaking too hard. When the soldier lunged, I didn't think. I reacted. I stepped between it and Lukas, who'd just sunk his sword deep into the gut of another soldier, flinging myself onto the back of the charging wolven, wrapping my arms around its thick neck, burying my fingers into the muscles. My friend was already wounded. I wasn't going to let anyone else close.

The beast yelped in surprise and skidded to a stop, nearly flinging me off, but I dug deeper, allowing the momentum to shift me into a better position on its back. I ground my knees into its sides as if it were a pony—a large, overly hairy pony with super sharp teeth.

Lukas shouted a warning. The wolven whipped us around again, attempting to throw me off and lunge at the drakken at the same time.

"No," I ground out, and dragged myself higher on its neck, sinking my teeth into its long, triangle-shaped ear as hard as I could. Blood filled my mouth. The wolven yelped in surprise, snapping its body around, claws reaching and legs flailing, trying to get out from under me. But I stubbornly held my spot. If it threw me off, it would kill me. There was no escaping that.

Spitting out the ear, trying to not swallow blood, I clawed at the monster's eyes, grunting when we crashed into the wall of cabinets. My entire left side went numb. Magic tingled in the air. Shit. It was going to shift. Before I could pull away, a sword plunged between the wolven's ribs, sinking deep into its chest and puncturing the heart, the point emerging a breath away from my side. The wolven gasped, reaching one last time for the new threat, before going still.

Shaking, body heaving with disgust and violence, I peered up into my savior's face.

Blood splattered across Viv's cheeks. A cut slashed across her forehead oozed more blood, and her coat was torn halfway down her torso. The beast's innards squelched when she pulled her sword from its body, and my stomach heaved. The coldness in her expression was unrecognizable as she scrutinized her kill. She wiped the blade on the wolven's fur, then remembered I was there, on the floor, and reached for me. I took her hand, my callouses slipping on the blood coating her skin, and collapsed against her when she pulled me in for a hug.

Over her shoulder, Aleksi bent over Lukas, applying pressure to the wound where the arrow had been, the offending piece of weaponry broken in half beside him.

Soren hovered nearby. "How is it?"

"He'll live." Aleksi swiped his arm over his face, smearing the blood. Sweat trickled down his neck. "It nicked his side, but avoided any major organs, else we'd be in real shit." He gritted his teeth. "The bleeding has slowed. I can patch him up, but he'll need some medical attention on the road."

"I'll help." I staggered out of Viv's grip and dropped beside Lukas, reaching for the bag I'd tossed against the wall. Everything inside me shook, the adrenaline slowing to a drip. "I've got supplies that will help. Lots of them." When we'd gone to the market the day before, filling my medical kit had been my top priority. This world I found myself in was far more violent than the one I'd left.

I carefully prodded the wound. Lukas grimaced, throwing his head against Aleksi's chest. The wound didn't look deep. It would need stitches, but nothing was broken from what I could tell. Even the wound I'd inflicted on his arm was shallower than I'd imagined. There would be a lot more blood otherwise. My fingers closed around the bottle of disinfectant I needed, along with a piece of gauze and a roll of bandages. Unscrewing the bottle, I looked Lukas in the eye. "Brace yourself, this is going to hurt."

He nodded and accepted the flat piece of bark I offered him to bite down upon. When he was ready, I opened the wound and poured the disinfectant on it, closing myself off to his muted shriek. A gray poultice went on next, sealing the injury until I could treat it properly later, and I slapped the gauze on top, winding the bandage around and around his ribs until I was satisfied it would hold.

Aleksi nodded with relief when he checked over my work. "Better than I could have done." He heaved Lukas' arm over his shoulders. "Whenever you're ready, my prince."

I stilled, staring at Soren. Interesting.

Soren didn't hesitate. "Works for me." He surveyed the room, eyes snagging on the dead wolven in the corner, and snapped at Viv. "Can you help Aleksi carry him? We need to hurry if we want to make it to the stables before they realize what's happened here."

My best friend sheathed her sword and nodded, hustling to Lukas, whose face had gone pale beneath his deep tan. Though he was still conscious, he was fading fast. Or he was about to be sick. Either way, he needed help.

"Here, suck on this." I closed his fingers around a hunk of dried whipple bark. "It'll work for now. I'll get you some stronger painkillers on the road."

He grimaced as he accepted it. "You really are useless with a knife, aren't you?"

Relief, real, wonderful relief, flooded through me. "You're the one who got in my way. It's not my fault it sliced right through you."

He shook his head and shoved the bark between his teeth. It took a few seconds for the effects to take, and he relaxed, eyes clearer than they were before.

I measured his pulse, pleased when it throbbed hard and steady under my fingers. "He's stable. We can move." Aleksi and Viv wasted no time hoisting the shifter to the door. I shoved my supplies into my bag and looked up to find Soren's attention fixed firmly on me, brows drawn tight in puzzlement.

"What?" I asked, not sure what to take from the intensity of his scrutiny, the way it burned as it worked beneath my skin and boiled in my very blood. This was a man taking my measure not as a woman or as a friend, but as an ally. I'd injured his companion through my own carelessness, but I'd also mended that injury. Soren stared at me like everything in his viewpoint had changed. My skin tingled, but I held his unblinking, black gaze.

Then he returned to himself, pulling forward that blank mask he preferred. As Viv and Aleksi argued over the best way to move Lukas quickly, Soren knelt, reaching beneath the table, and withdrew the knife I'd dropped earlier. He frowned at the blood streaking the edge—Lukas' blood—and wiped it on the leg of his pants.

"We've got work to do, you and I," he said, flipping the weapon around and snagging it out of the air by the point. "A lot of work."

22

Forget You Ever Heard It

"They've got a thing for fires, don't they?" I said, heart beating hollowly in my ears as we watched the flames flickering high into the night sky, partially obscured by the buildings. The wolven had set fire to Jester's Hideaway after we'd abandoned it in search of the stables. What if it spread? The buildings in Dowhurst were packed so tightly together, I imagined one building igniting another until the whole row was up in flame. I voiced my concern, and Soren shook his head.

"Barriers are built between the buildings to prevent that from happening." He pulled a strap around the unconscious Lukas, binding him tightly against Viv's front, where they sat on a horse. I'd finished treating the blond drakken in the stables while Aleksi rounded up our mounts, his so-called sparrows keeping watch out front. Lukas fainted the moment my needle touched his skin. It was amazing how confidently he handled pointed arrows, but a tiny silver needle sent him into spasms.

Soren checked his work, continuing his thought. "There are also wagons filled with water and teams of people equipped to deal with situations just like this. It's hardly the first time Dowhurst has dealt with a building fire. Aleksi looks after his city. He won't let it fall."

I glanced again at the red and orange flames, the black smoke only visible as it obscured the stars. After this and Solas and the forest of whipple trees, I would never look at fires the same again.

Viv tested the tension of the rope binding her to Lukas and nodded shortly. Blood had dried in her hair, matting it around her face. Soren strode to his own mount, swinging into the saddle with ease. "The captain here is just mad his men screwed up. They will question a few people like they always do when things don't go their way, but they won't get anywhere. Everyone knows who Aleksi is. They realize he's the reason they're able to live the way they do. They won't betray him—not to Fior."

But what about Soren? Did they know who he was?

Just when I thought I'd gotten a grasp on my situation, everything went sideways. I'd started to believe he was an outlaw, a vigilante intent on justice, a man rising up in a moment of necessity. Then things like today happened. He barked orders and held himself like someone born knowing their importance. My eyes skittered over the harsh line of the shifter's spine where he sat in his saddle, watching water arc through the air, momentarily beating back the flames. In the shadow of the trees, he appeared positively vicious.

Prince.

Aleksi had called him that, the title slipping out in the heat of the moment. The lines of my tattoo were soft where I rubbed my thumb over it. It could be a code name. But it could also be his title. It fit him disturbingly well.

Soren and Lukas had told me little of the role they played within the Requiem, but there was no doubt in my mind they were critical to everything that happened. Not only were they in the room with the supposed leader of the entire resistance, but they managed a number of issues in another city, acting as a go-between for Archer and the leader of this particular territory.

However...

The image of that boy fleeing Aeros flitted across the backs of my eyes. It could have been Soren. The hair color. The brooding expression. But how could that be?

Besides, the royal family had been slaughtered. The wolven had made a point to splash that particular information far and wide. The king, queen, and both their sons killed in the ambush on Aeros.

I climbed into my own saddle, staring at the pommel. Soren couldn't be a prince. If he were, that nickname would be damning. And Aleksi didn't seem the sort to mess up casually like that. It had to be ironic. Or perhaps tactical. A title for his position within the Requiem... or maybe the role he was prepared to accept if they succeeded.

Unsettled by the direction of my thoughts, I glanced at the city one last time. The flames had died down. The worn leather of the reins slid through my palms as I shifted, seeking a softer spot in the saddle. Pip perched on my shoulder, tiny head swiveling as she surveyed the forest, the lack of tension in her body telling me everything I needed to know. Ghost hooted an all-clear, relaying a call from Grim too far away for my human ears to distinguish.

Soren glanced at him. "They do come in handy, don't they?"

"Yes." The barn owl had earned his weight in mice. If not for him, I would have died in that kitchen. "Where are we going? They can scout."

"I second that. Where are we going, shortie?" Viv added. Metal clinked as she adjusted her stirrups. "Or was Tell's confession not enough to prove our loyalty to your cause?"

I knew she'd been listening.

No way would she have reacted that quickly to the attackers on the roof if she'd been sleeping. I would never discount her abilities, but that reaction time had been too fast, even for drakken.

Soren clicked his tongue. "I don't recall asking you to join, pest."

Viv smirked, thumbing her finger at me. "Where she goes, I go. We're a package deal." Her grin widened. "It's not like I was looking forward to being around your morose self longer than I needed to be, either."

He swung his horse around. "Azmarin. We are headed for Azmarin."

I exchanged a look with Viv. Another town I'd heard of yet had never seen, one roughly a three days ride west of here, the only city in the country with a population that rivaled that of the capital, aided by the fertile soil and relatively mild weather of the southern part of our country.

Viv waved her hand dramatically. "Lead the way."

* * *

We rode most of the day, only stopping to water the horses and scarf down rations. Lukas stayed asleep for most of it, though I periodically checked his bandages, applying salve as needed. Soren pushed onward until night fell, and probably would have insisted we keep going until I told him my owls needed to hunt if he wanted them to have any energy for the next day. Conveniently, I left out the fact I was about to roll off my horse in utter exhaustion.

Viv found us a small clearing filled with soft grass not far from a clear, cool pond. Soren helped me get Lukas out of the saddle before scouting out some firewood. Only when he'd vanished into the shadows did Viv bend in two, gasping and lifting her legs as if her muscles were on fire. "Thank the gods he listened to you. If we went any farther, I was going to die. I'm pretty sure the insides of my thighs are bleeding."

"I'm happy to check it out if you like. Just give me a minute," I murmured, medical kit open beside me, fingers swiftly undoing Lukas' coat to get a better look at his wounds. By no small miracle, the stitches remained intact, and I pressed two fingers to my lips, heart, then the sky, sending silent thanks to Zos for her mercy. So consumed was I in my work, it took a few beats for the awkward silence to crash into me, and when it did, I found myself taken aback by the fiery blush sweeping across Viv's face and neck, the red so dark it nearly rivaled her hair.

"What's wrong?" I asked.

I swore her color deepened, and she coughed into her hand, avoiding my eyes. "Nothing." She scratched her head, ringlets of hair bunching under her fingertips. "Never mind." Another pause. "I'll tie up the horses."

Baffled, I could do nothing but watch her scamper away, head tucked to avoid looking at me as she snagged the reins of our horses. She moved quickly for someone who, a moment ago, complained about her legs hurting—

Oh.

Heat prickled my cheeks when I realized what I'd said. How that could have been interpreted.

A roll of gauze tumbled out of my kit and I tried to scoop it up, missing twice. When I finally gripped it and the tape, I buried myself in redressing Lukas' wounds. The drakken was lucky that both injuries were relatively minor, narrowly missing vital organs and tendons. The bandages would annoy him and his muscles would be sore, but depending on how quickly shifters healed, he would be right as snowmelt in a few turns.

A hand stilled mine when I went to lace up his shirt again. Soren dropped beside me, crouching entirely too close for comfort. He'd washed his hands, and pale scars stood out in vivid relief against his skin. "Will he be alright?"

"Yeah, he'll be fine." I tugged a vial out of my kit and held it up, shaking the white powder inside. "This is my strongest sedative. I've given him small doses throughout the day. The sleep is good for him. It will help him heal faster. I worried the movement of the horse would tug at his injuries, making them hurt worse. I wouldn't wish that pain on anyone."

Flint hit steel, and the scent of pine needles and smoke wafted over us.

Soren tugged Lukas' shirt back into place, eyeing my open bag and the patch peeking out from behind a sheaf of bandages. "You're always so willing to help."

"He's helped me as much as you have." I smoothed his sleeve, ignoring Soren's flinch at the reminder of a conversation we'd had in a different forest about similar circumstances. "Besides, I can't stand anyone being in pain, animal or human... or shifter."

"Thank you."

The confusion in Soren's eyes snared me. The question that had burned inside me all day inched up. I only had vague memories of my time in Eversturm Keep, but I remembered watching the royal family from their balcony when they greeted the people, recalled the intensity of their gazes in the throne room, so similar to his own.

I couldn't hold it back any longer. I needed to know.

"Aleksi called you 'prince.'" Soren's expression guttered, but I pressed on. "What did he mean by that?"

Soren lowered his face, the light from the crackling fire accentuating the sharp angles of his nose and jaw, reminding me of the blade-sharp scales that slid across his skin in drakken-form.

"I wouldn't press that question if I were you." Lukas' voice crackled with disuse, golden eyes slitted and bleary. He groaned as he sat upright, inserting himself between Soren and me with a pained grunt. He clutched at his side. "Forget you ever heard it."

"Nah. I don't think I will." Viv ran her knife over a white stone she must have scooped from the river, sharpening the edge. The shushing sound filled the clearing ominously. "See, I heard Aleksi say it, too, and I'm far too curious for my own good." She glanced over. The blankness of her expression rattled me to the core. "Especially after my best friend basically vomited up her life story."

Lukas' hand shot out. "That was her decision—"

"Enough." Soren pushed Lukas flat on his back, careful to avoid pressing on his injury, pinning him against the horse blanket I'd spread out. "You need to take it easy or you're going to reopen those stitches."

"You can't be serious."

"Oh, I definitely am."

The men's eyes met and held, a silent conversation flowing between them that reminded me so much of how Viv and I interacted that I crossed to her and sat down, drawing a clear line between us and the drakken. I needed her beside me for what I felt would be an intense discussion. She rested her knife on her thigh and reached for me, her fingers threading with mine propped on my knee.

Lukas huffed, head rolling to the side. "Fine. Put yourself in danger. See what I care."

Soren rolled his eyes. "They deserve to know." He gripped his wrist in front of his chest, shoulders bowed in a defensive posture I'd never witnessed from him before.

"You know me as Soren, but my full name is Tristan Soren Ahlgren." Blood pounded in my ears. Darkness bled hazily around the edges of my vision. "Lone survivor of the Ahlgren lineage and Crown Prince of Idilea. I'm a leader of the Requiem, fighting to restore my kingdom and protect my people from the horrors inflicted upon them."

266

23

Your Kingdom Dies Today

"So you *are* an *akren,* after all."

Soren's admission stunned me into silence, but Viv didn't know the meaning of the word. Her thumb stroked the side of my hand, offering her a form of stable comfort, and I didn't miss the angle of her knife on her leg, perfectly positioned to grab and defend if needed.

"Hardly." Lukas snorted, face flushed from blood loss and restless sleep. He rubbed his bandaged arm, eyeing Soren, who had yet to peel his eyes from my face. There was more here. More than just the announcement of his royal lineage, a confession that merited a death sentence if a wolven happened to overhear. His fists clenched at his side.

"Do you know when we knew the wolven were invading?" Soren—the *prince*—asked softly. "When we realized how feeble our military forces actually were?"

I shook my head. The day of the invasion had started out like any other for me: waking with the sun, attending to the birds, and when the bells tolled noon—they didn't stop.

"We were in the throne room holding open court." Soren

referenced the session held once a week when anyone in the kingdom, regardless of name or status, could enter Eversturm Keep and make requests of the royal family directly. "Those days always seemed to be the longest, and that day seemed even longer than normal, with more issues than we were used to. My parents agreed to see one more group before breaking for midday feast, and three farmers entered. My brother and I were on the balcony above. They wanted us to watch the proceedings so we would learn from their example."

Soren heaved out a long breath. "My father asked the men how he could serve them. They didn't answer for the longest time." His eyes hardened, and he broke away from me, staring off into a distance I couldn't see. "I remember some members of the court laughing awkwardly, thinking they were simple. Or lost. Then one man who stood a little farther forward than the others stepped opened his mouth and said, 'Your kingdom dies today.'"

I drew my legs up against my chest, stomach squirming, balling myself up defensively. I wanted to cover my ears, bury my head, forget about it all. But the time for hiding had long since passed.

"I'll never forget that statement." Soren's jaw ticked. "My parents never had a chance. He reached under his cloak, pulled out two axes and threw them before our soldiers intercepted him. My parents died immediately."

Lukas reached out as if to touch the prince, but pulled away with a sad sigh.

"One of the others had a crossbow—this clever little contraption he hid in his bag. He tried to shoot us, but my brother pushed me to the ground. I remember the arrow shattering on the wall where I stood." Soren shook his head, eyes glazed. Even Viv had gone still, enraptured by the prince's pain. "Everything blurs after that. Eero got us out—stars, my brother always seemed so much older than me when we were only three years apart." A breath shuddered from him. "He knew we needed to get to safety and blockaded us into the chambers behind the throne room before pulling me into a closet. He tried to block out the screams by putting his hands over my ears, but I could still hear them."

A log shifted in the fire and broke in two, showering the dirt with orange embers.

"I don't know how long we were in there. After what felt like forever, we heard this rapping sound, like tapping on the stones. Eero recognized the signal from the castle guard that we were taught in our cribs." Soren rapped his knuckles three times on his sheath, paused for three beats, and knocked twice more. "He pulled us out of the closet at the same time this woman entered. She wore full armor and hefted a sword as big as I was." He motioned vaguely. "I remember her from watching the guards train. She was always so fierce.

"She saw us, pulled us close, and kept telling us she was glad we were alright. I remember her telling Eero how smart he was for hiding and blocking the route." Soren sucked in a long breath. "She said she and her men had rallied. She told us it was wolven who'd attacked, but we were gaining back the ground. I could see how scared she was, but she pretended it didn't matter and said she wanted to get us out of there as a matter of safety. A worst case scenario."

Soren gritted his teeth and jammed a stick into the fire. Flames sputtered around the green wood. "Eero kept protesting. He didn't want to go, he didn't understand why. But she told him she had a little girl our age and she would do anything she could to protect her—that was why she needed to save us. Not because we were princes, but because she cared for us." He blinked rapidly, face pinched. "Something crashed outside. The wolven were coming. I realize it now. She lied. Our forces weren't gaining ground. Our guards were dying. They were doing everything in their power to save the last of the royal family. Giving their lives in place of ours." His breathing quickened. "And despite their sacrifices, the wolven *still* almost found us."

A plume of dust rose when his fist crashed into the earth.

Lukas cleared his throat and arched his brow, mutely asking Soren a question. The prince shook his head in response. "The woman pushed us to the secret exit. She told us as long as we followed it straight down, we would end up near the stables where we could escape."

His breath shuddered. His eyes met mine and dread gushed through me, cold and oily. "Eero asked her her name. I think he knew then, because he always did, what was going to happen. I've never seen anyone in my life look so proud, even when beaten. She said her name was Captain Mia Falk, and she would give her life to save us."

I went numb.

I couldn't feel my face. My hands. My vision flashed black.

Viv's arm came up around me, tugging me against her, her face pressed against my hair, body shaking with emotion, but I couldn't look away from Soren. Couldn't break the spell he'd cast over me.

"Something about you, Telleree, has called to me—ever since I saw you standing in the smoking remains of your home. You, your story—the mystery of your life..." His face had gone gray, bloodless. "You said your last name was Falk when we met. I wondered if maybe you were her child, but that felt like too large a coincidence. But I wasn't sure, so I kept waiting to see. And then last night you shared the story of your mother leaving and you showed us the patch... and I knew. I knew you were that girl."

I nodded dumbly, too lost within myself to do any more.

Falk wasn't an uncommon surname. I could see why he wouldn't want to put those pieces together without further proof.

He rose, rounded the fire, and crouched before me. For the first time, he seemed uncertain about how to proceed. "The door splintered when she shoved us down the hole. I don't know what happened after that."

But he did. We both did.

Anyone who survived the massacre at Eversturm Keep was executed in the following days.

Someone protecting the princes? Helping them escape?

They would have died on the spot.

My mother had died saving the only survivors of the royal family: one of them the man who stood before me now, who'd saved my life more times than I could count. My mother had sacrificed her future so he could live his, and he had, unknowingly, rescued me in return.

She'd fulfilled her duties. She'd stood up for what she knew was right and had done everything in her power to see it through to fruition. Just like I wanted to do with my life—living in her legacy, emulating her selfless actions.

Tears dripped from my chin, splattering on my hands gripping my knees. Viv was muttering nonsensical words into my hair, apologies that weren't hers to give, clutching me as if she were afraid I might disintegrate in her arms.

If the tunnel let out near the stables...

I took Soren's hand. It shook as hard as mine.

"I saw you. That day. You and Eero and Lukas." The golden drakken had moved, now hovering against Soren's back. "My father and I were escaping. We were following the group of other survivors and he threw me over his shoulder because I couldn't keep up. I saw you rush around the corner and into the stables. You looked right at me." I squeezed his hand so tightly I worried I might break bones.

271

"And you reached for me. But your... brother pulled you inside."

Lukas seemed as stunned as Soren.

All these intersecting lines, our lives interwoven in so many ways.

And Soren said he didn't believe in the gods.

"It's like we were meant to find one another," Viv whispered, wiping her wet eyes. "All of us. My mother barely knew Tell's father, but he was the first person she ran to when she was trying to escape the chaos of the courtyard. She told me she felt like he would know what to do, that he was a man on a mission, with a plan."

"I barely knew Soren," Lukas murmured. "I recognized him as the prince because I worked with my father in the stables, but I didn't really know who he was. I just dragged them inside because my father told me to keep an eye out, to bring them in when I saw them. I guess the captain told him what was going on beforehand."

The fire popped, making me jump.

So many intersecting lives.

It couldn't be a coincidence.

My eyes found the moon, the curved crescent of the waning circle of light, and I murmured a prayer to Zos. Day by day, conversation by conversation, my path was becoming clearer. I trusted my dark goddess to lead the way.

24

Defend Yourself

"Are we supposed to call you 'Prince' now?" I eyed the tip of the dagger Soren pointed at me, nerves jangling at facing the point of the weapon and standing so close to the drakken who I'd studiously avoided during our morning ride.

"Nah. *Your Highness* has a better ring to it," Viv crowed. She sat cross-legged beside Lukas. Fresh, white bandages peeked out from the collar of his shirt, evidence of my afternoon's work. Those injuries would have taken me or Viv weeks to recover from, but Lukas had almost fully healed in two days. "But *akren* has such a... *ring* to it." She wrinkled her nose. "I'll stick with that."

"How about you call me Soren?" The drakken prince flipped the dagger around, catching the blade with two fingers and presenting it to me with a nudge. It was the knife he'd handed me at Jester's Hideaway, the one he stopped to grab before we made our hasty exit. "Neither of you grasp the idea of a *secret identity* very well, do you?"

Lukas chuckled as he mended a pair of tears in his cloak.

Viv rested her head in her hand, cupping her cheek. "Secrets? Tell, we don't know anything about secrets, do we?"

"Not a thing." I thrust the knife in front of me as if brandishing it at someone. Soren snorted at my stance.

This morning, I'd woken to the sounds of Viv and Soren sparring and had watched the two masters of sword craft go all out, hacking and slashing with a lightness and grace I'd never seen before. They threw taunts as frequently as they threw critiques, finding common ground despite their differences. They'd only stopped when sweat soaked through their shirts and dripped from their noses.

I recognized Viv's frustration, knew she needed the physical activity to settle the emotion dragged out of her by Soren's confession. I wondered if the prince also preferred physical challenges to mental ones.

When he strode past my bedroll on the way to wash up, he'd told me that he would work with me later, insisting I learn how to use a weapon, *any* weapon, to defend myself. He made it sound like he was being considerate, but I got the feeling he was pissed I'd cut Lukas. When I caught Viv's eye on her way to wash up, her thoughtful expression morphed into childlike glee.

Soren didn't realize how hopeless I was.

I nearly dropped the knife when Soren stomped toward me, brow furrowed. "You're holding the knife like it's a viper trying to sink its fangs into you." He rounded me and I held almost painfully still. "And your stance—it's wrong. All wrong. Here. Let me show you."

I jerked again when his knee pressed against the inside of mine, forcing my legs farther apart. He used his feet to tap mine into place, stopping only when he was satisfied. His arms came around me, shifting my back until it curved against his front, and his arms wrapped around mine, bending my elbows closer to my sides, the knife angled before me. "How does that feel?"

My throat struggled around the pellet blocking it. Tiny owlets fluttered in my chest, leaping and bouncing with frenzied energy. His heat surrounded me like an intoxicating cloud of burned lemon.

I understood the point of this, realized how he'd manipulated my form into a smaller target, a human weapon capable of standing her ground. But a much bigger part of me couldn't get past how close we stood, how firm his muscles felt through his shirt, wondered what his lips felt like brushing across my ears, down my neck...

"Fine," I squeaked, holding my breath, seeking a reprieve. I repeated my insistence. "Just fine."

"Good." Soren's chin rested on my shoulder, his hands firmly wrapped around the backs of mine, holding the knife in place as he angled it in a few directions. Warm puffs of air brushed my neck as he explained his movements.

I heard none of it through the blood rushing through my head, the dizziness that swirled with every touch of our bodies. I'd never been this close to anyone before, except for Viv. And she...

Her smirk held an edge. Sharp and dangerous, like the viper Soren had mentioned. Her eyes darted from my burning face to the prince's grip on my hand. Her lips thinned, whitening at the crease.

Feathers fluttered through me, quelling the leaping sensation.

It had been like this since I'd saved her.

Well.

Since she'd been taken.

This confusing twist of energy that came when I thought about her, how I obsessed over her safety and protection even though she'd always been the one protecting me was new. And then there were the sparks. The little jolts of energy when she threw her arm around me or the lick of flames in my belly that surged when we casually touched.

It hadn't been like this before.

The sensation of free-falling off the Spear had never struck me when Viv was around. Until now, I'd assumed I was alone in experiencing this change. I'd chalked the strangeness of my emotions up to knowing what it might be like to lose her.

But that press of her red lips, the narrowing of her emerald eyes. Maybe she experienced it, too.

"Are you paying attention?" Soren scolded.

"Y-yes." I shook myself, hunching inwardly. "All ears over here."

I needed to learn this. We weren't in the Owl Wood anymore. I couldn't keep relying on everyone to save me. For once, I wanted to know what it was like to protect those I cared about. The fluttery sensations disintegrated when I met Viv's gaze again.

I wanted to know what it was like to save *her*.

"Alright." He didn't sound convinced, but the prince moved around to my front, drawing a second dagger that matched mine in every way except the handle was black oak instead of white. "Defend yourself against me. I'll go slow so you can learn the rhythm."

I nodded and set my shoulders, folding into the stance he'd shown me as if I'd been liquefied and poured into a mold. How strange. I'd never felt that kind of assurance before. Inhaling deeply, I waited for him to strike. When he did, I moved, shocking myself when I caught the blade trusting toward my heart. Soren's brows lifted. Triumph flared, sparking and bubbling in the best of ways. Viv whooped, clapping her hands in approval. Even Lukas managed a smile.

"Again."

That was the one and only time I blocked the drakken.

Two hours later, we called it quits when my lack of coordination became woefully obvious. If Soren had meant his attacks, I would have died at least a hundred times over.

"Come now, you're not a failure." Viv snagged my braid and unraveled the end, brushing it over her fingertips. Most of it had come undone during training. "Though I admit, fat flurryfoxes would look less awkward holding a knife than you."

I grumbled something unkind into my water flask, but allowed her to continue redoing my hair.

Soren mopped at his face with his sleeve. "We'll try again tomorrow. The repetition will do you good. We get soldiers like you all the time, and we'll whip you into shape, too."

Lukas dragged his cloak over his shoulders, barely wincing at the way his body twisted to accommodate the move. "I think you are being overly optimistic. Soldiers as bad as she is are stuck with grunt work and you know it."

Soren's lack of response spoke volumes.

I chomped into a hunk of jerky, the saltiness soaking my tongue matching my mood perfectly. I really was a failure at this whole fighting thing, wasn't I? Why was I so bad at this? It couldn't be natural to be this uncoordinated. I drew my arms over my chest, stewing. Pip and Grim perched on a tree, heads bobbing and twisting as they listened for enemies. They were intent now, but I'd heard their warbling laughter while I'd sparred with Soren.

Chagrined, I shoved the rest of the meat into my mouth and licked my fingers clean. Across the plain, a bump emerged on the horizon, something gray and blocky. I hadn't noticed it before, but it stood out against the blue of the sky, as out of place here as I was with a knife.

"What's that?" I asked, pointing.

Lukas shaded his eyes against the sun. He hummed, paper rustling as he fiddled with his maps. Holding one up, he glanced between it and the blocky mass. He scratched his nose like he had a habit of doing when presented with a problem.

"We are south of the drakkentorre mines." He pointed at the x's on his map. Lukas never touched the page except with a pen, and warned me against doing so, lest I smear the decades-old ink or some nonsense. "Soren wanted us to avoid them, since patrol units monitor them, despite them being blown to shit." Soldiers from

Fior blew up the drakkentorre mines at the same time they attacked the royal family, effectively cutting untested drakken off from the supply of fresh stone.

Lukas brushed away a fly buzzing around his head. "We have snuck in and secured some stones to see if any untested shifters are among the soldiers, but it is about as welcoming as the tundras of sorrow in rezar."

I consulted the map. "We're too far north for it to be Aeros, right? We would have seen the lake by now." Aeros was built beside a massive body of freshwater dubbed Storm Lake. It fed much of the rich farmland around these parts.

Lukas chewed on his lip. Viv and Soren joined us, the reins of our horses in hand.

"If I had to guess, I would say it is one of our temples," Lukas concluded.

Tingles rushed down my arms, a cascading sensation that curled into my soul. I peered at the mass of stone again, squinting, mouth dry. "Which temple?"

He scratched an itch on his injured arm. "A few are clustered in that vicinity. Qet. Fen. A few others."

"I want to go."

Urgency ripped through me in a riptide, exhilaration riding the bumpy waves of excitement. Every muscle felt tight with anxiety, no, *eagerness.* So many thoughts rushed through my head, they blurred into one idea: I had to see what was there. Even when tracking the wolven who'd taken Viv and my family, I hadn't felt this *alive.*

"It will cost us about a day." Lukas consulted Soren, who dipped his head. "Archer wanted us back by the end of the week."

Viv tapped a knuckle against the back of my hand, following my gaze. "What'cha thinking?"

"I don't know." My hand curled against my chest, over the rabbit thump of my heart pushing blood straight to my head. Colors had never seemed so bright, the chill in the air so crisp. "I feel like I'm on the precipice of a cliff and I need to fall."

I felt her eyes burning holes in my cheek. "I'll go with you."

"We'll all go." Soren swung onto the back of his horse.

Lukas stared at him, jaw gaping. "But Archer—"

"It's been seventeen years. Archer can wait one more day." He dug his knees into the sides of his horse, who whinnied, directing her toward the temple. "I'm curious, too."

Viv slapped my back zealously. "An adventure within an adventure. How exciting."

Exciting was one word for it.

I shoved my foot in the stirrup and hoisted myself up.

So was trepidation.

25

So It Shall Be

The marble pillar proclaiming the name of the temple lay on its side, the lower half reduced to little more than off-white pebbles stained by time and weather. The wild had reclaimed this territory, and vines snared over the upper half of the rock, obscuring the image chiseled into the stone. With a grunt, Lukas swung from his horse and scrubbed at the surface, using his knife to hack away the worst of the growth.

Before he spoke, I knew what it would read.

"Zos."

I felt all three of my friends shift their attention to me, but I'd already nudged my mare forward, guiding her down the overgrown path. When these temples were run by priests and priestesses, the hip-high walls and tiled walkway would have been scrubbed to a bright polish. Now the black marble walls crumbled, nearly obscured by briarbushes. The tiles and their fine leafy patterns of reds and blues and greens were cracked, jagged edges poking through the rot of dead leaves and moldy branches.

However, nothing compared to the monument erected before me. Easily five stories high, a pair of obsidian pillars held up the massive arch of the open door. Its towering windows had long-since shattered, the jagged remnants of the red glass lining the edges of the frames were the only evidence of their former glory. The roof was domed, the coppery curve tinged green in patchy, ugly spots. I swung from the saddle outside the arch and tied my mare to one of dozens of hooks lining a long pole hung horizontally against the wall. It would have been used for just this purpose in the past, allowing travelers to stop and say their prayers.

Glass crunched underfoot, accentuating the eerie silence of the forest, as if the insects and animals recognized the atrocity that had been committed here and hesitated to encroach upon the sacred land. My friends joined me a moment later, Viv leading the way. She ran her hand along the wall, tracing the cracked designs of dragons chiseled into it.

"It's so sad," she murmured. "I feel the weight pressing down on me."

Lukas scooped glass into his hands, allowing it to sift through his fingers. "This is what all the temples look like. The soldiers murdered the priests and destroyed the relics in the days after the invasion. Qet's is the worst. I've seen it—if you can call a pile of rubble a temple."

Fior knew what our gods meant to us, how the dragons had gifted our people with their powers and guided our decisions. By desecrating these sacred places and killing those who served our deities, they destroyed our cultural identities, stripped us of our touchstones. Decimated our self-worth. It made sense they fixated on Qet. The god of light and wisdom had paved the way for our way of life. What he represented, the Fiorian people would have resented.

I hovered at the entrance and felt Soren at my back, hand on the pommel of his sword. He wanted to enter first, and though I did nothing to bar his way, I felt I held him back. He recognized what a monumental moment this was for me: to see the temple of the goddess I revered so mightily.

Darkness engulfed us as we stepped inside, my heart thudding hollowly in my breast. If Viv had found the outside of the temple sad, what the soldiers had done here was downright devastating. Tables and chairs were smashed, the wood reduced to little more than splinters. Pottery dating back hundreds if not thousands of years that would have depicted the various miracles performed by Zos and her followers lay shattered on the ground, a handle here and a chunk of rim there were the only evidence of what the works of art used to look like.

The floor used to be one massive chunk of obsidian carved flat by the patient hands of skilled artisans. Cracks now spidered through the center as if a massive weight had been dropped upon it. It didn't take me long to find the source. The marble head of Zos, blank eyes wide, flowing hair pulled back in a simple plait, rested on its cheek, severed from her body. Tears stung my eyes as I rested a reverent hand on the corner of her lips, the rest of her face too high for me to reach without help.

Shaking off the sense of ugliness and defeat, I pushed farther into the room, vaguely aware of Viv and Lukas and Soren fanning out, murmuring to one another when they found something of note. At the back of the temple, positioned square beneath another massive arch carved into the back wall, stood the statue of Zos herself, her leather armor and scarred cloak pooling around her feet. A sword hung from her hip and a series of vines representing her four deadly poisons wrapped around a bandolier strapped across her chest. One elegant shoulder crumbled, the barn owl depicted as her otherworldly companion sawed from his perch. A mass of rock at the statue's armored boots and the subtle arches of what would have been feathers spoke of what happened.

Pip landed on my shoulder, humming to herself uneasily.

I pressed my hands together, palms flat, thumbs resting against my lips. Silent tears trickled down my cheeks as I stared up at the goddess. The weight of the evil inflicted upon this place squeezed me so tightly I thought my ribs might crack.

"I'm sorry, Tell." Viv approached first, boots crunching on the pebbles. "I'm so sorry."

I shook my head, shrugging her hand off my shoulder, and knelt, shins flat against the floor, barely feeling the bite of broken rock, feathered cloak spilling around me, overcome by grief. By despair. I bent my head over my clasped hands.

I prayed every day.

Every single day when I rose and before I fell asleep. Rarely did I speak out loud, preferring to keep my conversations between me and the goddess who guided my way. Today I set that reservation aside, feeling more connected to the goddess than ever before.

"Oh Zos, oh holy Zos. How I cry for thee."

The goddess' most sacred prayer, a prayer reserved for the darkest of days, spun outward from me in ribbons of gold and black. Every word rang clear, my despair on full display. I'd never felt words more powerfully than in this moment. Not when I'd fallen from the cliff and had prayed for a miracle. Not when I'd laid my father and my people to rest. Not ever.

"And so it shall be."

The hairs on my neck prickled at the echo in the room, the feminine voice lifting with mine.

I opened my eyes. A soft glow reflected off the floor, one that had nothing to do with the setting sun. Slowly, I lifted my head, the light brightening with every incremental inch, until I met the blank eyes of the woman standing before me, not three paces away, a magnificent barn owl perched on her shoulder.

"Zos."

26

How Fascinating

The goddess smirked, the curling of her lips as sensual as it was dangerous. She stroked the head of her radiant owl, which preened under her affection. "Telleree Falk."

Knock me over and steal my soul. "You know who I am?"

I couldn't look away from her luminescence: the pristine smoothness of her supple skin, the curve of her cheek, the silvery details of the poisonous plants imprinted in her skin. Even the grace with which she moved was effortless.

"But of course." She pressed two fingers to her lips, then flourished her arm in a mocking motion. "The child driven from her home. The girl tucked away in the mountains. The unskilled swordsman and uncoordinated traveler. My most avid admirer, and the one who reaches out to me for every one of her whims. Telleree Falk of Solas. How could I not know who you were?"

The phosphorescence of my awe soured, reminding me where I was. I glanced to my right where the goddess had frozen Viv in place, her hand pressed to her heart as she bent her head in subjugation. If I were to look at Soren and Lukas, I had no doubt they would be locked in time as well.

I'd never heard of the Goddess of Vengeance and Death appearing before anyone outside of the battlefield, and she wouldn't have risen from her home in rezar today without reason. Unimpressed with me though she claimed to be, she was still *here* in front of *me*. And it seemed she intended to keep whatever she was about to reveal between the two of us.

Pip chirped her disapproval.

Wings flared and Zos' owl rose into the air, soaring to perch on the deity's severed head. The goddess eyed her severed limb with distaste and returned her eerie focus to me. I fought to conceal my shiver, hand cradling Pip's tiny body against my neck. She didn't have pupils or irises, just blank white spaces where eyes should have been.

"Your fixation is impressive." She withdrew a roll of parchment from a pouch at her hip and made a show of unfurling it, fingers trailing down the page. I bit back a smirk, imagining Lukas swatting at her for touching the ink. The hint of humor vaporized when Zos read, "'Zos, protect me in my sleep. I hear the wolves howling outside.'"

Every ligament in my body went taut, recognizing words I'd uttered as a child, not five years of age. It was our first winter in the Copper Mountains and we had only begun building the cabins of Solas. That winter was hard and unrelenting. Even the mighty etho wolves had difficulty tracking down food, and that drove them to encroach on the perimeter of our camp, like the ghosts for which they were named. In terror, I'd buried myself beneath my thin blanket under the thinner walls of our tent, praying to not be eaten.

"'Zos, I fear the grassweepers will destroy our crops. Their numbers are too many to keep away. Please tell me what to do.'" The goddess' braid slid over her shoulder when she turned her head, lips pursed in amusement. "You are aware the simpering fool who is my sister is the guardian of the harvest, correct? I'm not sure whether to be flattered you think me capable of accomplishing feats assigned to Lo... or to think you painfully foolish."

The priests who used to run this temple probably would have advised me against it, but I stood, needing to face her on my own two feet. The all-encompassing rage that engulfed me in the woods touched me again now, but I tamped it down. Barely. "You are the goddess of death and darkness. Crops can die as much as any other living thing, so it seems only natural to believe they fall under your jurisdiction, too."

Zos' grin widened, her halo of golden light bouncing off her straight, even teeth. "So it does, clever child."

Through her figure I could make out the lines of the bricks in the wall, proving that while she was here, she wasn't quite whole.

The goddess uncurled the parchment again, revealing another inch of spidery text. "'Zos, Viveca is trying so hard to master her new knives, but she cries herself to sleep every night. Would you show her the way to success?'"

The parchment rolled back with a snap, and Zos smacked it against her palm. My blood turned to ice. "Another misappropriated prayer—though I must say of all my siblings, Cas and I share similar temperaments, so I can see how you would be confused."

She strode forward, cloak sweeping regally behind her. Her boots made no sound. The goddess peered down her nose at Viv, whom she towered over by a good foot and a half. "Is this Viveca? The girl you always seek to protect?" Zos turned to examine the other side of Viv's face. "Shall I bless her today? A sign of my endearment?"

I moved without thinking. "Wait, please."

She couldn't touch Viv. I felt in the depths of my soul something very bad would happen if Zos were to make contact. Forgetting the danger she presented, I put my hand on Zos' arm to stay her movement. Golden light flared. My fingers burned, and I screamed, falling back, tripping over my feet as the goddess' attention snapped back to me. My skin blistered and bubbled where the light touched it. I cradled it against my chest, blood filling my mouth as I bit my cheek, holding back another cry of pain.

"You dare to touch me, human?" She bent so low the heat of her light burned against my face. The earth vibrated. The scent of scorched metal overpowering. "You overstep."

Hurriedly, I ducked my head, dropping to my knees, as much in subjugation as to protect myself from further harm. My tongue easily wrapped around the ancient language of the prayers I'd been taught, molding the outdated words to my needs. "My apologies, dark queen. I forgot myself in my eagerness to see you. I merely wish to know what you seek from me."

Rocks clattered and the walls swayed. I felt like I might shake apart. Then all went still. The searing heat vanished as the goddess returned to her dais. "Very well. You are young, and I'm aware of your foolishness. I shall forgive you but this once."

Stung, I kept my mouth shut, peering at her through my lashes. She had her back to me, head tilted toward the owl perched in the rafters.

"Humans lead such trivial lives, toiling away for the few years they are granted, mostly resenting and regretting their accomplishments, and then they die. It's all rather tedious. Though there are a few who make observing more interesting." Zos braced her hand on her sword, thumb tracing the stone on the hilt. I couldn't tell what color it was intended to be, since she only radiated gold and white. "You, dear child, have become interesting."

She said it like it was a good thing, but in my bones I knew it to be bad. Very bad.

Those who caught the interest of the gods tended to live very short, rather tragic lives.

I dared to lift my head, bloody palm pressed to my shirt, breathing shallowly, ignoring the way the gravel bit into my kneecaps.

"It was the fall from the cliff. It almost seemed like you'd accepted it. Until you didn't." Zos smoothed a nonexistent wrinkle in her tunic. "You prayed. You were in an impossible situation, faced with an ugly end, yet you had the presence of mind to pray. Not for yourself, but for those you held dear, those you tried to protect, even though you are terrible at such a thing."

Her lips thinned. "And it seems you saved yourself somehow. I did not send the prince to save you, nor did any of my other siblings, to the best of my knowledge. That was purely happenstance, and completely intriguing."

She crossed her arms over her chest. "How did you do it?"

My mind went blank. Completely, utterly blank. How had I conjured a drakken out of thin air? Was luck truly conditional on divine intervention? If that was the case, how was I supposed to understand what had caused the occurrence to happen otherwise?

"I don't know," I replied honestly.

Zos took a step forward. "I demand an answer."

"My dark queen, I'm sorry, but I don't have one." My palm screamed, blisters popping, the raw muscle underneath scraping against my callouses as I brought my hands together. "I have turned to you for my guidance all my life. I don't know what I could have done to change the circumstances of my life."

Her expression turned thunderous, and she took two more steps forward. My insides writhed, awaiting the next blast of heat, when Grim swooped down, talons extended, slashing at the goddess before sweeping out of the way. Pip shot forward as well, darting for Zos' eyes, chiding her irritations with the being. Zos swatted the smaller bird away and stared at Pip in amazement when she alighted on my shoulder once more, still chittering away. Ghost hooted from the rafters, Zos' shock evident on her face as she listened to them in a language I, for the first time in my life, couldn't comprehend.

"I think I understand." Zos smoothed a hand down her jawline. "It seems we are both being tested."

She stepped into the space between her statue's boots, cloak curling around her arms. "Guardian of the Owls is what they call you, girl. They dare to defy their creator coming to your defense." Her head tilted to the side. "How fascinating."

I stroked Pip's back with my good hand, dazed. I was what?

"It seems the curiosity that is you has more facets than I realized." For as calm as she appeared, Zos sounded absolutely furious. Even from several paces away, the heat she threw off was incredible. I cradled my hand to my chest, the heat causing it to palpitate again, trying to protect it as best I could. "I shall enjoy watching what happens to you next, Telleree Falk, Guardian of the Owls."

Her form faded.

"Wait," I called out, hurrying to my feet. "Please. Your kingdom is suffering, its people are dying. How can we save them? What can we do to drive out the Fiorian plague?"

The goddess paused. "If you need to ask me that, then you aren't ready. However, I will grant you this: when you understand your heart's conviction, and once you embrace it with all you are, the aid you seek will come in your darkest of moments."

Then she and her owl were gone.

Only the burn mark on my hand and arm, the skin seared from my skin, was evidence that she'd ever been there to begin with.

I stared at the spot where she'd stood, where the most confusing conversation of my life had taken place, not understanding what to make of it.

Footsteps pounded from across the room.

"What happened?" Lukas asked, as my legs folded beneath me. I saw no more.

27

Hate-filled Glare

Lukas made me recount what happened inside the temple three times before he was satisfied.

"The first known contact with the gods in more than fifty years," he exclaimed over his scribbling pen beside the light of the fire. "It was you who saw her, and me who gets to record it for the future. Astounding. The odds have to be…" His pen paused, and he mouthed a few numbers, eyes darting back and forth. He shook his head. "I can't even think."

I certainly could, though my thoughts were anything but pleasant. The goddess I'd worshiped my entire life had appeared before me, nothing like I imagined. In my childhood dreams, I'd pictured a woman dripping in the blood of her enemies, sword flung out to her side, a triumphant yet kind smile on her face for those who followed her. That image morphed the older I got into someone quieter and more vindictive.

In all my musings, I'd never imagined her mockery. It was my father who'd told me to find comfort in her embrace, to direct my prayers to her every night and every morning, promising they would reach her ears. Yes, they had reached her, but I hadn't expected her to throw them back in my face. Not only that, but she made it clear she hadn't been watching out for me this whole time—instead using my prayers as a means of entertainment.

Nausea swirled like a whirlpool in my stomach, and it was all I could do to keep eveningmeal down. Zos hadn't helped my father flee Aeros, and neither had she saved me from falling off the cliff.

Viv snipped the end of the white bandage and tucked it carefully into the folds near my elbow. I squeezed my fingers. The gauze around them felt awkward, but necessary. Fortunately, I favored my right hand or I would be in serious trouble. "I couldn't have wrapped it better myself," I assured her, hating the little furrows etched between her brows.

I'd woken not long ago, dazed by the encounter, my arm crying out in pain, lying flat on my back, surrounded by trees and my three companions. Lukas had given me a few drops of my pain relief medication, and when I'd settled down, I told them what had happened.

Viv had taken me at my word that I'd encountered the goddess the first time I relayed to them what had happened. Lukas wasn't convinced until he'd pored over my hand, demanding more answers from me upon the second retelling. And Soren—the man leaned back on his hands on the other side of the crackling fire, peering up at the stars. He hadn't said what he thought of my encounter, but I could sense his disbelief all the same. I was almost afraid to ask how he explained away my injury.

I stroked my thumb over Pip's head, cradling her in my lap against my injured arm. Viv sat beside me, occasionally brushing my arm or leg as if to reassure herself I was still alive. Still in one piece.

Exhaustion sank so deep into my bones, I wasn't sure it would ever subside.

Keeping my gaze fixed on the bandages, I exposed one of the raw nerves in my mind and asked the group, "What do you think she meant when she said she didn't send Soren to save me?"

The scratching of Lukas' pen stopped.

"Is luck truly independent of the gods?" I continued, staring into the depths of the fire, the rotating heating and cooling of the crimson coals in its center.

Lukas cracked his knuckles. "She is messing with your head. The gods are like this—cruel and manipulative. To think the seven of them have time to meddle with the affairs of all humans? To hand out all instances of luck? It is a gross overestimation of their abilities. Things happen because they are meant to happen, nothing more or less."

Though Soren and I often butted heads over issues of faith, Lukas had spoken little of his thoughts regarding religious matters. Now he hinted at belief in fate. Fascinating for a man intent on breaking down the facets of the world and examining each side for himself.

If fate was real, then my earlier suppositions were correct. The drakken and I *were* meant to meet again. The dead space where my heart used to beat felt a little less dark.

"It could have been another god, too," Viv argued, pulling her hair back in a pair of buns at the nape of her neck. "Just because you only pray to Zos doesn't mean she's the only one listening. Qet or Fen could have intervened."

"Why would they, though?" Lukas tapped his pen to the underside of his chin. "They have been very quiet for the past seventeen years, and now they decide to step forward?"

Viv snorted. "Just because Fior wants us to forget about them doesn't mean they're forgotten. For fuck's sake, you guys ripped off Zos' symbol to create your rune, and clearly she's doing just fine. I think they've been biding their time, waiting for the right moment."

"No." Soren shook his head, face bowed, bangs obscuring his eyes.

"I refuse to believe gods would let their people suffer—let them die—just so they could enact some grand scheme that somehow revolves around the three of us. That would be cruel." Disgust twisted his features. "No, beyond cruel. It would be abhorrent."

He spat on the ground and I felt it like a strike to the face. "The gods aren't listening because they aren't there. They don't influence luck or fortune or punish the wrongdoers. They simply don't exist. What happens to us is a result of our own actions."

I shot to my feet, thrusting out my arm in his direction, gritting my teeth at the heat of the fire. A hive of bees buzzed inside me. "Then how do you explain this, Soren? If the gods don't exist, then how did I get this burn? Do you think I just made it all up?"

He lifted his chin. "I think you triggered a trap left by the wolven. You were alone up there at the dais and must have hit something you didn't mean to. That burned you and you fainted from the pain." His eyes narrowed. "Your dreams took care of the rest."

"You—you seriously—of all the—you—" I fumbled with words, incapable of thinking straight, the whirring growing louder in my ears. He thought I dreamed that entire encounter? That I'd hurt myself out of foolishness, and now tried to save face by pretending I'd met one of the Seven? I brought my good arm around my chest like a bar. "I can't believe you are so close-minded that you refuse to entertain even the *idea* of other-worldliness."

He rose, dusting dirt off his hands. "I am firmly rooted in the reality of the situation in which we exist. My parents, my people, everyone around me believed in the gods, and where were they in our darkest time? Where were our so-called protectors, huh?" His eyes glittered in the light of the fire. "Nowhere. They didn't lift a finger. I don't need more proof than that of the lack of their existence. And if they do exist, they aren't worthy of our prayers because they're callous and unkind."

Lukas shifted uneasily between us. "Hey now, Sor—"

"I need to take a walk," Soren spat out. "If I don't, I'll stab something."

By something, he meant me.

The drakken prince spun on his heel, motions jerky, and left me in a haze of black clouding my thoughts. He could think whatever he chose to think. By no means was he required to believe in the dragons who had created our country, given him his very powers. But for him to be this resistant to amending his view of the world—

I threw myself on my blanket, legs lifted, foot tapping the ground. Between Soren's disbelief and the draining, humiliating experience of meeting the goddess I revered, I didn't know how many more hits I could take emotionally.

"Soren is... complicated." Lukas closed his book, pen folded between the pages, weighing his thoughts. "He was not always this close-minded, but you have to understand, the things he has seen, the people he has lost, the experiences he has had—they have changed him." He ran a finger down the spine of the ledger, tracing the bumps of the binding. "I think part of him wants to believe there are beings watching over us, protecting us, but I don't think he will allow himself the luxury of entertaining such fantasies."

"Whatever you say." The words tasted like rot. There was no doubt in my mind he'd gone through a lot of shit, that he'd experienced more pain than any shifter or human should ever go through. We all had. But if he wanted to be a leader of his people someday, I hoped he would reassess his absolutist way of thinking, assuming it transferred to more than just his thoughts on religion.

Then there was Zos.

My injured hand curled in a light fist in front of my stomach, where that rage still burned. It was as if something had permanently changed in my makeup, temper I'd never known before had finally awoken, teeth bared and nostrils flaring, demanding retribution.

"Tell." Viv cupped my shoulder, thumb rubbing circles into my shirt. I allowed her to comfort me, her touch banking those embers, though not quite extinguishing them. "Who cares what he thinks? He's just another person. You've never cared what other people think before." She smiled hopefully, those furrows still in place. "Wasn't it you who told me people can think what they want to think, as long as your resolve is strong, that's all that matters?"

I had said that, an echo of something my mother used to say when I misbehaved. My father was also fond of the saying, insisting we were in control of our actions and reactions.

"Yes," I gritted out, finally feeling the ugly, empty feeling melt away. "That's right."

Viv squeezed my thigh. "As for Zos, she could have been lying. Have you considered that? Maybe she's testing you and your beliefs. Lukas is right, the gods are manipulative. Don't let her get to you." The fire washed out the green of her irises, reminding me of Zos' blank stare. "You're stronger than this; stronger than you'll admit to even yourself."

I didn't know what to say to her when my thoughts were spiraling. "Alright."

"Good." Viv spoke with finality and tugged her blanket closer. "Now, you've had a really big day and you need to sleep it off. It will help your mind reset and give you clarity."

If the situation wasn't as dire as it was, I could almost appreciate someone else taking over the role of healer, and I bit back a grin. "Thank you."

"Anytime," she said, patting the ground as if that would make it softer.

"Soren can take first watch," Lukas decided, flopping back on his bedroll. He rotated his feet, attention fixed on the forest where the drakken had vanished. An owl hooted the all clear.

That worked fine for me. If the prince wanted to throw a fit, he could take the punishment he was due. Though as I rolled over onto my side, head pillowed on my forearm, I couldn't turn off my thoughts like Viv had asked.

Had my father been right telling me to pray to such a vengeful goddess? Had she really watched me this entire time, seeing me, hearing me, but never heeding my concerns? Had she laughed in that awful way every time my prayers crossed her—thoughts? Threshold? However the gods got their messages? And if she hadn't helped me before, what reason did I have to believe she would help me when she said she would? She'd already made it clear what she thought of me.

I didn't remember falling asleep, but I must have, because when I blinked again, the azure light of dawn was barely visible through the branches of the trees. Grim flapped his wings, settling deeper on his branch, beak tucked against his breast. Viv and Lukas whispered as they cooked breakfast. Across from me lay Soren. I'd mistaken him for sleeping until I caught his eyes hidden under the shadow of his arm, dark and gleaming and turbulent.

They caught mine and held.

And held.

And held.

* * *

I bent forward across the mare's back, the wind clawing at my hair, ripping pieces from the plait. Behind me, Viv whooped as Soren guided us along the upper edge of a small cliff. The lack of trees across the open plain was a refreshing change to the tightly-packed forests.

The snow had melted, signaling the last of the dying days of fret, and bits of green speckled the fields. A valley with cottages and fields carefully segmented by ramshackle fences was scattered below. The prince had pushed us harder today than he had any other, and catching up to him was like catching the wind.

The pace gave me time to think without Lukas or Viv attempting to draw me out of the dark place I'd tucked myself into in my mind. For the first time in as long as I could remember, I hadn't prayed to Zos before falling asleep. I also hadn't offered her my thanks upon waking, my mood blacker than dried dragon's blood, much to Viv's dismay when I rejected her offer of breakfast with a handful of bitter words.

It wasn't that I didn't feel the urge to pray gnawing at me, the bite of habit sinking in its teeth, but my confusion and frustration twisted me up, shaking me so I felt like a bottle of spiritwater bubbling and fizzing over. Then there was the matter of the ache in my hand, low and throbbing and constant. A reminder. I pressed my injury to my belly, willing away the pain. It was petty, but being the one to offer rejection rather than take it on the chin had a satisfying edge to it.

Though regret and guilt nipped at the edges of my thoughts.

The call of an owl rolled over me, but I barely heard it through the storm raging in my mind. I tugged harder on my reins and bit back a curse as the throbbing in my injured hand pulsed harder, the sensation tingling. Ahead, Soren pushed his mount faster, the black of his cloak flowing like a silken banner. Lukas trailed after, green cloak tucked beneath his saddle. His head swiveled, pace slowing, and reached around his back to unhook the bow he'd strapped there. I straightened, pinpricks of awareness rushing from my toes to my head.

Another call, this time from Grim. I barely grasped the end of it before it was gone. When Pip threw herself into my chest, talons clawing and scratching, I finally recognized the cries for what they were. Warnings. Dire ones, too.

A dozen dark figures appeared on the hill ahead, standing in formation on four legs, snouts pointed our direction. One moment they were there, the next they charged. I shouted and yanked on the reins so hard the mare went up on her back legs, throwing me from the saddle. My head hit the dirt first. I saw white when pain exploded from my nose and cheek, my battered body rolling over and over until it stopped. I coughed through the dust and dirt, prodding at the cuts and bruises, forcing myself upright. At least my nose didn't *feel* broken.

A wolven crashed into the side of Lukas' horse as he drew another arrow, shoving them—horse and rider—over the edge of the cliff. The horse's screams speared me as it tumbled down. Throat thick with sticky mucus, I raced toward the fight, bandaged hand pulled tight to my breast to protect it from further injury. Was Lukas alright? I couldn't make out the flash of golden hair among the mass of wolven muscle, horse flesh, and snapping teeth.

Metal clanged, and a wolf squealed. Soren swung down from his mount, landing in the midst of the charging wolven, his sword and daggers little more than ash-gray blurs as he stabbed and slashed, sprays of crimson arcing whenever he made a hit in his deadly dance of lethal precision.

A searing blast of awareness broke through the heated ribbons of panic tangling up my insides and I skidded to a halt when a red-furred wolven split from the main pack, having spotted me. Its lips pulled back, tail outright behind it, belly so low to the ground it almost touched. I ripped my dagger from its sheath at my hip as something big roared behind me, adopting the defensive position Soren had thrust my body into earlier, my arm shaking with a surge of fresh adrenaline.

Die. The soldier's order cracked, sharp as a broken bone in my mind, and it lunged, powerful legs pushing it high into the air. I tried to move, tried to run, but found my legs locked. It was going to crash into me. Kill me.

Then Viv was there, sliding seamlessly between us, her slender sword raised. Her blade sliced the wolven open from jugular to pelvis. I shouted when hot blood sprayed, coating my exposed skin. Something pink and gloopy smacked into my arms, but I turned away, swallowing a flood of bile that coated my teeth.

A golden drakken swooped, its shadow passing across me as it ripped another wolven away from the carnage surrounding Soren, who stood on a pile of bodies nearly as tall as he was. Lukas roared, lifting the soldier higher and higher, blood dripping from his legs and feet where the beast slashed him with his claws. And he dropped the soldier. I didn't watch, but I heard it crash into another approaching soldier with a sickly crunch, followed shortly by screams of agony.

I swiped blood from my face with the back of my hand. Viv taunted two wolven as she spun her sword expertly, first fending off one set of slashing teeth with an easy thrust, body allowing the momentum of the blade to pull her around, swinging at the last moment, cutting open the throat of the soldier who lunged at her. The wolven choked, tripping over the body of a comrade as it drowned in its own blood.

She crowed in victory, dropping the sword at her feet and reaching for the bandolier at her chest instead. With a whoop, she returned to face her next opponent, one with fur as white as a snowy owl's feathers, a pair of thin daggers in her hands. It regarded her more warily than the others, understanding the force it was up against.

"See what I did there?" Viv taunted. "You're next."

From where she stood, she couldn't see what I did: the black wolven slinking out of the shadows, one far bigger than any of the others my friends fought. Its golden eyes were fixed on my friend, hackles pulled back as it snarled. My head spun, and I fumbled for my weapon, patting my vest uselessly, trying to make my body work as it should.

Lukas shouted in conjunction with Soren, trampling a fresh wave of troops. I risked a glance up as I stumbled forward, finally finding the hilt of the blade at my hip.

The snowy wolven had backed off, moving jerkily on stiff legs, white fur drenched sticky red down one side. Viv spun her blades coyly, a move I recognized when she was ready to put an end to a fight. But the threat wasn't where she thought it was, and the white wolven knew it, too.

I couldn't shout. Couldn't even whisper. The words locked themselves in my chest. Blackness skittered across my vision when the black wolven made its move, shooting forward and sinking its teeth deep into her arm. Viv screamed and somehow avoided getting her stomach ripped clean open by the slashing silver claws. Everything inside me went icy cold, watching her fly through the air and crash into the ground. Her head snapped back when it hit a rock with a sickly crunch, and she went limp. The wolven circled back around, muzzle wet and dark with her blood.

A steely calm settled over me.

I wouldn't let her die. Not here. Not now.

Not ever.

I barely felt my body when I sprinted forward as the wolven charged, throwing myself in the path between it and my best friend. It hadn't anticipated the move, and lowered its mangy head a moment too late as I dropped to my knees, dagger raised. We collided. I smashed its muzzle with the bone of my injured wrist, screaming at the fiery pain. The wolven flailed, thrashed, but it was too late. The point of my blade sank deep into its fur, hilt buried between its ribs, disappearing deep its flesh. It grunted, eyes rolling, teeth caught in my shoulder, and it shook. Hard. I shrieked again, losing my grip on my weapon and wrapped myself around its tree trunk of a neck when it whipped me around once more, holding on desperately as we tumbled over the rocks.

Before we stopped rolling, I let go, landing on something with hard angles that dug deep into my arms and legs. The wolven found its footing, flipping around faster than I could have imagined, eyes burning with undisguised hatred as it wheezed.

I'd nicked a lung.

I reached beneath me, fingers slicing open on the blade of the sword Viv had flung away before I found the grip. It was in my hands before I could think. I needed to finish this one off, keep her safe, before any other predators found her body, limp and ragged.

I hoped she hadn't hit her head too hard.

The wolven was more careful this time, approaching me as it assessed my stance, its gasping growing more pronounced as blood spilled down its front leg, dripping from its paw. I held firm, ignoring the blood soaking my bandages, keeping myself between it and Viv.

She needed time to recover.

That one thought blinded me to all else, and I charged. The wolven saw through my bravado and anticipated my swing, knocking the weapon from my hand. Its claws raked a fresh set of wounds down my good arm, and I crashed into the dirt, bruised cheekbone cracking against a rock. Somehow, I ended up beneath the beast.

The dagger was still embedded in its chest. In another world, I would have applauded the soldier for recognizing the dangers of removing that weapon from the wound. Now I shrieked in triumph when I pulled the blade from its body myself, skin sucking and squelching in protest, and I thrust blindly upward, aiming for anything with hair. The wolven released a pained snarl as my knife sank deep once, twice, three times. A heavy weight raked down my front, thrusting me away, but it was too late. The wolven wheezed and panted, eyes glazed as it collapsed, blood gushing from its belly. I barely felt my own injuries over the buzzing in my head, the fresh horror sweeping over me as the knife slipped from my icy fingers.

Anyone could have killed me in that moment. I was as blind as I was deaf to everything except my staggering, gagging foe.

The wolven never looked away, legs twitching as if it longed to run one last time. Not when its head fell to the ground, tongue lolling from its mouth. Not when a mist stole across its eyes, glazing its hate-filled glare. Not when its chest heaved its last.

I'd done that. I'd killed a wolven. More than that.

Wolven were people—just in another form. A living, breathing being with its own thoughts and hopes and maybe even a family. My ears buzzed. Our fight could have easily gone the other way. The soldier could have torn my jugular from my throat if luck hadn't been on my side.

But I couldn't bring myself to care about that detail.

In my twenty-one years, I'd never killed another.

Until now.

A hand settled on my shoulder. Soren caught my arm when I swung it to do what, I didn't know. His black shirt was soaked and scarlet blood dripped from the hem and the ends of his hair. It had dried on his cheeks and he shook me, mouth moving with words I couldn't hear.

Viv. I needed to get to Viv.

I batted him away, red tinge marring my vision, stumbling over my feet until I dropped beside my best friend. She had yet to wake and my throat surged into my mouth when I bent over her, tears blurring her form, unsure if she was breathing. I thought to pray, but the words wouldn't come. The simplest of thoughts had been ripped from me.

Tears dripped onto her arm, smearing the blood, and I hovered a hand over her mouth and nose, my entire being waiting to see if her breath would whisper across it. I nearly collapsed when I felt it. Small, but there. A single breath. I flung myself on top of her with an aching sob, hands finding the back of her head, lifting her across my legs, cradling her against my ribs, fingers tracing her cheeks over and over.

"She's alright?" Soren sounded rusty.

I rotated, keeping Viv's head propped up on my shoulder. The bite to her bicep was deep, but the worst of the bleeding had stopped. It occurred to a remote, far-away part of me that most of the blood I could see was mine.

"She's breathing." I would know more about her condition when she woke up.

"Telleree. What you did—"

My breath stuttered. Black replaced the red licking at the edges of my vision. "Don't."

"But—"

"Not right now." A wall had come up, blocking the worst of my emotion, leaving me in a stunned state of harsh realization.

I'd killed someone. I'd protected the most important person in my life, but I'd still killed him.

Him.

A person even under all that fur.

And that wall blocking off how I felt about it, the guilt that crept along my spine like a centipede, it would hit me. But I couldn't let it right now. Not until Viv woke up. Not until we got out of here.

"Can we move her?" Lukas mopped his face with his shirt. His cloak hung in tatters. "I'd rather not be here when they send reinforcements."

He was right. We couldn't stay. I shook her again, but she didn't wake.

"Lukas, you carry her."

The man glanced at the prince. Whatever argument was brewing behind his eyes died. "Sure thing."

"I'll ride with Telleree." I barely heard him. The wall inside me had expanded, its black depths branching outward like poison leeching through my veins. On one side I felt me. The me that trusted and believed in the world, the goodness I knew was inherent to it. And on this side stood the other me. The one forced to fight, to do things she didn't want to do. The one who'd survived not out of skill, but out of desperation.

You should have died. The ugly voice of doubt nipped at me. *You know no skills, you have no experience. Your foolish actions will only get you so far.*

I tightened my grip around Viv when someone reached for her. Someone called my name. I didn't know who. I just sat there, a million thoughts swirling in my head.

My name. Again. I blinked. Viv stared up at me, eyes pained but soft as she brushed at my forehead. Sticky strands of hair peeled away. Her lips moved, and I recognized my name.

She was alive. She was awake. She would survive.

An emotion more powerful than any I'd felt before swamped me, relief and pain and affection threatening to swallow me whole. This time, when someone tugged her away from me, I let them.

Static hummed in my ears when a hand guided me forward, helped my foot into the stirrup. A warmth at my back. Arms wrapped around my ribs, hands gripping the reins. The wind tugged on the hair that had dried in patches to my face. Pip flew by, incapable of landing on my shoulder because of Soren holding me up. I recognized his lemonseed oil scent.

Only then did I release my chokehold on the wall strangling me.

Tremors started in my toes and worked up my spine until my entire body shook. I couldn't stop staring at my hands curled in the dark hair of the horse, the blood drying in the creases.

"Don't you give up on me now," the prince murmured over my shoulder.

The last bit of me that felt real splintered wide open.

28

Risk

"She's in shock." Soren.

"No shit, stupid." Viv's small, grimy hand closed around mine, obscuring the scarlet blood I couldn't stop staring at. A breath hitched in my chest, the first in what felt like eons. "You try coming face-to-face with the goddess you've revered your entire life, listen to her throw everything you've accomplished in your face, then kill someone when you've never liked the feel of steel in the first place, and tell me how you feel."

Lukas chuckled humorlessly. "If she doesn't snap out of it soon, I am taking matters into my own hands."

Something soft brushed my face and I leaned into it. Breath washed across my cheek. "I swear, men are so thick sometimes."

I blinked, realizing the darkness wasn't just the shadows behind my eyelids. We'd stopped for the night and settled in a semicircle in a clearing. The evening chill stung my cheeks, but someone had pulled my cloak around me so tightly the rest of my body hummed with warmth.

"It's alright. Follow me." Viv squeezed my shoulder, her grip on my elbow firm. I was helpless but to follow. Our feet crunched through dried leaves and I shuddered at the sound, imagining bones snapping with every step. "Let's get you cleaned up. Getting out of those bloody clothes will make you feel better, won't it?" Her rambling calmed the queasiness of my stomach, hidden knots in my muscles relaxing as I focused on the back of her torn shirt, messy hair tumbling from her bun. "You also reek of wolven, and the last thing we need is for your prince to fall into hyper-killer-mode again."

I stumbled and caught myself on her arm. *My prince?* What did she mean by that?

Viv steadied me, found my hand tucked away in the folds of my cloak, and tugged me forward again. The gesture peeled my arm away from my body, tugging on a series of stitches running up my arm and down my ribs. The jagged slash of memory of how I'd earned those injuries made me wince.

I'd killed someone.

I swallowed hard, trying to not fixate on that last detail. Unaware of my round-about thoughts, Viv hooked our arms together. "This is better, isn't it? Now I can hold you up if something tangles around your feet."

Like her hand tangling in mine, her skin felt soft as posy petals. I inhaled, casting my memories aside, breathing in a lungful of spring woods and the familiar scent of the oils Viv worked into her leathers to keep them supple. She must have cleaned up. I wondered when she'd had the time.

How long had I been away from myself?

We dodged the prickles of a briarbush, revealing a small but serviceable pond tucked between a pair of evergreens. Crickets trilled from the long grass, and the crescent of the moon reflected off the rippling water.

"Let's get this off so I can clean it." Viv tugged on my cloak and the heavy weight of leather dropped away. I drew a deeper breath, feeling more free outside of my bloodstained uniform. "Take as long as you need. I've left soap on the rocks. It'll be cold, much colder than it was earlier when we stopped, but I promise you'll feel better." Her voice sounded saccharine, but I didn't mind. I enjoyed the cadence of her voice. "I'll wait on this rock with your fresh clothing. Again, take your time."

Good idea.

It didn't take long to strip out of my grimy clothes, and though the darkness threatened to pull me under again, I chose to not dwell over the stains. Undressing revealed the sorry state of my battered and bruised body. A row of trim stitches bound the skin together along my forearm, and a thick roll of gauze wound around my shoulder where the soldier had bitten me. Carefully, I unraveled it, swallowing a gasp at the mottled purple bruise spanning from the cup of my shoulder to out of view along my neck. The wolven's teeth had shredded the skin, sinking nearly to the bone.

"That marrow root of yours works wonders," Viv remarked from her perch, working the fabric of my cloak in her hands. "Remember the time that fox bit me for getting too close to its den? I remembered you using that foul smelling yellow plant to stop the bleeding. It worked for us, too."

I closed my eyes, drawing a deep breath. Thank rezar she paid attention when necessary. I'd tried to teach her poultices and remedies before, but Viv's ever-racing mind rarely focused on such small details. Weakly, I nodded, turning my attention to the wrap around my hand and opted to leave it on.

Recalling Viv's warning, I tested the water with my fingertips, shivering when the chill stole the warmth from my skin. It wasn't the worst I'd encountered, and I knew better than to dwell over the rush of endorphins that was to come. Without further thought, I dropped into the pond with a sharp gasp and dunked my head, immersing myself in the icy chill.

The one-two punch of the cold and the dark crashed right through me.

The mental wall I'd propped up with mud and sticks crumbled, startling me into bright-eyed wakefulness. I found the soap scented with linseed, Viv's favorite scent, and washed hurriedly, not wanting to be in the water, exposed like this, trusting Viv to keep me safe from her spot on the boulder. She said nothing, but I felt her eyes on me, assessing every bruise as I scrubbed the remnants of blood from my skin and squeezed grime from my hair.

I wasn't sure how I should feel.

By my own hand, I had ended a life today. I understood the moral consequences of that decision, of choosing one life over another, but I couldn't grasp what it meant for me as a person. How was I to move forward? Could I accept my newfound title of killer, murderer, executioner—or would I fold beneath its weight?

With a moan, I ground the heel of my hand into my chest, at the crest of my heart, reassuring myself the heavy thump hadn't ceased. Viv had killed. Several times, in fact, since we'd left Solas, and she seemed perfectly fine. She barely glanced up when I snagged my clothes from the rock at her hip, her fingers attentively clearing blood from the vanes of a snowy owl feather.

Lukas and Soren had killed and they functioned well enough.

Well, Lukas did. Something in Soren had rotted—or maybe hardened—turning him into a lethal machine who slashed with sharp objects first and asked questions second.

Regardless, none of them had frozen, locked in their heads, recalling every grisly moment, every drop of blood. Even now, I couldn't stop remembering the soldier's eyes when they'd glazed over, how they'd emptied and gone glassy when his spirit vacated his material form.

Viv approached with fresh bandages, helping me bind my injuries again. The bleeding had started once more, but was nowhere near as bad as it had been. Still, I gagged while tucking my shirt into my pants, muscles pulling and shifting uncomfortably.

Viv offered me her cloak. "You'll be alright. Give it time."

"Were you like this? After your first kill?" My voice was hoarse.

She rubbed a slow hand down my back, curls shielding her eyes. After a long moment, she tucked my cloak under her arm and murmured, "We should get back before they come looking for us."

I knew better than to pursue the subject.

Pip found us on our way back to the drakken, tiny wings fluttering as she swooped around the circle and landed on my bedroll that someone had laid out. Viv promptly dropped down beside it, returning her attention to my soaked and dripping cloak. Knowing her, she would be up scrubbing all night, and I didn't feel like stopping her. I barely had the strength to keep my fingers from shaking as I bound my wet hair in a long plait, let alone fight my best friend about her fixation with perfection.

Lukas scooted closer to Viv, their voices low as they discussed something to do with the horses, and I settled on my blanket, trying to ignore the person who I knew was watching me. Kneeling, I pulled back the cover and froze when the pads of my fingers brushed something cold. Metal.

The dagger.

I recognized the curl of the dragon's tail that was the handle, knew if I pulled it from its sheath, the blade would ripple with sheets of metallic blue. A weapon designed for maiming and slashing and cutting and *killing*.

My chest tightened, my heart swelled. It hurt to breathe. Soren must have grabbed it. Closing my eyes, I forced myself to inhale deeply, in and out, allowing the hush of the grass and the gentle murmuring of a pair of silverfoxes to settle myself. When I opened them again, I was centered. Ready.

I wrapped a corner of Viv's cloak around my hand and knocked the weapon away. It rolled and landed in a bed of dead leaves beside my pillow. Without comment, still not looking at Soren, I pulled the blanket up to my shoulders, mind swirling as I stared at the hunk of metal, nearly a foot in length total and wicked sharp.

This would be a long night.

* * *

I hadn't slept.

The gray shadows beneath my eyes were obvious even in the rippling water of the pool, and I hastily scrubbed at my skin as if that would make them disappear. Freshened up and slightly more alert, I joined Viv on her bedroll, needing the feel of her beside me, watching her painstakingly clean the last of the feathers in the blue light of dawn. The shifters were still quiet, asleep. Pitching my voice low, I murmured stories about the owls whose feathers I'd chosen for my cloak as she moved across them, stories that reminded us achingly of home and the people we'd loved and lost there.

When streaks of pink and orange streaked across the sky, my shoulders felt a little lighter.

The drakken roused without much fuss, awakened by the same internal clock I lived by during the long months when the greenhouse crops demanded my attention.

We ate hurriedly and saddled the horses without speaking. Soren wanted to make it to Azmarin as quickly as possible, which meant another day and a half of hard riding. I felt his eyes on me as I carefully tucked my belongings into my saddlebags, steeling myself to address the questions he wouldn't ask. The weight clinging to my thigh threatened to pull me to the ground when I finished up.

Whistling, I dispersed the owls with reminders to keep us informed about scouting parties, and snagged Soren's sleeve before he slid his foot into his stirrup.

"A moment. Please."

He turned, body coiled like a snake preparing to strike. Lukas stilled, hands deep in his pack, and Viv rubbed the neck of the mare we would share, the line of her jaw stiff. I untied the knots holding the sheath of the knife to my leg and squeezed, revolted by the feel of the steel against my palm, before extending it toward the prince.

"Take it."

He assessed the weapon, face giving away none of his thoughts as his gaze shifted from the steel to me. I held steady under the pressure of his searching look, knowing what he would see: My resolve, the lack of tremble in my arm, the steeliness of my spine, the set of my shoulders.

I lifted my chin. "From here on out, I will no longer bear arms. I realize what that means, the risk I'm assuming and the burden I'm placing on all your shoulders, but I cannot and will not assume the responsibility of ending the life of another. Not in this fashion."

Stepping forward, I squared up against the prince, shoulders locked, daring him to take the weapon I pressed flat against his chest. "I remember what you told me, how everyone you travel with must be armed and prepared for battle. I assure you I'm more than ready for the second half of your request, I will make myself useful to you in any way I am able, but regarding the former, I am your weak link. I lack the strength and agility to properly wield all kinds of weapons and pose a greater threat to hurting one of you or myself than an enemy."

Soren's gaze slipped back to the knife which he had yet to accept. "And how, then, do you intend to help our cause? We need soldiers—"

"You also need tacticians," I cut in. "You need scouts and people capable of making quick decisions when they matter most. I've proven myself willing to do whatever is needed to carry out a mission, even put myself in harm's way if needed." Viv made a soft sound that caused me to tense up. "I will do whatever you ask within the parameters I've set." I paused, then lowered to one knee, head bowed. "My prince."

I'd never known royalty, but I felt the weight of that title now as I awaited Soren's verdict. A morning bird chittered a wake up call, unaware of the tension strung tight in the clearing. Still Soren didn't speak, stretching the moment to impossible lengths.

When I felt I might tear my skin apart just for something to break the silence, he crouched, knees hitting the earth in front of me, finger tilting my chin up. I'd expected anger, frustration—even resentment. The kindness I found instead on his face calmed the stormy lake thrashing inside me. "For someone struggling with her faith, it sounds an awful lot like you're putting your fate in the hands of the gods."

I couldn't disguise my wince, his remark hitting the soft spot I couldn't protect no matter how much armor I bore. "Some habits die hard." I wet my lips, gathering my thoughts. His eyes flicked down to follow the movement. "My faith and the questions I have about it are my own concern. They won't get in the way of our mission."

Soren tilted his head. "We'll see."

Yet he took the blade from my palm, the relief from its weight immediate, and slipped it into a deep pocket sewn inside his cloak, standing. "I accept your conditions on a trial basis. Prove you aren't just telling me what I want to hear, and you may do as you wish for the remainder of your days."

I blinked when he offered his hand, my vision expanding beyond the narrow tunnel I'd gotten trapped in. Viv kicked at the dirt, lips curved in a half smile, and Lukas grunted, turning his back to us as if he'd expected this outcome all along.

Soren's grip was gentle as he pulled me to my feet and he strode to his own horse, calling out, "Besides, this leaves more Fiorian bastards to die by my sword, doesn't it?"

29

Valuable Assets

Where Dowhurst screamed its vibrancy through colors, Azmarin voiced its history through jagged architecture. The city tucked among the rolling hills of the plains emerged without much warning. A vacant cabin here, an ancient tree there. Then we were in the middle of it, surrounded by buildings taller than any I'd seen before, their rooftops carved in sharp peaks with angles that would give even the most daring of skiers pause. The diversity of races and creeds and countries obvious in the streets of Dowhurst was absent here in the center of the country. Those who splashed through the chilled rain puddling in the cobblestone streets spoke in short sentences, the vowels stretched and rounded as a result of their thick Southern accents.

"Hurry inside," Lukas ordered, holding open the door to *Taft's Tailoring*. I wondered if he was aware of how his own accent had deepened.

Viv snagged my elbow and pulled me forward. She had neglected to pull up her hood and her hair hung in stringy ropes, bits of it sticking to her skin and clothing.

"Welcome, welcome. Hurry now, out of the rain." A woman with a pleasantly crinkled face and hands gnarled with work and age rocked in a chair beside a fire, a needle pinched between her fingers, hovering over a pile of fabric in her lap. "Poor dears, you're soaked. It's absolutely miserable out there." She shifted her work to a table beside her and creaked to her feet so slowly I felt her aches in my own bones, and beckoned. "Come now, give me your cloaks and warm yourselves. Wouldn't want you to catch ill."

"That won't be necessary." With a grin broader than any I'd seen on his face before, Soren removed his hood and shook rainwater from his sleeves. The woman gasped, and in three strides, the shifter was across the room, his arms wrapped tightly around her. I stopped in the middle of pulling off my cloak, blinking at the bizarre scene.

"Astounding," Viv murmured, squeezing water from her hair. "Maybe he's human after all."

Lukas snagged her cloak before it slipped from her shoulder to the polished wood floor and reached for mine, careful to keep the feathers hidden from view. "That is Madame Taft. She helped raise Soren. If you think he is vicious now—"

"Vicious as a kitten," Viv observed.

"—try seeing what he's like if you upset her. I warn you: don't get on her bad side." He hung our things from a series of bronze hooks on the wall. I'd kept my bag, looping it over my neck again, hand pressed to the small bulge in the side where Pip slumbered.

"She has a bad side?" I asked, wiping my boots on the rug, though it wasn't much use. Soren had already tracked mud everywhere.

Viv straightened her collar and checked the knife-like edges of her sleeves, clicking her tongue over a tear she discovered in the elbow. "She has to, right? I mean, how else would he turn out the way he did?" She curled her fingers in a mimicry of wolven's claws, though her bared teeth made her look more like a chipmunk. "I bet she assists when he's torturing people. Or maybe she's an assassin."

318

Her face brightened, the crinkles around her eyes almost vanishing. "I've always wanted to meet an assassin."

"Afraid not, dear." Madame Taft smiled warmly, hands clasped at her breast as she took us in, heedless of the shadow standing at her side glaring daggers at Viv. "These old hands have stabbed many a shirt, but never the fragile skin beneath."

"Pity. Though I suppose there's still time." Ignoring decorum, Viv threw her arms around the woman, who didn't look the least bit surprised. "But anyone who can tolerate that stick-in-the-mud for as many years as you have without slicing off a finger or two must be amazing."

The woman chuckled, squeezing my friend in return. The two separated, appearing for all the world like they'd been friends forever. The darkness inside me flared, and I curved arms around me in confusion. I didn't know this woman, and she certainly hadn't done anything wrong, so why did I feel such resentment?

Madame Taft moved forward, soft-soled shoes silent on the now-grimy floorboards. "Lukas? Was that you I glimpsed?" The golden drakken couldn't hold back his grin and stepped into the shorter woman's embrace.

"Don't be such a stranger," she chided, examining one of the larger rips in his shirt. She clicked her tongue, and I glanced at Soren, brow raised. So that was where he got that infuriating habit from. "I see you've been rough as ever on your clothing. This won't do; I'll find you some new things spick-spat. And the girls, too. They look even worse than you." Piercing gray eyes found mine. "Oh yes, don't think I didn't see you over there, little one." I hugged myself more tightly. "It's always the ones who wish to remain hidden who stand out the most."

She brushed past Lukas, but rather than reach for me, she smiled. It didn't meet her eyes, which bore an analytical sharpness. "Don't worry, child, I'll win you over yet. Even I would be hesitant around new people after that conversation you had with Zos."

Say what?

"Finnicky fool, that one," Madame Taft continued. "I'm partial to Lo, myself. A gentle spirit she is."

I could scarcely breathe around the pressure of my grip. How did she know what had happened at the temple? I'd barely spoken of it to the people standing closest to me, and I would have known if the shifters carried a messenger bird. We'd barely stopped to eat or sleep, and forget about free time—

"Come now." Madame Taft looped her arm through Soren's, guiding him toward a door at the back of the store. I'd assumed it was for storage, but when she opened it, a long staircase emerged, dropping into the darkness below. A single candlestick burning from a pedestal against the wall offered a small halo of light. Soren scooped it up and darted down the stairs, which didn't creak despite their age.

Lukas tugged me back as Viv studied the opening before taking Madame Taft's arm and helping her down the stairs herself. "Madame fancies herself a bit of a fortune teller, claims the gods send her visions of what has happened and what is to come." The panic swarming my mind like angry wasps lulled to a hum. I'd never heard of such an ability before. "I would say she's full of crock, but she is right about half as often as she is wrong, and when she's right—it's terrifying."

The mystery of Soren's cynicism regarding faith deepened, and I pondered that notion as we went down, down, down until the staircase ended in a long hallway lined with doors. Madame Taft opened the first and stepped inside, face up-tilted. I didn't trust that smile. "Archer, your company has arrived."

The hairs on my arms rose.

"Oh, really? This late? I never would have guessed." I'd only met the head of the Requiem twice before, yet I'd recognize his particular brand of grating sarcasm anywhere. I lifted my hand in a friendly wave when I stepped around the old woman into the surprisingly large, warm space. Silvery eyes narrowed. "Look who's alive. I see they found you before you did something foolish, after all."

The shifters chose to sit, but Viv and I remained standing. As much as she'd expressed her delight in meeting Madame Taft, Viv also didn't bother hiding her skepticism as she examined the man sitting on the edge of the bar, hands braced on either side of him.

"I wouldn't say that. They just aided me with my foolishness." I nudged Viv with my elbow, curious how we had equally opposite reactions to two people in such a short span of time.

The move drew Archer's attention and his haughty expression lingered as he looked her over so attentively even I bristled. "I presume you're the family Telleree wouldn't stop going on about?"

Viv stepped forward, gripping the hilt of a knife hanging from her bandolier at the center of her chest, and dipped her head in a bow that edged toward mocking. "Viveca Helvig. Huntress, blacksmith, navigator, and expert at all things practical at your service."

Lukas snorted. "I am not sure how practical checking your saddle five times before stepping into it is."

"Or if it's necessary to fold the hems of your sleeves precisely two inches back," Soren added, then coughed when Madame Taft cuffed the back of his head.

"Leave the girl alone. Peculiarities are to be celebrated, not mocked," she scolded, though she looked at me when she said it. I decided I didn't like her all that much. Her or the mystery she exuded. "I'll take my leave. Archer, be kind. And I'll have fresh clothes waiting for all of you, since some of you can't respect my work."

321

The door snicked closed at her back.

Archer braced his hip against the table, fiddling with the silver tab in his earlobe. "I take it your presence means you've opted to join our cause?"

"They have." Soren folded onto a chair. "And I want them at our next operation."

Lukas pinched the bridge of his nose, eyes squeezing shut. To his credit, Archer appeared to consider his offer, hand moving from his ear to brace on the table. "You think that wise?"

"Not necessarily, but I'm convinced they'll be valuable assets."

I was still figuring out the dynamics of the organization. Soren claimed the trump card of all titles, but it was clearly Archer who possessed the most authority. Whatever happened next needed his approval, which he clearly had reason to not extend after my first disappearing act.

"Listen. I told the prince—"

Soren cut me off with a sharp glance.

Archer's eyes went flat. Killer's eyes. "She knows? *They* know?" He smashed a fist against the table, making the assembly of half-consumed mugs of tea rattle. "What game are you playing here, Soren?"

"The one where we win."

"I can't believe you'd be so foolish as to—"

"You can stop reaching for that knife tucked in the small of your back any moment now." Viv stepped in front of me, her shoulder partially blocking my view. "I don't know who you are or what role you play, and frankly, it doesn't matter to me. If you won't have the courtesy of giving your opponent a moment to arm themselves for a proper duel, then I have no qualms about severing your skull from your spine."

Archer's silence was damning.

I leaned around her as he ran a hand through his silvery hair. He was about to kick us out, I could tell.

Then his quicksilver laugh lanced through the air, splicing right through me. I found Viv's hand and squeezed, a confusing array of pride in my friend and confusion over his conflicting emotions washing over me. Archer laughed again, a short burst of chuckles that seemed to surprise even him.

"You're good." He wiggled something free of his shirt and dropped it on the table. A knife. Soren rocked his chair back on two legs, a ghostly hint of a grin on his lips.

"What gave it away?" Archer asked.

"As if I'd tell you."

"If you do, I promise to present a greater challenge in the future."

Viv hesitated, her fingers firming around mine, torn between her desire to protect me and the challenge facing her. I tapped the side of her hand, giving her the all-clear. I didn't trust Archer, but I didn't distrust him, either. At the very least, I believed I understood his motives well enough.

"Micro-expressions. When you touched the handle, your lips twitched just so." She demonstrated the tiny flick of emotion, something warring between calculation and satisfaction.

Archer relaxed, the knife on the table forgotten. Lukas hunched over his bag, rifling through it, clearly done with this conversation. "And you?" Archer nodded at me. "Do you share her skill set? That wasn't the impression I got before."

I opened my mouth to tell him point blank I did not and would not carry weapons, but Soren beat me to the punch.

"You know as well as I do she'll make a solid tactician." The legs of his chair thudded back down. "And she proved it a few days ago."

Archer didn't ask to hear the story so much as he dropped into a chair and peered at us pointedly until Viv and I accepted our seats at the table, too. Lukas dropped a notebook, its cover soft and folded with use, in front of him. The drakken drew a deep breath, opened the text, and launched into the story of how I'd burned down a core chunk of the eastern forest to save my friends. Archer listened carefully, occasionally asking questions to clarify a point, but otherwise allowed Lukas to relay his report uninhibited.

When Lukas finished, Archer leaned back, chair creaking under his weight, and folded his arms. He ran a hand over his mouth and shrugged to himself. "Selfish. Destructive. Yet effective. Clearly." He tugged again on the silver piece in his ear. "Alright. I get it. But it's late in the game, Soren. We're too far along in the planning and she hasn't been there for any of it. Or for any of the war, for that matter. They won't trust a word out of her mouth, no matter how much you prop her up."

I would have bristled had I not agreed with him.

"Soldiers I can add all the time." The leader of the Requiem eyed me critically. "Those in leadership? Not quite so much."

Soren leaned on his elbows, his expression positively lethal. "Have you solved that... small problem yet?"

That didn't sound ominous. Things were rarely small in Soren's world, I'd observed.

Archer's brow knitted. "Not yet. But we're close to a workaround—"

"Let me handle it." There it was. The display of power I'd been waiting for Soren to use. It was remarkable to see him pull that prince card from his deck and throw it down like a weapon. I had no idea what he expected of me, but he exuded so much confidence I felt I could handle it. "All of it. I'll make sure we're prepared—in a week's time."

Archer pressed his index fingers to his temples, rotating them slightly. "I suppose you won't be telling me what you're up to in advance, either?"

"Nope." Soren popped the p. "How soon can you pull everyone together?"

Archer squinted as if battling a headache. "Theoretically, tonight. But tomorrow—"

"Tonight it is. Less risk of discovery that way." Soren kicked back his chair again, boots propped on the edge of the table. "Send out the missives. We'll meet you at the smithy in one hour's time."

Archer looked to Lukas, who lifted a shoulder, then to Viv, who fingered one of her many knives. After a beat, she said, "I may not like the *akren* here—" Archer's lips twitched with mirth—"but you'd be wise to listen to him. Sometimes he's got good ideas."

"Alright. Alright. I know when I'm outmatched." Archer went to the door, hand braced on the rounded knob. "One hour. And Soren, your desire for drama will be the death of me one day."

The door swung wide, and he nodded at Madame Taft, who waited outside with a large bundle cradled in her hands. Whistling, Archer vanished around the corner, footsteps fading as he hammered up the stairs. None of us spoke as the elderly woman swept into the room and started handing out the clothing with warm smiles. She smelled like cloves.

She handed mine to me last, squeezing my shoulder as if she knew how much of a mess my insides were. "Have faith," she murmured. "It's not too late."

Viv rounded on Soren, her braid whipping around so fast it almost cracked me across the cheekbone. "What exactly does this plan of yours entail and how screwed is my best friend?"

30

Restore Hope

"I don't like this."

I rolled my eyes as I straightened a navy tunic over my soft gray pants while Viv ranted at my back. "That's the fifteenth time you've said that, but we agreed to join this suicidal quest, and as such, are obligated to play whatever role they hand us. You not liking it won't stop it."

Not only had Soren refused to answer her questions, but he'd straight up refused to speak at all and swept from the room in a huff of heat and haughty arrogance. Lukas trailed, his expression far more apologetic.

"I don't care what it is." Viv ignored me like she had earlier. "If you aren't comfortable with what they ask you to do, we will leave. I don't care how many people I have to incapacitate to do so."

I held back a smile as I finished tying my bracers to my forearms, the knots loose so they didn't dig into the cuts and burns, and moved to my hair next, imagining Viv worrying her thumbnail with her teeth like she always did when the anxiety struck her worst. She hated biting her nails. It set her compulsions off something fierce, but she couldn't help the outlet it served.

"I know. But you have to admit you're curious." I released the scrap of fabric holding my braid together, fought out the loops, and ran a bristled brush through the snarls and burrs. We'd cleaned our face, necks, and arms in a small washroom behind one of the doors that connected us to the room where we'd met with Archer, rubbing our skin with soap scented with roseoil.

My cheeks burned when Viv started pulling her shirt over her head to clean her scrapes and I turned around, eyes averted, giving her a moment of privacy.

We'd changed in front of one another too many times to count, but our relationship wasn't the same anymore. I scrubbed at a spot in the center of my chest again, as if the touch could soothe the knot that tugged tighter when I recalled how the hardness of her eyes softened when her gaze met mine or how my skin buzzed pleasantly whenever we touched.

When the brush didn't catch on any more snags, I set it on a table and tugged my hair over my shoulders. It hung longer than I preferred, the ends brushing the soft spots inside my elbows. I pulled a chunk in front of me, appreciating its waviness, then shifted my attention to shoving my dirty things back into my bag. "When do you think Soren will return? It's been about a half hour."

When Viv didn't immediately answer, I searched her out and sucked in a breath so sharply I started coughing. She looked different, *good* different in her forest green tunic, its sleeves neatly folded up to her elbows, and straight black pants. She'd done something to tame her wild curls, but they still frizzled out from her head like corkscrews of lightning.

An expression I'd only glimpsed once before rose like the sun in her eyes, her hand clenched around her wrist as if she'd braced it there in an effort to stop her nervous gnawing. Her tongue swiped across her lips, her blazing eyes trailing over me, and my temperature rose under her scrutiny, shifting in the boots I hadn't been able to clean properly.

She cleared her throat, snapping whatever had been building between us. The corner of her lips lifted in a smirk, and she tugged on my collar. "I don't know what you would do if you didn't have me around." She proceeded to pull and shape my clothing and hair to her liking, my skin tingling with every brush of her knuckles.

At long last, and when I thought I might combust from the fluttering in my belly, she tied off my loose plait and tucked a stray strand behind my ear, her fingertips causing a rainbow of tingles to cascade down my neck. She ran a finger down the shoulder of the tunic. "This shade of blue brings out your eyes."

"Does it?" I leaned closer, drawn by the magnetism that existed between us, our foreheads nearly touching.

Viv swallowed, a tremble working through her hand, still on my arm, the roseoil soap weaving us tighter under its spell. "I must insist you wear this color from here on out."

Her breath was warm on my face and sweet like the chocolate she snuck into her pack when I wasn't looking. I wasn't sure what I wanted to do next, how I wanted to proceed, but I desperately wanted to close the hint of space between us, to see if she felt as soft as she—

We sprang apart like whisperhares when a loud knock rattled the door.

"Are you decent?" Soren asked.

I passed a hand over my face, the chill of my shaking fingers soothing the burning in my cheeks. Viv dragged her hair over her eyes, looking everywhere but me as she fiddled with the lower hem of her tunic. Biting back a curse, I hurried to my cloak and bundled it into my arms, calling for Soren to enter.

The prince swept in without ceremony, resplendent in his all-black attire. He didn't deign to glare at Viv as he strode past her, and stopped my arm when I moved to pull my cloak over my shoulders. "Nope, feathers out today."

I allowed him to take the cloak and turn it around, holding it wide for me to slip my arms through. Its weight settled over my shoulders, the dark browns and rusty reds and pure whites of the feathers coarse beneath my fingers. "Isn't this dangerous?"

Soren moved to my front, appraising, worrying the scar on his chin with his index finger. "Now's the perfect time for a little danger."

Viv groaned, her bandolier of knives clanking as she pulled it over her head.

"Lukas is rounding up Ghost and Grim. I figured Pip was already in here with you." He nodded his approval when Pip hopped from the bag to the chair at the mention of her name. I felt like I'd missed a critical part of this conversation, something explaining why he wanted my owls in the city. "I want you to use those loops at the bottom of your cloak, the ones you use to keep it out of the mud, and hook those around your thumbs."

Viv had gone still as if she had finally clued into whatever was happening.

"Soren, what's going on here?" I asked, not following his order.

He took my hand, his callouses scraping across mine, slipping my thumbs through the hooks. "Are you aware how much it looks like you've got wings when you do this?" He lifted my arms out from my sides. "With your hood up, you could almost be mistaken for an owl yourself. An ethereal creature born of the night and feather."

Viv sucked in a sharp breath. "You wouldn't."

"I very much would."

I stared down my front, taking in the material. I could see what he was describing, but the rest of the puzzle was still coming together. The prince read the confusion on my face and chuckled harshly.

"Telleree, you are an enigma. Your faith in your goddess, your cloak of feathers from birds who've been systemically slaughtered to near extinction, the birds who are loyal to you in a way I've never seen from any creature outside of foxes and dogs—it's striking, don't you think? Especially when you pair it with the rune for which we were created... and the one we revere?"

It hit me like a frying pan to the face and I took a quick step back. Soren allowed me to put space between us, dark eyes shimmering hungrily.

"You mean to turn me into an icon."

"I want to use you to restore hope to my cause."

Oh, he was good at that, pulling his authority taut around his fist when it suited him. Embers flared in my breast, hot with incredulity, but he cut me off before I could strip the scales from his hide.

"We are the closest we've ever been to restoring our country to our own hands." A muscle in his jaw feathered, and he braced a heavy hand on the table beside the door. "But the road is long and hasn't been easy. Every step forward has come at the result of two strides back. It's cost me everything I ever held dear—and still I keep fighting.

"That's where you come in. You and your mystery and your owls. You're the quandary we never saw coming." He shook his head at his melodrama. "I need—no, I'm *asking* you to be the beacon of hope I've been searching for; just like I need your owls to help me on this next mission that I swear to you will spark the wildfire that will engulf this nation."

I couldn't move a muscle, couldn't look away, ensnared by his passion that reverberated within me, stoking vicious and hopeful wonders I'd never felt before.

"I need you to trust this is the best for all of us." He closed the distance, the soles of his boots soft on the wooden floors. "I'm using

330

you, yes. But I'm using you with the best of intentions, and I'm being as upfront about it as I can. I see the faith you have in me, in what we're doing, and the last thing I want to do is shake that."

My cloak wrapped tightly around me, constricting in the implications of our future. I swallowed down a bubble of hope, pulling my ideals to the forefront. I couldn't—I wouldn't—

"You said on the road, when you gave up your weapons, that you would do nearly anything to aid me." Soren had never looked colder, meaner, more regal than he did in that moment, pulling my promise out of his sleeve like the ace it was. "Did you mean that?"

Damn him.

This wasn't a role I was meant to assume, one emulating a person blessed by gods, sent as a beacon to ignite the cause. The goddess I revered had crowed about seeing me as lesser, almost celebrating the power she wielded over us by refusing me my wishes and ridiculing me for my faith. She found me lacking—and though I'd buried my vulnerabilities deep, it hit a chord.

One that wouldn't stop humming.

Soren knew that.

Yet he wanted me to stand up for him, to assume the role I knew in my marrow I was never meant to assume. I was to follow his orders to free our country from oppression. To give hope where there was little to give.

My anger banked and my shoulders slumped when frustration fled. Who was I to stand between the people who stood so strong against the wrongness in the world? Though it felt like I'd swallowed a pinecone, I forced the words out of my throat. "I meant every word."

Soren closed his eyes, breathing out a sign of relief. "Then trust me now."

I felt Viv's eyes on me, the burn of worry eating her alive, when I reached for his hands. I squeezed them between my own, as if touching him would make this moment feel real. "I do."

He squeezed my hand and swung his arm toward another door, one that led to another hallway beneath the city. "Together, we'll conquer the world."

31

Ghost of the Goddess

The tunnel wound beneath Azmarin, lit intermittently by luminescent stones the size of my fist imported from Eritris, the land of insect hybrids to our south, and we followed it for what felt like eons. Soren led the way, confident in the path he chose, and I followed, fixated on the back of his neck, the sharp cut of his hairline as if a dagger had slashed across it. There wasn't a part of me that didn't ache, injuries that flared the longer I went without rest, but I refused to stop now. Besides, even if I wanted to sleep, I couldn't. My mind moved too furiously to allow such luxuries.

I felt sick. I was doing this, actually doing this.

Before my encounter with Zos, I'd never hesitated to share my faith or express my belief in her abilities. Soren and I had come to near blows over it on more than one occasion. But never had I claimed to be blessed by her. Never had I perpetuated being her chosen one or lauded the belief that she may have seen more in me than in any other.

Talons, if she hated what I was about to do now, she would surely strike me down.

Or get Qet to do it for her.

"Anytime." Viv's whisper hushed across the back of my neck as she crowded my space, careful to not step on my the backs of my heels. I understood her reminder of our conversation earlier, how she would go with me if I chose to run, and never loved her more than I did at that moment.

But I couldn't leave.

I'd given Soren my promise. I wanted to be useful, to find my place in the world. If that meant trusting him to guide the way, I would put my faith where my mouth was and believe in him, even if doing so shook me in a way I didn't trust.

A staircase emerged in the gloom. Soren took the steps two at a time and held open a door at the top for Viv and me to walk through. Peering past him, I frowned at what appeared to be another closet. Soren sighed. "Push through the clothes and you'll find another door. Open it."

I recognized the heavy weight of aprons meant for metalworking and the slide of chain mail that tugged on my feathers as Viv led the way, attempting to keep the weight from slapping me as much as she could. As promised, the door opened with a squeak, and we emerged in a large room that roared with heat. I tugged my collar away from my neck, and Soren nudged me aside as he closed the door behind us.

"I think it's time you elaborate on your grand scheme, *akren*," Viv hissed.

He wrinkled his nose at the slight. "I've called together the leaders of an operation we're about to lead to liberate the Silverkeep mines." I recognized the name. The mines in the western part of the country were named for their large stores of silver and sapphires; they were also the largest of our trio of remaining mines.

"Why these mines and not the Llyn Mines?" I asked, fighting

the bitterness that arose, recalling his dismissal of my pleas to take action a week ago.

Soren inclined his head, taking the hit on the chin. "More people, for one. It's the largest of our mines and also the most lucrative. Fior values sapphires more than rubies or emeralds, for reasons we are investigating." He scrubbed his hands together, glancing over his shoulder at a pair of barn doors erected on sliding hinges. "But more importantly, we've learned of a cache of drakkentorre stone located in the back of the caverns. Our spy got word out about a month ago—the last we heard from him."

I traded a look with Viv. More tearstone meant more drakken, and Soren had already mentioned the impossibility of accessing the original drakkentorre mines. If they could pull this off, they would not only liberate all those people but arm shifters with wings and scales again.

"It really could be the start of the revolution," I murmured.

"That said, we believe our spy is detained, most likely dead, and we need eyes on the mines to monitor their patterns. That information is necessary to our plans." He pointed. "That's where you and your owls come in." He gripped my shoulder, imbuing some of his strength into my spine.

His plan made sense. Birds were fantastic scouts: quiet, unruffled, and nearly invisible in the woods. Fior wouldn't know what hit them since they didn't know what to watch out for. That said, this operation had been in the works for weeks if not months, and I couldn't help but wonder if he had planned this all along—from the moment he'd learned of my ability to communicate with the raptors. I trained my gaze on my toes, arms clenching around my ribs, stung despite myself.

Viv toyed with her swordbreaker at her hip. "Alright. I see the logic in that plan. But why all the drama?"

"You're unknown. That creates its own kind of mystery, but add in all the other quirks and it makes sense to spin things that way." Soren rolled a pebble under the toe of his shoe. "I trust you stand with us, but they don't know you, and I don't have time to spend convincing them of your trustworthiness. The drama speeds things along, forces their hands." He scratched his arm. "If we don't get moving soon, I worry Innis will figure out our plans."

He knew his friends better than I did. If he wanted to deceive them—he understood their breaking points. I'd already witnessed first-hand the risks of waiting to take action. "What do you need from us?"

Soren glanced over his shoulder again. "Viv, you need to be threatening, imposing, a force against the gods themselves. You'll serve as Telleree's bodyguard. I didn't think you'd have any qualms taking up that role."

She scowled. "I'll show you threatening."

He flicked her a mocking smirk. "And Telleree, you just need to be yourself. Quiet, unassuming, and wholly devoted to protecting your best friend and your owls." I bristled. Unassuming? Was that how he saw me? "Wait for me to call and enter through those doors." He flicked his thumb at the barn doors. "The rest—follow my lead."

We voiced our affirmatives and a moment later, he was nothing more than a shadow slipping through the barn doors. From behind the wall came a smattering of guffaws and unkind curses. Viv and I slipped closer to the doorway to hear better.

"Well, look who it is," a gruff voice called above the din. "The commander himself. What took ya so long, Soren?"

"I've been busy."

"Always busy."

"Come now." I recognized Archer's voice. "We're *all* busy. Now let's get to it."

The voices dropped away and despite our proximity, Viv and I couldn't hear their conversation over the roar of the fires burning in the keep. Viv cleaned her nails with the tip of a knife, occasionally glancing between the cracks in the boards, and I focused on keeping my face blank, waiting for my voice to be called. My nerves made me twitchy. I wanted to scratch my muscles out of my skin, and I sank my nails into my palms, trying to settle my anxiety.

I didn't want to miss the cue.

When all the shifting in the world couldn't counter the numbness settling into my legs and feet, a woman's voice rose over the fire. "We can plan all we want, but we still don't have any idea how many soldiers are guarding the gate, let alone the mines themselves. And what about their patterns? It's reckless at best and a suicide mission at worst."

"Mel's got a point, Archer." That sounded like the man who'd greeted Soren. "Unless you've got some sort of miracle waiting in the wings, I don't know how this is gonna come together."

Silence. Then Soren spoke, his figure little more than a shadowy blur through the gap in the slats of the door. "You wanted to know why I was gone? I was searching for that miracle."

A series of chuckles and protests echoed that statement.

"And I found it."

"Stop kidding around—"

"I assure you, I'm quite serious." The figure with his back to the doors turned, arm extended. "Telleree, would you please join us?"

Viv slid two knives from their sheaths, her preferred Kris daggers as lethal as they were unassuming, and shoved the door open with a bang, mouth set in a thin, straight line. I followed, thumbs hooked in the loops of my cloak so the hem clung to my arms, head bowed beneath my hood, low enough to keep my face in shadow without obscuring my vision.

Several people gasped. One dropped to his knees, hands moving in the sign of Qet. A few drew their daggers, assuming defensive positions as Viv and I approached: a hooded figure resplendent in feathers and her weaponized guardian. Even Archer appeared taken aback, brow lowered, eyes narrowed as his hand rested on the hilt of the sword laying on the table before him. The flickering of the fire danced off the silver of his hair.

"It's a ghost," a man with a grizzled beard cried. "A ghost of the goddess herself."

I heard Zos' name murmured a few times, little more than quiet prayers.

"No need for that," Lukas said lazily, hand curling around his bow. "They come in peace."

Soren stepped beside me and carefully lowered my hood. The air felt cool against my cheeks without its weight. "Everyone, I'd like for you to meet my new friends, Telleree Falk and Viveca Helvig. You'll come to trust them as I do."

"Why would we do that?" the woman who sounded a lot like Mel from earlier spat. "You've brought spirits into our midst."

Viv let her dagger fly, the blade neatly embedding itself into the wood between the woman's fingers where they gripped the table. She jerked her chin as the woman gaped. "I assure you, I'm as real and as human as any of you."

"They both are," Soren agreed. "They aren't spirits or gods. They're people who escaped Aeros the day of the attack and managed to survive all these years, honing their skills, waiting for the right moment to emerge and enter the fold."

A man with a nose reminiscent of my favorite species of hawk stepped forward. "What do you mean? They escaped the palace?"

"Whose blood runs through your veins?" another woman asked, lowering her sword marginally.

"My father was Os Falk, head of the aviary. His wife and my mother was the captain of the royal guard—Mia Falk. I'm their daughter, Telleree." Several more people dropped their weapons, hands moving in the sign of Qet across their chests. "And my friend here is Viveca Helvig. Her mother was once a proud member of the blacksmith core." Bree had never shared the name of Viv's father, and it wasn't needed now.

"I believe her," came a voice near the back. "She's the spitting image of Mia, alright."

"And what of it?" Mel growled. "So you've found more survivors. Who cares? They crop up all the time. How can they be of use? They look like washed up rats to me."

Soren stroked a hand down my arm, leaving a trail of fire in his wake. I kept my face straight, remembering the role he needed me to play.

"Zos blessed Telleree. She's the Guardian of the Owls." It took everything in me to not close my eyes and bow my head at the blasphemy flowing from his lips, the mention of a title I didn't understand. "She wants to free our country from oppression."

I recognized the command, pressed my lips together and whistled. Pip popped up from the bowl of the hood where she'd hidden, finding her familiar spot on my shoulder. Several people cried out at her appearance. Others shrieked when Ghost and Grim emerged from the rafters, wings spread as they landed on the backs of two chairs, rustling and preening as they waited for instruction.

"Soren says you need scouts," I said. "I'm prepared to assume that role."

"How?" asked the gruff man who stood beside Mel. I had a feeling these were the people Soren needed to win over—quickly.

"I understand them." Finally, some footing I felt comfortable with. "They can spread through the trees, speak with other birds, assess

339

the situation and get into areas where you can't. Through that information, I'll be able to tell you everything you need to know."

"How can we believe you?" asked a woman standing beside one of the fire pits, hand raised.

Archer spoke, a small smirk on his face. "A test. We'll have Telleree here prove herself."

Lovely. Just lovely.

32

See the Way Out

Viv had yet to put away her knives.

I rocked on my heels, uncomfortable with the number of eyes on me. My greenhouse; the woods outside the Llyn Mines; staring down Colonel Kohl: they were all places I would rather be than standing in the middle of a smithy surrounded by a crowd of people who could be described as hostile, yet curious.

I understood their concerns. I did. These men and women had fought together, worked together, toiled together for months if not *years,* and then along came me—someone claiming they could help their cause in new and uncomfortable ways. Those whose faces I could see appeared to be of similar age to me, but in experience, they far outweighed my own.

"Relax," Viv murmured. "They might not like us, but they fear Soren more."

The prince hadn't left with Archer, Belfer, and several other members of the Requiem to set up whatever trial they had planned. Instead, he leaned against a wall, alone, arms crossed and eyes closed, while Lukas made the rounds with his trusty notebook, scribbling notes as he caught up with various members of the team.

"Respect." It was Mel who approached first, back rigid with resentment, a long strip of fabric dangling from her hand. "You said we fear him, but it's respect. And a whole lot more of it that you *puntataras* couldn't possibly understand."

I'd never understood the slur about pigs myself and shrugged off her curse. Pigs were honest creatures with simple needs. I wished we could have raised some in Solas, but their hides weren't hardy enough for the Copper Mountains.

"Really?" I asked. Sweat rolled down the sides of my face from the heat thrown by the smithy's fire, but I didn't wipe it away. "You must not know him very well, then, because he's one of the scariest beings this side of the continent."

Maybe super hearing was part of a drakken's skill set, because I could have sworn Soren's lips curved upward as if I'd paid him the highest of compliments.

Mel scoffed and threw the wadded ball of fabric at my head. Viv snagged it out of the air with the flat of her knife and coiled it around her hand, eyes narrowed to slits.

The other woman jerked her chin. "Put that on. Archer says they're ready for you."

Gaze still locked on Mel, Viv passed the material over and I ran it through my hands. A blindfold, and a sturdy one at that. Pip nudged my hand with her beak and I trailed a hand down her back in reassurance before winding the strip around my face, embracing the darkness, appreciating the metaphor for how I'd lived my entire life until now.

Mel checked the knot, fingers rough as they tugged and twisted, ripping out strands of hair, but I waved Viv back. Let Mel think she was in control. There was no one more powerful than one perceived to be weak. Her actions were out of my control, so I focused on the task ahead.

Archer wanted to test my relationship with my owls. I could handle that. The muscles in the back of my neck relaxed. For a minute I'd thought they might want me to prove my connection to Zos—who thankfully hadn't struck me down yet for my blasphemy—or throw me off a mountain again... but this was most definitely in my wheelhouse.

When Mel finally deemed me fit to move, I asked, "Will my owls be safe?" I could feel Pip on my shoulder, but wasn't sure where the others had gone, only that I couldn't sense them any longer.

"Ghost and Grim are fine. Lukas is taking care of them." Soren replaced Mel over my shoulder, and I flinched when a hand brushed my elbow.

I swallowed. "Lead the way, then."

Mel scoffed, the sound louder now that I'd lost sight of the world around me, and a hand curled around mine. Viv's. I recognized the size and shape. "Follow me. I'll make sure you don't trip."

This couldn't be more easy. I trusted Viv with my life. Pip would warn me if necessary, and Soren had a lot riding on this. Between the three of them, I would be alright.

And so we walked. I was aware of doors opening and closing, the sensation of the earth closing in around me, our footsteps rebounding off the walls of what I imagined to be another tunnel. I nearly slipped on rocks a few times, but Viv was always there to steady me, her grip warm and comforting around mine. Another door opened, and we stepped onto what felt like grass, the earth springy and light beneath my boots. I couldn't sense any walls or ceilings and the air smelled crisp after the evening rain.

It might snow.

A signal must have been given, because Viv dropped my hand with a whispered, "You got this," and I felt everyone drift away from me, leaving me alone. Not alone. The sensation of being watched was one I was becoming well-acquainted with. Pip also remained, the pinpricks of her feathers scraping against my neck, rising and falling as she breathed, head swiveling as she took everything in.

"Do you know where you are?" Archer's voice drifted out of nowhere.

I wet my lips. "We're outside, but aside from that, no. I don't know where we are."

"Are you able to see anything through your blindfold?"

I wasn't sure my eyes were open, it was so dark. "No."

"Mel, did you give her this blindfold and watch her put it on?"

The woman's voice came from my left, hard and grating. "I did."

"Did you keep an eye on her the entire way here to ensure it stayed on?"

"Yes."

Archer wasn't ready to release her yet. "And did you test this blindfold yourself?"

"I did, sir. I couldn't see anything." It sounded like she was eating rocks to admit that.

"Very well. Any objections?" Archer paused. Leaves rustled in the wake of a passing breeze, small ones. Aspen? If I could feel the bark, I would know for sure. Archer continued, "So we proceed. Telleree, you've offered the use of your owls to scout the Silverkeep mines. You say you can understand them and they understand you. You believe you can communicate them well enough to pass along the information they relay. Is that correct?"

Pip's beak brushed my throat, and I stroked her back, my voice raw. "I trust them with my life."

Archer's voice lost its hard edge. He sounded almost... amused? "We wish for you to demonstrate the connection you share. Before you is a maze, one that is both complex to maneuver through and filled with danger." That meant traps. Pitfalls, snares—maybe worse.

"Your hands will be bound. You are not permitted to use them to guide your way, and your *human* friends may not call out hints." A few people chuckled. "You may only rely on your owls to guide you back out. If you fall, you're out. Though you're permitted one mistake."

Let them laugh.

If there weren't so much at stake, this would have been fun.

Two crates creaked open and a pair of wings beat the air. Pip's feathers brushed my cheek as she, too, took flight, finding her spot in the trees.

A hand guided me forward. Archer, I assumed, not recognizing the spidery grip on my arm. With an apologetic squeeze, he lashed my hands behind my back with what felt like twine and tugged on it, testing the give. There was none. "You have a half hour to complete the maze. Time starts now."

I could do this.

I used to do stuff like this back home all the time. Tuning out the feeling of eyes boring into my head, I rocked my neck on my shoulders, getting comfortable. "Sound off."

Grim hooted from the right, Ghost from the left. Pip was the farthest away, straight ahead. The Requiem was smart to choose a maze that required thinking logistically. For many animals, this was an impossible test, or at least one they would need several attempts to pass.

But owls were among the most intelligent creatures I'd ever met, and I'd raised these.

I refused to let them be underestimated.

"Are you ready to play a game?" I asked.

Pip adored games, and she trilled happily, her energy spurring Ghost and Grim who hooted their agreement. I sensed the ripple surge through the crowd, though none of them so much as whispered.

"This is a maze," I explained. "There are two openings. One path connects them flawlessly. I'm going to enter from one opening and you're going to get me through to the other side without putting me in danger. Does that make sense?"

Ghost hooted.

I pushed thoughts of the ticking clock from my head. They would only serve as a distraction. Centering myself, I asked the owls a series of questions about the maze itself, trying to understand what I was walking into while giving the owls time to analyze the way out. As I listened to their responses, an image formed in my mind.

The maze took up most of the clearing, a square about a hundred feet both wide and long with the crowd of Requiem soldiers watching from my left. The path itself was simple, branches from briarbushes and other fauna formed pathways wide enough for me to walk through. The walls were about as high as my hips. Snares had been set and holes dug periodically around the maze, simple traps that would be far more difficult to navigate blindfolded.

The only thing I couldn't grasp was the shape of the maze itself.

"Can you see the way out?"

All three owls chimed their affirmatives.

Here we go.

Pip trilled again, and I stifled a grin. That bastard. Archer had intentionally placed me facing a wall, not even at the entrance of the damn puzzle. I took three steps right, imagining his foxy face crinkling with amusement. "Let's do this."

I'd relied on my owls before, and I wholeheartedly meant it when I said I trusted them with my life, but there was something surreal about being the instrument to prove their worthiness. We moved slowly, every step made with confidence, only stopping when the owls quarreled. Ghost proved the most capable when it came to navigating the nuances of the maze. Grim was most helpful in keeping me in a straight line, and Pip guided me around the snares and pitfalls. As I moved deeper into the maze, the clock I'd pushed to the back of my mind crept forward.

When I rounded a particularly difficult corner complete with not one but two traps, Lukas' voice split my concentration: "How many people are watching you right now, Tell?"

I nearly tripped over my feet and clenched my teeth, fighting to stay upright with my center of gravity thrown off. The question ruffled Grim's feathers, and he screeched his displeasure at being interrupted. They must have wanted to complicate things. Maybe we'd already exceeded their expectations, and they wanted to see how far they could push us.

"Pip?" The owl chittered her answer. Huh. More than I thought. "Twenty-three."

A murmur went up, and I managed a few more steps before another question volleyed my way: "Can you check for enemies within a thousand paces?"

Soren. If I hadn't sworn off violence, I would have strangled him. Guessing this was a new part of the game, I removed Pip from the maze and told Ghost and Grim they would have to manage on their own. Two corners later, the screech owl issued the all clear.

"We're safe," I relayed, knowing full well that three of those watching recognized Pip's call. Wings rustled, and I imagined Pip landing near our audience, eyeing them with interest. "Any other questions?"

Having picked up the fresh aspect of this challenge with relish, the questions started coming quicker, things like what people were wearing or how many trees were in a certain area. Some questions were too difficult for the birds to interpret: specifics about types of plants or colors of attire, which I informed the watchers about with growing frustration. I also fielded questions about myself, and while I wasn't comfortable sharing some of these details, I didn't want to risk my standing within this tight-knit community.

A headache pounded in my temples, the result of navigating the six or seven voices all demanding things of me, fracturing my attention. Grim hooted, informing me we had just twenty feet left. Almost to the end. It was at the peak of my frustration that a question knocked me off-guard and I made my first mistake.

"Are these your only owls?"

My toe caught on the edge of a pitfall and I flailed, going down hard, my burn screaming in pain when I landed on my arm awkwardly. The murmuring of the crowd died, leaving me in eerie silence. Even the owls went quiet. I couldn't see anything, but still I squeezed my eyes shut, forcing back the tears that welled in the back of my throat.

That was all it took. A simple question and I was back on that mountain cradling the torn and shredded bodies of my birds, salty tears staining their beautiful feathers. I could smell the black smoke and the charred flesh as the flames devoured their bodies. It reminded me of why I was here, standing beside Soren and his team. I couldn't allow anyone else to experience that kind of pain again. That ugly, horrific, preventable death.

"No," I ground out, rolling so to my knees, hands still bound at the small of my back. I still wondered where Clyde had ended up: stupid burrowing owls and their stupid habits. And the wild snowy who'd traveled with us momentarily, abandoning us for no reason at all.

"I have lost many. And there are still others who I call family that I haven't been able to find."

Grim whistled, alerting me to my proximity to the wall, and I stood carefully, curving around the corner with ease. A few more steps and I would be out. Ghost, this time, alerted me to the danger, a bigger dip than before, this one with rocks at the bottom. Screw this. Screw this test and these prying questions. I turned to those assembled, aware of their focus.

"But Zos help me, I will find them."

I raced forward and leaped, imagining my cloak flying out behind me, the feathers ruffling in the wind. Ghost's chime told me I'd cleared the danger. Three more steps and I was out. I fumbled with the knot Archer had left for me to tug loose, freeing my hands, and ripped the bandanna from my head, heel of my hand pressed to my temple, scouring the crowd for Archer. There were more than twenty-three people now. Word had spread.

"Did I make time?"

The leader of the Requiem glanced at his silver watch. "By two minutes. You passed." He tugged on his earring. "Congratulations Tell. Welcome to the team."

33

Trapdoor

The following week passed in a blur of unfamiliar faces, dark tunnels, and pounding headaches.

Pleased with my success in the maze, Archer summoned me early the next morning and instructed me to work with both those who led the Requiem and the foot soldiers who would carry out their plans. I saw little of Stavanger proper, spending most of my time navigating the tunnels that wove beneath the city and its walls, and it was hard to believe Fior controlled this territory given the sheer number of rebels I met on a daily basis.

"That's the beauty of it," Archer told me the second evening, tweaking my nose cheekily. "We allow the grand duke to think he's in control, pretending to be meek and cowed, but really it's the perfect cover, giving us the freedom we need to run our operations with them none the wiser. We don't have the numbers to take on the army alone, but with sneak attacks, we stand a chance."

The attack on the Silverkeep mines appeared to be the biggest of sneaky moves, the culmination of years of recruiting and training and deceiving. When I wasn't meeting people within the Requiem, I was learning about those who operated outside of it: the leaders of Fior's northern military, the lords and ladies who occasionally visited Aeros, the soldiers who were trusted in key areas. I drank in the information, knowing it would help me understand the scope of the situation so I could provide the best information.

Archer had pulled Viv from my side immediately, wanting her to start training with their elite troops. From what little she told me in the minutes we shared in our room beneath Madame Taft's shop, she couldn't be more delighted with the role she would serve.

"The front lines," she'd breathed, eyes glowing with excitement. She slashed with her knife as if imagining slitting the throat of an enemy only she could see. "We take out the worst of the baddies first, get as close to the entrance as we can, and then the second wave comes in, cleaning up our mess and taking care of any stragglers."

The more her excitement grew, the greater the dread in my chest expanded, its brutal branches winding deeper inside me, twining around my heart and snaring my lungs so I could scarcely think or breathe around the worry. Every time it became too much, typically when I was tucked in the darkness of the tunnels between meetings, I had to brace myself, remind myself this was what she wanted, what she was *good* at.

But no matter how deeply my dread burrowed, I couldn't bring myself to call upon Zos.

Part of me still flinched away from her ridicule. Another part didn't want to draw any more attention to Viv than needed. I didn't think I would ever forget the way Zos had stared at my best friend like a ripe berry ready to be plucked from the bush. She'd spent so many years protecting me, the least I could do was redirect the attention of the goddess of death herself.

Since that night in the tunnels, we'd scarcely talked, let alone touched, and it became easier to convince myself I'd misunderstood the shivers her fingers had invoked. I told myself I imagined the desire burning in her eyes when she allowed herself to be vulnerable.

My wounds healed, and the bandages came off. The burn took the longest, and Viv was with me with I finally made the call to unwind the bandage. The itching had finally stopped. Together, we soaked the stained cloth in warm water and peeled it away. I gasped at the white scar that appeared beneath the bandages, one barely visible against my skin.

"That can't be normal," Viv said reverently, tracing the raised edges of the scar. "If Lukas wasn't convinced you met the goddess already, this would prove it to him, surely." She'd been spending a lot of time with the drakken lately, relying on his expertise to help her understand the inner-workings of the Requiem. "It looks like a plant wrapped around your wrist."

"It's queenkiller's lace," I marveled, tracing the wispy flowers gracing the tips of the vines. If we had stumbled upon it in the forest, its berries would have been red as heart blood and its stems the palest shade of green.

Viv dropped heavily beside me. My skin prickled beneath her finger wandering around the whorls of the vine. "That sounds dangerous."

"It's an incredibly rare plant," I added. "Its berries produce the one of the most toxic poisons in the world. As far as I've read, it's second only to a poison produced by a duchy in Eritris—and there's some dispute over whether the strongest poison is naturally grown or manufactured."

I traced the lines again, transfixed. "Queenkiller's lace is one of the poisonous plants Zos claims as her own—most of which are about as rare as this one. To see it in real life would be a miracle."

"We both know how unlikely miracles are these days." Viv wasn't looking at the scar when she said it. She was staring straight at me, the crests of her cheeks brushed with pink, green eyes sparkling with wonder. "Right?"

I swallowed hard against the feathers fluttering softly down my chest, tugging my sleeve down around the scar, and didn't answer. I couldn't answer. Not when she looked at me like that.

"What do you think it means?" Viv asked when the silence became too much. She toyed with a finger-length knife she'd pulled from a sheath along her forearm.

My heart clenched painfully, recalling my thoughts in the temple about the tragic ends met by those who the gods and goddesses chose to carry out their heroic deeds. I was no hero, but I was certainly wrapped around her finger. Somehow, I felt that was worse. "Nothing good."

Viv leaned back on her elbow. "Nothing?"

"It could be a warning."

"Or a blessing."

She had a point. But I couldn't dismiss the feeling of a specter looming over me, dark and dangerous and deadly. No, this felt like a warning. One I shouldn't ignore.

* * *

I threw myself into my work after that, obsessing over the minor details because it was the only control I had given my situation. Often, that meant working with my owls, hurrying them outside the walls to the clearing where I'd faced my first major test, teaching them new words and commands.

Two more days passed where I scarcely slept or ate, let alone visited the rooms I shared with Viv. Archer must have noticed my wan appearance and told me to take an hour for myself, to find something to do to take my mind off of things. Between my scar, my responsibility, and my confusing relationship with Viv, I couldn't relax, so I returned to the woods, scaled a tree and darted from branch to branch like the squirrels I'd loved to mock in the Owl Wood, delighting in chasing my birds. They were clever enough to stay within sight, but not close enough to snare their tails or wings.

When I dropped back in the clearing, hot and sweaty from exertion, but feeling freer than I had in weeks, I encountered a dark shadow leaning against a tree. "Soren?"

The prince was busier than any of us. He and Lukas were called to meeting after meeting, working on last-minute details required of such a huge operation. It was nice to see him like this—alone. Quiet. Non-conflicted. He straightened and offered my cloak. I'd dropped it on the ground, preferring the freedom that came in its absence.

"It's a shame you don't have wings," he observed. "You move like you deserve them."

I allowed him to slip the cloak over my shoulders, the scent of the lemonseed oil he worked into his scales washing over me. I sighed. "Is that possible? To find your inner drakken when you're older?"

Like all children borne of Idilea before the invasion, my parents had taken me to the temples to test out the bits of drakkentorre kept in bowls. I recalled the slick slide of the beads in my tiny toddler fist, so smooth and slippery. Though she would deny it later, my mother hadn't disguised her relief when I failed to feel a tremble of power. My father had laughed and thrown me over his shoulders, promising to gift me wings of a different sort.

Soren hummed and twisted the bracelet on his wrist, the one that hid his shard of stone. "Intriguing question, and one we've discussed at length, actually—Archer, Lukas, and me. Archer and I believe it must be possible to come into shifter abilities well into adulthood. There are children born within the last seventeen years who've never been presented with an opportunity to discover their inner talents. I also refuse to believe those children can't possess their drakken just because they couldn't touch some old stones before they turned five."

He sighed. "But Lukas thinks they're out of luck, that our next generation of shifters will come after we free our kind and we return to our traditions. He says because it's never been recorded in history—people coming into talents after they're older than seven—that it simply isn't possible." He shoved his hands in his pockets. "What a depressing way to look at the world."

"And that's coming from you."

There was that grin again. The one that I knew he only allowed a few spare people to see. The one that caused my heart to twist. "Yes, I suppose so."

He pulled open the trapdoor, cleverly concealed between a pair of trees, brows bunching as he peered into the depths. "My torch must have gone out. I swear I left it burning."

"No matter." I ducked beneath his arm and hopped the ten feet to the ground below, bending my knees to take the impact of the drop. "I know the way back."

Only a few tunnels had luminescent stones bored into the walls, and this was not one of them. When the door closed, what little light filtered in vanished with a snap. Soren dropped beside me a moment later. He crowded the hallway, our clothing rubbing together. Side by side, we walked in silence, straining to hear danger approaching in the dark. I'd settled into a comfortable rhythm when the mood shifted, darkened.

"I'm worried about this operation." Soren rarely admitted weakness, let alone concern. He'd exuded nothing but confidence, even arrogance, about their plan to free the prisoners in the mines, and to hear him expressing doubt shook me.

Badly.

I snagged his sleeve, dragging him to a stop. I couldn't see his face, but I guessed where it was in the darkness, and planted my hand firmly on his chest, feeling his lungs expanding and contracting. "Soren, you are going to pull this off. You have a good plan, you've got good people. I've listened to Archer go over every detail ad nauseam, working out the kinks until everyone involved is satisfied."

"But that's Archer—"

"And Archer wouldn't do this if he didn't think you were prepared to handle it." My fingers dug grooves into his shirt. "He would not risk lives—your life—unless he was positive in the outcome. You're so close—it's going to turn out."

His chest heaved and his hand came up, circling my wrist. "I'm putting so many people at risk for this. What if—"

"Stop it." I pushed up against him. "Don't you say another word in doubt. This will work. It *will*."

Silence. His thumb stroked my pulse, chasing goosebumps across my skin. "How are you like this? How do you have so much faith in the world, even when it turns against you?"

He always did this: turned situations back on me, on my faith and the questions I had about it. I was growing weary of it and went to pull away, suddenly uncomfortable with our proximity, when Soren tightened his grip, keeping my palm flat over his heart.

"I may not believe you met the goddess, but I saw the change in you after we left the temple," he said. How ironic then, that he squeezed the scars of the burn that remained from that encounter, scars I hadn't decided whether I wanted to show anyone else. He continued, "Whatever you experienced there, it changed you. I haven't heard you pray once since then, not a peep. And trust me, I got used to hearing you calling on that god of yours all times of the day."

Soren's arm circled my back, pulling me closer. His warm breath brushed my lips. "Your god betrayed you, but even now you're telling me to believe. To believe that we can pull this off, that we have the skill and the ability and the element of surprise necessary to land a significant blow to Fior."

His hair flopped forward, the strands falling against my face, tickling the bridge of my nose. "To succeed where my brother could not."

With my free hand, I brushed those strands out of the way, mind spinning. Though plenty of time had passed, I had yet to sit and think about my feelings regarding Zos, frankly feared the analysis and what it might mean for my future. But I wasn't a coward. I questioned more now than I had in the Copper Ridge Mountains, but at the core of it all, I was starting to understand myself.

My words were soft, pulled straight from the well of faith I knew would always exist within me. "This is bigger than one goddess, Soren. This is bigger than all the gods, and even if Zos won't stand with us, there are six others. One of them must believe in our cause." It just about killed me to face the ugly teeth of that truth.

"This is for the sake of Idilea, for your people, for all of drakkenkind and the humans who live alongside them. You are their king, their protector, their savior. You and Archer and Lukas—all those people who follow you. They believe *you*. They believe we can pull this off. Don't discount their faith, because that's bigger than the gods. I have faith in that faith."

Soren's response was immediate. "But what if I'm not the savior they need? I'm so cynical. I've heard Archer's analysis, but I have my doubts." His body shook against mine, an echo of a sob he couldn't contain. "Eero was the best of us, the smartest and strongest. They had a soundproof plan, but they failed." His hand fumbled around mine, linking our fingers together and squeezing. "He and Lukas' father and so many others were captured and executed at the hands of those dogs when they failed." His voice hardened. "It almost cost us the Requiem because we lost most of the fighters who remained. If my brother couldn't pull this off—" his breathing stuttered—"what hope do I have?"

"Stop it." I pressed flat against him, stepping on the toes of his boots as my temper flared, acidic as snake venom. "You are enough. I've seen your passion, your love for this country. Your loyalty is second to none, and I count Viveca among that number. If anyone can pull this off, it's you." My hands found his face again, thumbs brushing the creases of his cheekbones, and I shook him, demanding him to see the determination in my face, even in the absolute darkness.

His chest heaved, our breaths coming in pants. My frustration twisted, not in outrage at his doubt, but with a new kind of passion. I felt lightheaded with our proximity, lost in his scent and warmth. He was so strong, every muscle honed and for his cause.

I dragged one trembling hand down his cheek, to his jaw, then back around his neck where I brushed the soft, short hair that knifed across the back of his head. "Do you hear me?"

"I hear you." His voice shook.

"Do you believe you will succeed?" I needed to hear him say it.

His hand spanned against my back, his fingers rubbing down my spine. "You make me want to believe it."

"Not good enough." Our mouths were practically touching, we stood so closely together. His breath mingled with mine and my head went so light I imagined it floating away. "I need more."

"And I need you." His response was swift and heartbreaking, though I didn't have long to dwell on the pain because his other arm came up around the back of my head, fingers curling in my hair. "I said it already, Telleree. You make me want to believe, to find faith in something I can't see, and it frightens me. I want to understand your passion, your mind, how you think—but right now, I can barely—I can't—I... I need you."

358

He was shaking so hard I feared he might rattle apart. His forehead pressed against mine, his thumb finding my cheekbone. "May I? Please?"

I knew what he was asking. Twin flames of fear and exhilaration twined around one another, burning hot and high, and despite the danger, I craved more. "Yes."

Soren's lips brushed mine, soft and cool, drawing me in. His grip on my scalp shifted, fingers dancing down the back of my neck, resting at the top of my spine where he kneaded the muscles, carefully shifting me in his arms, angling my head to his liking. Our kisses grew harder, more insistent, our wandering hands more secure as we explored one another's bodies.

I sipped on his lips, loving the hitch in his chest when I pressed my open mouth to his throat, how he shivered when I moaned at his touch. He tasted like sweet and shadow, a blend that fogged my brain, drunk on the sensation of *him*. How long we'd danced around this, our bickering bordering on something more.

He needed me. I needed him.

A fever coiled within me, the flames spreading farther and wider than they ever had before, tingling in my fingertips and toes. I needed more. Impatiently, I dug my fingers into his hair, pulling him closer, my lips parting, chasing the sparks that danced between us. With a groan, he gave in, his lips parting. His arm around my back was firm but steady, and I knew if I wanted, I could pull away, break the spell, and he would let me.

"Fuck, you have no idea how long I've wanted to do this." He maneuvered me backwards, our feet artfully dancing around one another until my back pressed against the wall of the tunnel. Pebbles pattered around my feet, scraped off the wall by my cloak. "You feel so good."

Our kisses softened, turning tender. Deeper. The sparks that had flown hot and fierce in my breast transformed into feathers, twisting and turning, their wildness tamed. As those feathers drifted and settled, I went still in his arms. Tears threatened, and I closed my eyes against them, pulling my lips from his, hands planted on his firm chest.

Soren was an avalanche. Given the opportunity, he would swallow me whole.

"I can't."

When I truly craved the sun.

"Of course." The prince gave me space, though didn't fully release me. It made me a terrible person, but I didn't want him to, even though it was what I needed him to do. He pressed a kiss to my forehead, his hand gliding up my spine. The sensation, soft and tender, almost drew me in again, but when his lips ghosted down my nose, seeking my lips, the crack in my chest widened, opening a dark void that roared in haunted agony. I pushed against him and the hand cupping my head stilled, his thumb tracing small circles on my temple.

"I'm sorry," I whispered, only partially sure why I was interrupting this moment, but needing to put it out in the open for both of us to see. "I'm so sorry." I made no further move to pull out of his arms, another crack splintering wide in my chest at my hypocrisy, at my clinginess, even if he wasn't who I trusted with my life. My heart.

For all the violence he exuded regularly, none of it was evident in his hold now. If anything, his compassion swamped the bitter anger that wrapped around him like a blizzard as he sought to understand my conflicting signals. He pressed another kiss to my forehead, nose brushing the hair on the crown of my head. "You have nothing to apologize for."

Shuddering, shaking, I wrapped my arms around him, my chin finding a comfortable spot on his shoulder as he settled into the embrace. I hadn't allowed myself to imagine this moment, neither the heat that flared or the tenderness that lingered, too afraid of what it meant. But I knew now those sparks were hot enough to burn, and I wasn't sure he would stick around long enough to put them out.

He made me feel things I hadn't felt before, and I basked in the warmth of his embrace, recalling the heat of his glower and the way my stomach flipped when he aimed that half smile my way.

"I can't. It doesn't feel right," I repeated. "I wish I could explain, but I don't think you'd understand."

His chest rumbled. "But I do."

Sensing my surprise, Soren drew back enough for me to peer at him, eyes adjusted enough to make out the silhouette of his face. He stroked my cheek, brushed the corner of my lip, then slipped around my neck. His chest heaved with a long, harsh shudder. If I hadn't known better, I might have believed it to be a sob.

"I'm too late." Dirt crinkled against my collar, as if he'd drilled his fingers into the wall, forcing it to absorb the breadth of his pain. "Too fucking late and I knew it."

My brain, still recovering from the surge of endorphins, recognized the throb of disappointment. I couldn't be the one to reassure him, but I wanted to. I reached for his shirt again, prepared to pull him back to me, to tell him he had it all wrong, that he wasn't the one to blame, when light flared, orange and bright. The opening appeared at the end of the hallway and a door swung on its hinges.

I squinted against the brilliant flare, the bed of snakes that was my dread and guilt writhing, hissing and spitting in warning. I hadn't realized how close we were to the end of the tunnel until a figure traipsed down, the bob of her hair flaring around her head when she stopped mid-step. Viv's mouth dropped, the color leeching from her skin as she stared at me, then Soren, then our bodies entwined around one another.

My stomach clenched, and I shoved Soren away, reaching for her. "Wait. Viv. It's not—"

"I don't—what?" She clutched her hand to her chest. "I can't—"

Barely one step forward and she was already scrambling through the doorway, torch abandoned on the ground where she'd dropped it. The door slammed shut and her boots pounded against the floor of the smithy. Another door crashed into a wall.

Halfway up the stairs, I recalled the prince, and turned back to him, his eyes dark and mournful.

"Go," he said. I'd never seen him look more defeated. "Get her. Tell her the truth."

Which version?

"I'll be back." I promised.

Then I was gone, chasing my friend through the streets of Stavanger.

34

Matters of the Heart

"Viv." The door crashed into the wall before I could catch it. "Wait. Please." I was gasping, chest raw and screaming, snot streaming down my face. My best friend in the world stopped in the center of the tailor's shop, which was, thankfully, empty of patrons. "Please."

"Yes, Telleree?" She planted her boot and turned, arms coming up around herself, clutching the edges of her cloak. "What exactly do you have to say to me?"

Telleree. She only used my full name when she was pissed.

I fumbled the door closed, wiping my face, and opted to not move deeper into the room. One wrong step and she would bolt. "What you saw in the tunnel. It wasn't how it looked." A cramp flared in my side, and I flinched, squeezing the injury with a grimace. "Let me explain."

"Oh, so you weren't kissing the prince?" A shadow shifted in the back rooms where Madame Taft kept her extra supplies. I recognized the tip of the boot that emerged and pressed the heels of my palms to my eyes. "You know, wrapped up in Soren? The bloodthirsty boy who's, I don't know, using you for purposes you don't agree with and has zero qualms about doing so? That boy?"

I smoothed my hand over my frazzled hair, wondering where it had all gone wrong. Not half an hour ago I'd centered myself, and now it was all messed up. I'd abandoned one man to the tunnels, his eyes haunted and empty, and the woman who I was still coming to terms about what she meant to me was beyond mad. My heart rabbit-kicked against my ribs, pounding so quickly I couldn't differentiate the beats.

"Yes. Alright. We kissed." I held out my hand, palm flat, staying her rebuttal. "But it didn't mean anything. It was—"

Viv barked out a laugh, a pained, beaten whimper of a laugh. "It didn't *mean* anything? That man has been moon-eyed over you since I've known him, and it meant nothing? That's not how it looked when I so *inconveniently* interrupted."

My heart dropped through my gut. "Viv. It didn't—I couldn't—" I clutched at my chest as if I could rip my heart out and present it to her. There were so many options, so many avenues to take, but I couldn't stray from the path of brutal honesty. Lying to my best friend was never my forte. "Yes. You're right. It did mean something, but not how you're thinking it meant. It was one moment, and it didn't—I will never—"

I was failing. Absolutely failing at this, my thoughts like dandelion seeds scattered by the wind, impossible to gather again. What was I trying to say? About him? About her?

"Listen." Viv's voice softened, but I recognized the danger that posed. I'd only ever witnessed her this angry three times, and never had her fury been directed at me. My spine curled, my body caving in on itself, waiting for the poisonous barbs to hit.

"You can kiss whoever you want. I'm just surprised it was him, of all people. *Him.*" She dropped her arms, her face expressing a different truth, one of betrayal and defeat. She looked so much like the prince I'd abandoned for her that I wanted to scream. It made me want to smash something, to shake her, demand she hear me out. If only I could figure out what to say.

She attempted a smile. "I want to make sure you're thinking clearly about this. You are two very different people with very different upbringings with extremely different views of the world." Her voice cracked, betraying her attempt at clinical observation. "He's a prince and you're a wild girl he saved from the mountains."

I knifed backward, my shoulder blades slamming against the door I'd forgotten. Hot tears welled in my throat and I swallowed them back down.

"Make sure you think about that." Viv trailed her fingers through her hair, a curl catching and springing back into place. "Think about the fact he's probably going to die getting his throne back if someone doesn't stop him. And Telleree, no offense, but you don't have the backbone to do anything about it."

This time when she spun, red hair flaring around her head as she strode for the doors to the tunnels leading to our rooms underground, I didn't call to her. I let her go, one hand curled into a fist against my chest, the other pressed flat against the front door, shaking, torn between screaming and breaking something as a fissure cracked my heart in two.

The door to the tunnel snicked closed, and I sagged, legs finally giving out, crumpling at the base of the wall. Moisture trickled down my cheeks and I swiped at it uselessly, tears dripping from my chin, speckling my tunic. Too far. She'd gone too far this time. Yes, I had failed to articulate my feelings about Soren, but what she'd said bordered on cruel.

I felt bigger around the prince, stronger and more sure. He embodied the danger of living in the mountains and twice as much exhilaration of the sharply angled slopes we skied on, but none of the comfort that came with the familiar. No, my home belonged somewhere else, with someone else. Someone with wounded doe's eyes who I wasn't sure how to talk to anymore.

Someone who had always accepted me.

Until now.

"Oh, dear girl." Madame Taft emerged from around the corner, a soft blanket in her arms. She flipped the lock on the door and sank beside me, wrapping the wool around my shoulders as she bundled me against her, rocking slowly back and forth. I choked, allowing the tears to flow more freely, tiny sobs hiccuping from my lips. My hand pressed to my mouth did nothing to quell the noise. "Matters of the heart are always so complicated, aren't they?"

"Why?" Tension knotted my shoulders, invoking a new kind of shaking. Taft hadn't been here alone. Lukas had been here, too, listening to our argument as we ripped each other apart. I'd seen his boot and heard him follow Viv into the tunnels, no doubt to soothe her like Taft was doing for me. I braced a foot beneath myself, ready to charge after her and make her see reason, but Taft gripped my arm in an unbreakable hold.

"Give your friend some time. She's had a shock," the weathered woman warned. "How you're feeling now? She feels the same. Understanding what others mean to you and what you mean to them is part of growing up." A wrinkled finger scraped across my cheek, collecting my tears, and when she bundled me closer, I found myself incapable of resisting, my face jammed against her shoulder. "You're both hurting. And it's alright to hurt. I've watched you girls. I know this will work out. Give it a little time. I promise, you'll see I'm right."

She sounded so reasonable.

And I allowed myself to pretend that she knew best. If only time were a luxury I could afford.

* * *

Viv and I didn't speak for two days.

She abandoned our normal tunnels and favorite businesses. I didn't know where she was staying, but I had a feeling it was somewhere close to Lukas. Mel informed me the two of them had become inseparable following our fight.

Tracking Viv down would have been easier if we weren't so busy preparing to leave for the mines. I welcomed the work, embracing how mentally consuming my tasks were, leaving little room to obsess over my relationships for long stretches of the day. Archer placed more demands on my head as if he knew my predicament, from running from one end of town to the other relaying messages, to sending out the owls to check on some detail, or preparing carts and gathering armor.

Even Soren proved elusive, leaving Azmarin with the first batch of soldiers bound for the mines. Archer demanded I linger with the last party bound to leave Azmarin, insisting I was necessary to the closing operations. Yeah, he knew. He had to know. And I allowed him to twist me around his finger until we finally departed the dreary southern city, Viv and Lukas in tow.

Azmarin was the last major city on the way to the mines. They boasted a small trading town that was little more than a main street lined with a handful of businesses—primarily a bank, a general goods store, and a bar. Mel told me long, tall buildings lined with tiny windows boasted single-bedroom lodging.

Before the invasion, working in the mines had been considered an honor. Many of those who dove into their depths emerged wealthier than they ever could imagine. Idilea also had strict laws about working in the mines: limiting the times of operation, ordering basic amenities be met on a daily basis, and restricting time spent working them to three months before taking two years away.

Now those laws were dust.

Our people slept in the sweltering depths of the caverns, sweating nutrients from their skin, growing weaker by the day, working their bodies until they gave out. The lodging that used to house the workers was now inhabited by Fiorian soldiers.

I slumped over the neck of my mare as she plodded through the trees on the outskirts of Azmarin, fingers twisted in her dark mane, staring miserably down at nothing. Exhaustion stained my thoughts, blurred the edges of my vision, yet I couldn't sleep. Not without horrors chasing my heels, breathing in my face, slashing at me with knife-tipped fingers. Hooves clopped, approaching from behind, but I couldn't be bothered to look up. With my feathered cloak folded away and my hood up, I was scarcely recognizable behind my maroon scarf and freshly fitted shirt and pants.

"You didn't tell her the truth, did you?"

His voice was like a physical touch down my back, and I shivered. Soren had returned to escort us. Holding a hand against the pale gray of the afternoon sky, I could make out the outline of the prince in my periphery, the way he sat tall in his saddle, refusing to bow to the flurries sweeping around him. His hood was down, hair in rare disarray. For as regal as he appeared, I couldn't find the energy within myself to uncurl my back to match him.

What a mess we'd made of everything.

"What do you want?" I asked.

He ran a hand over the curve of his stallion's neck, scratching lightly along the mane. "There are a great many things I want, Telleree." I would never get used to how he said my name like that, the way he always said it in its entirety, his tongue curling around it like fine wine, and I wanted to slap myself. I knew how I felt about him and how I refused to allow him to sweep me away in a chaos of blurring snow and blinding feelings. But my heart hadn't caught up with my brain and it craved one more touch.

One more kiss.

Soren cleared his throat. "I want to wipe away your misery."

I chuckled humorously. "I don't think there's anything you can do about that."

"No? Have I told you my view on challenges?" He angled his horse closer to mine, our legs nearly touching. "They're meant to be overcome."

I shook my head. "Stop. I need to be alone and think about—"

"The last thing you need is to be alone. You've had two days of alone time. Archer's helped you with that—and yes, I'm aware of what he's been up to." His breath clouded in front of his face and he guided his horse around a fallen log. "Right now you need a friend to remind you of how exceptional you are and how talented that cantankerous friend of yours is—vulgar though she may be."

The laughter that burst from me felt real. Between Soren and Viv, I was hard-pressed to pick who was more vulgar. As quickly as it surged through me, the burst of joy faded. I squeezed the reins, the stitching digging grooves in my gloves. "You still consider us friends?"

My cheeks burned at the foolishness of my tongue. Of all the things to ask...

"You're asking all the hard questions today, aren't you?" Soren went quiet, but it wasn't a tense silence, one that demanded to be filled or broken. No, this was companionable silence achieved by two people who understood the need for such a thing, who appreciated the way a horse's hooves landed on the ground and the way the wind tangled around the bits of snowflakes around us.

"Yes, we're friends. We'll always be friends." He brushed his fingers across my upper arm playfully, successfully drawing out a smile. "I may have wanted more, but I can look beyond that, you know." He puffed out his chest. "I held back for weeks and I'm sure given more time, it will fade. Besides, it's not like I won't have a whole mess of bigger problems to attend to."

His eyes were over-bright, his smile too wide, but I permitted him that lie as my heart broke for him. For the man who craved simple pleasures in a world where he wouldn't find many.

"You're right about that." I adjusted my scarf to fend off the worst of the puffy flakes. "We'll get through this fight and the one after that, and when you're back on your throne, I'll figure out my next step. I won't put you through—"

"You misunderstand." His horse shook its head, sending snow flying every which way. "I want you by my side when this is all said and done. You and Archer and Viv and everyone who has helped us get this far." He grinned up into the clouds. "Lukas is always reminding me of the attributes I need to fix when I become king: I'm too impatient, too blood-thirsty, too aggressive—too morally black. I need someone like you around, full of life and light and promise—who looks at the world like it's this bright, shiny place."

I snorted. "I've never seen the world like that, you know."

"No. But you see it much differently than I do." He was barely whispering now, and I had to strain to hear the syllables. "It's why it's for the best we don't get our emotions too tangled in this friendship. I need to rely on you like I rely on the sword in my hand."

Yet again, he said the last thing I expected. I could scarcely see beyond the immediate problems we faced, let alone a future where a king would want me by his side. All I'd ever wanted in the world was my owls and my greenhouse. I wasn't prepared to handle court life and the responsibilities and trials that came with it.

But I could see it. See myself standing where my parents once had, envisioning their proud faces as I reclaimed their legacy.

And what an image it was.

Until I turned it away, buried it in a jar in my mind reserved for hopes and dreams. We needed to get through one problem before thinking about what came next. We had prepared for the battle ahead, but that didn't mean we had evaded the threat of all risk.

Death was still on the table.

"Soren, you're looking at the world the wrong way," I managed. "You're loyal to a fault and you love your country. You're capable of great compassion, but you've never had a chance to find that side of yourself and allow it to sweep you away. Once the battle is behind you, I think you'll see yourself more clearly."

Silence settled again. Our horses moving side by side, hooves sinking into the drifts. Eventually, the silverpines swallowed the aspens. Archer's voice rang out from up front, summoning the prince to his side.

"See," Soren said before breaking away. "This is why I need you here. You give me hope. Hope for a better future, a brighter outlook. We'll always be friends. No matter what."

35

Anything Could Happen

The Silverkeep Mines ran as deep as they did wide, their tunnels twisting far into the roots of the soil, according to Lukas. Three entrances led to the shafts below, each heavily patrolled by soldiers. They had removed sweeping swaths of trees in arcs away from the mines, making it more difficult to approach without notice.

Archer and I crouched behind some pines bordering the southernmost entrance, monitoring the movements of the soldiers and the slaves they kept down below. Though I'd been briefed on the landscape and why my owls would be so helpful in this terrain, it wasn't until now that I realized exactly *how* helpful.

"They're prepared for war," I murmured three hours into our shift. "Have the mines always been so heavily armed?"

Archer sat with his back against a tree, poking at an old map he'd laid flat on the dry earth. Though we'd passed through a storm on the way out, the snow hadn't reached the mine far out west. But it would soon. I could smell the energy in the air, the wild scent of ice and fury brewing over the horizon.

"Yeah. First order of business for the Fiorian command, in fact,"

Archer answered my question. "They took their first round of prisoners, marched 'em below ground, then put a policy in place with no one in, no one out unless you're wolven or dead."

A shudder worked down my spine, and I whistled for Pip, who plunged through the foliage to land on my shoulder, murmuring quiet whisperings deep in her throat. I stroked her tiny head as she spoke, listening attentively to her update as Archer watched on, his interest undisguised.

"Want the good news or the bad news first?" I asked.

The leader of the Requiem smirked. "When have I ever wanted good news?"

"The other entrances are as heavily armored as this one. About fifty Fiorian soldiers are positioned at each. Most stay above ground, but a few must be relegating things below, too, because the number shifts by about seven each turn of the clock." Icicles formed in my stomach. They gave their own people breaks, but many of our people hadn't so much as seen the light of day in months or years. I fought to restrain my temper by focusing on the branches scraping together in the subtle northern breeze. Though tucked away, shouting and raging would draw the wrong attention.

Archer's pen scratched on the page. He rubbed the back of his hand over his mouth. "Fifty, huh? I'd expected more, but I suppose they are wolven. One of them is worth five humans, at least."

I scooped some up some pine needles and clenched them in my palm. We needed three hundred soldiers, but we only had about half that. And about two-thirds of the people we did have were fully trained. Soren, Lukas, and the Requiem's third drakken named Ivan offset the odds a little, but not by much. Requiem leadership outside of Archer was banking on help from the hundreds of prisoners hidden beneath the earth. I ground the needles deeper into my skin, their bitter scent clouding the air. What they didn't talk about was how bad the conditions of those prisoners might be. What they had in numbers would be significantly diminished by being overworked to the point of near death, combined with lack of sleep and proper nutrition.

Pip hopped to my leather bracing, talons hooking into the curved fold of the leather. Again, I reminded myself we couldn't dwell on the impossibilities: only focus on what we could fix.

I translated her twitters for Archer. "They're well-stocked. Pip and Ghost saw them unloading fresh rounds of ammunition." I shook my head, struggling with the terminology. "Arrows forged from metal, armored plates garnished in gold, boxes of swords—even some sort of—" I broke off, glancing at Pip, who hooted crossly— "black powder?" I frowned and mimed with my hands. "It's stored in boxes about three feet wide and two feet tall. I'm not sure what it's used for."

"It sounds like blasting powder." Archer whistled between his teeth. "I'd heard rumors of it appearing in shipments on boats that dared trek across the Caswich Sea. If it's here, that's more than a little worrisome." He caught the confusion on my face and clarified. "Blasting powder is difficult to come by on this continent and is not widely used. Something as simple as an errant spark or a strike from flint on steel can set it off and cause an explosion, similar to a dragon blast."

It was difficult to imagine such a thing. The power of such a weapon stole the breath from my lungs. Archer nodded somberly. "If they plan to use it here, all it would take is one blast in the right place to block off an entrance or bring down an entire shaft." He twiddled with the edge of his map. "Did your scouts say how many boxes of powder they saw?"

Pip's head had swiveled one hundred eighty degrees to watch him as he talked, understanding the leader perfectly. The owl plucked at the ties holding the leather to my arm. I shook my head. "Grim didn't see any, so he's not sure. Ghost saw two boxes. Pip saw one."

"Fair enough." Archer scratched a few more notes. "See if they can keep an eye on those stores. We need to get to the powder first if possible—before they blow anything up."

Pip bristled and flew into the tree over our heads, intent on getting back to work.

"What was their good news?" Archer asked.

I'd almost forgotten, and the reminder brought forth a grin I couldn't disguise. "The owls say there's plenty of small game. They're quite full."

Archer blinked as he measured that statement, his mouth twisting, and he buried his mouth in the crook of his arm to muffle his laughter, shoulders shaking mightily with the effort. He clapped my back. "I needed that."

After shoving his map into the small pouch he wore on his hip, he leaned forward, a small mirror in hand, and flashed a signal at a pair of rebels situated about a hundred yards away, keeping watch. Archer wanted rotating shifts no more than five hours long, insisting anything longer than that would cause unnecessary strain and stress. He wanted everyone to stay sharp.

Tomorrow would be a big day—hopefully in our favor.

"C'mon, let's head back," he said, gesturing east.

I whistled to Pip, filling her in on our change in plans, and trudged alongside him. It was easy being with Archer, almost like having my father back again. He posed an intimidating figure at the helm, but he was easygoing and didn't sweat the small things. He also lacked Lukas' snark, Soren's restrained violence, and Viv's harsh criticism. He took things in stride and refused to let them ruffle him.

"Eero would be proud of how far we've come." Archer plucked a dead leaf from a red maple and twirled it between his fingers. "He also hated sitting still, so all this scouting would have caused him a ridiculous amount of anxiety."

It wasn't the first time he'd mentioned the elder Ahlgren brother in the past few days, but it was the first time he'd spoken so casually.

"What was he like? Anything like Soren?"

Archer ducked beneath a low-hanging limb. "Soren wasn't always this bad, I'll have you know. But no, he and Eero couldn't have been more different. Eero was optimistic, always laughing about something, a ray of sunshine in the murk of resentment and pain swirling around us." Archer's throat clicked when he swallowed. "I think he was that way because of Soren. He was only older by three years, but the murders of their parents forced the responsibility of raising Soren onto his shoulders. Eero took that seriously."

Leaves crunched beneath his feet and he glanced down, brow raised. "How are you always so quiet?"

I motioned to several mossy spots and bits of rock barely sticking out from the earth. They seemed obvious to me, but I was coming around to realizing how unique my perspective was. "If you take more care, you'll be more quiet. I can show you what to look for."

He shook his head. "Whatever you say." But he motioned for me to take the lead so he could watch what I did and mimic it. He was good at that, correcting his mistakes.

"You were saying," I encouraged.

"I was saying that Eero was my best friend, even if I'm not sure he would have said the same about me." Archer continued, his tone bearing no resentment. "He loved everyone and wanted to be friends with everyone. I was just a guy too stubborn to leave him alone."

He stepped on a stick, cracking it in half, and cursed softly. "When he died, it took a lot for me to pull myself back up and remember my place in the Requiem. Soren's the one who talked me into coming back. Did you know that? This scraggly scrap of a kid I'd always considered my little brother walked right up to me, shoulders thrown back, chin tilted, and looked me straight in the eye. He said his brother would have wanted me to pick up where he'd left off. He would have wanted us united and fighting for our freedom, no matter the cost. And godsdamn did he make an impression."

That was why they seemed so close, because though their blood ran different, they were family. Brothers unified by their experiences. Like me and—well. That might not be the best description of my relationship with Viv anymore.

We crested a hill and peered down, the tops of several tents in various shades of earth barely visible between the budding branches. Archer twisted his earring around and around.

I lifted my eyes, scanning the wispy clouds frothing over the deep blue sky. "Soren tells me you believe drakken can come into their powers well beyond the age of childhood." I paused. "Is that why you fiddle with your stone so much? Because you believe one day you might uncover your inner drakken?"

Archer's fingers stilled on the piece of silver. "How did you know?"

"You get this look in your eye when you touch it, like you're seeing an entirely different reality," I replied. "Soren and Lukas also mess with theirs like that."

A shout carried up the side of the mountain and something heavy clattered below.

"This one is my dad's. The last piece of him I have left." Archer ran his hand down the scratchy bark of an aspen, plucking at a stray curl. "He died about six months before Eero, one of the last truly free drakken. He was killed in a skirmish outside Aeros. Lukas' father was with him.

"Pops never pressured me about not being able to shift, but I knew he was disappointed when we came back from the temples empty handed. He loved his career in the navy and the freedom afforded him by the open sea and the sky." Archer inhaled deeply, eyes fixed on the clouds as if imagining drakken exploring their expanses. "Even after that first failure, he never gave up. He would grab my little hands and squeeze them in his big, rough ones and tell me, 'Son, until the day you breathe your last, there's always hope.'" His fingers found his earring again. "Whenever his ship docked, we would visit the market and he would coax me to try the drakkentorre, always waiting for the right piece to find me. Then the invasion happened when I was eight, and those dreams vanished."

I plucked at a corner of my cloak, crumbling the mud that had dried there. Certain bloodlines were associated with producing shifters, but there was no rhyme or reason as to who would develop the gift. It was our nation's greatest mystery—and sometimes its greatest equalizer.

A corner of Zos' rune peeked out from the edge of my sleeve, bound in the poisonous vines of my scar. I traced it absently.

"I know it's stupid, but there's this part of me that still dreams about being able to shift. Maybe one day I'll unlock that hidden piece of magic within myself and make him proud." Archer ran his hand through his hair, the sunlight sending silvery bits shooting through the strands. "But I have to face reality. The odds of that happening are nearly impossible and I have a war to win. I'll leave the heroics to the real drakken and those fighting on the front lines. My job is to put them in the best position to succeed."

A wind kicked up, rustling the trees, and Archer sighed again. "Let's get eveningmeal. If you're anything like me, I doubt you're hungry, but we'll need our energy for the morning."

"I'll be down in a minute."

With a long look, Archer left me to it, pondering his words and the dreamscape he so desperately wished he could believe in.

It took much longer than a minute for me to leave that corner of the woods.

* * *

No fires burned in the camp that night. Those who dared speak kept their voices low, wary of the sound carrying to the ears of the soldiers patrolling the mines. Our last strategy session concluded as the last dribbles of light bled from the setting sun, mostly an analysis of the new information I'd gleaned from the owls and the shifting of troop patterns to accommodate them. Overall, we knew the roles we would serve and who would be positioned where.

Now it was a matter of seeing if we could pull off a miracle.

I stuck close to Archer's side, lost in my thoughts, barely hearing Soren and Lukas when they returned from their shifts keeping watch over the mines. I'd eaten mechanically and couldn't remember falling into a light and fitful sleep shortly after. But when I opened my eyes to Archer's gentle nudge several hours later, the remnants of my nightvisions lingered and my fear morphed into anger, complete with gnashing teeth and slashing claws. I spared no time storming across camp, my thoughts a silver arrow.

"Tell, now's not a good time." Lukas shifted to block my path with his body. Dark fingerprints of purple exhaustion smudged the skin beneath his eyes, but his spine was straight and his jaw set as he squared off against me. "She's barely slept in days and the last person she needs to see right now is—"

"No offense, Lukas, but there's never been a better time." I slapped his hand away when he reached to stop me. The perfectionist and the know-it-all would have become best friends, wouldn't they? Though I was glad Viv had made a friend, one willing to protect her from even me, I wouldn't allow him to come between us.

My temper had settled after hearing Archer's story, icing over like the vast tundra north of our borders. In its wake remained sharp, cool resolve. It rankled that she hadn't come to see me, that she'd shut me out in these most vital of moments. We had always been partners, from standing up to our parents to taking punishment for not finishing chores to exploring the Owl Wood. I understood she was hurting, but so was I. This couldn't wait any longer, not as rebels emptied supplies from saddlebags and hooked swords and knives to their belts and bandoliers.

"She may be upset with me, but she's the most important person in my life, and I will say my piece." I shoved at the drakken's chest. Viv was right there behind him, her hair bound in a tight knot at the nape of her neck, back to me as she fiddled with her bag, but the stiff set of her shoulders gave away the fact she was listening to every word coming out of my mouth. Lukas glowered, and I rose on my toes to meet his challenge.

"You hurt her."

"She hasn't given me an opportunity to explain," I snarled. "If we were in Solas with all the time in the world, that wouldn't be an issue. But we're in the middle of a war, in case you forgot. And we're about to head into the biggest battle this country has seen in some time." A tendril of fear strummed inside me, a chord that rang so clean and commanding I couldn't ignore it. "Anything could happen."

This time, he allowed me to knock away his arm, and I stormed around him, stopping just shy of where Viv crouched. My best friend. The woman I'd charged halfway across the country to get back with little more than a thought and a prayer. The warrior livid with me when she was just as guilty of omitting her truths for the sake of protecting herself.

Protecting us.

My hands fisted at my sides. "I'm sorry, Viveca. I'm sorry for hurting you. It wasn't my intention to make you mad or drive you

away, but I also don't regret what happened between me and Soren."
It was important to me that she know that, even if it stung. I still
had my questions, but that kiss had crystallized a large segment of
my reality. "There's always been this spark between us, and I'm glad
we finally addressed it. Because now we can move forward, beyond
it. You should know that being with him... it didn't feel right." I
swallowed hard, fighting the burn creeping up my neck and cheeks,
aware of more ears listening to our conversation than just Viv's.
"Maybe in another world we would have worked out. But here? I
felt guilty. It felt like betrayal."

Viv shifted, the curve of her cheek visible in the azure light. Several
soldiers in mud-stained clothing led horses past me, avoiding eye
contact as they followed the murmured commands of the officers.
In fifteen minutes, this camp would be void of all living things.

"It's you and me, remember? Us against the world. I want to talk
to you again, confide in you like I always have, tell you how I really
feel, but I can't do that when you're this mad at me." My breath
shuddered out of me, relief mingled with apprehension. "But we
will talk when things have cooled down, and I want you to know I
care about you. More than care about you. So don't you dare get
hurt, because that might just break me."

I fisted my cloak in my hands, trying to muddle my way through
these last thoughts. "Archer has me stationed at the main entrance,
but don't think you're getting away that easily. I'm sending Grim to
keep an eye on you, and you know he will. Don't fuck this up."

Without waiting for a response, I spun on my heel, cloak swirling
around my legs. I couldn't say any more. Not with tears clogging
my throat and her pretending she couldn't hear what I was saying.

I hesitated when I drew alongside Lukas. As one of our three
drakken—the third being a young man with hair like straw and
a personality to match—he would be stationed with her at the

easternmost mine. If we could secure that one, countless lives would be saved.

"Same goes for you," I bit out. A look of surprise skittered across Lukas' face and I shook my head. "I'll be pissed if you allow anything to happen to yourself, but I'll let Soren rip at you first. So do your best to not mess this up either."

I darted around horses and people, dashing the tears streaking down my face while Pip cooed against my neck. Once, I thought I heard my name, but I was too far away for that to have been possible.

36

How to Breathe

I nibbled a thumbnail as I stared down at the map and its many colorful markings.

"Do your scouts have anything new to report? Any strange activity?" Archer tapped the black x's representing the main line that would rush the largest entrance. Pip had already touched base with Ghost, Grim, and the network of smaller birds they had coaxed into helping. Her head bobbed twice from where she stood on the corner of the map closest to Soren.

"Pip says their behavior remains unchanged," I translated. "Everyone is where they should be."

A dozen guards were posted outside each entrance, the movement in and out of the three openings as constant as the rise and fall of buckets of water from a well. Something about this felt off, but when I'd shared my feelings with Archer before this gathering, he'd told me nerves and paranoia were a natural part of war. He assured me anyone could win a battle on any given day, no matter how large an army they had at their backs.

Rather than find comfort in his assessment, my paranoia mounted. Sure, anyone could win, but anyone could also lose.

"That settles it." A bearded man named Tugs, whose face bore long ropes of smooth, red scars, slapped his hands together. "The archers take out the soldiers standing outside the entrances." The arrows were tipped with fast-acting poison, so even if they didn't hit true, their marks would still go down. "On Archer's command, my contingent charges the main entrance, taking out any Fiorian dogs who cross our path, ordering our people out—"

"—where the healers will be ready to treat them," a willowy woman with long hair twisted into a severe bun said. Despite my skills with herbs and other medical remedies, I hadn't had much opportunity to converse with Lenore, who managed the "odds and ends" of our rag-tag rebellion. From the small healer unit to managing supply runs, there was little her sharp eyes didn't oversee. "We'll be ready to care for them once we get them into the trees."

"The next signal will be for me," Soren said, smoothing his hands over his thighs. He'd abandoned his cloak and sword in anticipation of his shift, insisting they would only weigh him down, and he looked strangely naked without his human armor. "Archer signals the go-ahead after the initial charge. I fire two blasts of fire into the sky, and the right and left flanks launch their attacks on the other two entrances."

I fixated on the circles representing the right flank. Viv's battalion. The smallest of the units, yet one Archer assured me was filled with highly skilled warriors. The only thing giving me the smallest amount of relief was that Lukas was also positioned to the east. Soren took the center mine. And Ivan would take the west.

I'd interacted only briefly with the third drakken in the mess hall. He radiated a natural sense of calm that had silenced my anxiety. He'd spoken little over dinner when I sat nearby one night, mostly listening to his companions chat. When I finally gathered the nerve to ask him about the color of his scales, he gave a lopsided grin and merely said, "Blue."

It was a shame we didn't have more shifters. Drakken stood a better chance against wolven in a fight, so our best bet was to free the ones trapped in the tunnels, get their hands on the limited drakkentorre we'd recovered, and hope they would fight alongside us in the name of revenge.

I refocused as everyone discussed the minor details of the operation, details they'd already worked out in the days and weeks leading up to the attack. I swept my thumb over the tattoo on the underside of my wrist. Hesitantly, I laced my fingers together and closed my eyes.

One long, drawn in breath later, I dared to pray. My fingers shook and the corners of my eyes stung, but for the first time in a long time I *wanted* to pray to Zos. I'd always turned to her for protection and guidance in the past. Now I prayed for her to look over Soren, Lukas, Archer... Viv. Myself.

The breath I'd held in my lungs released with a slow whoosh, and I shook out my trembling arms. I was far from making my peace with the goddess of the darkness, but we could use all the help we could get.

I would be stationed with Archer in a tree off to the side of the main entrance, listening for signals from the owls who were also keeping watch, so I was in a good spot to help defend the leader of the Requiem if needed. As for the others—they would need to watch their own backs.

"May the blessings of Zos guide your sword." Lenore pressed her fingers to her lips and held them to the sky, following her concluding prayer, one often issued in the midst of difficult situations. I must have missed the meeting wrap up because everyone was splitting off to get into position.

"Alright, let's head out," Tugs ordered, dragging two of his subordinates through the mouth of the tent.

Archer spoke with Lenore about some nuance as he folded up his map, and when I turned to leave, Soren stepped into my path. He cupped my elbow, drawing me close enough to inhale the sweet scent of the soap he'd washed with earlier.

"Are you alright?" he asked.

I shook my head. "Everything feels wrong. I know what the owls are telling me, and I understand the logistics, but I feel like everything's about to go wrong." I wrapped my arms around my belly, willing it to settle. "It's the last way I should be feeling right now, but I don't want anything to happen to any of you."

He ran a firm hand down my arm. "You don't think that's how any of the rest of us feel right now?"

I quivered. No, it hadn't occurred to me.

"Nothing is assured in war. Preparation and skill can aid in success, but they're far from determining factors." Strands of hair fell across his eyes. "I threw up twice this morning thinking about what's about to happen. This battle... it's huge."

It was a deciding point. A turn in the war.

And many people would die achieving it.

Soren's gaze flickered over my shoulder, and his lips firmed. "I've got to go, but you take care, alright? Keep Archer safe for me. I can't do my job if I'm worried about him, too."

Everything that rattled and shook around inside me stilled. Soren—the drakken who lived for blood and gore and violence—felt the same way I did. Uneasy. Uncertain. Nervous. Maybe Archer was right, and I needed to cut myself some slack. Stomach finally settled, I squeezed Soren's shoulder and turned to Archer so I wouldn't have to watch him exit the tent.

He scratched his temple, something in his expression begging to be released, but he buckled it in when I cocked my hand on my hip.

"Ready to go?"

* * *

Archer's fingers were stiff around his bow. A quiver of ebony and scarlet-fletched arrows hung from his shoulder as he surveyed the battlefield. My nails dug into the rugged bark of the oak tree we perched on, my feet sure and steady on the branch I'd deemed strong enough to hold both of us. Pip huddled in a bundle of branches over me, wide eyes fixed on the expanse of dirt leading up to the mine. A few boulders rested around the entrance, which I guessed were left in place for added protection.

I rolled my shoulders again, relieving the tension strung between them. The left and middle flanks were set. Now we awaited the all-clear from the right. An itch worked up my nose and I pinched it tight, stifling a sneeze.

Because of it, I almost missed Pip's quiet hoot, one that made the hairs on the back of my neck stiffen. A rock had risen in my throat and I swallowed it down, raising three fingers and waving them so Archer could see them. He nodded, silky hair rustling in a sudden draft, drew a deep breath, and raised his bow.

A long pause.

The arrow hit the base of a log in the center of the field.

A soldier carting a bucket turned toward the sound, only to stagger back, water spilling everywhere. An arrow pierced his eye. The few other guards in the clearing also went down quickly, signaling a nearly perfect start to the first wave of our attack. When the last of the twitching bodies went still, hands clutching the shaft buried in his throat, Archer shot another arrow at the log, splitting his first arrow in half.

My head went light as dozens of men and women dressed in the grays and greens and browns of the Requiem emerged from the foliage, swords and bows in hands, picking their way across the field. They scarcely made a sound as they crept forward, attempting to remain out of sight of the guards lurking inside the cave.

Tugs and a group of men I didn't recognize at a distance reached the cave first, lingering outside as they waited for more people to catch up. Archer lifted his bow, scanned the clearing again, and at my nod, released a third arrow into the stump. With a roar, Tugs threw himself into the mouth of the black hole, sword overhead, a group of men and women shouting as they followed suit. My eyes watered from staring at the opening so intently.

Archer motioned me to crouch, breaking my revere, and released an arrow across my back into some bushes where Soren was crouched. A flash of black burst from the undergrowth, and the drakken flung himself into the skies, wings pressed flat to his spine, a burst of fire billowing from his mouth. A second blast followed the first, and he released a mighty screech. The final signal had been cast.

Whether I liked it or not, what happened next was in the hands of the gods.

Soren shot through the burst of orange and yellow flame, wings pumping, the sound echoing. His tail jerked, his sinuous head swinging around, and he released another wild cry. Pip screeched in warning.

"Fuck," Archer snarled, snapping to his feet, jerking another arrow from his quiver. We'd missed it. One of the boulders propped against the wall of the cliff that I'd dismissed earlier had rolled aside. Dozens of Fiorian troops spilled out of the opening it revealed, many of them in their wolven forms.

Soren swooped low, talons extended, attacking a wolven at the forefront of the charge, scooping him up by the neck. Rebels who remained outside the cave quickly realized what was happening, the ambush taking place right behind them, and raced toward the new threat. Screams and metallic clangs filled the air along with the sharp, bitter bite of blood.

Archer swore, firing arrow after arrow at anyone who came within his reach. I could barely keep up with the movement, from the sun glinting off the silver swords, to the black blood spilling from gashes of wounds, to the drakken winging around, lips peeled back in a grimace, incapable of using his fire or risk burning his own people.

"The others need to know," I murmured. If we were under attack here, the odds were good the other mines were equally prepared. I needed to—

An explosion shook the earth, violent enough to nearly toss us out of the tree. I gaped, heart crashing as a geyser of rock and earth and smoke blasted high into the western skies. The shriek of the blue drakken caught in the blast was as unmistakable as the brilliance of his scales as he pinwheeled, wings shredded, flailing, caught in the explosion.

"They blew up the mine," Archer snarled. "They blew up the fucking mine. But if they—"

A second almighty roar ripped across the skies before Archer could finish his thought. I barely caught his arm when he slipped from the branch, dragging him to safety before he plummeted two stories to the ground. A matching geyser of debris rose from the east, this one darker, blacker. My heart shot up to my throat. Viv's battalion was there. Gold flashed as Lukas dove, weaving between the boulders.

"No," I screamed, clutching at my shirt. My skin had gone numb. "I have to get to them."

"Stay here," Archer ordered, yanking me against him. "If they blew up the other entrances, it's entirely possible they will blow up the one here. That said, they need this mine more than we do, so they might hold off, but we have to stay sharp."

My fists pounded against his chest, my vision blurred. "But Viv and Lukas are over there. They are—"

"I know they are." His eyes were wild, his fingers claws that dug into my shoulders. "But we have to trust they can take care of themselves. Lukas is sharp, and you saw that he's alive. Your friend is also intelligent. You have to believe she wasn't caught up in that mess and focus." I winced when his fingers drilled deep into my muscles.

"Focus on our fight or we will lose," he continued. "We need to keep this mine open so people can get out. We need that stone more than anything. That means I need you looking for risks, calling out new tactics. I need a sounding board. There's only so much I can handle while firing arrows. That's your mission now. Got it?"

My head cleared. Archer needed a second-in-command. I could do that. Nodding, I pulled away from the man and refocused on the fight ahead.

Soren roared and Archer reached for another arrow, aiming for the wolven with white fur who'd latched onto the drakken's leg, bearing him to the ground. With a gulp, I forced the panic down and scanned the clearing again, monitoring for threats, debating tactics I might relay to the Requiem leader.

We seemed to have the edge here, but I wasn't sure how long it would hold. We had to keep the mine open. People clothed in little more than rags, their bodies marked with burns and welts, were spilling from inside, prisoners we'd set free.

We had to keep the entrance open for their sake.

Pip chortled, calling my attention to one enemy soldier in particular. He moved strangely despite his height, hunched over, sword still in its sheath as he ducked and wove around the edges of the battle.

A spool of what looked like thick black twine unraveled at his side as he moved away from the mouth of the cave. I didn't know what he was doing, but something deep inside me told me it couldn't be good.

Even worse, no one else seemed to have noticed him.

"Archer, you said our priority was keeping the mine open, right?" The leader risked a glance my way. "Yes."

"I found a threat, and no one else is near. I'm going in." I dropped from the tree, ignoring Archer's frantic protest. I rolled like we'd practiced, bouncing back to my feet without wasting a moment.

My legs pumped, shoving people out of my way as I darted around bodies and ducked arrows, flinging myself across the field. A wolven standing between me and the soldier I was after snarled, a strip of pale flesh dangling from its maw. It pawed the ground, teeth bared. I flinched, ducking back as if it might save me, when a black arrow sprouted from the beast's throat. He dropped, hissing and spitting as he died.

With a prayer of thanks to the leader of the Requiem watching over me, I launched myself at the soldier pressed against the wall, fumbling with a little metal box in his hands. He dodged the fist I threw at his face, only to put himself in the path of a swinging sword. It crashed into his head, denting his skull, and he dropped. With a shout, I rolled, reaching for the device as it tumbled from his limp fingers, and landed with a crash against the wall of the cliff. Stunned and fighting back a rush of vertigo, I peered at the metal box cradled against my chest, amazed I hadn't crushed the lever sticking out the side. Pulling my knees up against me in an effort to make myself as small as possible, I examined the twine protruding from the box. It snaked into the mouth of the mines, and I recalled the explosions we'd witnessed on the horizons.

My ears buzzed like a barrel full of bees, and my stomach bottomed out. Maybe those blasts had been caused by something similar to this. I had to sever that connection.

"Zos, don't you fail me now," I shrieked, and ripped the cord from the box, curling in a ball, hand cupped over the back of my head as I prepared for an answering explosion to rip through the ground.

Nothing happened.

The device tumbled from my arms, clattering to the ground, nothing more than a square of steel and wire. My arms shook too hard from the surge of adrenaline for me to pick it back up and I rose to my knees, shaking and stunned that my rash action had actually worked. I'd diffused whatever that box was. As long as they didn't have a back-up tucked away somewhere, we still stood a good chance of getting the people out of the mines.

Now I needed to get back to Archer.

Someone shouted my name in warning. I ducked as a sword passed over my head, close enough that I felt the air displaced by the weapon brush against the nape of my neck. Scrambling backward, I dodged another blow, one that would have cut off my leg. The Fiorian soldier bared his teeth, gleaming golden armor buckled to his chest, arms, and legs. He spun the sword in his hands and spat at me, pulling back for another strike. I rose on my elbows, scrambling against the side of the cliff, trying to escape when a black blur dropped from the sky. The man barely had a moment to scream before talons ripped his head from his body, spraying me with blood.

I gaped when that vicious, triangle-shaped head swung my way, ears flattening against his skull. A hiss slipped from Soren's throat, the sound not dissimilar to a screaming teakettle, and his wings heaved. Teeth sank into my shoulder and agony seared like fire as he lifted me off the ground. Not a second later, a trio of arrows crashed into the ground where I'd been.

Arms around my neck.

Soren's voice carried a metallic sheen as it echoed through my pounding skull. Either I was delirious from the pain, or this was a form of communication he'd never shared with me before.

Hurry. Can't hold.

Every pump of his wings made the pain that much worse, and I fought back a wave of nausea as I wrapped my arms around his reptilian neck. The edges of the scales sliced holes in my shirt and pants as I wrapped myself around him, clinging to his back. I nearly screamed again when he released my shoulder, using his massive wings to lift us higher.

The cloak hanging from my neck and arms weighed me down as I worked backward, finding a more secure position. The rhythmic beat of his wings and the sharp edges of his scales proved challenging, but I figured out how to best avoid slicing myself too badly. After a little more maneuvering, I found the best way to hang on was to hook my knees against the joints of his wings, feet tucked underneath me, and grip the ridges of bone protruding from his spine.

"I'm good," I shouted at the drakken, hoping he could hear me over the wind. He must have, because his body straightened, neck lowering to make himself more aerodynamic. Swallowing hard, I allowed myself to look down through my hair flying around my face.The world seemed almost pretty this high up.

It was a sentiment I immediately regretted when Soren angled straight down. My scream was lost in the wind along with my stomach. Squeezing my eyes shut, hands gripping the bone like my life depended on it, I flattened myself against his body, praying for the sickening rush to end. With a jerk, he snapped again, wings pumping furiously, and blood sprayed as he ripped open another trio of soldiers.

A beat later, we were flying high into the sky. When I remembered how to breathe, I straightened on his back, shoulder screaming with the effort, cringing as I wiped red from my eyes and cheeks. I didn't dwell on it because movement to the north snagged my attention.

"Wait," I yelled into his ear. "Look to the north."

A rumble went through him, rattling my bones, when he, too, spotted the contingent of wolven approaching from the trees. They were about a hundred soldiers strong, their golden armor obvious even from the depths of the woods. It wouldn't be long before they reached what remained of our forces to the east—assuming anyone had survived the explosion.

"Can you fire another blast?" I asked, recalling Lukas' warning about drakken only having the ability to launch a few fireballs before they needed to rest. My hands slipped on the blood turning his scales slicker than ice. Much of it was mine, weeping from a thousand tiny cuts.

Yes.

"We need to create a fire barrier. If they can't reach our troops, they can't fight."

His head bowed in what I imagined to be a nod and my stomach dropped again as he dove, skimming the tops of the trees to stay out of sight. He flapped faster, winging around at impossible speeds to approach from a different direction. Sneaky. No doubt they were aware of his presence to the south, so coming from the north would hopefully catch them off guard.

"You know, we make a pretty solid team," I said.

I felt his rumble of answering amusement shake against my legs before he opened his mouth and unleashed a stream of fire. The heat smacked into me like a wall and I buried my face against his neck, praying my cloak would shield the worst of the burn. People shrieked, many of them engulfed in flames. The fire caught in the trees, crackling and roaring, spreading as it burned hotter than the most dangerous of wildfires.

Clear.

I lifted my head, realizing we'd winged into the skies again. Though my skin was red in some places, blisters already swelling, the heat was gone. Beneath us, flames roared through the forest, a long line of trees disintegrating in the line of fire that had effectively created a barrier between our forces. Hopefully, our men and women would have enough time to work their way south to safety.

"Nice job." I ran a hand down his neck. "Let's head back to the main—"

I screamed, clinging to Soren like a parasite when he flattened his wings against his body, edges of the flaps covering me, and rolled, body spinning like an arrow aiming for its target.

"What was that for?" I shouted when he pulled out of his dive, searching for something in the trees. "What were you doing?"

Bolts. They're firing at us.

Bolts? Like crossbows? I leaned sideways, trying to see around his neck. Soren's shadow drifted over the body of the blue drakken, Ivan's body twisted at an impossible angle, three spears sticking from his chest. A fourth pierced his wing, the leathery membrane shredded.

Tears pricked my eyes. "We need to land."

I agree.

Soren wheeled, intent on finding a clearing, when a streak of black blurred past on his left. *Too late.* We'd figured out where the bolts were coming from, but I couldn't see through the trees. Soren reared back when another bolt emerged from the trees. It was too late to change course.

It was going to hit us. We were going to die. He tensed as I clutched him hard.

A wall of gold flashed.

Lukas screamed as the bolt crashed into his breast, wings crumpling as he pinwheeled to the ground.

"No," I shrieked, Soren's voice echoing in my mind.

The black drakken plunged, talons reaching, desperate to stop Lukas' trajectory. Everything inside me cried out. We'd almost reached him when something heavy crashed into us, knocking Soren off kilter. He roared, struggling against the strings pulling tight around him. A net. He bucked violently, a roar ripping from his throat, and I lost my grip. For a moment, I was weightless as I slipped through a hole that hadn't closed around him. I reached for him, tendrils of fear squeezing tight around me, knowing there was nothing he could do as I fell.

I was still processing what had happened when I smacked into the densely packed limbs of a pine tree. The branches bowed beneath my weight, giving way, and I curled as I tumbled downward, needles dragging against my skin in a chorus of painful bursts.

With nothing to hold on to, I landed on my bad shoulder at the same time the black drakken sank to the earth, twisting and snarling as he fought the golden strands of the net ensnaring his body. Violent black waves of agony riddled the edges of my vision as I clutched my dislocated shoulder. Heaving, I cradled it against me, wondering if this was it. If I had met my end.

When the world finally settled beneath my feet and there was nothing left in my stomach, I rolled over, bringing Soren into view. He was still thrashing, but his movements had slowed, turning more painful as the golden strands pulled tighter.

He needed help.

Ignoring the shooting stars that were every single scratch and bruise and puncture arching through my body, I stumbled forward. I'd almost reached Soren when he morphed, the net wrapped tightly around his human form like strands of a massive spiderweb.

"Help Lukas," Soren cried, motioning to my left where a large figure lay, the broken spears of trees sticking up around it. "There's something magical about this net. I can't get it off and it feels sticky. Worry about me after you help him."

Alright then. Limping through the trees seemed to take forever, especially when I wanted to scream every time my shoulder twinged. When I finally reached the golden drakken, I couldn't hold back the tears that stung my eyes and dropped beside him with a cry. His beautiful wings hung in long bloody shreds. The heavy metal bolt sticking from his rib cage had pierced one, and the trees had taken care of the rest. I ran my hand over his scales, muddied with blood, and he flinched, a shriek whistling from his lips. A golden eye opened, bleary with unbridled pain.

"Hang in there, Lukas," I murmured. "I need a moment to see what I'm working with here."

Miraculously, the bolt had missed his heart and lungs. However, it had shattered bone in his shoulder, lodging itself underneath his clavicle. If he survived, it would take a miracle for him to use his left arm again. Urgency drove me into action. The soldiers would have seen where the drakken had fallen, and it wouldn't be long before they found us. I dipped my hands in my pockets, feeling for the medical supplies I'd shoved into them earlier, and emerged triumphant with a small bundle of moss commonly used to accelerate clotting.

Lukas had passed out from the pain, and still I whispered soft, consoling words to him. With any luck, he would stay asleep, because what I needed to do was going to hurt.

A hiss escaped his teeth as I circled him, trying to get a better idea of what I was working with. The bolt was about as thick as my arm and as long, too, its serrated iron tip punching through the plated scales on his back. Pulling it out would be impossible. That meant pushing it forward, which would hurt like rezar. My shredded shoulder twinged in sympathy.

I shook the drakken awake. "Don't bite me. I'm going to get that bolt out of you, but it's going to feel like I'm killing you."

He closed his eyes with resignation, and I came around his front again. "One. Two." On three I shoved against the fletching. Lukas heaved, body rippling as he fought a roar. With every last ounce of strength I had in me, I threw myself against it and it emerged with a squelch, landing in a mess of blood and gore beside him. Teeth clenched, I kicked it out of the way and started shoving moss into the hole in the drakken's shoulder.

The blood gushing from the wound slowed and stopped.

A long breath shuddered from between Lukas' teeth before he passed out again.

"He's okay," I called to Soren, shifting my attention to the drakken's battered wings. The blood had dried, but I wasn't sure I could help him right now.

"If I prayed to the gods, I'd thank them."

That was a huge admission coming from the prince.

Twigs cracked, and I spun when I heard pounding feet approaching. Soren's face was stricken as he tugged uselessly at the ropes that clung to the earth as powerfully as they stuck to him.

"Leave me," Soren demanded. "Go. Now. Don't let them find you."

"But—"

"Go! That's an order."

When I took a step back but found myself incapable of taking another, he launched the last arrow in his arsenal. "You need to find Viv, remember?"

With a sob, guilt spinning spider's webs inside me, I launched into the trees on watery legs mere moments before a trio of soldiers emerged from the foliage around Lukas. When I was far enough away that I was certain they couldn't see or smell me, I scrambled up a tree, one with limbs I could climb without relying too heavily on my arm, biting down on my sleeve to muffle my agonized whimpers.

Soren had fought his way through the tangle of rope so he stood, back straight and eyes fixed on the snarling wolven circling him, his posture regal despite the precariousness of his situation. One by one, the wolven morphed into their human forms, fur fading into skin and joints cracking and bending in unnatural angles as they straightened to stand on two legs.

A second group circled Lukas, who had also shifted into his human form, taking care not to touch him as Soren looked on, calm as the quiet that settled before the most vicious of storms. Five soldiers formed a ring around the prince, and a man who'd transitioned from the whitest of the wolven stepped forward.

"Lookie who've we've got here, boys." The man rubbed his hands eagerly. "We've snared ourselves quite the *royal* catch."

I bit down harder on my arm to muffle my gasp. They knew who Soren was?

"You're a difficult one to pin down, *Tristan*." He turned his back on the prince and ambled toward Lukas, circling the golden shifter with his hands in his pockets. "And your little friend here—quite the mastermind of your antics, I'm told."

"Don't you fucking touch him," Soren snarled.

The man stroked his trim, white beard and crouched, forearms braced on his thighs. "A little respect would go a long way, don't you think? Especially given your situation." He ran a finger down Lukas' cheek, smearing the blood drying on his skin. He raised his hand to the sun as Soren snarled, struggling against his bounds. "You know who I am, right? You should be begging me to spare his life. After all, it's only you we need."

I squinted at the man, but didn't recognize him. He stood head and shoulders taller than his drakken counterpart, bulky shoulders square, hands locked behind his back. The sun glinted off his bald head, and he scanned his men with a critical eye.

"You and Innis can go fuck yourselves for all I care." Soren spat at the man's boots. "I'll never bow to you."

The man eyed the glob of mucus, and in a move that seemed almost lazy, he punched Soren in the face. I winced, flinching against my tree as the prince staggered, raising his arms defensively. The next punch was more vicious. Soren fell, and the man kicked him in the ribs. Blood flew from Soren's mouth. The prince coughed, spat, and glared up at the man with undisguised hatred.

"That's *Grand Duke* to you, disgusting *travetry*." The man kicked him again. "His name is too rich to be uttered by the likes of you swill. And me? You can call me General. If I hear anything else out of your mouth, your friend here will suffer." He angled his head lazily toward Lukas.

General. There was only one general I knew of in the Fiorian army. General Markus Rosewood, stationed firmly in the capital, the grand duke's right-hand man. The one in charge of the three colonels who roved the lands, monitoring our eastern, western, and northern borders. If the general himself was here—I swayed on the limb. We'd been betrayed.

We'd fallen into a trap.

I cradled my head in my hands. Even if we retook the mines, losing Soren, Lukas, Ivan, and countless others would deal a massive blow to the Requiem. The soldiers guffawed, their jeers and shifting bodies drawing my attention once more.

The general hauled Soren upright by the collar of his tunic, toes grazing the grass, glaring at the prince. "Say that to me again and I'll cut your tongue out myself."

Soren bared his teeth. "Innis would cut yours out in return. Maybe take your whole head with it, if we're lucky."

The general snapped his fingers and a soldier guarding Lukas kicked his head, catching him under the chin. Lukas' head jerked with a snap and I gasped in horror. The general went eerily still, head tilted, and I realized my mistake. Blood pulsed in my ears and my insides went icy as I stared in horror at the bite marks in my bracer. I'd forgotten to muffle the sound.

"I grow bored of this." The general swirled his finger in the air. "Wrap them up and let's get moving. We have what we came for and then some." He chucked Soren under the chin. "The grand duke will take extreme pleasure finding ways to use him to make you bleed, boy. Just like he used that *travetry* brother of yours to torment the other traitors the last time."

Soren threw himself against the soldiers restraining him. "I'll end you—"

The general punched him in the face again and Soren's head rocked back, dark blood pouring down his nose and mouth. "You never know when to shut up, do you?" he murmured as Soren struggled to stay upright. "Try to stay awake, though. I want you to hear the screams."

Screams?

Soren lifted his head, one eye blackened and swelling, blood dripping from his chin.

The general grinned wolfishly. "You didn't think I'd forgotten about your little friend, did you? The one who so kindly stopped your accomplice from bleeding out? The owl girl who's been following you since your excursions in the north?"

I'd never felt so cold.

They knew where I was.

The general pointed over his shoulder and two men shifted into their wolven forms, mouths open and panting. "The one hiding back there watching all of this? I want you to hear her screams as my men

401

tear her limb from limb."

If Soren had a snappy comeback for that, I didn't hear it. I'd already rushed away, hopping from tree to tree, adrenaline numbing the pain splintering from my broken shoulder, panting as I scaled higher, pushed deeper into the woods, angling southwest, back to the main line.

I told myself they couldn't catch me. Not up here. I wouldn't let them.

I refused to let Soren hear my screams.

37

Red Clouds

I escaped my wolven trackers using tricks of the shadows and my instincts of moving through the woods to my advantage. They almost caught me a few times, but each time I managed to slip out of their grasp. That said, I couldn't give myself all the credit. It was entirely possible they'd grown bored with the chase and decided to leave me be.

They'd already captured the prince. What did a gangly girl matter?

The battle was long over by the time I made it back to the main entrance of the mine. Judging by what the general had said, they'd accomplished what they'd intended by imprisoning the prince and bringing down our drakken and had pulled back, leaving us to our own devices.

Exhausted, I dropped out of the tree, clutching my wounded, throbbing shoulder, and stepped out of the shadows into a circle of light that was the roaring fire built in the middle of the clearing. Dozens of tents had been erected and people were scuttling everywhere, treating patients laying on blankets, clutching wounds as they screamed and groaned—or lay silently, asleep where the pain couldn't reach them.

A few were dead.

"You there." I turned at the voice and found a trio of soldiers heading my way, swords and spears raised. "Hands in the air where we can see them."

With a sigh, I lifted my one good arm, swallowing a moan as the full weight of my shredded and dislocated shoulder settled back into place. "Please don't shoot. I am a friend."

"I said, hands in the air, girl," the lead soldier snarled again, skin pulling around the stitches binding a long slash across his forehead.

"This is as good as I can do." Blood and yellowish pus dripped from my fingertips, evidence of the scabs splitting apart.

The second soldier circled his spear at the fluid. "Ay, I think she's tellin' the truth."

My voice was hoarse, rough around the edges from screaming. "I need to see Archer, please. He will know who I am." The flat of a sword braced beneath my chin as the lead soldier advanced, tilting my head up so I could meet his eyes. "Talk to him before you kill me."

"Hey, Gil, wait a sec." The second soldier pushed forward, spear angling toward the ground as he eyed first my face, then my cloak. "I think it's her. The owl girl."

"The owl girl?" the third one echoed, dawning awe lighting up his face. "I saw her tackle that wolven and stop them from blowing up the mine." He peered more closely at me. "You do kinda look like her. Can you bare your teeth a little? She had teeth like a fox, that one."

The second one batted away the third's reaching hand. "No, the one who flew with the prince and stopped the wolven advancing on the east wing. I saw them swooping overhead." He nodded, scruffy face relaxing into a half smile. "Gave us enough time to evacuate."

Elation rose inside me like Soren shooting for the clouds. The eastern wing. Viv's wing. I almost threw myself at him, then remembered the steel at my throat. I glared at Gil, who narrowed his eyes in return, then directed my attention back to the second man. "Did you see a girl about my age? Lots of red hair and angry at the world? The odds are good she beheaded a few people without a second thought, if it helps."

"A girl with red hair." The soldier scrubbed his face, thinking. "Nah. That doesn't sound like anyone I saw, and I'd remember something like that." My heart tumbled to the base of my spine. "You know her or sumthin?"

"She's my best friend."

"Enough." Gil pressed the blade hard enough against my throat to split the skin. Any more blood loss and I'd probably pass out on my feet. "Turner. Gibs. Are you saying we can trust her? Because I don't think this wisp of a girl is capable of all you've said she is."

I glanced between the soldiers, begging them to see reason.

"Aye," the second man said a firm nod. The head of his spear rested firmly on the ground. "The cloak says it all, even if she didn't look summat familiar. I've heard others talkin' about her. About how she's always with the prince—fitting since they flew together an' all. An' she's got all those owls with her all the time." He scanned the woods at my back as if searching for the birds themselves. My chest squeezed. I'd called for the birds multiple times, but they had yet to make an appearance.

The third man nodded gamely. "Let's get her to Archer. What's the harm? He'll kill her himself if she's not who she says she is."

Reluctantly, as if he regretted not severing my head from what was left of my shoulders, Gil lowered his sword. Before I could breathe a sigh of relief, he grabbed my good arm and shoved me to my knees, roughly patting me down, snorting when he found nothing in my pockets but bits of dried herbs and moss. He ordered the scrawnier of the men to bind my hands with a bit of rope, then prodded me in the back, forcing me to walk. "Looks like you're getting your wish, missy."

A few people glanced our way as we marched through camp, but most were too busy chopping vegetables for the stew or aiding the healers with the wounded to pay much heed. Gil cut a clean line through the chaos, aiming for a tent set up in the center of the crush of activity. A group of people clustered around a makeshift table composed of a few boards propped up on barrels, pointing at curling documents and shouting orders. To my disappointment, I didn't recognize any of them.

"We're here to see Archer," Gil told a woman standing guard at the flap of the tent. She barely glanced at me before peeling back the fabric, eyes dull and fatigued. I wondered who she had lost. My captor shoved me inside with a snarl, almost knocking me to my knees once more. I whipped around to give him a piece of my mind and came face-to-face with the man I so desperately wanted to see. Relief, pure and powerful as a pounding waterfall surged through me. I would have thrown myself into his arms if not for Gil holding me back with a painful grip on my wrists.

Instead, I settled for a quiet, "Archer."

"Tell?" He blinked as if seeing a ghost. "I thought you were—how are you—" He gripped my upper arms, then dragged me against him in an awkward hug. I inhaled the clean pine scent that lingered beneath the sweat and gore. Home. I was finally home—of sorts. Archer jerked me back, a question in his eyes. Black swam in my vision, my blood whooshing painfully in my ears, and I knocked him away in time to drop to my knees and vomit up a bellyful of bile.

Archer crouched, ignoring the mess I'd made, and cut away the ropes binding my wrists. I sagged, rubbing the raw edges of skin, inhaling in counts of three to steady myself, listening to the play of conversation around me.

"Boss, you know this girl?" Gil asked. His obtuseness would have riled me if I weren't focusing on staying conscious. Archer recognized me, for Zos' sake.

Archer clearly felt the same. "Yes, of course I know this woman. We've been looking for her everywhere."

"Oh, holy Zos." The third soldier this time. "It is her. Owl girl. Turner, can you believe it? The woman touched by the gods herself. And I met her."

"Get. Out." Archer snapped. "Thank you for bringing her to me, but return to your post." His tone turned lethal. "And tell no one of who you found until I meet with you again."

"Sir, yes sir," the third man said. My stomach had finally settled, and I imagined the guard holding his hand to his head in a poor imitation of a salute.

The second man—Turner—scoffed. "Knock that off and go. You can find us at our post, Archer." A pause. "Owl girl, I'll think on what you asked some more. If I remember anything, I'll make sure you're the first to know."

His sincerity touched me. "Thank you."

Boots shuffled, and the flap drifted shut, the voices of the men trailing away, leaving us in silence. Archer waited for me to open my eyes before speaking. "I'm sorry you had to deal with that. I do have several trusted rebels searching for you, but I tried to keep your disappearance contained. You've become a bit of an icon, and it would have been devastating for morale if people knew you hadn't returned with the rest of us."

I nodded shortly. So Soren's wish of using me as a symbol had come true.

It was as brilliant as it was aggravating.

"I'm sorry for not realizing how badly you were hurt."

A mocking smile curled my lips, and I finally met his silver eyes. "You mean this old thing?" I jerked my chin toward the gaping, weeping wound. The blood had dried my shirt to the injury and tugged against it uncomfortably. "I've had worse."

"You and just about everyone else here," Archer muttered, leading me to a chair which I sank into gratefully. "If I had any sense, I'd get you to the medical tent."

I shook my head, the last of the dizziness withdrawing. "Is Viv here? We saw what was left of the eastern wing and it sounds like some people have made it back." I clutched his arm. "Was she among them?"

Archer closed his eyes and dropped onto a bench, rubbing his brow. "Honestly, I'm not sure. I know we're still getting survivors from both east and west wings. We have people scouring the woods in both areas bringing back those they can find, and our medics are doing what they can to bind them up. But it's taking time." He ran his hand through his hair, molding sweaty ridges in its normally coiffed shape. "I wish I could give you better news, but it's been chaos here."

He leaned forward, elbows braced on his thighs, pleading with eyes that looked as exhausted as I felt. "Where is Soren? We saw Lukas go down and then Soren got tangled in the net. We saw you fall—and that was it. Now you're here. Alone. What the rezar happened?"

The breath I'd been holding shuddered out. "They were taken captive." Archer's face went hard, fury knotting his jaw. He motioned for me to continue and I launched into my report, starting with everything Soren and I had accomplished from the air to the moments when I'd lost the wolven tailing me on my way back to base. When I finished, Archer took a moment, leaning forward, elbows braced on his knees, fingers steepled.

"Fuck," he finally spat in disgust, leaning backward, one arm slung across the table in the middle of the room. "We knew we'd been double-crossed given how quickly they acted with those explosions. What we couldn't make heads or tails of was why they retreated so abruptly." He shook his head. "When Soren went down, the wolven vanished. It was the weirdest thing. If they'd kept pushing, they would have overrun us. I know they would have. We didn't have half their numbers, let alone their training. One moment I was sure we were about to be slaughtered and the next they were gone." He snapped. "Just like that."

He cupped his mouth in his hands, voicing thoughts I'd already come to terms with. "They wanted Soren. They knew taking him would crush our spirits. And nabbing Lukas was about as bad. Rezar, they took out all three drakken. That's enough to kill any momentum we gained." He straightened. "If I knew who betrayed us, I would remove their head now, but I haven't had a chance to even think about who it might be." He barked a laugh that lacked all humor. "I don't even know who's still alive who *could* have betrayed us."

I didn't blame him for that. The chaos of the camp already spoke volumes.

"How many prisoners did we save?" I asked.

He stared at the blank brown canvas of the tent. "Not enough."

Damn it all. How many thousands of lives had been lost in the blasts and how badly off were those we'd recovered? "Alright."

I stood, scanning the room.

"What are you looking for?"

I spotted what I was looking for on a long table up against the wall and picked up the kit marked with a red cross. I shouldered the bag, appreciating its weight.

Archer stopped me before I exited the tent. "Where are you going?"

"You have work to do. So do I." Viv was still out there somewhere.

409

I wouldn't rest until I knew someone had found her. While I waited for the scouts to finish their work like Archer had indicated, that meant I would find a way to make myself useful.

* * *

Amputated limbs. Broken bones. Burns. Gashes. Slashes. Sucking wounds. Rashes inflicted by poison ivies and sulfurous gasses. I lost track of the number of wounded I treated.

The healers hadn't blinked when I showed up covered in blood, clutching my medicine kit. They didn't have time for questions. One woman filled my shoulder with clotting moss after popping it back into place. I'd anticipated every step she would take, but I still hadn't been prepared for how much pain that process caused. A few quick stitches and a roll of gauze later, I was as right as snow. I could even use my injured arm again.

Without a backward glance, the healer pointed at a table with a delirious man sporting a missing leg tied off with a tourniquet at the knee and told me to do what I could to make him comfortable. They were asking me to watch over him until he passed away.

I did them one better. I handed him a sprig of whipple bark from the stash in my bag, ordered him to bite down, then found an attendant to hold him down as I cauterized the wound. He screamed. He passed out. He woke up. And he would live. His life wouldn't be easy, but he would at least have one to live.

After that, the healers asked me to help when they needed a spare set of hands, gradually gaining greater trust in my abilities as they realized the depth of my knowledge. A few hours later, I was largely on my own, tackling some of the most critical cases, leaving other healers available to deal with the masses. I didn't mind the work. It kept my mind off my worry for Viv, the concern for my missing birds, my fear for Soren and Lukas, and my deeply rooted sense of guilt and failure. It didn't matter how frequently I told myself I wasn't the one to blame. I couldn't stop thinking about our failure to see the double-cross, how I'd missed the giant crossbows that knocked the drakken from the skies. And mostly—my failure to free Soren.

I'd saved Lukas' life, but if I'd worked faster or understood what I was dealing with sooner, I might have done more than that. I might have gotten both of them out before General Rosewood had caught up. When I caught myself dwelling while scrubbing my hands with soap, I shoved them into the water and forced my thoughts to swirl down the drain with the red clouds of blood.

Pausing to gulp down what felt like a tankard of water who knows how long later, I asked the orderly who brought me the bottle if he'd seen a girl with red hair and green eyes, probably spitting mad and covered in blood. Like the soldier, the description didn't ring true for him, but he'd passed my request down the line. Occasionally, a nurse would prod my arm and ask me to look at a patient. Sometimes a doctor would pull me over with the grim look of someone who'd just held someone's hand while they'd died.

Each time, my heart pounded so loudly I wondered why the earth didn't shake.

Each time, my fears were unfounded, and I'd turned to the next patient, working through the night until the sun rose again.

As bad as the injuries were on those who'd been caught up in the explosions, nothing compared to the wounds of those who'd survived the mines. The ones who'd been below ground for months or years. They fought with those who sought to help them and screamed when the sun slanted across their eyes. We sequestered them inside, strapping them to cots to keep them from bolting, many battling their heliophobia so hard they ripped open their skin and re-broke bones in an effort to escape. One of the doctors finally thought of a solution, procuring blue-tinted glass the patients could hold over their eyes as they sat outside. Healers often used the glass to build boxes where they stored and preserved herbs and other medicinal plants that couldn't be kept in complete darkness but also wilted in direct sunlight.

It wasn't just their sensitivity to light that caused issues. Many were missing teeth or fingers, their bodies gaunt with lack of nutrition, whittled down to little more than skin and bone. Most bore signs of frequent beatings and whippings, sores that spoke of short nights on the hard ground. Scars that couldn't be explained. They all craved food, and it broke my heart to keep it from them, instead putting lukewarm cups of bone broth in their outstretched hands. The surge of vitamins and protein would overwhelm their systems if they consumed too much.

It was Archer who finally pulled me away from the tent, dragging me behind him as he handcuffed me to the rail of a cot bolted to the ground.

"Enough," he said, shoving me onto a threadbare mattress that felt softer than any mattress in the history of mattresses. "You're going to eat what's on that tray." He pointed at a sheet of metal loaded with soft bread, cold meat, and a pile of boiled vegetables. My stomach rumbled. "You're going to sleep for at least four hours. And you're not going to complain about any of it. Hear me?"

I nodded mutely, saliva pooling in my mouth as I reached for the loaf, which was still warm, fresh from the oven. Archer's lips twitched when I shoved it into my mouth, choking when I accidentally inhaled the fluffy dough.

"Your help is appreciated, and I know you're worried about your friends, I am too, but if you don't take a moment to turn your brain off, you will collapse. That's not what Viveca would want." He shook his head when I opened my mouth. I shoved more bread into it rather than say what was on my mind. "And not what Soren would want. You have to care for yourself and then you can worry about them. I promise we'll wake you if we learn anything you need to know. Sound good?"

The gray fog swirling around in my head intensified during his little speech, and it was all I could do to shovel the mushy vegetables in my mouth, scarcely taking a moment to chew, let alone taste what they were. I'd never been so exhausted in my life, and I knew I was on the verge of collapse now that my feet were no longer on the ground.

Taking my silence for the acquiescence he'd hoped for, Archer scrubbed his knuckles over my head in a gesture that felt paternal, murmured something about sleeping well, and left. The last thing I remembered before I lilted to the side, head resting on the flat pillow at the head of my cot, was the flap to my tent falling closed.

I awoke to someone shaking me, their hands resolutely pinning me down. I recognized Archer's features in the dark. Behind him, perched somewhere over his shoulder, the heart-shaped face of a barn owl practically glowed in the dark, its eyes shut in slumber. "Ghost?" I scrubbed at my eyes to clear the sleep from my fuzzy thoughts. How long had I been out?

"Tell. It's Viv." Those three words breathed a world of life into me. Lightning crackled through my blood and I shot upright, fisting Archer's shirt. "We've found her."

Holy Zos. I shoved him off me and I planted my feet on the ground, swaying as I stood, thankful I hadn't bothered to remove my shoes. I didn't like how he'd said that. They'd found her. Not that she was here. Or awake. Or even alive. Just... found. "Where is she?"

He passed me my cloak. The owl didn't so much as shift on his feet, and I wondered if I was seeing things.

"The healer's ward." Archer cursed as he grabbed me, keeping me from falling on my face when my legs collapsed from under me. "Pull yourself together. She needs you right now."

Alive. She was alive. The callouses of Archer's hands were rough as they folded over mine, and I barely saw the faces of those we passed as he led me through camp, though I got a vague sense things had significantly calmed since my arrival.

"They brought in the last round of survivors we found from the eastern front," Archer said. "One of the orderlies recognized her."

Recognized her. So she hadn't been awake. Mad as she was at me, I doubted she would have casually sauntered into camp and not demanded to see me immediately had she been conscious. What did that mean? I struggled to keep calm. The better part of a day had passed since our assault had ended. She might have been exhausted and fallen asleep when she was back in allied hands. That had to be the case.

"How is she?" I asked, dodging a cart filled with firewood.

Archer shook his head. "I'm not sure. I haven't seen her myself. I got the alert and came to see you."

I squeezed his hand a little harder. He'd kept his word.

The inside of the healer's tent was far better lit now than it had been when I'd left. Candles flickered between the rows of patients evenly spread out on blankets. Most were asleep, but a few watched us pass with bleary eyes. Healers picked their way along those rows, offering water and handing out bits of whipple bark. At the back of the tent, several white sheets had been pinned to the roof. Through them I could make out the silhouettes of a dozen or so healers bent over patients still requiring intense care.

"How long was I out?" I pondered.

Archer glanced back, distracted. "About eleven hours, I'd say. We checked on you after about six when Ghost flew into camp—" So he hadn't been a figment of my imagination—"but you were fast asleep so we left you be." I nodded, my rising anger reducing to a simmer. I followed him toward the back of the tent.

"This should be the last of them. We aren't finding any other survivors, anyway." His voice was faint, little more than a mosquito buzzing around my ear. "We lost about two thousand in the mines. Maybe seventy soldiers. From what we've gathered, they hid most of the prisoners in the two mines they blew up. They didn't care about the cost to them, only that it killed as many as they could."

My skin tingled numbly. Thousands of lives. Gone. Just like that.

About half of our force decimated.

All in one afternoon.

"We got some drakkentorre out. A few prisoners thought to grab sacks of the stuff when they realized what was happening." Archer paused. I wondered if his thoughts mirrored mine—debating whether the cost of the stone was worth the lives spent gaining it.

It was a difficult question to ask.

He shook himself and drew back the curtain, revealing the operating area. At the end of the line, by herself, lay Viv. I recognized her hair and the owl perched on the cot beside her chest. Grim. I forgot about the doctors. The nurses. Even Archer. I flew across the room, cloak flaring behind me, and fell to my knees beside her cot. Grim ruffled his feathers, hooting in greeting.

For a moment, all I could do was stare. Blood flecked across her freckled face and several deep scrapes on her neck had been stitched shut. Her chest rose and fell steadily. The heavy blanket covering her body up to her chin was miraculously unstained by blood and gore. I would have to thank the orderlies for their thoughtfulness later.

"Viv, it's me." She didn't stir. "I came as soon as I heard."

Still, her eyes remained closed, her breathing unchanged. I

wondered what had happened to her because what I could see of her looked fine. Battered, but fine. I fumbled beneath the blanket, seeking her hand. When I couldn't find it, I lifted the blanket to see better and my momentary relief vaporized.

Hesitantly, I drew back the blanket, draping it over her hips. A trio of deep gashes started at the base of her throat and disappeared beneath the collar of her gown. Another series of precise stitches held the claw-marks shut. As gory as those wounds appeared, it wasn't the worst of what she'd fared. I reached out, fingers brushing the coarse material of her gown, not quite touching her, trembling.

Her right arm ended with a stump several inches above where her elbow would have been. The wound was cauterized using the method I'd shown the healers earlier. It looked ugly, but the lack of pus oozing from the injury was reassuring. If the wound was infected, it hadn't presented yet. Bandages were wrapped around her other arm and hand, and when I lifted it up, I bit back a curse at the pink flesh. Third-degree burns ran up her arm and shoulder and wrapped around her rib cage. Were she awake, I wouldn't have judged her for screaming.

I lifted her hand, moisture dripping from my chin and staining the gauze. From what I could tell, her ring finger was missing, possibly more. Yes, she was alive, but with these injuries, I wasn't sure she would ever be the same again—physically or mentally. She'd always been a weapon, using her body to its greatest potential.

These wounds had the power to change that.

Grim hooted hollowly, echoing the sob that ripped from my chest.

I finally focused on him, smoothing a hand over his feathered head. He nipped my arm in recognition, crowding a closer. A chunk had been taken out of his wing and he was missing two talons from his right foot. Huge chunks of feathers had been ripped from his back and I wondered what he'd survived. If I had to guess, he'd not only been caught up in the explosion, but had fended off an attack from a wolven, too.

I swiped at my face, smudging the tears, and drew a shuddering breath.

"Viveca." I stroked a shaking hand across her cheek, her shallow breath fluttering against my skin. Her lashes didn't twitch. "I'm so sorry." A shudder racked my body, and I pressed my forehead to hers, my tears streaking down her cheeks. "I missed something along the way, a sign or a clue about what was going to happen. I should have done more to ensure you would all be alright and now everything has gone to shit. You're badly hurt. Grim isn't much better. Soren and Lukas are prisoners. And so many people are dead." I choked on a sob. "Dead."

I squeezed her remaining hand hard, bringing the bandaged digits to my lips, pressing kisses to them. Something soft landed beside Grim and a hoot echoed his sorrowful mourning. Pip. A tiny part of my soul that had been missing was back. She seemed more intact than Grim, but was weary, barely holding her head upright. Whatever they'd gone through didn't matter. They were here now, with me, and that was the last damn twig, the one that shattered the dam inside me.

I cradled Viv's head, eyes closed as I sobbed, not caring who witnessed the magnitude of my grief.

How could this happen?

How could we have been betrayed like this?

For many long minutes, I allowed myself to fall into the darkness behind my eyelids and sink deeply into the depths of that wasteland of nothingness. When I surfaced, Viv's breathing remained unchanged. My tears had dried.

And my resolve was set.

With great reluctance, I drew the blanket back over Viv's body, tucking it in around her to keep her warm. "You stay here and get better, alight? I need to talk to Archer and sort some things out. Grim, will you stay here and keep her safe?" The massive gray owl chortled and moved closer to her head, confirming he had zero plans to go anywhere. Pip opened her bleary eyes and hopped to my shoulder, her fuzzy body finding its familiar spot against my neck.

No doubt, Archer was in damage control mode. Now that things were settling, he could finally focus on finding out who had betrayed us, and I wanted to do everything I could to help with that effort.

"Thank you," I said to the healers as I passed, appreciating what they'd done to help her. They'd known the odds were not great of her coming back in one piece, and they had tended to her respectfully. I nodded somberly at the ones whose hands I couldn't shake. "Thank you for all your help."

I made my way through camp blindly, still not sure where everything was positioned. I'd only followed Archer out of necessity. One of the blacksmiths pointed me in the right direction, and I finally found the tent I was looking for. The flap was closed, but a candle inside revealed the silhouettes of several people standing around the table in the middle. No one guarded the entrance, and I hesitated outside, gripping the edge of the flap, listening.

"We need to return to Azmarin to reassess," Archer said.

"Archer." That was Tugs. The beast of a man who'd lead the charge into the mine. It was good to know he'd survived the fight. However, he'd been nothing but eagerness before the battle and now his voice was weighed down. Fatigued. "It's over. The general captured Soren and Lukas. Half our remaining troops are dead. Those we saved from the mines are on the brink of death. And anyone who can still walk is doing just that. Their morale is dead. The Requiem is in shambles. You're in denial if you don't acknowledge that."

"No," Archer sounded sharp. "This isn't over. We've got to keep moving—"

"My staff feel the same," said Lenore. I would recognize her sharp, even voice anywhere. "They're scared. They watched the drakken fall and the mines explode. They're afraid for their lives and the lives of their families. They watched so many die only to save how many? Seven hundred? Maybe? And those numbers are falling. The ones we freed are simply too wounded, too beaten down, too battered."

Archer tried again. "But we can still—"

"Enough." Tugs again. "The ones who survive won't be able to fight for months—even years—and that's *if* any of them choose to stand with us. There's no direction right now. You know better than any of us, the other mines are being fortified as we speak. They allowed us this opening because they knew what was coming. Now that opening is gone. They got what they wanted, and that was Soren. You know what happens next."

Silence settled around us like snow.

I understood what Tugs wasn't saying.

Soren was as good as dead—assuming they hadn't killed him already. Though they could be pushing for a public execution, I supposed.

We had failed. The Requiem was crushed.

The grand duke and his cruel general had won.

Carefully, I released the flap of the tent. Outside, I was calm and collected, but inside I was a blizzard. A raging, whirling chaos of fury and frustration and utter, debilitating helplessness.

How had it come to this?

How?

I couldn't accept it.

I needed answers.

My thumb stroked across the tattoo staining my wrist.

If no one here would give them to me, then I would demand them from the gods themselves.

38

Destroy Your Legacy

Hail pelted my face, and rain lashed at my clothing, soaking me to the bone. I crouched lower on the horse as purple-hued lightning forked across the sky, urging her to sprint faster, harder. For the better part of two days, I'd done all I could to not think of Viv and her injuries and how difficult her recovery would be. I had yet to open my pack, hastily thrown together when I'd fled from the command tent and stolen the mare, arrowing eastward. I'd pushed the poor thing to the brink of collapse before calling it a night, only to be awoken by the storm. We hadn't stopped since. I embraced the violence of the clouds, the anger of the gods, using it to fuel my inner rage.

Hooves clattered on the fragmented tiles as we wheeled beneath spindly trees and around broken branches. This trip lacked the luster of my last visit to Zos' temple, the lightning highlighting the gaping holes in the ground and casting snarled shadows from broken masonry. The mausoleum rose ahead, dark and gray in the swirling mists. I swiped rain out of my face and swung from the horse's back before she'd fully stopped, hastily tying her reins around the fractured post outside.

Five strides later, I was inside, hand trailing the same path across one of the columns holding up the massive arched entrance. I ripped my hood from my face, barely feeling the tail of wet trickling down my back. "Zos," I cried into the musty darkness. "Show yourself."

Water dripped from the cracks in the roof, the breaks in the stone periodically highlighted by bursts of crooked thunderbolts. A shiver trailed down my spine, a tingle of electricity, and a powerful boom echoed through the chamber.

"I know you're here."

I paid the decapitated head of the goddess little heed, her stone cheek pressed against the floor, blank eyes wide and staring. The rest of the statue loomed before me, staff in hand, broken bird at her feet. The pale marble seemed to glow in the dark, and I threw my arms wide, soggy cloak dripping.

"Why did you do it?" I shouted. "Why did you betray them? Betray me?"

A flicker of white branched across the ceiling.

"This is your country, your kingdom, and it's crumbling beneath your very eyes." I mounted the three steps to the raised dais. Pip flew from my bag and perched on a pillar above me. "First, you permit Fior to overrun our borders. Then you let them kill the king, the queen, and all our nobles. And for seventeen years our people have toiled in the mines, flinched at the destruction inflicted upon our cities, hiding from the prying eyes and reaching claws of our invaders. Seventeen years you've allowed them to wreak havoc and destroy *your legacy*."

The toe of my boot caught the edge of the step and I crashed down, knees cracking, hands barely catching me before my face hit the ground. Another boom rattled the chamber.

"This was our chance." I rose to my knees. "Our opportunity to push them back and reclaim our land, our people, our passion. But you *abandoned* us."

My heart cracked open like an egg. "I prayed to you every day since we fled from Aeros. I devoted my soul to you. The Requiem took your symbol and its people embraced everything you represent; they gave you new purpose, new anger, new vitriol. They took the vengeance you've offered so many times in the past, and this is what you do?" I slammed my fist into the stone at my side, pain radiating through my bones, voice breaking. "You abandon them when they need you most."

I crawled forward on my knees, hands in my hair, and screamed. "Where were you? Why have you cursed us and your country? Have we not sacrificed enough, offered enough? Bled, cried, slaved, broken enough for you?" I gripped the edge of Zos' boot, nails breaking to the quick, my blood streaking the marble expanse. "When will you stand with us? You blessed us with our drakken, but they're gone and so is the prince. The Requiem is disbanding. And me—us—your faithful subjects…"

I broke off with a sob, throat raw. I bent low, forehead pressed against the stone I'd practically wrapped myself around, then lifted my head, peering at the broken cracks of her neck. Behind her I imagined the flare of ghostly white wings, her barn owl peering down at me with black, black eyes.

"I'm lost." I wasn't sure when I'd finally acknowledged that truth, but I whispered it now in the dark and still and ruin. "You said you'd be there for me when I needed you most, but you left me. You mocked me. You cursed me. And I don't know what to do." My voice cracked. "I listened to my father, I heeded his warnings, and I gave you everything. And now I don't know what to do. Where to turn."

Tears mingled with the drying rainwater streaking my face, splattering the smooth stone between my hands.

"I'm scared. You shook me, you rattled me, you—you hurt me." I sucked in a breath, ripping apart my shredded lungs. "I stumbled and because of that, I stopped praying. But turning against you hurts so much. I can't bear it anymore." I dug my hands into my chest, fingers spearing my ribs. "Despite everything, I still turn to you. I'm here now, aren't I? What do I have to do? What *can* I do?"

I licked the salt from my lips, head light as I fought to breathe between sobs. The words slipped away, and I allowed myself to cry. To feel every ounce of guilt, pain, and anger. As the storm raged on around me, I remembered Soren's doubt, Lukas' criticism, and Viv's bright-eyed anguish.

It hurt. Everything hurt.

From the moment I'd stepped into the woods to check on my owls under the light of the blood moon, I hadn't stopped hurting. I didn't think I ever would.

Slowly, like the receding tide, my tears dried, little more than bubbling jolts shaking my chest. I felt drained, dehydrated, and blissfully, wonderfully clear-headed.

I rested my head on the toe of Zos' boot.

She hadn't come. She wouldn't come.

Because I was thinking about this all wrong.

Who was I to demand answers from the gods? That wasn't how faith worked. Not true faith. The gods and goddesses couldn't and wouldn't come and fix everything just because they could. Not for mere humans, their subjects. But they could work through us. Despite everything I'd gone through, I still believed that.

My hands curled together, fingers interlocking. The rain had dried on my skin, turning the texture chalky. I could no longer hear the thunder or feel it rattling the floor.

The storm had passed.

"Forgive me, for I have strayed." I murmured the first line of confession normally uttered to Qet, yet I offered myself up to Zos like I always had. I had to come to her and allow her to work through me. More than ever, I needed to ground myself in my faith and allow her to guide my way.

That's how faith worked.

The gods provided guiding light, but ultimately, it was up to their people to make our wants and desires a reality. I needed to believe in myself and my abilities. Sure, maybe it was faith or coincidence that brought Soren and Lukas to my aid when I fell from the Spear. Maybe we were always meant to collide, a collage of worlds and colors coming together and spinning brightly out of control.

I wiped my nose on the back of my sleeve. My hair hung in damp threads around my face.

However, no matter where my journey had taken me, I was the one making the decisions. I drove us back up the mountain to assess what remained of my village. I was the one who stepped in front of that terrified girl at the tavern and faced down a monster. It was my stubbornness that made me track my best friend across half the country, who set the forest on fire, who risked deadly hallucinogenics to save people bound for a terrible situation. I had followed my instincts and my morals—only looking to Zos for guidance and understanding.

Whether she gave it was up to her.

The fickleness of the gods was one of the first lessons my father had taught me. And I'd forgotten. I'd strayed from my path, lost myself in the blur of seemingly never-ending struggles. But here, now. In this dark night, bound by the ribbons of the rain and the glow of the emerging moon, I found myself again.

I pressed my lips to the tattoo imprinted on my skin, mesmerized by the warmth that flared in my heart. A familiar feeling of belonging sweeping through me. Comforting. Relaxing. A feeling I'd missed more than I had realized. Pip settled on my shoulder once again, beak nuzzling my hair now that my anger had dissipated.

"Your guidance I seek," I whispered, curling up on my side, cuddling the owl to me. "I understand now what you were saying when you appeared before me—and what you have been saying all along. I was lost, but now I'm found."

I licked my salty lips, eyes closing as the darkness of sleep dragged me under.

I scarcely felt the rock digging into my hip, the ache of my limbs against the bits of rubble and debris. Because I finally felt home again. As close to home as I might ever get.

39

Castle Werentra

Something jabbing my side woke me up. I recognized the toe of a boot digging into my ribs, careful yet persistent, and groaned as I shoved at whoever was bothering me. I rolled to my side, pushing myself up, so I balanced on my hip, hand braced on the ground, scrubbing at my salt-crusted eyes. When I could see properly, I blinked at the marble boot in front of me and the squared edge of a stone sword dangling a few yards away, hanging from the goddess' hand.

Qet's teeth. I'd passed out in the temple. Dawn had come and gone. Clutching at my cramping stomach, hunger gnawing at me like a parasite, I nearly tumbled over when I crashed into a pair of legs standing beside me, the hem of a green cloak streaked with mud dripped rain on the tiles where I'd laid.

I followed the path of those powerful legs upward, over the gold and emerald tunic of the Fiorian army, across a broad chest, and met the unflinching gaze of a pair of familiar golden eyes. Colonel Kohl rubbed absently at the corner of his scar as he peered at me, stance eerily similar to that of Zos' statue: cloak, expression, hand on the pommel of his sword, and all.

Talons.

I closed my eyes, sending a silent prayer to strovara, and pushed myself upright. If he planned to arrest or kill me, I would much rather be standing. "Colonel."

He frowned, scanning my damp and muddied form. My eyes felt puffy and I could still feel the creases carved into my cheek from where I'd rested my head on my arm.

"I never gave much credence to deities before," he said, voice as low and rough as I remembered, "but I'm starting to think you might actually be a goddess incarnate."

I couldn't help but glance down at myself, then the immaculate form of Zos towering above us, trying to see the situation as he did, and couldn't get there. If he was going to stab that sword through my chest, I wished he would already.

"I'm not a deity." My hair had dried against my neck and itched fiercely. I scrubbed at it, wondering where my tie had gone and if my horse was still outside. If she was, I could make a break for it. Though, the stiffness in my joints and the crackling of my spine warned me I probably wouldn't make it to the arches before this wolven in peak form ripped me to shreds. "I'm a normal girl with supremely abnormal problems."

Minus my aging body.

The captain silently followed me as I creaked down the stairs, clutching a stitch in my side. That was the last time I slept on a stone floor. The more I moved and got the blood flowing through my veins, the more I awakened, the precariousness of my situation wrapping around me in ropes and chains.

My heart thudded hollowly in the cage of my chest, yet I forced myself to act casual as I threw one last look over my shoulder at the grand statue of the goddess and walked away from the man with the sword. And the sharp teeth.

"Yes, I can see that much," he said wryly. "Only a human would move like a reanimated corpse."

Excuse me? I halted at the edge of the purpled shadows, right at the precipice where the edge of darkness met the sunshine glinting through the arched entrance.

"So tell me, how did you survive that fall from the cliff?" My heart rate increased. He did recognize me. "And the blizzard? And escaping that wildfire that killed dozens of our best soldiers and drove many more mad? Were those all coincidences? Or were they part of a far larger, more elaborate plan?" The colonel spoke matter-of-factly, like he wasn't affected by any of it.

I released the cramp in my side. "If you want to kill me, just get it over with already." I spun, arms held out, parallel to the tile floor. "It's been an incredibly difficult last few weeks, and just when I thought things couldn't get more difficult—they did. I know you can outrun me in just about every way, and I'm in no mood to tell you all my secrets, so if you plan to kill me, please do it now." I paused, considering. "Though I'd appreciate it be as painless as possible."

He quirked a brow, hand braced haughtily on his hip. "What, may I ask, would you consider painless?"

I opened my mouth and then closed it again. That wasn't a terrible question. Falling from the cliff hadn't been pleasant, and I never wanted to get trapped in a fire again. Drowning might be peaceful, but it seemed pretty awful up until the end. He did have a sword, but even if he speared me through the heart, it could take some time to bleed out… so that left…

"Beheading or poison, I guess."

The other half of his mouth quirked upward. "You guess?"

"The other options leave time for an extreme amount of agony and retrospective thinking. I'd rather it just be over quickly." Another pause. "Queenkiller's lace would be fast-acting, assuming you can actually find some."

He dragged the toe of his boot over the floor, dislodging a bit of mud stuck between two tiles. "It must be your lucky day. I failed to bring any poison with me and I'm not in the beheading kind of mood, so I guess you'll just have to remain among the living for a little while longer."

My mouth dropped open. From outside, my mare nickered, no doubt eating the variety of leafy plants left to grow wild. "Let me get this straight—you're not going to kill me?"

"Nope."

"You plan to take me prisoner?" I hesitated. "I won't talk, if that's what you're after. I'm not very important to anyone." The lie sounded false even to my ears.

The colonel's boots squeaked as he crossed to the fallen head of Zos. "Nope, not looking for a prisoner."

What kind of insane world had I awoken in? "Then you're just... letting me go?" I gestured at the opening and the freedom it offered.

"Negative there, too." He seemed far too amused for his own good.

The colonel had to be twisting my words; my questions hadn't been very precise. I imagined an army lying in wait outside, ready to fill me so full of arrows it would make a hedgepig jealous. Or maybe he didn't want to take me prisoner because he planned to use me as a hostage instead. The more my mind swirled, the greater my anxiety grew, and I clutched at the ties of my cloak, gasping.

"Would you calm down?" The colonel stood right in front of me, gripping my arms, holding me steady. "Whatever you're thinking, it's not true."

The lack of fear I felt in his presence concerned me, and I quickly stepped out of reach, shaking off the feeling of him touching me. "You don't know what I'm thinking."

His brow lowered. "I actually have an excellent idea what you're thinking, because you can't possibly have guessed the truth."

"Which, I assume, does not end with me dying nearby?" I stroked the feathers of my cloak, wondering where Pip was.

"No," the colonel said. "Killing you would defeat all my best efforts of keeping you alive."

I jerked backward, the past flickering before me, all the times we'd met up until now. He hadn't actually taken action against me—either to injure or kill.

"I don't understand," I managed through my confusion. "What are you trying to say?"

"I'm saying I was sent here to help you." Colonel Kohl checked the buckle on his sword belt. "I know who you are and who you work with. My entire purpose in this country is to find the leaders of the Requiem and extend an offer of assistance from a very powerful place."

I almost didn't want to ask, but I had to. "What kind of powerful place are we talking about?"

"Castle Werentra in the capital of Fior."

The primary residence of Fiorian royalty.

* * *

I ran my hand over the mare's neck, smoothing the coarse hair. Everything felt surreal, like Colonel Kohl and I were living on different planes that had somehow united, and I was having a difficult time wrapping my mind around it.

"Explain it to me again," I demanded.

The colonel sat on a crumbling bench outside the temple, scooped a handful of pebbles into his gloved hand, and ground them together. "Where would you have me start?"

"From the beginning makes the most sense to me," I said haughtily, then checked myself with a glance toward the archway towering overhead. Zos hadn't spoken to me the night prior, but this felt like a test. "Forgive me. This is just—it's a lot to take in."

"I understand." He tipped the stones into his opposite hand, gray dust sticking to the leather. "I work for a powerful entity within Castle Werentra, one who does not agree with the motives behind the war or the treatment of your people in the aftermath. They would like to put an end to it without their name being in the mix."

He refused to tell me the name of the person he worked for, insisting that information was only fit for the leader of the Requiem. However, the way he spoke and the anonymity upon which he insisted made me believe we were taking about royalty. To my knowledge, this was the queen's war, and the king had died shortly after the attack, so it couldn't be either of them. I believed there were two princes, but I wasn't familiar with information about either.

"The emergence of the Requiem presented this individual with a prime opportunity to insert their assistance into the war and hopefully see it to the conclusion." The colonel flicked pebbles to the ground, one by one. "They instructed me to infiltrate the Requiem, to make the contacts necessary to form an allegiance, and report back immediately."

I paced along the edge of the path. A small trail had already formed beneath the steady stomping of my boots. Definitely royalty—or someone high up in the chain of nobility—to get someone placed so high up in the ranks on such short notice. Archer himself had said Colonel Kohl was new to the military forces in Idilea, and had only been in command of the North for a handful of months following the death of his successor before I'd collided with the resistance effort.

When I asked him if he played a role in the atrocities committed in the mines or the massacres of our children, the colonel gave me such a look of vile rebuke I couldn't help but believe him when he said he wanted to do everything in his power to rectify the rape of our country.

"But your position held you back," I continued, fiddling with a vine dangling from a tree.

"Positions of command have a way of sucking up time," he acquiesced. "They also make it difficult to endear one's self with the native population. Though I don't agree with any of the orders I'm instructed to carry out, I must maintain the farce for my mission to succeed."

Pip hooted the all-clear from the east. She'd been working her way clockwise around the temple, making sure we weren't being watched. Her presence hadn't surprised the colonel, making me wonder what he knew and had seen.

"I wasn't making much headway within the towns themselves—your people are extremely distrusting, and I applaud them for it. I had nearly given up hope when I heard a rumor that a band of survivors of the massacre in Aeros had been living in the Copper Mountains all this time."

A hint of a shadow danced across his lips as he stood, brushing his hands to remove the powder clinging to his gloves. "I saw an opportunity to appeal to those who might not be so biased against my kind, and took it. Unfortunately, one of my captains also heard that intel and launched an attack the same day." His lip curled. "He hoped to curry favor with the general by taking down some of the last known survivors of Aeros."

"And you found me." I braced my hands on my hips, staring into the foliage, listening to the trills of the birds flitting among the branches. "And killed your comrade."

A grim chuckle. "That's right. You were the one foolish enough to fall over the edge when I asked you to move to more solid ground."

433

I locked my hands behind my back. "And the tavern? When I defended that girl, you weren't about to rip my head from my shoulders."

"Nope." He grinned. "Though you gave me a bit of a shock, because I was convinced you had died during the fall. No normal person would have survived it, anyway." He cast me a reproachful look. "I was trying to work out the best way to squirrel you to safety when your *friend* saved you. That's when I led my men on a merry romp around town to give you time to escape."

Oh Zos. I wouldn't have believed him if I hadn't recalled the strangeness of our conversation on the Spear. It felt like it made sense, how we'd danced around one another all these weeks: him trying to make contact and me running at every opportunity. Though, had I a chance to go back and do it all over, I didn't think I would change a thing.

"I also hid your trail when you escaped from Stavanger. My reach beyond the northern territory is limited. The general is wary of me, you see. He doesn't like me much, given my social connections."

I liked this man. Zos save me, I was really starting to like his attitude. Given my impression of the general from several days ago, I was willing to bet Kohl and the general had come to blows before on far baser reasons.

"Because of that, I couldn't help much beyond my immediate territory. I certainly wasn't aware of what was planned at the Silverkeep Mines." His expression told me he knew what had come of it. "But I was called down to monitor patrols while everyone else converged on the castle with that prince of yours. I'm sorry I couldn't be of more help."

I nodded, not trusting my voice at the reminder of all we'd lost.

The colonel sighed and reached for the canteen of water he'd set beside the bench. I shook my head when he first offered it to me, then screwed off the top and drank deeply. "I wasn't far from this temple, in fact, when I received reports of the Owl Girl—yes, that's what they're calling you now—racing across the countryside in the rain." Looking back, I had acted rashly, taking little care to protect myself or hide my tracks. "The storm kept them at bay, but they spotted you before you entered the woods here. I told them I would deal with you myself."

He tilted the canteen my way again. "And that is how I saved your life *again*."

A rabbit darted from beneath a briarbush when I came too close, white tail flipped high as it darted for more dense underbrush. Everything the colonel said made sense. His arguments were compelling. I wasn't sure if I believed him on all counts, but enough of the timeline added up with other things I'd been told that I wanted to believe him. Except...

"What do you get out of this? I know what your *friend* wants, but what about you? Surely you aren't so selfless that you don't have your own reasons for going along with this scheme."

He bent until his golden eyes filled my vision. "Slavery is wrong. Period. My position gives me a chance to rectify some wrongs committed by my country. We have no reason to be here. Our fight is elsewhere. Bringing our ideologies together will help both of us in the long run." His face was so very serious. "That's enough of a reason for me. Will it be enough for you?"

Again, I couldn't help but feel that Zos had answered my prayers, presenting me with an opportunity to correct the course of the nation and set things right. This sounded too good to be true, but we desperately needed a miracle right now. Without one, we were nothing.

"You think I'm connected to the Requiem?"

"I know you are." There was that half smile again, one that made me wonder how many of my secrets he'd cracked. "One isn't spotted in the company of Prince Soren, his best friend and known strategist Lukas Trygg, or the designated leader of the Requiem himself—Archer Skojare—without being intimately involved in the effort."

"And you want me to bring you to him?"

"Simple as that."

"How do I know you aren't being followed?" I argued, clinging to this last argument. "That this isn't a ruse to destroy what's left of the Requiem?"

"Because your owl has told you as much." He reached out, almost touching my arms. I stared at his hand, nails rounded, dirt wedged beneath them. "Given the victory of General Rosewood, no one outside of Aeros will be interested in much beyond the fact that your prince is in custody, being primed for a highly public execution. They will not inquire about my whereabouts for several days, plenty of time for me to concoct a cover story."

He was good. Very good. "You say you'll help us get Soren and Lukas back?"

"And everyone else I can."

I shouldn't believe him, let alone give him what he asked for.

Archer would tell me I was being foolish, reckless. Stubborn and obstinate.

But against all advice...

"I'm Telleree Falk, a lost woman from the Copper Mountains, looking to find her way." I held out my hand. "But you, my reluctant ally, may call me Tell."

He stared at my hand, lost for words. When I thought he wouldn't accept my offer, he seized it, his much bigger hand folding neatly around mine. "Colonel Julian Kohl, a traitor in Her Majesty's army, ordered here to right the wrongs of the past—who also happens to specialize in helping people find their way."

We grinned at one another, a mutual sense of uneasy trust and cautious hope weaving a delicate web between us.

"Get what you need," I ordered. "For Zos' sake, disguise your uniform, and saddle up. I'll get you where you need to go."

40

Owl Girl

We rode hard until evening fell, only stopping to water the horses and scarf down food stuffed in our saddlebags. Kohl had changed into a standard black tunic and gray trousers, the embellishments of his rank neatly hidden away. Like mine, his cloak was double lined, and he flipped it so the black side faced outward, careful to keep the emerald tucked around his body. Periodically, he scanned the terrain, and urged us one way or another, keeping an eye on the sun as we went. Pip kept an eye out for patrols when she could, but she wasn't getting enough rest to trade off like she would if the other owls were with us, and eventually sought refuge under my hood.

The farther west we moved, the more my faith in Colonel Kohl grew. It didn't appear anyone was following us. Pip would have picked up on such a thing for sure by now. He also knew the routes the soldiers rode and took care to guide us around them while wasting as little time as possible. If he sought to double-cross us, surely there were easier ways to do so.

No, I recalled the betrayal at the mines and the now-familiar anger that burned constantly in my belly flared, pushing me harder. Our mole was working from within, someone who already had intimate knowledge of our operation.

When we stopped to rest, I asked him the question that had nagged at me all day. "You really know how to get them out?"

The colonel paused, smoothing wrinkles from his bedroll. His sword lay beside it, freshly polished, the leather treated. "You should have a fortnight. This is a huge moment for Grand Duke Brandt. The last living Idilean royal and one of the men who threatened to ruin his operation are finally in chains. He will want to make a spectacle of their executions."

I sagged against the tree I'd settled against, the bark digging into my back. That meant more Fiorians at the capital than normal. Likely more nobles, too. The challenges we faced had just multiplied—literally. I pinched the skin between my brows. As with everything else with this damned war, just when things seemed desperate enough, they somehow got worse.

"But I know where they're being held. How to get in and how to get back out." He slipped under the blanket, his back to me, hand resting across the flat of his sheathed weapon. We had agreed I would take first watch. "If that beloved goddess of yours can spare any luck, we could use some of that, too."

I blew out a hard breath and levered my way up the tree rather than respond.

As I settled among the freshly budding leaves, fingering a slender green branch, I couldn't help but allow a splinter of hope into my heart. A fortnight wasn't a lot of time, but it was time. I didn't want to think about what Soren and Lukas were going through in the dungeons of Eversturm Keep, the torture they were likely enduring.

But I vowed I would get them out.

Even if it cost me everything.

* * *

It was easy to think from the back of a horse. Almost too easy, given how silent the specter of a shifter was beside me was, scanning the landscape for threats. We clattered across a road paved with stones and passed a caravan of farmers returning from market, cloaks pulled to their chins, shoulders hunched from a hard day's work. A few women looked up at the pounding of hooves, their eyes catching first on the man in black out front, then me.

And they lingered.

One woman pulled a little boy into her lap, pointing, worn face glowing as she whispered into his ear. Other children took notice and started whooping, flaring their arms wide and hopping up and down as if they were wings, their cheers following us until they disappeared from sight.

The colonel shot me a meaningful look. "Like it or not, you're writing a story."

I kept my eyes fixed on the long, rough hairs of my mare's mane.

A story. That's how Soren had seen it, too. Manipulating the world to send the message he wanted to give, encouraging dreams and beliefs instead of the cold, hard facts of the reality they *knew* to be true.

The blessed one.

The Owl Girl.

The colonel was right. Mine was a tale that had been in the works long before Soren had concocted his plan to use me as a symbol for his rebellion. He'd merely tossed oil on the flames. I'd seen the way Aleksi had considered me, the caution his sparrows had taken around me. I was reminded of how many of Soren's followers had dropped to their knees when I'd first appeared in Azmarin, and I'd heard the whispered rumors that followed me. Even after the battle, the awe of the soldiers was evident, and the healers had started to respect my abilities.

Whether I approved of his tactics was beside the point. Soren was right in a very big way.

I dug my knees into my mare's sides, encouraging her into a full gallop.

That gave me an idea.

41

Interesting Company

We rounded the southern edge of Azmarin and slowed our horses to a trot, warily eyeing the city as we rode by. Everything appeared to be in order. No homes or businesses on fire. No screaming. It almost made me second-guess my instincts.

"They will have increased the patrols, if that's what you're thinking," the colonel murmured. "But they won't be obvious about it. Their priority at the mines was capturing your prince and killing as many of your leaders as they could. Now that they've had a few days to regroup, they will be after the rest of you."

I guided my mare deeper into the woods. "Why did they pull back, anyway? They had us cornered. A little more pressure and they could have destroyed the rest of us then and there. They already blew up the mines. Why not burn the forests, too?"

The colonel went quiet for so long I thought he might never answer, though it was among the least treasonous of the questions I'd asked so far. Having found the clearing I was looking for, I slid from the saddle and looped the reins around a tree.

"Leave your enemy enough hope to hang themselves with."

I paused, gripping the handle of the trapdoor that led to the tunnels beneath the city. With any luck, these hadn't been compromised yet. "That's a cruel concept."

"Cruel, but effective," the colonel said. "It's an old idea ingrained in our military teachings. Fior used to be two countries. Several generations ago, the two clashed over differing ideologies and the northern territory of Fin successfully crushed and absorbed Rainette deploying that tactic."

I flung the door wide and hopped into the darkness of the hollow. Colonel Kohl grunted when he landed beside me, pulling the door closed behind him. "It's impressive, the things people will attempt when they're desperate, and leaving them that tiny bit of hope is often enough to drive the most reckless into action. Keep in mind, when you're the one leaving the opening, you can anticipate the actions that will probably be taken." He touched one of the luminescent stones gracing the wall. "The loss you suffered is also designed to crush spirits and destroy hope elsewhere."

That's what Tugs and Lenore had told Archer. Too many people had given up on the cause, devastated by what they'd witnessed in what should have been a defining moment of glory. Few devoted soldiers remained, and it would take years if not decades for the Requiem to reassemble its strength.

"This wasn't the Requiem's first major attack," I said. Dirt flaked under my fingertips. I hadn't bothered with a torch, but I remembered this path. "It must count for something that you haven't completely broken our spirits after seventeen years of this bullshit."

More silence followed, accentuated by only the soft thuds of our shoes.

"It's what gives me hope," the colonel said.

I nearly stumbled when my fingers hit the smooth surface of the wall where Soren and I had shared our tumultuous kiss, closed my eyes against the memories that rose unbidden, and pushed forward faster, down another pair of tunnels that forked. Eventually, I scrambled up the ladder to the door that opened into one of our escape houses. The colonel followed without hesitation.

The first few doors didn't yield much, just storerooms hastily filled with barrels of mead and bags of potatoes and other supplies. Someone had been here recently, but after flinging door after door after door open, I forced myself to accept that no one was here. They'd stayed in the forest, after all.

Maybe the wounded were too weak to move back into town. Or maybe enough people had stayed to fight after all and Archer was rallying them while I wasted time here.

If that was the case, then hopefully Madame Taft knew something. Doubling back, I dragged the colonel toward the second fork in the path and went left instead of right. A long staircase emerged, and I hustled up the steps, Kohl on my heels. Murmuring for him to stay put for now, I shouldered open the door, and stepped from the closet into a narrow hallway with candles burning warmly from their sconces. Cinnamon and sugar spiced the air. Muted voices grew louder as I walked toward the main room. Desperation to find a familiar face drove me forward almost recklessly, and when I rounded the corner, I stopped in the opening.

"Archer." I breathed his name like a prayer, barely registering the welcoming smile of Madame Taft. A full breath of air filled my lungs. "You're here."

He and Taft stood before the crackling fire, arms crossed. Archer's face was ashen, his eyes bloodshot. The shadows beneath them were more purple and pronounced than I'd ever seen them. I hadn't been gone long, but it appeared as if he'd lost twenty stone, and that weight had settled upon his shoulders instead, forcing his spine to bend. In several quick steps, his arms came around me, his hand cupping the back of my head as he pressed it to his shoulder. I wrapped my arms around him, wishing I could transfer my strength to him.

"You're not an *akren*, right?" His whisper was soft.

I squeezed harder before stepping out of his embrace. "Don't tell me you think so highly of yourself that you'd be the one I chose to haunt?"

"No, I suppose not." The worry lines engraved on his forehead eased as I intended.

Wooden rings clattered against a rod as Madame Taft checked the street behind the curtains drawn over the windows, careful to keep the room obscured. "What he means to say, dear, is he's thankful you're alive. You left everyone in a right state when you up and left like you did."

My cheeks burned at her quiet admonishment. "I'm sorry. Archer, I meant to talk to you before I left, but I overheard the news in your office, about the Requiem ending and everyone calling to disband. And I kind of... lost it."

My eyes flew open when Taft's warm, weathered hand squeezed my arm. "Given you left that friend of yours behind, we assumed as much. Well, *most of us* assumed as much. Archer thought you were likely to get yourself killed." She hummed, shifting my cloak aside to examine my stained and torn clothing. "I'll get you some new attire. Take a seat. I'll be back shortly."

Chagrined, I sank into a chair beside the crackling fire, searching for shapes in the shadows thrown by the flames. "I really am sorry."

"I know you are." Archer dropped into the chair opposite me, elbows finding their familiar spots on his knees as he braced his chin on his palm. "We had eyes monitoring the routes into Aeros, but none caught sight of you. If you didn't leave to hunt down Soren yourself, where did you go?"

"I needed to see Zos." I ran a hand down my face. How foolish it seemed now, rushing to a god to demand answers. "It felt hopeless." I clenched my fists in my lap. "I was half-insane with fury. Frustrated at myself, at our failure, at the gods. I wanted to know how they could have allowed this to happen, to tear us apart like they did. Everyone's dreams were crushed. I…" I quirked an abashed smile. "I kind of demanded answers from the source herself."

Archer focused on the path my thumb wore over the tattoo on my wrist. He could have done so many things in that moment: berated me for my childish impulses; laughed at my juvenile intent; left the room at my folly. Instead, he wet his lips and leaned back in his chair. "And? Did you find them?"

I'd never been more thankful for his assertive presence in my life. "Of sorts."

"I certainly hope those answers you found explain why this young man was skulking around my linen closet." Madame Taft pushed the tall form of the colonel into the room. Archer clattered to his feet, and I rushed to intercept him, fingers digging into his arm, holding him back.

Despite the softness of the tailor's words, there was a certain amount of steel in her eyes which she had yet to remove from the colonel. Almost too quick for me to see, the blade of a knife slid up the sleeve of her shirt into a sheath she must have obscured there. "It's fortunate I have a policy of asking first and gutting later."

"You have my endless gratitude." I closed my eyes at the hint of mockery in the colonel's voice.

The old woman jabbed him deeper into the room. "You may laugh at my knives, Mr. Kohl, but it's my shears of which you should truly be afraid."

He regarded her with a raised brow. "You know. I actually believe you." A smile lit upon his lips when he turned to me. "Interesting company you keep, Tell."

Archer's muscles bunched under my palm and I stepped in front of him, a physical blockade between the men. I was under no illusions of my physical power here. My friend could have knocked me aside and attacked the colonel the moment he'd appeared in the doorway, but out of respect for me—or maybe fear for Taft—he stayed put, boots planted as if stitched to the floor.

"Telleree," he said evenly. "Explain why one of the three colonels of the Fiorian army is in the middle of this shop." Silvery eyes slid my way, frigid in their ferocity. I shivered. I hadn't felt this much animosity from him since I'd first met him. "And why he appears to be on friendly terms with you."

He stepped back, the distance he created accentuating the betrayal he felt. That was fair. He didn't need to give me this opening to state my case or hear me out. I knew how many weapons he kept on his person and how easy it would be for him to make me and the colonel bleed.

"Explain." Archer snarled when I failed to answer quickly enough. An order, not a request.

"He says he can help us free Soren and Lukas." I dragged my thumb down the seam of my cloak, straightening the cockeyed feathers of the great horned owl that lined the edge. "He's not the enemy we've believed him to be."

Archer eyed his enemy. My enemy. Former enemy?

"We ran into each other at Zos' temple," I hurried to continue, not certain how long Archer would restrain himself. "He wasn't trying to kill me on the mountain. He was searching for the Requiem. He has information that can help us and wants to offer an alliance."

I shifted closer to the colonel, forcing my shoulders to not bow under the weight of the betrayal apparent in Archer's stare. "Colonel. Please. As you explained to me, please explain to him. Surely you

447

recognize Archer Skojare, Commander of the Requiem and best friend to Prince Soren? He's the one you've sought this entire time, right?"

"So he is." The colonel took a moment to size up the man standing opposite him, then lifted his shoulder in a mollified shrug and launched into the story of what he'd told me at the temple. The more he talked, the more Archer's anger faded into quiet puzzlement, and he sank again into the plush chair beside the fire. At the conclusion of his tale, the colonel dug a large ring, a hunk of drakkentorre, and a letter from a pocket inside his cloak and offered them to me to give to Archer.

I put them on the table at my friend's elbow instead, reluctantly awaiting his verdict.

"Your story is intriguing. I'll give you that much." Archer sounded utterly exhausted, though a hint of hope dawned on his face. I risked a glance at the colonel, noting the quirk of a grin on his lips. Archer's response so closely mirrored mine back at the temple, it was almost laughable.

The commander first touched the signet ring, tracing a finger over the emerald pounded into the flattened facet before dismissing it for the drakkentorre. He leaned over the stone roughly the size of his thumb, but hesitated to touch it. "Where did you find one of our relics?"

A relic? That meant it was one of the seven original tears. My hand fisted in my pockets. It was utterly priceless.

The colonel examined the cut of a shirt hanging from a hook on the wall. "It was a gift to the crown upon the signing of our last peace treaty, entrusted to the care of the crown prince."

It was Madame Taft who crossed the room and dared touch the stone, rolling it around in her palm, milky eyes soft and distant as she squeezed it.

"He speaks the truth. I remember hearing of this decision, a bold one to entrust another country with one of our prized artifacts." She closed her eyes, weathered cheeks falling. "I'd forgotten until now."

"Is it Qet's?" I asked.

Archer frowned at the stone, taking it from Taft. "No. We have Qet's stone secured." The original drakkentorre, the first drop of sacrificial liquid that allowed our people to tap into their shifting abilities. I shifted on my feet, wondering if my question had been foolish. Of course, we wouldn't have given away our most prized possession.

Archer gently placed the polished rock on the table and picked up the letter, running the pads of his fingers over the creases in the yellowed, wrinkled paper. He rapped it against the flat of his palm, staring into the fire for several long moments as if asking it for guidance. A log crackled and resettled against the grate, snapping him from his stupor, and he slipped a nail under the fold. He scanned the page, running his hand across his chin, then handed it to me.

The message was short:

If you're reading this, then I dare say Julian has achieved the impossible for what may very well be the eighth time in his storied career and found you. Should he be gravely injured or found out for his duplicity, he's under strict orders to destroy this missive.

Had I anyone less stuffy—or irritating—on my staff equally qualified to deliver this, I would have sent them in my stead. Alas, please tolerate his impetuousness.

Now to the point: I wish you no evils, I bear no lies. My support I offer freely should you desire.

Nik.

I read it three times over, my puzzlement growing with each pass.

What a strange note. Something about the name at the bottom rang a bell, but I couldn't place my finger on it. Archer accepted the letter when I offered it back, folding it back into its original square form.

"Say I believe you, Colonel Kohl." He ran his nails over the edge of the page, sharpening it to a blade-like edge. The wolven angled his body toward us, but didn't look away from the fire. "Say I believe you are who you say you are, this letter is from the man it claims to be from, and you both mean the offer you've presented. What happens next? How firm in the conviction of his words is your prince?"

Holy Zos. Nik. Crown Prince Dominik. The second-most powerful person in all of Fior. I could have sworn thunder boomed overhead, I was so amazed.

Royalty. The colonel worked for royalty. I'd been right all along.

The Colonel's shoulders lifted. "That's a conversation between you and the prince."

42

Good Reason

"You couldn't be serious."

Archer apparently agreed with my cry of disbelief, because he shot to his feet, discarding the note beside the rest of the offerings. "You're telling us the prince is here? In Idilea?"

"Yes."

No way.

I must have spoken again, because the colonel rolled his eyes. "Yes, way." The colloquialism sounded strange coming from him. The writer of the letter knew the bearer quite well. "That information isn't public knowledge, but yes, he's here in your country."

How peculiar, to realize our rogue prince who'd spent most of his life traipsing around the country in one form or another was now in custody and another rogue prince in disguise was also running around, apparently intent on uprooting his mother's plans. My mind raced with the possibilities. Were other princes here, too? Perhaps from Eritris?

"Why is he here?" Leave it to Archer to cut to the quick of things.

The colonel picked at a speck of dirt dried on his sleeve. "I told him I was close to making contact."

"And?" Me this time. Our capitals weren't anywhere near close enough for that kind of trek. It wouldn't make sense for him to be so close to our borders, even on a whim.

The colonel scratched the irregular stubble flecked around his scar. "And royal presence has been requested for what will be a highly publicized execution."

Though we'd spoken about it previously, I closed my eyes against that reality, a hollow void expanding inside me. The realization that if I was wrong about the colonel and his intentions, if we didn't get Soren and Lukas out soon... it would be the end.

The colonel didn't wait for me to collect myself. "Grand Duke Brandt believes the capture of your prince to be the final feather in his cap of conquering your country. You and your people have proven it well by now: You are more than willing to rally behind those of royal blood. First Eero. Now Tristan. By extinguishing their presence, he extinguishes the flame of your burning rebellion."

Archer didn't contest that line of thinking.

Not that he would, even if he trusted the colonel.

"The queen is eager to divide your land among her loyalists. As such, she's ordered the crown prince be present at Prince Tristan's execution, to bear witness to the fruit of the grand duke's labor."

My stomach knotted. This was happening. The worst-case scenario was tumbling toward us at breakneck speed, and if we didn't act soon, we wouldn't have time to act.

Archer pinched the bridge of his nose. "Well, Tell, what do you think?"

Of course. We were among the few who remained committed to the cause, but still the fact that he asked me my thoughts had my spine hardening to steel. I smoothed my thumb over the tattoo of Zos and eyed the drakkentorre. "I believe him."

"Why?"

There was a reason Archer wanted to hold this conversation before the colonel himself, and I wouldn't question him now. "Because if this is an elaborate plot concocted by the prince, or someone pretending to be him for the sake of argument, what do we have to lose? Soren? Lukas? Our lives? The Requiem?" I hooked my index fingers in the collar of my shirt. "Sorry to say, Archer, but of those four, we've only got one left. And our lives and the lives of our people are over if Soren is executed."

I tucked some hair behind my ear. "You said over and over, the attack on the mines was our first shot at restoring greatness. What if that battle isn't over yet? What if this offer is an extension of that battle?"

The fire crackled as Archer thought that over, pacing a well-worn trail across the floor. A group of people walked past the entrance to the shop without knocking, their voices muffled through the wood. Madame Taft propped her shoulder against the wall, thoughts hidden in the folds of her face, while Colonel Kohl kept his attention fixed firmly on the sad state of his attire.

"We can only offer assistance." The colonel added, almost as an afterthought, "Within reason. We cannot fight this war. The crown prince doesn't have the clout or resources to pull off what he's attempting through any… legal channels. He will do everything he can to render aid as a silent partner, but he cannot risk being seen as a traitor to his country since he wishes to continue serving them as the sovereign they need down the line."

Archer exchanged a long look with Taft, one rife with history and a wealth of trust.

"Will you take part in our discussions, Tell?" Archer asked. "If you believe this is the best course of action to take, will you stay with the Requiem to see this plan is carried out?"

I blinked. Of everything I'd expected him to ask…

"It never crossed my mind to leave."

Archer's brow lifted, and I flushed, remembering how my actions could have been interpreted. "That was different. That was fear and frustration speaking. I wanted to find answers for you." I squeezed my cloak tight in my fists. "That wasn't me abandoning our cause..."

Oh.

My mouth went dry.

"You see where I'm going with this?" Archer prodded gently. "You could leave all of this behind and find the peace you so desperately seek. The Requiem doesn't have to be your future, especially given the shape it's in. I know your desire has always been to reclaim your isolated part of the world, but if we're going to do this, I need you committed to the cause. If I'm to listen to your council, I need to know you're with us.

"This plan, assuming we choose to ally with the prince, means more war is coming. When we save Soren and Lukas and break the final chains of the remaining prisoners, the bloodshed will return and difficult questions will be asked." I quivered at the conviction in his tone. "You may not bear the sword or shoot the arrow, but you will be responsible for decisions that will result in deaths, likely many of them."

He crowded my space, which should have made me uneasy. Instead, I only felt a strange sort of resonating calm. "Given how closely you hold your morals, can you live with that on your conscience?"

How my world had changed. I knew Archer was offering me an out, an opportunity to split from the rebellion I'd never intended to join and would never have sought out had I not crashed into Soren. Literally. He was giving me a chance to cut my losses and retreat to the Owl Wood to salvage what I could of my future.

Maybe when I'd traversed down that mountain in search of Viv, I would have rejoiced this opportunity. Now it soured in my stomach. Abandoning our mission meant abandoning everyone I cared about: Viv, Soren, Lukas, those toiling in impossible conditions, the villagers who cowered when the soldiers passed by them in the streets.

"I won't abandon them." I squared my shoulders, aware of our small yet intimate audience. "I'll find my peace, but it's no longer what I dreamed in the Copper Mountains. Peace doesn't mean a snowy clearing with a warm cabin and owls gathered around." It had once. But not any longer. "I will never know peace as long as my country is at war. I must do everything in my power to bring the dreams of those who believed in revolution for far longer than me to fruition."

I blinked, envisioning Soren kneeling on a platform, his head lowered to a block of iron, the executioner's sword ready to drop. Another blink and it was gone, replaced with the lost man who'd snagged my hand, something broken behind his eyes when he'd asked how I could so easily believe in something neither proven nor tangible.

He'd drawn me into this world.

I would keep him in it.

"Now there's a response I can stand behind." Taft's approval split my concentration, shattering it into a million shards. "Well Arch? What will you do?"

The leader of the Requiem, the age-old friend of a fallen prince, the man who would light the path through which we would rally, hooked his arms behind his back. "We'll meet with the prince."

* * *

Rather than saddle me with monitoring our newest ally, which would have been entirely fair given I'd brought him into this whole mess, Madame Taft smoothly drew the colonel away after we settled on the last details of our plan. He promised it wouldn't be difficult to reach his prince through some pre-established means, and would set up the meeting at the location of our choosing.

"I need to talk to a few people about what we're about to do," Archer told me, shrugging into his cloak. It was still too cool outside at night to go without it for long. "Will you be alright here? No offense, but you look like you haven't slept for a week. I'd like for you to recharge while you can."

"I'll be fine, but I was actually wondering where—" My heart fluttered in my throat, turning my words into little more than a squeak. "Where can I find Viv?"

It had nearly killed me to not ask until now, holding off on my selfish desire to see the one person who'd stood at my side for my entire life, for the betterment of society as a whole. Now that things had settled, I needed to check in on her. I had to measure her improvement with my own eyes, rest my fingers on her pulse. No assurances from anyone else would settle the anxiety coiling like vipers in my belly.

Archer was kind enough to not say anything, though I knew he'd watched every thought pass across my face. "She's in the tunnel that runs beneath the smithy. It's where we're keeping all the patients who don't have anywhere else to go right now. She has her own room." He twisted the knob. "She's doing better, but you'll want to brace yourself. Negative energy won't help anyone healing from those kinds of wounds."

Before I slipped away, I remembered something. "Did you find the traitor?"

"Yes." Archer closed his eyes wearily. "One of our newer recruits. We found classified documents copied in her own hand in her pack.

She's been dealt with. Don't worry about it."

I nodded sharply. The shiver that rattled me had nothing to do with the cold that sucked all the heat from the room when he shouldered through the door. Without wasting another moment, I vanished through the door at the back of the shop, and all but fell down the stairs in my haste to reach the tunnels. I found the area Archer referenced easily enough, and after a few false tries, I finally found the right room. I caught the door before it before it swung wide, struggling to control my panting as I took in the unsteady light cast from a single candle in the crack between the door and the stop.

She was here. Right on the other side of this door.

My best friend.

And maybe someone meant to be more than that.

Tamping down the unease bleeding through me, I slipped into the room, closed the door, and approached the cot propped up on spindly legs. Someone had tucked the blankets firmly around Viv's form, bundling her in a cocoon of warmth. Grim was with her, perched on a chair in the corner, head tucked into his back as he slept. Viv's chest rose and fell steadily, never changing, even when I hovered over her, taking stock of her hand resting on top of the blanket, the flush of her pale cheeks, the tangle of her rich hair.

"Hey you," I breathed, casting my fears and doubts aside and lowering to my knees beside her. "Look at me getting the drop on you." Viv was always aware of her surroundings. Even as children, she was impossible to sneak up on when we played games in the trees.

I squeezed her hand, smoothing my thumbs over the back of it while gazing at the fold of flat fabric that draped against her opposite arm, remembering how the healers had severed it at the elbow. "You look better than the last time I saw you, though I think you would have preferred the healers leave you covered in blood and gore just so you could show off."

They'd done a nice job bandaging her chest and neck. My fingers itched to pull back the cotton fabric to check the stitches underneath, but I didn't dare disturb the wound. The burn needed to remain covered for it to heal correctly, and I'd already witnessed the fine work of the healers.

The bar of the cot pressed into the indent of my stomach as I brushed some stray strands of hair off her forehead. Her eyelashes cast thick shadows across the tops of her cheekbones. Close up, I realized she had a little more color to her skin than I'd first thought.

"I'm sorry I wasn't here to help carry you back to Azmarin, and something tells me the only reason they succeeded in bringing you here is because you're out like this. Mad as you are at me, I don't think you would have let them take you without knowing where I was." Or so I hoped. Our relationship may have fractured, but I didn't think it was a void we couldn't cross. "I want you to know I wouldn't have left you if it weren't for a good reason."

The bed bit into my ribs as I hunched over her, but I could more easily see her face this way, measure the rise and fall of her chest. Content in her company, I told her about my cross-country trip and finding the colonel. I also filled her in on the conviction with which I'd spoken to Archer about understanding my new path forward in the world, telling her she would have been proud of me for speaking up. The sound of my voice filled the cozy room, and I kept talking even when the candle guttered out. Aside from gripping her hand in mine, I didn't touch her again, though I longed to. That wasn't a call for me to make.

When I finally thought I'd run out of words, I found a handful more.

"I'll make you proud, Viv." The bed creaked when I rested my back against it. "There's more I want to tell you, but I need you to come back to me first. Please." My fingers folded tight in my lap. "Zos bless you."

43

True Renegades

Archer knelt beside a fireplace the size of a small bookcase, dragging steel over flint in a soft hushing sound. Sparks hit the bits of twisted white paper he'd thrust among a pile of dried maple sticks. The room was cool without the fire, given the temperatures had plummeted again, a reminder that rapt was a fickle season.

I motioned for Colonel Kohl to sit in a nearby chair and snagged a lit candle off the table before circling the room, searching for more lanterns. We'd entered this little cottage in the middle of Azmarin from the kitchen and had followed Archer into a small living space scattered with dinged furniture boasting faded cushions. I traced the grooves of the metallic pins on the back of the settee, the curve of the wood smooth beneath my palm, and held the flame of my candle to the lantern set into the wall. The amber light illuminated a painting of a silverpine forest beside it.

"There we go." Archer closed the grate, orange and yellow flames leaping greedily behind their barrier, and dusted off his hands. "It'll warm up in no time."

The colonel remained quiet, sharp eyes missing nothing. He

claimed to have passed Archer's message on to his prince about meeting here, though Archer had his doubts.

I tugged on the ties of my cloak and wandered to another painting, this one of a wide, flat lake with the arching towers of a castle off in the distance. Eversturm Keep. A memory flickered, gray and black with age, but before I could snatch it up for examination, it drifted away. Grudgingly, I lit the last lantern and set the candle in the holder on a small coffee table situated squarely in the center of the room. The gaping maw of a staircase opened beyond the backs of two armchairs, but Archer didn't seem particularly concerned about that as he picked his away around the room, straightening things.

"Who lives here?" I asked, hanging my cloak from a hook on the wall. He wasn't wrong. It hadn't taken long for the cottage to warm. Pip hopped from her spot in my bag and bounced to the arm of the second chair, head swiveling as she examined her new surroundings. The colonel watched her with interest.

Archer shoved a sheaf of documents into the drawer of a table against the wall. "I do."

"Seriously?" I scanned the room again with fresh eyes, taking in the muted blues and subtle greens of the fabrics, the hand-carved embellishments in the corners of the baseboards, and the thick stack of dusty books shoved into a case in the corner with titles I recognized. Books of philosophy and strategy. Of war. "I can see it."

"Cut it out." Archer's hand dipped into his hair, smoothing it unnecessarily. He shifted from foot to foot, avoiding my eye. "Your wandering is making me itchy."

I tugged on a tassel on a set of navy blue curtains, marveling at the feel of the silk. I'd only handled the fabric once in my life and that was by mistake. "It fits. I can feel you in here. All spick and span but secretly comforting and cozy."

I flashed the commander a grin. "I'm surprised any of you have your own residences is all."

A clock ticked on the wall, the longer hand edging closer to the hash mark at the top. Archer fiddled with his earring and shrugged. "It was my father's, but he registered the paperwork under a different name. After he passed, I couldn't find the deed to sell it off. So, here we are."

Liar.

I swallowed back the retort, keeping in mind the company staring at his hands folded in his lap, likely marveling over the lack of ropes and chains binding him, and dropped into the sofa, rubbing winding patterns in the pale green velvet. I wondered how Archer felt about opening his home to not one but two sworn enemies. Sure, we were running low on secure places, especially since he wanted to keep the vast extent of our tunnels a secret, but this level of personal invasion was monumental. It was obvious to me how much he cared about this place, one of the last remnants of his father, and to risk it like this...

A knock sounded at the door. Three raps. A pause. Two more.

The colonel rose, hands coming around his back so he stood at attention.

"Let's get this over with." If he second-guessed his decisions, Archer didn't show it and strode to the door. A figure dressed in black swept into the room with a gust of chilled wind. He tugged off his gloves as he stepped into the room. Zos, he stood as tall as Colonel Kohl. Maybe taller, even. What did they feed the people down south for them to grow so massive? The man scanned the room from behind the veil of his hood before scraping it off his head.

The gods could have carved him from the side of a glacier, his features were so sharp and so fine—almost feminine in their beauty. Where we Idileans bore scars and skin toughened by the bitter chill of the climate, the prince appeared delicate yet arresting. His wheat-pale hair was bound at his nape and he stood straight, the stance of a royal who'd never known what it was to look up at another.

His brow arched as he took in the silence, then shoved his gloves in the pocket of his vest so the fingers stuck out. "This is not how I pictured meeting my first group of true renegades."

What?

Kohl smacked his clenched fist over his breast, snapping the tension, and bowed low. "My prince."

"Julian, we've been over this," the newcomer chided, failing to introduce himself to either Archer or me, which would have been the polite thing to do. "No titles in enemy territory."

My brows lifted and I caught Archer's surprised glance my direction. The colonel straightened but refused to relax. The boy eyed him again, then swept the room across the room and snagged my hand before I could react. "I hear you, Owl Girl, are the one to whom I owe my thanks for keeping my best friend's head on his shoulders." He brushed a kiss across the backs of my knuckles in a gesture that made my breathing dangerously thin. "For your cool-headedness—and kindness—you have my deepest gratitude."

"It was nothing." I tugged my hand away, rubbing the spot his lips had touched as if he'd scorched me with his charm. Though he moved with authority, this close up I realized how young he was. Maybe a winter or two younger than me, his build gangly, his face unlined.

He winked haughtily and spun, tugging off his vest which he threw over the arm of the settee, then pointed at Archer. "You are a difficult man to track down, Archer Skojare."

Clearly suspicious of the prince's airy attitude, Archer's fingers twitched at his sides as if beckoning me to join him. That wasn't happening. "You're Dominik Zeit, the crown prince of Fior?"

"Nik, please. Shall I slash open my arm and prove my blood runs blue?" He sank into the sofa beside me and promptly propped his boots on the very table he'd gestured to with such impetuousness. "Alas, I'm not a fan of pain, especially when self-inflicted, so I suppose you'll have to take my word for it."

A laugh bubbled up in my breast and I fought it down. Colonel Kohl cast me a sidelong look, telling me he'd warned me this was how things would be, and sank back into his chair.

"The way I see it, as charming as this place of yours is, the longer I stay, the more danger I put you in." The prince folded his hands in his lap. "Shall we proceed?"

Archer dropped into the remaining chair. "Your associate says you sent him to track us down because you wish to offer us your support. Is that true?"

"Julian doesn't know how to lie."

"And I only acknowledge straight answers."

A disturbing flash of cunning flickered across the prince's face. "Yes, I sent Julian on a suicide mission to seek out those behind the Requiem. I wished to speak with you about how I could offer my support to your cause. That was a season ago, however. You and your people have proven quite reticent in staying hidden."

"Why would you do that?" I asked. "As part of the crown that ordered the invasion of our territory, why would you not only turn against your people but offer to support their enemies?"

The prince settled deeper into the sofa. "I may be the crown, but I don't stand with the crown."

"Remember what he just said?" I flicked my thumb at Archer who was rubbing his hand down Pip's back in short, soothing motions. "About straight answers? That applies to me, too. You're the one who wanted to meet with us. You're the one risking your title. Either talk straight or leave. We don't have time to play games with princes, especially foreign ones."

A smile danced upon his lips. He was enjoying this. Playing with us. Or whatever he was doing. As charming and rude as he was, I got the impression he did very little without thinking it over first.

"Strong words for such a slight girl, especially since you need me more than I need you." He leaned forward and I realized his eyes weren't translucent blue. No. They were the metallic shade of the sky at the edge of a blizzard, tinged with all the danger that came with it. "However, I'll level with you. I appreciate those who aren't afraid to call others out on their bullshit, especially when they're royal."

Archer stroked his beard. "So why do you want to help us? Your mother has all but beaten us into submission. Your grand duke has our prince in custody. We're one week away from our back being severed in two."

The prince waited. The crackling of the fire filled the silence.

"Because I am not my mother and I never want to be mistaken for her." Prince Dominik brought his foot up to his knee. "I was two when our nation invaded yours. I had nothing to do with the decision to invade, but every step in the course of my life since then has been guided by it.

"Some of my earliest memories include tutors telling me about the treachery of your country, how your king had amassed an army unlike any other, planning to overrun ours for our resources and a desire to implant your false gods in your stead. My instructors told me your sovereigns had been planning the attack for years, and our crown responded in the only way it could: by attacking first and halting the plight before it could begin."

That couldn't be right. My mother and father often talked about

465

the strength of our small military. Though the ones in service were powerful, we barely had the drakken necessary to maintain our army and navy, preferring to focus on farming and mining than on acts of aggression. We'd believed our climate too unforgiving, our threat of fire and air power too daunting for anyone to actually attack.

Archer's brow knit. "But King Ahlgren had just returned from signing a new peace treaty with Fior a half season prior. He went to your country, stayed in your castle, brought gifts of our dedication to that cause. Why go to such lengths if he only meant to invade?"

The prince nodded, eyes alight as if Archer was a particularly bright student. "Duplicity knows no bounds. Are you familiar with the concept?"

Archer's gaze flickered to the books in the corner. "Give the perception of one kind of action while carrying out another."

The prince threaded his fingers together. "For most people in our country, that's enough of an explanation. The influx of wealth from your stolen gems doesn't hurt, either. However, that reasoning never settled right for me. The story didn't add up." He brushed the edge of his nose. "Though a child, I remembered meeting your king on that trip. He gave me that stone, the one I left with Julian to give to you."

I fisted that stone in my pocket now, the curves of the oval familiar against my palm.

"I remember the kindness in his eyes when he knelt to give it to me. I don't recall his voice, but he said I reminded him of his own son who was about my age and how we would never tolerate one another if we met in real life." The prince threw his arm over the shoulder of the sofa, incapable of settling. "I couldn't reconcile that memory, the benevolence of that man who shook hands with my father with the one of a bloodthirsty king presented in the books my instructors put in my hands.

"It also didn't make sense how a nation that reportedly had been preparing to attack us for months if not years, would fall so quickly. An army as large as the one you were purported to have would never have fallen in a single day." He shook his head, the silky strands of his hair catching on the embroidery of his collar. "Even if you had been caught off-guard and your king assassinated, your drakken would never have been conquered as easily as they were, gold armor and nets or not."

The prince stood, his lean body filling the room, hands shoved deep in his pockets, eyes flinty.

Archer had settled back, the tension drained from his shoulders. I couldn't tell if he believed the prince, but he certainly seemed more relaxed than he had in some time. "So you didn't believe the accounting of your country's take on how the war started. There's still a large gap from not agreeing with the whys and deciding to commit treason."

The prince halted before the painting of the forest, the silvery limbs of the pines heavy with freshly fallen snow, the glow of the sun trapped behind the gauze of the cloudy sky. "I didn't stop my investigation until I proved myself right. I found the documents proving not only had my mother but my father ordered the attack on your people. When I finally figured out why they had turned against one of our oldest allies—"

He bit back something, his back straight and sharp as one of Viv's arrows.

"My family history is somewhat twisted and I won't bore you with the details. To keep in brief: my father ordered the invasion, but it was my mother who crafted the plan and pushed him to it. She was certainly the one who issued the order to commit genocide to maintain control following my father's death."

He turned back to the room, jaw set tight. "I won't stand for genocide. I may have had nothing to do with this invasion, but I will do my part to end it. It's shameful and despicable, the actions my country has taken: for breaking your trust, for overrunning your people, for doing our best to massacre your culture. I want to restore my nation's pride, and I can't do that standing behind my mother. I understand why they felt they needed to invade, the corner they were backed into—" he bit something off again, a hint of the political undercurrents I knew ran far deeper than what he was telling us—"but it's wrong. They never should have made this call, and while I am in a position to do something about it, I must, even if it means committing treason and ending this war only to start another."

Archer exchanged a look with me.

"I'm not following," I confessed.

The prince shook his head. "It's not your problem and it never was. Fior is being blackmailed in a very nasty way with the threat of invasion hovering over our shoulders. Your gems are holding our enemies at bay for now, but those will run out eventually, and we will need to deal with that threat at some point." He leaned against the wall. "Frankly, I'd rather deal with it now, but I need to establish the pieces to do so. And that means ending our occupation of your country and moving on to the greater issues at hand."

Archer inclined head. "You're looking for a political alliance down the line. That's what you get out of this."

Prince Dominik looked at him approvingly. "Your country will get its sovereignty back and we will be prepared to pay recompense for our egregious behavior. In the meantime, I will deal with the unsavory matters at play within my own borders, restore my crown's dignity, and work to forge a new relationship between our countries that will be of mutual benefit. Seems like a fitting solution, does it not?"

"It will take time," Archer cautioned, but he didn't say it was inconceivable. I didn't think Soren would be happy about it, but we were backed into a corner and having the help from someone on the inside would be invaluable.

"I'm aware of that," the prince said. "But at least we will have time—assuming we can band together and save that prince of yours, given you've hinged your country's future on his shoulders."

Archer glanced at me. "Well, Tell?"

I knew what he was asking. Did I believe this stranger? Did I think he could help us? Was he truly on our side? I squeezed the stone in my pocket. The mark of the Requiem peeked out from behind a portrait of a woman I didn't recognize. The symbol of Zos, twisted to reflect our country's needs, a sign of hope and persistence.

Zos had indirectly led me to Colonel Kohl, and the colonel had led me to Crown Prince Dominik.

I would be a fool to not heed her guidance.

"I believe him." I held up the stone, its opal depths flashing with secrets. "Together, we will be able to save Soren and Lukas and put this whole situation right again."

"I concur." Archer stood. "You think you can help us get him back? Save him from execution?"

The prince smiled, his teeth white and sharp. "Absolutely. Now tell the people you've got hiding upstairs to come down so we can hash out our plan like civilized creatures."

44

Quite the Ruckus

Tugs and Lenore worked their way downstairs, stairs creaking under their feet. The bear of a warrior appeared first, his beard more grizzled than the last time I'd seen him, with large patches missing, scorched away by fire. Lenore's face pinched tight as she scanned the room, fingering a heavy bit of gauze wrapped around her neck, obscuring a nasty cut she'd gotten in the fight at the mines.

Though Archer said they'd caught the traitor, he'd admitted to me he only trusted a handful of people anymore, and he trusted these two above all others. They'd been with him the longest, going as far back as Eero's rebellion, and offered some of the wisest council.

"If you think this is wise—" she started to say to Archer, who shook his head.

"I believe him."

"So do I," Tugs grumbled, rifling around in his vest for his pipe. "I'll never trust a Fiorian, but I believe this one wants to end this war for his own godsforsaken means."

"My thanks," the prince said dryly.

Lenore pressed her lips so tightly together they went white, but she dipped a shallow bow all the same, opting against speaking for the time being. I understood her hesitancy, appreciated her for it even. None of us were comfortable with this situation, and while we had few choices available, it was good to have someone openly second-guessing things.

The scent of cloves melded nicely with the fire as Tugs drew in a puff of his pipe. Archer accepted a document from him before introducing the prince to the newcomers. With the pleasantries out the way, he unfurled the page, motioning for me to pin down one curled end while he held onto the other, revealing a map of Aeros.

Azmarin and Dowhurst were sprawling cities, growing outward rather than up. The centers of the cities were packed business districts with limited housing options, but the streets wound outward in all directions, transitioning to rural farmsteads that extended deep into the hills. In contrast, Aeros rose vertically, locked within the firm confines of its rectangular outer wall. The first king had designed the city with defense in mind.

Its outer walls stood three stories tall, built of gray rock dug up from the depths of Storm Lake nearby. Twin walkways ran the width of the wall: one at the top, the other about halfway down. Slots cut evenly into the stone gave archers access to the outside. Aeros' four entrances were located in the four corners of the walls, and the twin gates were positioned at 135 degree angles. One gate lowered from above and the other swung outward. When both sets of gates were locked, the city was impenetrable from the ground.

The city itself was divided roughly in half. The poorer working class worked in the northwest half of the city, while the richer nobles and upper class merchants staked their claims to the southeastern side. A long, wide road served as a dividing line between the two sections, and the street that started in the southeast led to Eversturm Keep, which was situated on a hill surrounded by another rectangular wall, this one about two stories high. Its single gate allowed entrance from the ground, but seven half-moon 'balconies' jutted out from the wall in regular intervals, places for drakken to land. The king and queen used to deliver speeches and welcome dignitaries from those balconies as well. Now they served as places for the grand duke's personal guard to patrol.

I scratched my chin, trying to imprint the map on the insides of my eyelids. I'd never seen Aeros outlined in such detail before, and appreciated Lukas' work. It would be a simple matter to get through the outer gates as long as we were careful, but the inner walls were more challenging. Rumor had it the gate to the castle rarely opened.

The prince crowded closer, his arm resting against mine. "Julian briefed me on your goal, but would you outline your objective again so I can be sure we're on the same page?"

Archer tapped a long building situated northeast of the southwest entrance. "We need to get Prince Soren and his advisor, Lukas, out of jail as cleanly and quietly as possible. Our eyes in Aeros confirm they are being held in the cells below ground. Once we get them out, we can reconvene and reconsider our plans."

I reached forward and circled the castle. "Why keep them in the jail? Wouldn't the castle be more secure? They could lock them in one of the towers or any of the rooms without worry."

Archer walked to the kitchen and emerged with a kettle. "I have a few theories about that." He hung the pot over the fire. "Our contacts have seen soldiers escorting the prince between the castle and the dungeon several times. I believe that's a power move: the grand duke flexing his muscles in front of the people, showing them he has their prince in custody and he can do whatever he wants to them or to their future." Archer leaned against the wall, gazing into the fire. "I doubt he's concerned about security issues. He believes the Requiem to be disbanded and any attempts to save Soren would involve a small group hardly capable of going up against his army. There are just too many soldiers."

Tugs nodded. "It could be arrogance. Brandt makes no effort to hide his vanity. It could be he doesn't want to live in the same place as one of the dirty drakken he's worked so hard to suppress."

The prince tapped his knee thoughtfully. "That sounds exactly like Innis. He's always been one to flaunt what he has, especially in excess, most likely because he came from nothing. He's arrogant enough to want to live separately from his enemy *and* to make a power play out of it." He folded his arms haughtily, expression schooled into something gloating. "'Ha, look at how close your prince is, but you'll never get him back because I have him so tightly guarded. You'll never trounce me, I'm too powerful.'" He dropped his arms, head angled coyly. "Something like that."

Archer shot Prince Dominik the same look he gave me when he thought I was being petulant, and removed the kettle from the fire when it shrieked. "Arrogant though he might be, Brandt isn't stupid. He has increased both the soldiers keeping watch in the dungeon and the patrols circling the jail at all times of day."

The prince flashed those too-white teeth. "So you need help getting in."

Archer returned to the kitchen and Tugs pulled a ring of heavy, iron keys from his vest. I eyed his pockets, wondering what might emerge from them next. "Years ago, only one key was needed to unlock all the cells in the jail. The system was designed to be simple and the justice system worked quickly, so people were rarely housed there long enough to worry about them breaking out." He held up a skeleton key. "Based on recent intelligence, we don't believe that has changed—and if it has, we should be able to pick the locks."

"All we lack at this point is the opportunity to get in," Archer said, emerging with a tray of steaming cups. Though we all accepted the tea, none of us drank.

The prince cracked his knuckles, looking entirely too pleased with himself. "Fabulous. This is when being royalty really pays off."

Pip cooed and I lifted my arm, offering her my brace to land on as she eyed the newcomer with a heavy amount of contrition. He regarded the owl critically in return, then addressed the room.

"I want you to consider something before I reveal how I can be of service." He sipped his tea thoughtfully. "You'll recall, mother dearest sent me to your country to bear witness to your prince's execution. With Tristan out of the way, the threat of revolt diminishes, dissenting voices fall silent, and I wouldn't be surprised to see those who aren't necessary for day-to-day operations be sent to the mines for no reason other than living.

"You should consider the implications that has in the near future. If their plans go accordingly, Fior will be in a position to fully assimilate Idilea into its borders and hand over your land for our nobles to claim and occupy."

A tremor shivered through the room. An unpleasant taste filled my mouth. I'd thought it was bad enough to be occupied in a military state, but I'd never considered what came next. The final step in any conquering nation. They'd toppled our religion, enslaved our people, and obliterated our economy. Parsing up our land would come next.

When I met Archer's eyes, I realized he'd already known this and had made his peace with it long ago. The weight he carried on his shoulders wasn't an act. He knew precisely what would happen when the Requiem gave its last and hope trickled away.

It might be generations before we worked up enough energy to fight back.

Or it might be never.

"That's horrible," I murmured, wrapping my arms around myself.

The prince's gaze softened. "I have no desire to rule this territory. To reiterate: I want nothing to do with claiming your people or dictating your ways of life. My mother only needs to concern herself with what's happening now; it is I who must worry about what comes next. My country has enough problems without worrying about when another revolt might come from the north. I would rather cut your shackles now than keep you bound." He shrugged. "I realize you don't trust me. That's fair, because I don't trust you. But I hope that my actions now will guide our conversation moving forward."

For as haughty as he seemed, Prince Dominik actually appeared to care about his kingdom. If we got Soren out alive and survived this war, would he grow into a strong and thoughtful leader like this man appeared to be? Soren was so focused on the here and now, on righting the immediate wrongs, it was difficult to imagine the prince strategizing about what came in the future.

"You mentioned a distraction," Archer prompted, draining the last of his cup.

"I did." That smirk was back. "If there's anything royalty is good for, it's causing a big fuss over nothing, and I have a bit of a reputation back home for being the fussiest and most frivolous of all."

Though their people occupied our lands, I knew very little of what went on in Fior. But given my impressions of the prince now, I could easily see him using his arrogance to his advantage.

"When I was handed my marching orders, I called up the biggest caravan I could to come north with me. I need all my little trinkets and servants, after all. Can't pack light even if I only intend to stay for a few days." Prince Dominik shoved his hand in his pocket and emerged with a fistful of tiny jewels. "In fact, I've stopped at a few towns and villages in Fior along the way, spreading goodwill of the crown. As you can imagine, all those wagons and horses—and the people we're picking up along the way—it's already causing quite the ruckus."

Tugs' eyes lit up, and he elbowed Lenore, who looked less than thrilled to be jostled around. "That activity is sure to fluster the guards at the gate," he said. "Dealing with all those people and horses alone will be an ugly task, let alone getting them through the streets and to the castle itself. They'll need all hands on deck to pull it off without starting a riot." He tugged on his beard, chuckling. "What an awful situation."

"Especially if I inconveniently arrive a day earlier than anticipated."

The room went so silent we could hear the muted conversation of a group down the street.

"It's kind of brilliant," I said, imagining the chaos with mirth. "Causing enough of a distraction to pull soldiers away from the jail that we have time to move in and get Soren out without anyone being the wiser."

Archer couldn't contain his grin. "We'll still need to knock out the guards on the inside, but it's insane enough that it might work."

"Not might. Will," the prince corrected. "After your men are out, what you do with them is none of my concern." The colonel shook his head, dissuading Dominik from saying whatever was about to come out of his mouth, but he went for it, anyway. "Are you positive you don't wish to do more? Freeing the prince could be a linchpin to much bigger things. You will be right beneath Innis' nose. I realize your numbers are thin, but I could—"

"No," Archer said. Firm and steady. "We go in, we get the prince, we get out. End of story. We aren't prepared to launch a full-scale attack, not without more people and planning. Besides, the city will be a hive of enemy activity. I know Brandt is drawing in most of his high-ranking staff to bear witness to Prince Tristan's murder. We simply can't risk it."

"I see." Prince Dominik disguised his disappointment behind his smirk, one that was looking less arrogant and more like a mask. "In that case, allow me to handle the fuss of causing a little chaos and you do what you need to."

He drew his hood over his head. "If you require anything further, I'm leaving Julian in your care. Feel free to kill him if you think me duplicitous… or if he irritates you enough. He's only my best friend, but I won't hold it against you."

The prince flicked me a look.

I felt there was more to this. Something he wanted to say but couldn't.

It was clear he hoped Archer would take advantage of the opportunity, but even I agreed with our leader. Now wasn't the time to take a page from Soren's book. We needed to act with deliberation. The only people we could trust were in this room and a handful of others.

Reclaiming the kingdom was out of the question.

So what was with that look? What was he planning that I couldn't see?

A gust of icy wind rattled the map as the foreign prince blew back out into the night.

45

It Wasn't a Dream

"I still don't like this," Lenore quipped the moment the door closed. "I say we do as he suggested: kill this monster here and work on a new plan."

Archer ignored her. "Would he really be fine with us killing you?" he asked Kohl.

The colonel lifted a shoulder, unconcerned. "Hard to say with Dominik. He does as he pleases most of the time. I try my best to keep up."

"He seemed genuine to me," I said, leaning into the velvety cushions. The sofa was more comfortable than it looked, especially when I wasn't sharing it with someone else. "But you all know I don't like painting an entire race of people with a singular brush."

Lenore sucked air loudly through her nose as if I'd slapped her. "If you knew half of what—"

"Wolven drove me from my home and massacred my entire family for doing nothing more than living beyond their jurisdiction," I cut in. I was late to this game, any later and I probably wouldn't have been part of it at all, but I had suffered my losses as much as any of them had. "I have as much of an ax to grind with them as you do,

478

but I'm willing to give them a chance to prove themselves. We won't get anywhere unless we start trying to do something about it."

"I agree." Archer smoothed the wrinkles from the map, leaning over it again as if trying to coax more secrets from the ink. "Like it or not, we're out of options. We either accept their help or leave it. We'll suffer the consequences of whichever action we choose."

Lenore glared at the wolven. "Does he need to be here? How do we know he isn't planning on betraying us right now? I don't like it."

"He stays." Archer's tone brooked no argument. "That's the last I have to say on the issue. We need his help to get past the guards. Without him, we don't have enough swords to go around, so yes, he needs to be part of this conversation."

"What are you thinking, boss?" Tugs took a drag on his pipe. "The prince causes a ruckus, the soldiers disperse to deal with the mayhem, and—"

"Tell will be waiting from the bell tower of the courthouse." Archer tapped a square north of the jail, the only building taller than three stories in a ten to fifteen block radius. "She and her owls will be able to see the prince's caravan approaching from there. After we surround the jail, she can give us the go-ahead to enter."

It floored me, the faith Archer had in my abilities in this situation. I stroked Pip's head with my fingertip. "I recommend using mirrors to communicate. That frees up my owls to scout farther ahead. You will be able to see the shimmer from just about anywhere, and anyone could mistake it for light reflecting off the bell if they happened to catch a glimpse, too."

Tugs smoothed his mustache. "I like that. Simple methods yield the strongest results."

Archer tapped the map again, this time circling the jail. "While Tell is keeping watch, we prepare to attack. Two go for the main entrance and another two go around back. That way, if one group gets tied up, the other still stands a chance of getting through."

Lenore took a delicate sip of her now-cold tea. "You said something about eyes in the city, Arch. Who's left?"

He tugged on his lower lip. "No one you need to worry about." He banged his fist on the table suddenly. "Now come on, help me find the weak points. Where are our best places to hide while we wait for the signal?"

Tugs jumped at the opportunity to show his expertise of the area since he'd been stationed at Aeros before the war broke out, and though I listened, part of me couldn't focus, still fixated on Archer's answer to Lenore. Archer had said he trusted Tugs and Lenore above all others.

But what if he wasn't certain about that, after all?

* * *

I stood outside Viv's room, hand on the knob, forehead pressed to the wood. I visited her as frequently as I could, but this time might be my last before we left for Aeros. She remained in a coma, her mind and body still healing, and transporting her to the capital city was out of the question.

Biting back a burst of fear, I stepped into the room and closed the door at my back, waiting for my eyes to adjust to the dark. She hadn't moved from her prone position, head cradled on the pillow, injured arm crossed over her chest, body swathed in fluffy blankets. I dragged a three-legged stool to her side, wincing at the grating of wood on wood that broke the quiet, and interlaced our fingers.

"We are working with a new ally, Viv, but I can't decide if you would call us fools for trusting him." I plunged headfirst into my story, relaying every detail of Archer's house, of the meeting with the prince, and the post-discussion about positioning.

Viv probably would have called us out for trusting in this gamble, but hope fluttered in my breast, bits of dandelion fluff blowing in the breeze. Sure, Dominik was imperious and more than a little rude, but he seemed genuine beneath the facade. If he wanted to rip away the last vestiges of our resistance, he had plenty of ammunition.

But I didn't think he would.

"I believe he wants to rectify the wrongs his country has committed, even if he has to betray his people in doing so," I reasoned with Viv, the coarse pad of my thumb catching on the edges of the bandages twining around her palm. "It's interesting to me how much he appears to resent his mother and how close Soren was with his own family. Royals and commoners really are more alike than we were led to believe."

I studied the walls encasing us. This place was all wrong for Viv, with its lack of color and clutter. She'd filled her room in Solas with dried leaves and flowers, chunks of glittering rocks from the caverns inside the mountains, stray bits of metal harvested from the forge, and long branches slathered in paint that she claimed made the best walking sticks. By contrast, this space with its gray walls and thin quilt didn't match the vibrancy of the woman I knew so well.

"I wish you were here," I whispered. "I miss you so much. What I said to you before the fight—I meant it. There was more I wanted to say, too. So much more." My voice hitched, emotion clotting in my throat. "I wish I hadn't walked away, that I'd made you hear me out. I shouldn't have left things like I did. It was so foolish of me. I miss you. So much."

Hesitantly, I lifted her hand and brushed a butterfly kiss across the back of it. The gesture was at odds with the twisted, mangled mess of thoughts writhing around my gut: hope, fear, regret, pain, anger. I couldn't separate them to save my life.

Her hand twitched.

I froze, staring at her fingers. I had to have imagined it. A frightful fancy. The healers didn't expect her to awaken for at least another week. There wasn't any way she had—

This time I saw it, the bend in her knuckles and tightening of her fingers around mine. My eyes flew to her face and my heart gave a devastating lurch, nearly exploding from my chest when I found her watching me, lids at half mast, eyes tracking the tears dripping from my chin. She squeezed my hand again, more firmly this time.

"I don't think you're foolish," she said, voice thin as spider's silk. I leaned forward to hear her better. "You might be stubborn and act on emotion, but that's what I like about you." She sounded stronger, blinking back the dredges of slumber.

My heart soared on owl's wings, eclipsing the moon. Fear and worry vaporized, blown away like ashes in the wind, leaving nothing but peace and joy in its wake.

There was so much I wanted to say. So much I needed to tell her. But words weren't enough.

Before I could second-guess myself, I closed the last few inches between us, my lips finding hers, little more than a whisper of touch before resting my forehead against hers. She went still beneath me, the rise and fall of her chest barely detectable. Just when I thought I'd made the greatest blunder of my life, she sighed and shifted, her arm coming up around me, pulling my face back down, applying pressure in all the right places.

Relief washed through me like a rushing river, the chill so brutal it was almost boiling, searing away every thought save the softness of her lips against mine, the silk of her hair slipping between my fingers as I cradled the back of her head, the warmth of her breath like life itself. All too soon, I drew back, shuddering at the effort it took, and cupped her cheek, needing to see the wicked glimmer of her green, green eyes.

I swallowed hard, swamped in the heat and awareness shimmering brightly back at me. I understood why she'd reacted the way she had when she'd encountered me and Soren in the tunnels, but everything leading to this moment fell into place with a snap: The way she gravitated toward me, protecting me even when I didn't need it; the subtle ways she brushed against me, touching me whenever she could; the way she always coaxed the best out of me.

I wasn't sure when her emotions had shifted, when she'd started seeing me as something more than her best friend—but there was no mistaking her feelings as her thumb erased the remnants of my tears.

Her soft smile had never appeared more radiant. "It took you long enough to figure it out."

A chuckle burst from me, sharp and wet. I smoothed her hair behind her ears, appreciating the way her ropy scars contrasted with the rose petal texture of her skin. "I wish you'd told me."

"You needed time." Her thumb caught on the corner of my lips and lingered. "You weren't ready, and neither was I."

I kissed her again, desperate to feel her against me, a mixture of wondrous pleasure and exploratory excitement bubbling up between us. "When?" I asked when we parted again. "When did things change for you?"

Her lashes lowered, severing my view into her soul. "Years maybe? I've always admired you, and that grew into something more. I always wanted to be with you—it was why I was always trying to convince you to leave with me and tackle the world together. I thought we had time... until we didn't." I inched back, tracing long lines down the side of her neck, enjoying the goosebumps that pebbled in the wake of my touch.

"I finally embraced how I felt when I saw you charging through the smoke in the forest outside the mines, careful and calm as you freed us," she continued. "I almost couldn't bear it when I thought you'd died in the fire. I felt half of me break before Soren dragged you out."

She brought her arm up as if to clench her fist against her heart in a familiar gesture of comradery, then froze, gaze trailing down to the bandages wrapped around the stump of her arm. I nearly choked on the pain that flared inside me, watching her process her loss. She stared at her injury for a long time, thinking, analyzing. Understanding. Finally, she said, "So it wasn't a dream."

I gave her room to sit up, finding subtle ways to keep touching her. A hand on her leg. A brush against her ribs. "No. But you're alive. I don't care what condition you're in, whether you have all your arms and legs or none. You're here with me now, and that's all I need. Ever."

Viv moved her hand again, taking in the flex and pull of the tendons beneath her skin, comparing it to her injured arm and the limb she had lost. She swallowed, throat working as she forced the emotion down. "I can still hold a sword."

"Yeah." I choked on a grin. "Yeah, I suppose you can."

"Then that's enough for me."

Zos, she was too much. I snagged her hand and cradled it in mine. "You sure?"

"No. But it will be for now." Her grin turned coy. "Besides, I refuse to stay here, laying on my back while you're off saving that stupid prince and his best friend."

She'd heard me. Every little bit of it.

"Hold on a minute—"

"Tell me more." She snagged my wrist, keeping me pinned against her side. "Tell me everything."

Helpless against her will, I did as she asked, and told her everything I had yet to say.

46

Pretty Perfect

I shouldered my way through a throng of people, Viv's grip on my arm keeping me from tumbling when my foot snagged on the edge of someone's shoe. The man glared as if I were in the wrong, not he and his friends for taking up half the street. Viv tugged me along.

"It's not worth it," she said, dusting off my collar. "He's not worth your time. Besides, we're supposed to be invisible, right? Creating a scene in the middle of Aeros is not what Archer meant by blending in."

So practical. I allowed her to straighten my cloak and fix my hair, shifting the weight of the bag slung across my back into a more comfortable position. The bell tower of the courthouse loomed over Viv's shoulder, black and pointed and ominous. "I'm still not sure how you talked Archer into letting you come along."

"He knows better than to question logic when he hears it." She knuckled the small of my back and we rejoined the crowd. "Besides, I think he was worried about you being all alone. With me around, you stand a chance at defending yourself."

I eyed her injured arm and the sleeve sewn shut to cover the bandages. It was healing well, and Viv never complained about the pain. The very afternoon she'd awoken, she'd shoved herself out of bed and tracked down Archer, insisting she be included in our plans to rescue the prince. He'd told her there was no way in rezar she would be joining us in her condition, and she'd challenged him to a fight, insisting she would hold her own, even without one of her hands.

Maybe pity had swayed him, or perhaps her insistence had done the trick. Whatever it was, he drew his sword and leveled it against her dagger. Minutes later, she had him flat on the ground, the point of her blade pressed to the bulge of his throat. That evening, I learned she would be accompanying me to the bell tower, helping me keep watch over the city as the rest of our group got into position around the jail.

"People sure are testy here, aren't they?" Viv complained, eyeing a shop keep haggling with a customer over a bag of lumpy potatoes. "Doesn't it feel foreboding to you? Like when the sky billows black ahead of the storms?"

It did. I'd been twitchy since we'd joined the stream of farmers and merchants trickling into Aeros an hour ago, uncomfortable under the weight of their glares, shoulders hunched to hide in the thick of the crowd. Irritation and frustration buzzed around us like a haze of flies. The soldiers picked up on the emotion and rode on horseback with their hands braced on the pommels of their swords and grips of their whips, circling the crowds.

I guided Viv around a group of gossiping women, their hoods pulled low over their heads. "Maybe they're always like this, but this feels intense."

I eyed the poster hanging on the wall beside the women. "I think it's the execution. The grand duke is being... ostentatious."

Viv snorted, glaring at the slashing black font proclaiming the date and time of Soren's execution over a black and white sketch of the prince and his closest advisor. "That's one word for it."

The posters were splashed everywhere, pinned to walls and hanging from balconies. A few were even slapped on the outer wall of the city in celebration. Brandt did nothing to hide his glee over the fact he'd finally taken custody of the last living royal of Idilea, and apparently planned to make Soren's death as showy and monumental as he could.

As he should, given his position.

With Soren gone...

I couldn't stomach the idea of what happened next.

A Fiorian soldier riding alone cut off a group of merchants struggling to get their donkey to move through the people clogging the street, and one of the men started shouting at the soldier for interfering. The soldier slid from the back of his horse, whip in hand, and I turned away when another soldier joined him, forcing the man to the ground. I flinched at the sound of leather cracking against flesh.

Others didn't look away, their faces blank and jaws tight as they formed a circle around the display. More than a few appeared ready to fire off their own thoughts on the matter, if their shaking bodies and clenched fists meant anything.

I ducked my head and pulled Viv into an alley. This city was on the verge of exploding.

"We're almost to the bell tower." I pointed at the spire looming overhead. "Archer's contact says they work in twelve-hour shifts that rotate out at 2 a.m. and 2 p.m." The bells had rung twice when we'd walked through the gates, our timing perfect.

I rifled through my bag and emerged with the small glass lantern I'd shoved inside. A handful of dried weeds tied with ribbon lay across the wick. I would light it when we were inside the tower.

Viv pulled her hood low over her brow, hand shoved inside her vest, toying with the knives she'd sewn into the lining. "Are you sure burning atler roots will knock them out for long enough? I've only ever heard of it working for six- or seven-hour increments."

I shook my head. "No, I have extra with me. As long as we tie them up, we should be fine."

It wasn't the best solution, but my options were limited. I hadn't originally planned on Viv joining me when I'd concocted this plan with Archer, but she wasn't in a state to knock two burly men unconscious, no matter her protests otherwise.

From what we knew, the guards who manned this tower primarily watched for problem spaces down below. Occasionally, they would toll the bells to alert the guard tower a few blocks to the west if help was needed, otherwise they didn't do much. It was the responsibility of the soldiers on the wall to watch for approaching convoys or problems beyond the city's borders. While I could see over the walls, I would also be listening for their unspoken commands.

Viv accepted the rough, gray mask I handed over and wrapped it around her mouth and nose, mimicking me by pulling her scarf over the top of it. "Let's go."

Getting into the courthouse proved easier than expected, and once through the wide doors engraved with a trio of scales, we turned into a stairwell, following the hand-drawn map given to us by Archer's unidentified contact until we found the door that marked the bell tower.

Viv tested the knob and shook her head when it stuck. I eyed the gap between the door and the floor, knelt, and lit the fire inside the lantern, setting it close to the gap. My friend tugged her mask higher as I blew gently on the smoke, wafting it beneath the door. A few minutes later, twin thumps hit the ground.

I couldn't put out the fire. There was a chance it wouldn't light again, so I removed my lock picks and thrust them into the door. I wasn't as adept at this as Viv was, but I would make it work. Sweat slicked down the side of my face as the metal pieces clicked together, carefully following Viv's whispered instructions. The bolt popped, and the door jolted on its hinges. Success.

Viv squeezed me in a rough side hug and thrust the door open, disappearing into the winding stairwell with a flick of her cloak. While I dealt with tying up the guards, she hurried up three flights of stairs, lantern in hand. When I finished securing the last guard, I heard Viv shout, "Fire! Fire!"

Boots clattered. A low, male voice murmured something. Then nothing. I crept up the stairs, appearing at Viv's back, her presence warm and solid. When no one emerged after several minutes, I motioned us forward, testing my luck. Sure enough, two more guards slumped on the stairs, one bleeding from a cut on his head, their weapons several steps down, where they'd dropped them.

I grabbed the lantern as we entered the belfry, relieved to find it empty. The room at the top of the circular tower was wider than I'd expected, with clear views of the city in all directions. I blew out the fire and tugged my mask down so it hung around my neck while shielding my eyes from the sun, gazing past the smaller inner wall at the castle beyond. I imagined the grand duke was ordering a feast ironically fit for a king ahead of tomorrow's execution, laughing and gloating over his victory.

"It's beautiful up here," Viv breathed, bracing her arm on top of the wall. "Think we can come up here more often when we take this city back?"

I butted my shoulder against hers. "Sure. But when we take our *country* back. How does that sound?"

"Sounds pretty perfect to me." She swung around, casting her face in the shadow as she eyed the path that wound the circumference of the tower. A waist-high wall separated the floor from the hole where the ropes draped below. A pair of brass bells hung over our heads, their clappers swaying in the slight breeze. "We just have to wait for the prince to show up and alert Archer and the others when they're in the clear?"

"That's about it." I removed a round mirror the size of Pip's head from my bag and shoved it in my pocket. I had a spare in my pack if we needed it. The others should be getting into place around the jail, ready to break in the moment I flashed our signal. My owls would also be coming up to check on us soon. "We will meet up at the base of the bell tower. Then it's on to the stables and we escape."

"It sounds so simple when you put it like that."

"The best-laid plans are," I replied. "Ready to bring up the guards?" We needed to group them together so we could keep an eye on them.

"Absolutely." Though Viv sounded strong and sure, we both knew she shouldn't be here. However, I also knew she would have followed us on her own, permission from Archer or not. Now we just needed to get through the evening, pull Soren and Lukas out, and escape. That would give all of us the time we needed to heal and plan and figure out what we were going to do next.

47

Master of Masks

I brought the spyglass to my face for what felt like the millionth time, scouring the streets for trouble while Viv dozed with her back against the wall. We had waited through four bells which operated on an automated pulley system, and the sun was starting to sink low in the sky, turning the horizon amber.

I focused the lens on a man at a fruit stall arguing with a soldier who'd snatched an apple, his arms waving wildly over his head. The soldier appeared to take his wrath for a few minutes, casually taking bites from the fruit, before two more soldiers rode up. One tugged the man's hands behind his back, handcuffing him and leading him behind a building where I lost sight of them.

Petty arguments similar to that had played out all afternoon, some more violent than others, and I lowered my glass. The city reminded me of that black powder we'd found at the mines, scattered about and ready to detonate the moment flint hit steel. How many people were arrested every day? What happened to them? Surely there wasn't enough room in the jail for all of them.

Ghost landed on his perch along the wall, talons clicking on the stone, hooting that nothing had changed. The others were scattered around the courtyard, maintaining silent vigil over their charges. I rubbed an itch behind my ear, the same one that had started tingling about an hour ago when the prince missed his first deadline. He'd said afternoon, but it was now dusk. Any later and things would get trickier in the dark—when people grew more bold and more paranoid, emboldened by the heavy cloak of night.

Viv tugged on my sleeve. "I can hear you worrying from down here," she murmured, voice mushy with sleep. "You need to chill. You hit the guards with more of your smoke not too long ago. We have time. Just be patient."

"How can you say that?" Without the prince, our whole plan went cockeyed. "If he double-crosses us now or doesn't show up—"

"Then we'll deal with that when it comes." Viv swiped her sleeve over her eyes. "Worrying for worry's sake is a waste of energy. Do I trust him? No. Do I think you're taking a gamble with this plan? Yes. But I'm here now and there's nothing more we can do at the moment."

Momentarily appeased, I raised the spyglass again and dropped it in my lap when a trio of bells clanged in a steady yet unrelenting rhythm. Those bells had nothing to do with our tower. Viv shot up beside me, her shoulder pressed against mine, her own glass in hand as she scoured the fields beyond the wall. "They've spotted him."

"There. In the east." I pointed needlessly when she swung her glass around, dial swiveling as she zeroed in on the caravan of carts and carriages and horses and people slogging toward the city, emerald banners snapping in the wind, emblazoned with the image of a moon and sun eclipsing over a pair of crossed swords.

The Crown Prince of Fior had arrived.

A wide smile split my face. Dominik hadn't bailed on us; our plan was officially a go. Shouts from the streets rose on the winds, lifting up to us three stories in the air. As expected, the soldiers were caught off guard as their prince approached. Men on horseback yelled at those who weren't, while still others banged spears and swords, shouting for backup. I rounded the tower, keeping an eye on the guard post a few blocks away, chuckling when a man in a starchy uniform emerged, tugging a hat on his head, face red as he snapped at the men and women under his command milling about, watching the crowd grow.

And it was growing.

Archer's contact was right. This particular series of bells must be new to the civilians, because it drew them to the wall and the main road like flies to a carcass, people tripping over one another in their haste. I heard some crying out that the prince was approaching and that drew even more civilians to the chaos.

Enemy or not, royalty was still royalty. A man in a brilliant green cloak clattered down the stairs bracketing the gate where the caravan approached, waving haphazardly at the woman to his right who bobbed her head, sending a series of commands down the line. Those orders traveled all the way to the jail, where, to my delight, a dozen soldiers spilled from the entrance, shouldering their way through the crowd.

Viv laughed, a crystalline sound that soothed my clanging nerves. "Look at 'em run, Tell. That prince of yours was right. They really aren't prepared for him to arrive so early. At this rate, it'll be nearly impossible to get him through the gates, let alone through the city."

She wasn't wrong. The S-shaped road that wove through town was congested, barely leaving enough space for a cart to pass. Vendors hustled to erect makeshift stands, hawking their wares, while children scrambled up on crates, trying to see above the heads and shoulders of their adult peers. More soldiers poured in from every which way, scrambling to organize the mess. Some succeeded in establishing a level of control. Others—not so much.

"Watch the jail," I told Viv. "I want to keep an eye on the prince."
We traded spots, calling out updates while the chatter from the crowd below intensified. The caravan drew closer, and the soldiers regained some of the upper hand, successfully carving a path through the masses. It wasn't a large path, but it would work for what they needed. Ghost hooted updates, keeping an eye on the signals from the other owls below. By my estimate, we would be in the perfect position to strike when the prince breached the wall at the pinnacle of the madness.

"Signal Archer and the others to get ready," I yelled to Viv, not worried about our voices carrying over the din. "Maybe fifteen more minutes and they'll be clear."

I brought the glass to my eye again, honing in on the blond head of the prince riding a massive black stallion at the front of the assembly. I recognized the regal set of his shoulders, the twist of his hair clasped at the nape of his neck. His smirk was gone, replaced with a lazy grin with a sardonic quirk that could be mistaken for amusement. His limbs were loose and relaxed as he leaned against the pommel of his saddle, ear half turned to listen to whatever the commander of the wall was saying. Occasionally, he lifted his hand and waved at the crowd, arrogance seeping from every pore, seemingly oblivious to the hostility brewing and bubbling hot around him.

"A master of masks," I murmured, turning my lens to scan the rest of the procession.

"What's that?" Viv asked, coming to stand beside me. She, too, fixed her spyglass on the train. "My, my, he is a pretty one, isn't he? Far prettier than our homegrown version. Sure you don't want to trade them?"

I shook my head, returning to Prince Dominik, who was gesturing at something behind him. "He may be pretty, but I get the impression he's as brutal as Soren, just better about hiding it. I'll take the straightforward type any day."

"What's wrong with the wagon?" Viv asked. "Are they stuck?"

Down the line, a boy covered in mud strained against the back wheel of a wagon, which stood almost as tall as he did. The driver twitched the reins, and they attempted to lurch forward, but the wheel got stuck mid-turn. The boy fell, landing in the dirt, covered in sweat, shaking his head at the driver.

"Looks like something is broken," I volleyed back. Whatever the reason for the hold-up, it was causing bigger issues with the crowd. People kept crushing up against one another, jostling for a glimpse of the royal family who had uprooted their lives.

The captain stepped away and gestured another soldier forward, a slight man with a bristly mustache. He beckoned to a group of soldiers working crowd control, and together they were able to partially lift and shove the cart off of the road. The driver of the cart directed them to the stables, mouth moving as he relayed orders.

Ghost hooted from the corner, his feathers glowing orange in the evening light. Almost clear. Just a little more mayhem and the last of the soldiers would be clear of the jail, leaving it free for Archer and the others to invade. I angled my lens on the prince again. Something wasn't adding up, but I couldn't put my finger on why.

Dominik edged his horse forward, lifting his hand again in a wave. A roar rose with the gesture, and not a kind one. I shook my head. He was going to get himself killed if he kept that up. Then I choked on a gasp when he swayed in his saddle and looked straight to the top of my tower. If I hadn't known better, I would have sworn he had found us. He tilted his head toward the wagon being slowly pushed into the depths of the barn connected to the stable.

I spun the dial of my telescope. The horses strained on their ropes and I could almost hear the wood groaning as they forced the wagon to turn in an angle it didn't want to go.

"Something is inside that wagon," I murmured to myself. "He wants us to know it's there."

What could he have hidden, and how would it help us? I nibbled a thumbnail. I would have to convince Archer to let us search the stable before we left, even if it disrupted our delicate timeline.

"Tell, we're in the clear." Viv waved her hand from across the bell tower, the sun catching on the brass of her telescope. "Ghost gave the signal."

Abandoning the caravan that was finally edging toward Eversturm Keep, I rounded the gaping hole in the middle of the floor and dug my mirror out of my pocket. Nerves jumbled wildly in my chest, hissing and zapping with urgency, and I angled the device so it caught the sun, flicking it once, twice, three times. A ten-beat pause. I repeated the signal.

I didn't repeat it a third time.

From the shadows, two figures garbed in dark cloaks and hoods slipped from their hiding spots and rushed toward the entrance of the jail. The other two were around back where I couldn't see them. When they vanished inside, Viv and I ducked down so our heads were barely visible over the edge. Viv blew out a breath, her hand finding the curve of my shoulder where it met my neck, kneading the knotted muscle she found there.

"Now we wait," she said.

I eyed the fiery sliver of the sun against the horizon, then the shadows stretching longer around the jail. There wasn't anything more I could do but hope and pray.

48

Too Easy

"Something is wrong." I smoothed the feathers of my cloak over and over. The sun had set half an hour ago—far longer than it should have taken our friends to get in and out of the jail with Soren and Lukas in tow.

Viv sat on the stone floor of the tower, watching me as I paced. Earlier, she'd urged me to be patient, reminding me all plans came with unexpected challenges, but now she fell silent, brow scrunched with concern. I glanced at Ghost, his moon-shaped face swiveling as he waited for the signal from Pip telling us to make our way to the base of the tower.

"They should have assembled at the relay point by now," I muttered. Candles now burned in the windows of the castle, hundreds of them illuminating the night. "At least one of them should have escaped."

The crowd had dissipated when the last of the showy wagons rolled through the inner gates, which closed behind it, locking out any interlopers. Our plan had been for Archer and the rest to slip into the mix of people in the market after things returned to normal and before the soldiers resumed their posts.

"No way they'd leave us to our own devices, and the owls certainly wouldn't miss them." I turned too sharply on my heel and almost stumbled into the hole that shot straight down the center of the tower. Adrenaline burst through me in a wild hiss of static, and I slammed my hand to my heart to calm the wild beating. "They must have been caught."

Or worse.

I closed my eyes, hands clasped as I sent a silent prayer to Zos— easily my sixth or seventh since they'd entered the jail. Viv had lit the lantern in the stairwell not long ago, burning the last of the herbs I'd brought with us.

"Does it seem too easy to you?" Viv broke her vigil and sniffed wetly, wiping the back of her glove across her nose. "Our part of the plan?"

I frowned. Something about this whole thing had felt off, but I'd chalked it up to nerves. "What are you thinking?"

"Well, the placement of the guards, for one. They were positioned perfectly inside the door. It's possible they didn't see the smoke, but still, they went down without much fuss. And the two at the top of the tower..." she trailed off, picking at the bandage wrapped around her wrist. "They were knocked out pretty easily, too." She shook her head. "Earlier, I thought it was laziness, and they weren't prepared for the possibility of an attack. But what if it's something else?"

I sucked in a breath. "You think we were double-crossed?" Again, I was reminded of the mole that Archer claimed to have eliminated. In his house, I hadn't been sure of that statement, and that feeling had only grown in the days since.

"I think somehow the grand duke found out about our plan," Viv clarified. "Either he guessed or he was tipped off, I can't say for certain, but he knew, and now it's too late."

I ran my knuckles over the stone, ridges of skin catching on the rough grout. There was always the prince and Kohl to consider, too. The outliers to our equation. They had everything to lose by helping us, and I'd witnessed how easily Prince Dominik donned different masks to fit the occasion. My nerves balled into a knot in my throat. I'd believed his sincerity and was won over by Kohl's no-nonsense attitude. So had Archer, his suspicions dissuaded by the prince's mission and the hope it offered. Maybe Lenore had been right to cling to her concerns, to bring them up time and time again.

If we had been sold out, our friends taken into custody or killed or worse... "We need to move."

"Way ahead of you." Viv drew a long coil of rope and several anchoring hooks from her bag. She grinned cheekily, fastening one of the rappelling hooks around the line. "It's been a few months, but surely you haven't forgotten how to scale a mountain."

I accepted the clip she offered with a roll of my eyes. "As if I could ever forget."

For as much as she blustered about wanting to leave the Owl Wood behind and start fresh, Viv was as graceful among the rocky terrain as the goats who called the Copper Mountains their home. We'd grown up with the forest as our playroom and were used to adapting to its challenges.

"Will you be alright?" I asked, eyeing her empty sleeve while she fed rope down the hole in the center of the tower. Of the two of us, she had always been the faster climber, but she was still recovering from her injury. More than once, I'd noticed her trying to use her amputated hand, forgetting she didn't have it any longer.

She anchored the rope and gave it a hard tug, approving her work with a grunt of satisfaction. "Don't worry about me. There isn't a cliff that's intimidated me yet. What's one little tower?"

I peered down the dark hole, a shiver rattling up my spine at the gaping depths. I understood why we had to go this way. If we had been double-crossed, no doubt they would be watching for us to scale the outside of the tower with troops also positioned inside the church, monitoring the only other way out. But just because I understood the logic didn't mean I had to like it. "Is our trap set on the stairwell?"

"Of course it is."

That might buy us some time. "I'll go first."

"Naturally." Before I could drop into the hole, Viv snagged my wrist, her lips finding mine in a hard kiss full of angst. It caught me off-guard, the sudden assuredness with which she moved, and when my brain finally caught up, she had already released me with a shy little smirk. "Now go. I promise I'll give you a better present at the bottom."

"I'm not sure I want to know what that means," I muttered, heat stinging the crests of my cheeks as I dropped into the hole, hands gripping the edge as my toes found footholds in the stone. If the bell tolled while we were down here, our eardrums would burst. "Here goes nothing."

At first, my movements felt awkward, limbs remembering how to work in tandem as I set the first two grips for Viv as she swung over the edge. The light dimmed, and I settled into a rhythm, paying careful attention to the feel of the wall against the soles of my shoes, listening intently to the catches in Viv's breathing, the slamming of my own heart against my ribs.

Down, down, down we went.

I lost track of time and space until my boot kicked the ground. Hurriedly, I dropped the last foot and unhooked myself from the rope. "We're here."

"Thank the gods," Viv breathed, nimbly dropping beside me. I couldn't see her, but when she sagged against me, I felt her cradling her bad arm to her chest. Worry curdled like sour milk and I pulled her close, inhaling the scent of her oiled leathers. She reciprocated, burying her head against my shoulder until she wasn't gasping.

I cleared my throat and squinted at our surroundings. I was certain the door to leave had been to our left when we rappelled down. Slowly, I edged clockwise, testing for gaps in the bricks. Finally, my fingers found the edge of a door, crumbling and rotten with termite residue. I called Viv over and she felt the soft surface, her nails barely making a sound as she scratched it. I tested the knob. It squeaked, but worked.

"Think anyone is waiting for us out there?" she murmured.

"Zos save us, I hope not."

Together, we shoved the door open, throwing our bodies against it when it refused to budge at first. I stumbled for a few steps, squinting against the light thrown by the streetlamps. To our luck, no guards seemed to be around. When I gave her the all clear, Viv stepped out beside me, cheeks smudged with dirt and grime. Her nose wrinkled.

"It smells like it does right when you've lit a fire after a storm," she said. "Kind of woodsy and green and your heart is all tangled up as you watch that tiny little flame eat through the pine needles, praying it will catch."

I rolled my shoulders, understanding her completely. "Let's get to the stable. If anyone made it out, I think they'll be there."

We only saw a few people as we ducked around corners and darted across roads, feeling like bandits stealing away with the crown jewels. Those we did encounter kept their heads down, hands shoved deep in their cloaks, sticking to the shadows. Vaguely, I wondered where everyone had gone.

"I don't see anyone," Viv said when we emerged across the road from the stable. "But maybe they're hiding inside—or in the shadows."

Something about the sight irked me, a small sense that something was wrong, that I wasn't seeing something right in front of my eyes, but no matter how hard I scanned road, squinted into the shadows, I couldn't figure out what bothered me.

"Let's go," I said, snagging Viv's hand. We sprinted the last few yards, only slowing when we entered the flickering shadows around the side. Still nothing. In the distance, someone shouted, but it quickly cut off.

Viv edged around the corner, peering down the length of the barn. "I don't think—"

"Tell. Viv." The hairs on the back of my neck stiffened when a woman darted across the street. Viv slid against me, our sides practically glued together, her hand curling around the knife in her pocket. She didn't release it when Lenore called out to us again, breathless. "Thank goodness I found you."

"Where is everyone?" Viv asked. I watched the alley from which she'd emerged, unease growing.

Lenore shook her head, hood falling back far enough to reveal the purple hue of her black eye, the long scratch across her cheek. Fingerprints of blood stained her jaw, red and mottled as if it had been dragged across wood or stone.

"They knew we were coming." She braced her hand on the wall, trying to slow her gasping. "We made it inside just fine, but then it all went haywire. I stayed as lookout in the main area while everyone else branched out. The wolven caught 'em in the cells." She stared at the wall blankly. "I heard them fighting and yelling. One of the soldiers caught me." She dragged her hair back from her cheek, revealing more dried blood. "I only barely made it out."

Viv shot me a look. "Soren? Lukas?"

"I'm not sure." Lenore licked her lips, hands shaking as she wrung them together. "I didn't have time to look for them then, but with you here, we can go back and look. I know they're trapped in there.

I think I know another way in. One a little less obvious."

My nerves solidified, settling at the base of my gut like rocks. I'd almost believed her until she made that suggestion. Going back now without knowing what had happened or a plan? That was the last thing we needed to do. It was like we were begging to be caught. And if she had this much muster to return now, why hadn't she gone alone? Before the enemy had a chance to rally?

"If the prison was overrun, how did you get out again?" Viv asked, a low note in her voice that made my insides clench. "You're a good fighter, but how did you make it out when the others couldn't?"

Lenore's eyes flashed. "What are you accusing me of? I fought like rezar and only barely escaped. You see what they did to me."

Yeah. I did. And I also noticed how only her face was bruised. No blood on her clothing. No tears in her shirt or cloak. Her slicked-back hair appeared untouched. Every time I'd fought with wolven, I'd walked away looking like a steak a cook had pounded too thin.

Viv replied with something I didn't catch, because something else had occurred to me. The battalion of wolven with the spring-loaded crossbows at the mines and the ones equipped with bolts big enough to bring down a dragon had come from the west—the front where Lenore's soldiers had been stationed. Even with everything happening in that immediate vicinity, the wolven shouldn't have made it as far as they had as quickly as they did. There was no reason for them to seek out the eastern flank—not if they believed the explosion they'd survived was as violent as I'd been led to believe.

Lenore had taken another step back, hand stretched behind her as if feeling for something to brace against.

"Something's been bothering me," I said. The street remained quiet, though a few people passed by a few blocks over, their shadows stretching across the road. "We moved up the attack on the mines by two days. Two full days. Yet the wolven were fully prepared. How did they find out we'd moved up our timeline?"

Lenore's eyes glinted, hard and furious. "What are you accusing me of?"

"—only twelve people who met on a daily basis knew about the change. All regular soldiers were kept in the dark." I shook my head, recalling the woman who'd asked me where Lenore was on the morning we advanced on the mine. I hadn't seen her that morning at breakfast, which she ate religiously.

I hadn't recognized her treachery because I'd wanted to believe Archer when he'd insisted the mole had been taken care of. Maybe he had, and maybe that person was also a traitor, or maybe they were an accomplice of Lenore's. Where one mole found its home, more were sure to follow.

"Are you saying—"

Viv lunged, her knife raking across the taller woman's throat with practiced ease. Stunned, Lenore didn't have time to reach for the sword at her hip as she clutched at the gaping wound, the blood ripping down her throat and pooling in her collar. She gurgled, dropped to her knees, gagging, and went still.

"I couldn't stomach any more of her lies." Viv wiped the flat of her blade on her thigh. "She's been feeding the grand duke information this whole time. Her two-faced duplicity make me sick."

I stared at the body and the blood soaking into the dust and dirt. Soren and Lukas had been captured because of her. Hundreds had lost their lives because of her actions. Viv would never wield weapons the same, because she had ratted us out.

I hoped Zos made her burn in the afterlife for her sins.

"If she sold out our plan to break out Soren and Lukas, the odds were pretty good Brandt knows about Dominik's assistance, too," I said. "For all we know, both princes are being held captive."

"We need to get out of here." Viv peered around the corner of the stable. "You know as well as I do we can't break them out. Not on our own, and we're no use to anyone if we're dead."

I didn't agree with her, but I couldn't think through the fog of my mind. Couldn't visualize a plan that would help us get our friends out alive. Viv pulled me around the front of the stable.

"Where are the guards?" she asked, halting before the warm, well-lit barn.

Everything about the night felt surreal. From the prince showing up to the jeering crowd to the realization of who exactly betrayed our cause. Even the townspeople were acting strange, and the streets were far emptier than I felt they had any right to be. Now the guards had disappeared, and I really wanted the smoke growing thicker around us to go away.

The smoke.

I inhaled deeply.

"Viv—" I said, when she jerked backward so quickly her elbow rammed into my stomach. A figure emerged in the doorway, a pair of swords jutting up over his shoulders. The man peered down at us, scarred lips quirked in a half-smile.

"Admiring my handiwork?" Aleksi asked.

49

We are the Requiem

Viv kept her knife out, stepping smoothly between us as I wheezed. "Did you betray us, too? In Dowhurst? Did they find us because of you?"

Aleksi's grin fell away. "Archer is my brother, and the crown has owned my service since the day the king swept me off the streets—a dirty, tired, mangy little orphan—and gave me a home. I would die before I allowed any harm to come to them."

The stones in my stomach left over from Lenore's treachery dissolved. Viv seemed to believe him, too, and lowered her knife. "Sorry. Lenore was your rat about the mines, but I've taken care of her."

Aleksi absorbed that information with a blank face, his heavy stubble muddling his features. "Archer? Soren? Lukas?"

"They're in custody, from what we can tell," I murmured.

Heavy bells clanged, and we peered at the tower and the flames shooting from the alcoves. Shadows raced around the ramparts, shouting and throwing water on the fire. So they had finally gotten tired of waiting and broken the door, knocking the lantern into the pool of accelerant we'd left as a trap. "We're the only ones who escaped."

"Nice work." Aleksi gestured at the stable. "Let's get out of the street before they find you."

I swallowed hard when we walked past a pile of wolven bodies crumpled against one wall, the hay slippery with blood. That explained where the guards had gone. Viv cast them an expressionless glance, her eyes lingering longer on the blood than on the bodies, as if she longed to scrub away the mess.

"I assume you were looking to escape?"

Viv said yes at the same time as I shook my head no. He crossed his arms, amusement flickering in his gaze, and Viv humphed, glaring at me like she didn't know who I was anymore. "No," I reiterated. "We aren't leaving."

"That's good," Aleksi said. "You'd have a hard time of it, anyway."

Viv offered her hand to one of the horses. It sneezed at the blood drying on her fingers. "Why's that?"

"They shut the gates and locked 'em up tight." He settled against the door of a stall, surveying us with heavy-lidded eyes. "The whole city is in an uproar. First time they've closed all four gates for as long as anyone can remember. Even the invasion happened too quick to shut them against the Fiorian army."

My unease felt justified: the scent of smoke that refused to dissipate, the strange tension gripping the air, and the lack of people in the streets. Throw in the posters announcing Soren's impending execution and Aeros was a tinderbox on the brink of explosion.

"Where is everyone now?" I asked.

Aleksi inclined his head. "Word is everyone is gathering along the inner wall—south side." Where the balconies named for Zos and Qet bracketed the gate that opened to Eversturm Keep. "There's also a gathering on the north side. That one's not as big, but the soldiers are having a tough time keeping everyone calm. That's what my sparrows say, anyway."

It hit me. "You're Archer's contact, the one he's been relying on for information from inside the city."

Viv rolled her eyes. "Don't tell me you're just now figuring it out."

Aleksi laughed, short and sharp. "Would he trust anyone else?"

That laugh reminded me of Prince Dominik and how he'd pinpointed me in the bell tower, as if trying to tell me something of great importance. The wagon. Where was the wagon? Ignoring the questions from Aleksi and Viv, I slipped into the adjacent barn and strode down the aisle, keeping an ear out for movement, and finally stopped when I found the cart against the wall on the far side. It was leaning, one of its wheels removed, tucked in among some hay bales and odd bits of machinery.

"They looked it over pretty well when the prince insisted they leave it here," Aleksi said as I stepped on the hitch to get a better angle. "Damn near picked it apart from what I saw. They didn't find anything. Just a bunch of dry goods and a broken axle that needs some explaining."

Or not. I hopped up into the back. Something told me the axle had been broken on purpose. I pried open the lid of a barrel and dove my hand deep into the grain, fishing around. Nothing. I tossed the lid aside with a clatter. Viv climbed in behind me. "What are we looking for?"

"Anything that's out of the ordinary." I kicked away the hay littering the floorboards of the cart, pounding the heel of my foot into wood in a few different places, trying to hear if anything sounded different. "There has to be something here."

Aleksi pried open another barrel and reached in, dried corn spilling through the gaps in his fingers. "Why are you so certain?"

"The prince looked at me in the tower. It seemed like he was telling me that he'd left something important with this wagon." I shoved my arm into another barrel so deep my shoulder almost disappeared as I sifted through the grain. The sweet, musty scent of it filled my nose. "It's no mistake this cart was left behind."

Aleksi shrugged and followed my lead, shoving his arm into more corn, coming up empty-handed a few minutes later. Viv eyed the bags and barrels with distaste, thumb hooked in her belt loop, and mimicked my stomping from earlier, shuffling in a precise pattern across the floor.

Two barrels later, I finally felt what I was looking for. The velvet of the pouch was so soft I nearly mistook it for grain, but when my fingers went back over it, the folds of the purse the size of my fist became obvious and I tugged it out with a yelp of surprise. Aleksi and Viv joined me as I turned it over in my hands. The ties were pulled taut, and I dug my nails into the knot, struggling to free it. Viv's breath warmed my neck as she breathed over my shoulder. Finally, I pried it loose and tipped the contents into my hand. Aleksi sucked in a gasp and my mouth went drier than the hay left out for the horses.

Viv was breathless. "Is that what I think it is?"

"Drakkentorre." I couldn't look away from the dozens of glittering stones nestled in the palm of my hand. More drakkentorre than I'd seen in seventeen years. Aleksi plucked one of the smaller ones from my hand, muscles stiffening and eyes growing wider than the wagon wheels.

"What's wrong?" Viv asked, reaching for the gem.

He shook his head, moving out of her way. "It's the strangest thing. I feel like... I could fly. Like there's this new part of me that I've never noticed before. It's calling to me." His eyes met mine, bright with wonder. "It's exactly like my friends described it when they found out they were shifters."

Viv poured over the stones, frown deepening, but didn't take one.

"How's that possible? You're not a child."

Aleksi shook his head, still and silent, as if he'd forgotten we were here.

"Archer was right," I murmured. "Age doesn't matter. Just like blood, gender, and social status never mattered. Maybe it's possible for everyone to transform." I shook my head as my thoughts bubbled over in a rush of electrifying questions. "Maybe children are better able to tap into that side of themselves because they're so young and malleable. I also wonder if it's about want and desire: those who want to be a drakken enough can become one. Or maybe—"

"Maybe the gods pick us after all." Viv scratched her arm. "Maybe they know we need an army and with these, we can make it happen."

"Do you feel anything?" Aleksi asked, nodding at my bare palm.

I shook my head. Everything inside felt the same. No thrilling jolt of awareness, no creature rearing its head. Maybe I wasn't meant to shift. After all, I had my owls and my love of nature. And I had Viv. Now all I really needed was my kingdom back.

Carefully, I poured the stones back into the pouch. Aleksi tucked his stone under his armband, keeping it pressed tight against his skin. "You know what this means, right?"

The tension. The growing violence. The many, many people finally rising up and gathering in defiance of the wolven. Brandt may have driven them to this, may have wanted them to gather and bear witness to his final assault, but I saw a much bigger possibility.

"We start a riot." My grin felt wider than my face. "And take back our country."

* * *

We found four more bags of drakkentorre hidden deep in the barrels of grain, corn, and barley. Viv also recovered two small pouches of blasting powder tucked under hollow panels in the floorboards. I wondered if the prince had anticipated the double cross and sought to give us options, especially considering how disappointed he'd been when Archer had refused to commit to a larger plan to end the war. Or maybe it was a trap. Either way, it was too great an opportunity to pass up.

Aleksi squeezed the waterproof skeins of powder as Viv explained what she'd witnessed at the opening of her mine, indicating the powder had been stuffed into small cylindrical containers tucked against the entrance. Those were ignited with a length of twine, similar to the mechanism I'd ripped apart at the main entrance.

"Sounds simple enough," Aleksi mused. "I think we can use this to blow open the inner gates. The explosion will have the desired effect you're looking for among the crowd, and it will give us an opening to Eversturm Keep." He stared out over the rows of horses. I wondered if he was thinking about the castle, his memories there, realizing that this plan could destroy it all. A mob wouldn't stop for memories.

"If we retake the castle, we retake the kingdom. There's no escape route for Brandt unless he can grow wings." Though he had access to drakkentorre, we knew he had the ability to shift into wolven form, and no one had heard of a dual shifter before.

"Viv and I will stir up the crowd, giving you the distraction you need to lay the groundwork," I said. "Who's to say the riot doesn't bring down the gates without the help of the powder? There are a lot of very angry people in this city who've been simmering for far too long."

"I like it." Steel hushed over stone while Viv sharpened her knives. "There's probably, what, seven-thousand people who live here? Plus travelers? A mob of that size versus three- or four-hundred wolven sounds like a pretty good bet to me, especially if we can give them the gift of transformation."

We all agreed shifters were hidden among the civilians, those who had successfully escaped notice from the wolven. Those people combined with the many who had yet to embrace their abilities should, in theory, be enough to level the playing field, especially since they could access their power immediately.

"I guess that's it then." I handed Viv two bags of stones and squeezed Aleksi hard, realizing this might be the last time I saw him. Anything could happen to any of us now. "May Zos protect you."

He smirked. "Pretty sure that's Qet's role."

"That guy's got enough on his plate."

Aleksi chuckled and ducked out the door, disappearing into the shadows on the other side of the street. Viv hovered at my elbow. "You sure about this?"

"As sure as I was about joining the Requiem."

"Good enough for me." Her grin was sharp.

It didn't take long for us to slip through town, sliding through side streets and ducking around corners. The closer we got to the inner gate, the louder the chanting and the heavier the smell of smoke became. I pulled my hood over my head when we finally worked our way past the stragglers lingering along the edges of the crowd. The sheer number of people gathered outside the wall was immense, and it was remarkable to me that Brandt hadn't ordered the wolven to break it up.

Then again, he had said he would execute Soren at dawn...

Viv gave me a nod when we reached the last row of businesses. Several hundred feet of grassy space separated the city from the wall, providing a level of green space and open area for the guards to monitor for trouble. That area was packed with people, and we would need to work our way through them after starting the riot to ensure our plan succeeded. Viv and I had agreed to split up to disperse the stones more evenly among the crowd. As long as neither of us were killed before we had a chance to stir everyone up, we stood a halfway decent chance of pulling this off.

My heart throbbed, knowing we had to separate, but fearful of what might happen. I drew a deep breath. "As sure as the dark meets the light..."

"We will meet again," Viv finished, a soft smile on her lips.

I ducked into a doorway and flipped my cloak inside out, smoothing my hands over the glossy feathers, revealing them for the first time in what felt like months. I slipped it on, pulled the hood over my head and the loops along the hem over my thumbs, then dipped around the side of the building. It was easy enough to scale the gutter, and I made it to the red-shingled rooftop in no time.

I'd picked a good spot. The building stood two stories tall and was positioned not far from the gate. The soldiers were scattered. Some crouched on rooftops like me, but most were on the ground in wolven form, snapping and snarling at those who came too close. Every now and again, someone would point at the half-moon shape of the twin balconies where hidden fires burned.

Once upon a time, they'd served as landing places for drakken. Merchants and vendors had set up mobile shops there, people congregating in small droves as they looked out over the wonder of their city. Now the balconies stood largely empty, large swaths of stone that would soon be awash in royal blood if we didn't do anything to stop it. Movement to my left snagged my attention, and I caught Viv's wave as she leaned out over her own rooftop.

Go time.

Zos, lend me your strength. I believe in you. Please believe in me.

I searched for an opening, anything to use as fuel to start this fire. It wouldn't take much. Something like—there. Below, a guard shoved a woman to the ground, cursing at her as she glared defiantly up at him. A ring opened up around them as he paced, teeth and claws elongating. "Watch yourself, you *travetry*. If you don't, I'll—"

"Hey you." I stepped to the edge of the rooftop, cloak pulled around me, voice as loud as I could make it without shouting. I pointed at the soldier. "Who do you think you are?"

The wolven stepped back, searching for me. He snarled when he finally picked me out among the alcoves of the rooftop. Several people followed his gaze, turning their backs on the wall, waiting to see how this would play out.

"You think you're big because you can transform into a wolf, don't you? Because you've beaten our country and our people into submission," I cried. The wolven began to shift, teeth pulling back in a snarl. More heads were turning, more faces tilting up to find me, my face hidden in the depths of my cloak. "But that's what we *want* you to think. We've made you think you're in charge, that we've given up. But we haven't." I braced my hand against my heart. "While you've pillaged our country and taken our people hostage, we've been planning."

Impossibly, my voice grew louder, as if the gods were infusing me with hidden power. I thought about Archer, channeling his quiet strength, imagining what he would say in this dire moment. At least a hundred people were looking back at me, some nodding while others whispered to their neighbors, scowls deepening.

Two more wolven joined their companion, hackles raised.

"We've been giving you time to underestimate us. And why is that?" I slashed my arms out, the wings of my cloak flying wide, feathers fluttering. A gasp went up from the crowd, the whispers growing louder, coming faster. "Because we're coming for you. You took our prince? You planned to murder him right before our eyes? That's where you messed up. We will crush you like the slime you are—the filth not good enough to stain the bottoms of our shoes."

A roar went up around the crowd. Many stamped their feet, clapping and shouting in agreement. More wolven were pushing through the masses, swords and bows drawn, trying to fight their way over, but not getting very far. The soldier I'd called out stalked forward, eyeing the building speculatively. Several blocks away, two more wolven jumped from tiled roof to tiled roof. I was running out of time.

"You may be wolves. But we are dragons." I drew the pouch from my cloak. "You caught us by surprise the first time, but guess what? Wolves will never beat dragons again." I poured the stones into my hand, taking care to catch the waterfall in the firelight, so the gems radiated with the unmistakable luster of drakkentorre. I looked out over the crowd, addressing them directly for the first time.

"Are you angry?"

A cheer went up around me. I poured the stones into my other hand.

"Are you tired of being pushed around and being abused? Are you sick of having these disgusting invaders take your homes and your land and tell you that you're not good enough?"

Another cheer. Not just a hundred now. Hundreds. More people were shoving back against the advancing wolven, taking advantage of the strength they bore in numbers when the soldiers dropped back, snarling and snapping at heels and hands.

"Of course you are," I cried. "Why? Because you're Idilean. We are Idilea."

A feminine voice whispered in my head: *Duck.*

I dipped as an arrow soared right over me, the bolt sinking into the chest of one of the wolven leaping from the rooftops. A roar went up from the crowd when I straightened, wondering why that voice sounded like the goddess I'd met but once. Anger simmered and snapped from those gathered below, fiery in its ruthlessness.

"You see that? You see what they did?" I pointed at the wolven's body draped over the gutter, blood spilling over the edge. "They're trying to silence me—to silence *us*. They know we're bigger and stronger than them. That we are Idilean. We are dragons. And this is the Requiem."

A chant rose. *We are Idilea. We are the Requiem.* Over and over again. I threw my hands wide, my cloak billowing around me.

"Where are my drakken?" I shouted over the din, barely able to be heard.

A few hands went up. Then more. "Come on now. There are more of you out there. All of you. We are drakken. And now we will take back our country."

I threw the drakkentorre out into the crowd, a hundred shimmering gems that flew wide and far, just as a wolven jumped onto my rooftop. I backed away, shouting our rallying cry one last time. In the distance, people were throwing themselves against a mob scrambling for stones that Viv had thrown. She was no longer in sight.

To the wolven, I snarled, "We are the Requiem." And I jumped from the roof as the first drakken exploded into existence, violet scales and all.

50

Not Drakken

A pair of burly men caught me before I crashed to the ground, saving me from a concussion and several broken bones. The bigger man set me on my feet and entered the fray of fighting that surrounded us while the slightly smaller man hovered, asking if I was alright. I brushed him off with a nod of thanks.

The wolven I'd taunted from my rooftop perch had followed me down, but struggled against a dozen people holding him back. Some slipped punches through his guard while the girl who'd glared at him so acidly tore at his golden armor, ripping it from his frame. Everywhere I looked, people were yelling, screaming, fists flying, and legs kicking. Some chanted variations of, *"We are Idilea, we are drakken,"* with blood streaking down their faces, and others tackled the soldiers mid-transformation, uncaring of their hooked claws and mangy snouts.

My plan to incite a riot had worked too well.

A pair of screeches sounded over my head as two more drakken took flight, flexing their turquoise wings experimentally. One dove, tail lashing, talons extended. Someone screamed. I shouldered my way through the first opening I found, ducking a fist that flew at my face. I needed to get to the gate, but it wouldn't be easy crossing the wide plaza on my own.

A hand with wiry veins spider-webbing across the back of it snagged another fist that flew my way. The man from before, who'd hovered after I jumped. I'd forgotten about him. He offered a thin, gap-toothed grin. "Where ya going, Owl Girl?"

I pointed at the gates of the inner wall, their doors shaking against the force of the people crashing into them below. My surprise savior dipped his head, snagged my wrist, and pulled me through a ripple of people in the crowd, his height giving him greater advantage. As we slipped away, I threw a glance over my shoulder, hoping for a glimpse of Viv. Her rooftop remained empty. Hopefully, she'd escaped before the wolven had caught her.

We are Idilea. We are vengeance.

The roar of the crowd picked up strength and volume, the chant sparking and crackling as it spread, fueled by fiery magic of its own making.

I winced when the first bell tolled. Then another. And another. All six bronze bells positioned on the landing balconies now sounded in rhythm, matching the pulse of the blood surging through my veins. Our warning system was being used against us.

It wouldn't be long before Brandt was forced to fight back.

I lost track of time and space as I pushed forward, uncaring of the hands that clipped my shoulders and face, some reeling back when they caught sight of the feathers on my neck and back. Twice, we passed the bodies of wolven soldiers, their skulls caved in, blood soaking into the ground. More drakken burst into existence as the gems we'd thrown into the crowd were passed along the writhing group of people.

I tightened my grip on my helper's hand as a drakken lifted a wolven up by his armor, claws slashing at her face and neck as the soldier snapped and squirmed, blood streaking his matted brown fur. We'd worried our newfound shifters would fly away, leaving us bereft, but those concerns were washed away now. There had to be at least twenty drakken slashing away, with more bursting into existence by the minute.

The clanging of the bells changed, the rhythm picking up pace. Something jumped in my periphery, a flex of muscle and dark hair, the wolven's mouth open wide as it sought my throat, only to be brought down by a woman no bigger than I was, a sword clutched in her hand. She'd somehow found the gap in his armor and slipped her blade between his ribs. She panted, back bowed, and wrenched the blade from his body. She swiped it across his heaving back and joined my side with a nod.

"My sister told me about you. She says rumors of the Requiem dying were just that, and if I ever saw you, to trust you." The woman casually punched a man who recklessly charged through the bodies. I thought I recognized something in the curve of her cheeks, the sunken quality of her eyes, but someone screamed and I lost my train of thought.

Together we moved, picking up more people along the way who either recognized me or our intent. Our pace increased as they forged a path through the crowd, forcing the wolven and humans back. Once, I glimpsed a drakken with scales so dark I thought it might have been Soren. My heart tumbled to the bottom of my stomach when it flapped its wings and released a roar, dipping into a dive. It sounded nothing like him.

A bolt as wide around as my forearm slammed into its torso, cutting a gaping hole in its abdomen. Blood sprayed, and the drakken shrieked as it crashed to the ground. Tremors ran up my spine and I glared up the wall again. The massive crossbows that had brought down Soren and Lukas now ringed the balconies, soldiers cursing and sweating as they loaded bolts into place. Another mechanism, one wider and taller, snapped back, releasing a net that snagged around the emerald body of another drakken and caught fire.

"Holy Qet," one of my helpers cried in shock.

Our group had stopped, staring at the writhing, screeching drakken struggling to free itself from the ropes that pulled tighter the more it thrashed. Several people jumped in, trying to help, only to fall back when the flames seared their hands. It wasn't long before the shifter stopped moving. It wasn't the only one, as more nets and bolts were released into the crowd.

I spun in place, hand on the back of the woman with the sword, seeking the gates. We were maybe fifty paces from the wall, yet the gates were still more than a hundred yards away. We'd cut through the quickest, fastest route, which had led us beside the balcony symbolizing Zos, the black stone rimming the parapet obvious even in the darkness.

The fact Aleksi hadn't blown the gates wide open meant something had gone wrong.

I opened my mouth to urge our group onward when shadows shifted against the flames of the torches roaring on the balcony overhead. A pair of figures emerged. My blood sang, terror slicing a wide swath through my stomach. Soren. Even two stories away, I could make out the bruises marring his face, the blood that soaked his clothing. His hands were bound behind his back and a gag was shoved in his mouth. Someone had shoved a crude crown of broken bones onto his head, and blood trickled down the sides of his face.

The prince strained against his bonds, muscles in his arms bulging as he took in the sight of his people fighting, the drakken wheeling and screeching, and the fires raging out of control through the city. The odors of blood and gore and smoke and sweat and pain all mingled into one coppery, tarry mess. Soren was shoved to his knees, and a man emerged from the smoke, a golden sword swinging at his side. Grand Duke Brandt Innis.

I'd never seen the man before in my life, yet I would recognize him anywhere.

He lifted a long, circular tube to his mouth. "People of the kingdom once known as Idilea, I've heard your pleas and I've chosen to answer them."

Panic ripped through me. The shouts and screams quieted as people turned from the fighting to crane their heads back, eyeing the figure standing tall and proud overhead. Seizing the opportunity, I surged forward, shoving my way to the wall, gasping sharply when my hands finally met stone.

Brandt drew his sword, the sound slicing through the shouts like claws through flesh, and leveled it at the back of Soren's neck. "You see this man here? He's your prince. Your last drakken prince. And if you don't back off, I will destroy him here and now."

I'd ended up against a support beam carved into the outside of the wall. The higher it went, the wider it got to support the weight of the balcony. I tested the stones, each about a foot and a half long and a foot wide, stacked on top of one another and sealed with grout. An idea occurred to me as I gripped the worn, chipped rock. I tipped my head back again, but I'd lost sight of the grand duke, who was still shouting for obedience.

"What are you doing?" The group of the men and women who'd gotten me this far had followed me, and it was a woman shouldering a sword that stood as tall as she did who spoke.

I pointed at the wall. "I need to get up there. I can save him."

"How will you do that?" a man with a crossbow asked. He must have scooped it up from the hands of a dead wolven.

"I'll climb. Will you make sure they don't bring me down?"

He brought the bow to his shoulder, a dark scowl twisting his handsome features into something ugly. The girl smirked, lifting her sword in a partial salute. The sturdy man who I'd trusted to get me this far crouched, fingers twining together in something like a hammock. "Need a boost?"

Nodding, I shoved my hands in my pockets and scrubbed them dry with some of the herbs I found inside. Viv and I used to stuff pouches full of gray dust to dry the sweat from our hands while we climbed, but I didn't have that luxury today. I would have to rely on my instincts and a whole lot of luck to make this climb. My stomach trembled and the muscles in my back ached, but I forced those distractions aside and stepped into the cradle of the man's hands. He boosted me up, shooting me at least five feet higher than I would have otherwise, and I found my first hold, toes wedging their way into a crack in the grout, my fingers wedged in another.

The group encouraged me onward, but I didn't dare look anywhere but at what was in front of me. It was my father who had taught me looking up or down created an optical illusion. It was best to only worry about finding my next foot and handhold, ignoring everything else happening around me.

As I picked my way through the cracks, relying on the corner of the wall to help me when I could, I was aware of the bolts that crashed into the stone beside my body, spraying me with debris. A net narrowly missed falling on my head. The soldiers on the ramparts had seen me, and I hoped my newfound friends would buy me enough time to reach the top. I was making steady progress, but as sweat sluiced down my neck and I wiped my free hand on my damp sleeve for what felt like the hundredth time, I started to worry I wouldn't make it. There wouldn't be time.

The noise from the crowd had dimmed, and Brandt's shouting had grown louder. "Gone are the days of dragons. Now it's wolves who reign supreme. If you don't disperse now, I will carry through with your prince's execution. Where is your Requiem now?"

I shook my head, dismissing his lies. Soren would die today, regardless of what the crowd did or did not do. To my surprise, I wasn't the only one who realized that fact.

"We are Idilea. We are drakken." The chant started out small, thready. I hoisted myself up another block, back and neck burning fiercely. The crowd picked up on the chant again, growing stronger. More angry. "We are the Requiem."

The fire in their voices pushed me higher, forcing my slippery fingers and reaching toes to find the necessary grips. I screamed when my fingers curled around the curved top of the stone that marked the edge of the short wall designed to keep small children from tumbling down. I hoisted myself up and over, one leg dragging over the wall, and nearly tumbled to my death when a soldier rushed at me, sword drawn. I ducked out of the way, and he wasn't quick enough to counter.

His screams died shortly after he tumbled over the edge.

Hastily, I pulled my other leg up, edges of my vision dark with exhaustion as I willed more adrenaline to pump through my veins. Two soldiers stood nearby, giant crossbow abandoned, their heads inclined to the left, toward the gates. I couldn't see what they were looking at.

Brandt had his back to me, the sword in his hand steady as he pinned Soren down on his knees.

"Enough," he was shouting. "Enough. All of you."

I wiped my bleeding hands across my tunic as Brandt tossed the tube to the side. Only those closest to him could hear what he said next. "Then take what you deserve."

I surged forward, terror driving fresh waves of horror through me. Only thirty paces separated us. Thirty running steps. The grand duke drew back his sword. I forced myself to run faster, harder, feet crashing on the stones as a scream I wasn't aware I had left tore through my throat.

I wasn't going to reach him in time.

My arm outstretched.

Brandt started to swing down, Soren's muscles taught, fighting the soldiers holding him down.

A roar unlike anything I'd ever heard—louder than raging blizzards and boulders crashing together during an earthquake, louder still than any beast I'd ever imagined—tore across the land. I dropped to my knees, opening jagged bloody scrapes as I bent over, hands splayed on the stones, gazing upward. The sound stayed Brandt's hand as a spectrum of color burst from the clouds. Seven drakken, each larger than most buildings, flapped their monstrous wings, creating gales that crashed against the wall in thunderous waves.

Not drakken.

Dragons.

Our gods had finally answered our prayers.

51

The Dark Prince

The biggest dragon with scales the color of moonstone descended first. An inferno exploded from his maw as he approached the wall, incinerating the wolven fleeing his approach. When he wheeled overhead, swiveling back around, several soldiers from another balcony fired arrows, striking Qet's lustrous hide. He paid them no heed as a dragon with wings of the deepest sapphire swept them from their perches. Lo had always been depicted as the gentlest of the goddesses, but even she had a vicious side.

I stared, heart in my throat. A dragon with obsidian scales dipped and ducked through the streets, legs and arms sticking from her mouth as she crunched down on the soldiers she found, blood dripping from her angular jaw. The appearance of the dragons had reignited the riot below. People threw themselves at their oppressors with more fervor than before, weapons and fists flying as they attacked in earnest. The flames of the inferno roared higher, devouring homes and businesses alike.

The sight of my people fighting as if there was no tomorrow, and the vision of Zos wreaking her retribution, spurred me forward.

The grand duke had frozen, his hand in Soren's hair, sword dangling at his side, watching the destruction. I couldn't see his face, but I imagined his jaw slack, his eyes wide as they reflected the flickering of the growing fires.

I sprinted, fighting sore and drained muscles every step of the way, fumbling in my pocket for the smooth shape of the stone I'd shoved deep inside it this very morning. I'd made it about a dozen steps, a third of the distance to the two men, when I was thrown to my knees by an almighty explosion.

Rock and wood shot through the air, chunks of it shooting every which way: remnants of the gates that no longer stood. The rumbling of the wall sent me crashing to my hands and knees again, my bones protesting the sharp, unexpected movement. I screamed when a plank of burning wood landed not six inches from my outstretched hand, and I scrambled upright, scanning the skies, desperately trying to discern any more objects flying my way.

Most debris rained down over the crowd and on the opposite side of the wall, sparking more fires as it landed. People surged through the opening, some falling to stray arrows as they rushed toward the castle, nearly tripping over one another in their haste.

A surge of pride soared through my breast. Aleksi had done it. He'd actually done it.

I had a spare thought for Prince Dominik, hoping he'd found a safe spot to hole up with his closest advisors, before turning back to the grand duke, who'd snapped from his stupor. He'd finally noticed me. Icy cold speared my limbs, and I rushed forward again. His lips drew back in a snarl and he raised his sword, but he was too late. I slid under the sweep of his blade and snagged Soren's hand, ripping him from the soldier's hold through sheer momentum.

The dark prince and I went tumbling, head over heels, and crashed into the low wall which saved us from near-certain death. I couldn't hear past the ringing in my ears, and I forced my body to unfold, reaching for Soren. He found me first, tugging me close, eyes desperate as they flashed across my face.

I shook my head, incapable of voicing what I wanted to, and shoved the stone gifted to us by the Fiorian prince into his hand. Soren planted his hand on my chest, shoving me back as a sword came down between us, sparks flying on the stone where my head had just been. When Brandt drew back with a snarl, the sword caught me in the shoulder, slicing a thick line across it and up the side of my neck. I scrambled backward toward the middle of the balcony, clutching the injury.

Brandt towered over us, a vision of fight and fury as he swung again, his haste making him sloppy, missing Soren by inches.

"Finish him off." I was screaming, scrambling back from the swipes of the weapon, putting distance between us, my throat raw though I couldn't hear a word of it. "Finish him. Now."

In my periphery, a black dragon swooped, talons extended as she snatched up a half dozen soldiers rushing our way, including the general resplendent in his full-body armor.

Soren dodged another attack and finally registered the stone in his hand, the realization of the gift I'd given him dawning in his eyes. To my horror, he shoved it into his pocket.

"What are you doing?" My back crashed into the wall, my head rattling with the impact. Why didn't he just transform and—

The prince ducked another of the grand duke's attacks, then popped to his feet, arms twisted at an impossible angle as he wrestled the sword from his grip. Brandt slipped and caught himself, somehow staying on his feet, swaying precariously close to the edge as the prince approached. I could feel the burning vengeance emanating from his form as Soren strode forward, grip sure where the grand duke's had been shaky.

He drew the sword back and shouted, "This is for my family."

And he shoved the sword into Brandt's heart.

The man responsible for the oppression of our people, the one who gave the orders to cast them into the mines, the wolven who'd led the charge on the castle that had murdered the king and queen, the sick individual who'd executed Soren's brother and Lukas' father, stumbled. His mouth moved, hands gripping the blade shoved clean through his chest. His knees locked.

Soren stood coldly over him as he tipped over, skin pale, and went still.

A heavy thud shook the balcony again. The impact came to me as though from a great distance, and I spared the black dragon a single glance as I used the wall to pull myself upright. Zos spread her wings, a guardian watching over her prince. I clutched at my fresh injury, bunching my cloak around the wound, trying to staunch the flow of blood.

I felt drained, emotionally and physically. Every muscle in my body ached, and I wasn't sure if my torn and bloodied hands would ever be the same again. I dragged myself forward stiffly, right leg dragging from an injury I wasn't aware I'd gotten, and fumbled for Soren's hand as I drew level with his side. At first, he didn't respond, then his fingers firmed around mine.

"You did it," I heard myself saying. "You got your revenge."

Black eyes slick with unshed tears and bright as the fires burning along the outer wall found mine. I touched his cheek, leaving a streak of fresh blood, an imprint of the danger I'd endured left on him. He didn't seem to understand the magnitude of this moment, the realization of what had just happened.

The fighting below was dying down as our people raced through the streets, searching for wolven who'd escaped the immediate massacre. Smoke trickled from a hundred different spots in the city, curling and spiraling in thick, gray puffs. Drakken flew side-by-side with the dragons, their bodies tiny next to the gods, monitoring the fields for enemies trying to escape.

We'd done it.

I didn't know if Viv or Lukas or Archer—Aleksi—if any of them were still alive.

But we'd done it.

I wet my lips and pulled my hand away, the weight that had fallen upon my shoulders the moment I'd looked out over the expanse of my burning village, closed the wide eyes of my dead father, finally lifting. Bones creaking, I lowered to one knee, peering up at the prince through my one good eye. "Idilea is yours, my prince."

Zos prowled forward, the talons of her wings scraping against the stones. She, too, lowered her head in supplication. Two more dragons landed on the wall behind her, Ner's scales a fiery red that blended well with the light gold of Vey's perfect build. Two figures slipped from the gods' backs. My heart surged when I recognized the blond of Lukas' hair and the fiery gaze of Viv. They, too, dropped to their knees, and the dragons joined them in bowing their heads. The beasts crouched so low their jaws touched the ground.

I lowered my head as Soren spun in place, keeping my gaze fixed on his boots, giving him time to register the presence of the gods. His friends. I wondered if those below noticed the dragons and the singular figure standing atop the ruins of a city he'd been born in, and also bent the knee.

He knew. He had to know. This was it. The moment we'd all been fighting for.

The moment we retook our country, and he reclaimed his throne.

Another heavy thud rocked the balcony. The air swirled, tugging at my hair as the large being transformed from dragon to human. The man stepped forward, pale and glowing. Though I'd seen Zos more times than any other human alive, I didn't dare look up now, couldn't bear to meet the milky gaze that I knew must belong to the most righteous of the gods himself.

"Well fought, King Tristan," Qet said. "Your father would be proud."

52

Champion

He was the prince, but no one had properly prepared Soren for the role of *king*. He didn't know how to respond to his friends let alone the gods prostrating themselves before him—which I realized as the ache in my neck muscles grew with the weight of holding my head at such an awkward angle.

"I dare say that's enough of that." Zos' brashness saved us from what could have been days of bowing while Soren wrapped his mind around the reality of our situation. "I'm too old for things like bowing."

"Sister, you've only bowed thrice in your life," noted a third dragon with a voice like chimes muted by mist. Voices. Actual voices. Not the whispers that slipped through my thoughts. I lifted my head. A woman in long, sapphire robes embroidered with silver doves and long, black hair that pooled around her feet shot Zos a look.

Lo. In her human form.

All the dragons had assumed their human forms. From Ner with his bare chest slicked with black gore and oily blood, a hammer the size of his head clenched in one hand, to Vey with his wispy tunic and colorful gems dripping from his ears, neck, and arms, to Qet who shone so brilliantly it hurt to look his direction.

Idilea's seven gods and goddesses were all here, standing before us, gossiping as if we weren't bathed in blood, stinking of sweat and smoke and triumph.

"I fear there is still much to accomplish." Cas could have been Zos' twin. The sword hanging from the God of War's hip matched hers in every way except length. He tucked his bronze helmet under his arm and shook out his sweat-streaked hair. "I'm not sure how long we will be able to remain on this plane, but I certainly would like to rip a few more heads from bodies with what little time we have left."

"Here, here." Fen, with her catlike eyes, stroked the head of an owl. Not just any owl. Pip. I blinked. My bird perched on the goddess' shoulder, preening into her hand. Of course Pip would get along with the God of the Travelers and Messengers.

Viv stood with a grunt. She stood closest to the goddess and kept shooting her puzzled looks, as if not sure when she'd appeared. At her side, Lukas scowled around his broken nose, occasionally wiping blood that dripped from it with the back of his hand. Viv pointed at him and mouthed to me, "He lost his pen."

Qet inclined his head toward Soren, who had just helped me up. His hand locked around mine, grip so tight I felt my joints grinding to dust. "Shall we usher in a new era, King Tristan?" I fought a flinch at the unfamiliar title. "Your country has suffered much, but before it can heal, my brother Cas is correct. We still have much work to do."

Soren's grip relaxed, and I nearly moaned in relief.

"My gods, goddesses, may I extend the highest thanks from myself and from the people of Idilea for coming to our aid," he said. I flicked a look at him through my lashes, a little caught off-guard by the formality, though appropriate for the situation. "If you would, the

Fiorian army still exists far beyond the borders of Aeros. Would you help us track them down so we may expel them from our country?"

Cas didn't need to be asked twice. He jammed his helmet on his head and spun his sword, voice faintly metallic. "Fuck yeah. I want Dowhurst. Payback for what those bastards did to my temple."

Fen shooed Pip away. My owl launched herself at me, tucking her small body into the curve of my crossed arms in apology. Ner stepped to her side, rotating his hammer. "We'll handle the north."

"Do take care with the architecture," Vey drawled, twisting a fat ring rife with rubies on his middle finger. "I'll leave the bloodletting to you, but try to not create more work for me on the back end."

Qet raised his hand. "I'll head west. Come now."

Without a look back, the five dragons transformed into their more fearsome forms and launched into the sky, the wind from their wings threatening to knock the rest of us from the balcony. Soren watched them go with a faint smile, and though he shot Zos and Vey a look, it was to me and the approaching Viv and Lukas to whom he spoke. "I don't know how you pulled this off, but I'll never be able to thank you for your help."

Viv punched him lightly on the shoulder. "As if you need to pay us back, shortie. I had plenty fun breaking into the prison and releasing, well—" She brought her index finger to her chin, eyes glimmering. "Everyone. Archer. Tugs. Lukas here." She rapped her knuckles against his. "A wolven named Julian who told me to tell you he wouldn't die so easily, Tell." I shook my head, relieved he'd escaped after all. "And a bunch of other drakken locked away behind bars. I think they're the ones responsible for most of the destruction down there, anyway, pissy bunch of firestarters."

She grinned at me, tugging me to her side. "But I can't lay claim to the appearance of the gods. I'd say that's the doing of this one here."

I sputtered. "Hardly." But even as I said it, I recalled Zos' words at the temple, where she'd promised her assistance even as she mocked my very existence. But still. "They came when they were most needed, that's all."

Soren's eyes bored into mine. "You came for me; you saved my life and gave me the tools to take my revenge. When I check in with Archer later—" he swept his hand over the battlefield and the drakken soaring between the buildings, the flames flickering off their scales, disguising their colors. Much of the fighting had died down and many of the rioters had given up their hunt for blood and wandering around, dazed. "—I have a feeling he's going to tell me that you played a significant role with what we've achieved here today."

I studied my boots and the rips in the toes where the fabric had snagged on the grout. I didn't want recognition. Nothing I'd done here was out of selfishness—except maybe keeping my friends alive. This war and what came next was Soren's battle, not mine.

Yet that wasn't true either.

The moment I'd crashed into him, my life had irrevocably changed. No longer was I content to live alone, in silence, in the woods. The peace I had once sought had morphed, and though the grand duke was dead and much of the Fiorian army destroyed, I found myself craving more.

There was so much work to do and I wanted to be there for it. I wanted to stand by Soren's side as we rebuilt this country. I wanted to help Lukas fill books upon books with knowledge and drink in more of Archer's infinite wisdom. I wanted to explore my budding new relationship with Viv and learn how to tell vulgar jokes like Tugs.

I found the strength to look Soren in the eyes. "Whenever you want to talk, I'm ready."

"Can we get to work now?" Lukas grumbled, his words slurred

thanks to his nose. "If I stand around any longer, I am liable to fall asleep, and we should stop them from destroying *everything* in the castle before that happens."

I jolted. The castle. There was a chance Prince Dominik remained inside. He might be the enemy, but he had helped. We needed to find and secure him before something awful happened. "We need to go there now. It's a long story, but the Crown Prince of Fior helped make this all possible, too, and he's probably holed up inside. We need to help him."

Soren frowned, absorbing the crush of information. "Alright. Telleree, you come with me to the keep. Viv, you go with Lukas and round up the stragglers. Don't let them kill any more of the soldiers. Lock them away if possible." He paused. "The prison isn't too badly damaged, is it?"

Viv's tone was saccharine sweet. "I left it intact, if that's what you're asking. Figured you would want to use it at some point." Her expression turned positively wily when she pulled me close, bringing my lips to hers. I pulled her flush against me, realizing what she was up to even as bubbles of happiness burst in my chest, my arms snaking around her torso, lips softening against hers, turning her need to stake a claim into something more tender.

She was here, in my arms. Sassy. Alive.

When we'd parted ways in the midst of the crowd, I'd thought I might never see her again. Yet here she was. I swept some of her hair behind her cheek, slanting my mouth against hers twice more, then drew back. Moisture glimmered in her eyes, making the green sparkle in the torchlight. Her throat worked as she swallowed. "Stay safe?"

"Always," I replied.

She spun away and jammed her index finger into Soren's chest, the prince's expression unreadable. "When I tell her to stay safe,

I'm really telling you to keep her safe, got that? Anything happens to her and you will answer to me." She smacked her chest and the bandolier of knives she still kept strapped there. She would need to adjust the handles when she had time, so they hung from the side where she could reach all of them easily.

"Sure thing, spitfire." But a heavy emotion passed between them, despite the lightness of Soren's words. "Let's go before anything more happens."

"A moment, please, before you all righteously take back your city." I wheeled when Zos spoke. Vey had seemingly vanished for the time being. "Ms. Falk. A few words?"

Viv tugged on my cloak and Soren gave me a look that said he would tell the goddess to shove off if I asked, but I waved away their concerns. Whatever she had to say to me, I was strong enough to hear.

Five paces to the goddess and I stared up at her, towering over me, even now. She'd transformed from the woman I'd first met at the temple. That mocking smirk, the haughty tilt of her chin, the inflated chest puffed up with pride were gone, though the raw power in her iris-less eyes remained. She evaluated me, still standing, refusing to bow in her presence.

"You've grown into the woman I'd hoped you would become and more."

It took everything I had to not rock back on my heels. I'd promised myself I would feel nothing, would take whatever critique she doled out without protest. But I hadn't anticipated praise. It warmed parts of me I'd feared would be cold forever.

Zos glanced to the skies and the moon that hung low in the clouds. "You stumbled. You fell. But you pulled yourself back up again. You found your purpose and reclaimed your guiding light." She braced her hand on her sword, thumbing the clear stone pounded into the top. "Everyone loses faith, but only the hardiest find it again—even fewer truly embrace it in their darkest, most miserable moments."

I lowered my eyes. The temple. She was referencing the second time I'd visited her. When I'd sobbed and raged and spilled all my hurt and frustration and anger.

Zos' touch on my chin was icy cold, a stark contrast to the heat that had seared me the last time we'd touched. She lifted my face to peer directly into hers. "I'm proud to call you my Champion, Telleree Falk. May we one day meet again."

I couldn't explain the feeling that surged through me, like the crashing of a blizzard meeting the warmth of a fresh spring day—all of the most beautiful moments I'd ever experienced in my life balled up into one. As she walked away, arms spread as she unfurled her dragon's wings, swathing herself in the cloak of night once more, I couldn't move, struck by her parting words.

Zos' Champion.

Me.

Soren approached. I'd recognize the heaviness of his stride anywhere. He said something that got snared in the sticky webs of my thoughts while I watched her dive to the city and the wreckage below.

My fingers found the tattoo on my wrist and I squeezed.

53

Do You Trust Me?

Cheers went up. Soren wheeled overhead with me on his back, and the hundreds of people lingering outside the castle pumped their fists in the air. Some foisted torches that reminded me of the stars sprinkled across the heavens. I doubted any of them recognized him as royalty, but the mere sight of a drakken was like water presented to a dehydrated woman. Now that the shifters had reclaimed their birthrights, I hoped they would remain a frequent sight around the capital and our country.

Using my knees to brace on Soren's back between the rhythmic pumping of his wings, I pointed one gloved finger at the tallest spire of the keep, the one where the royal family had once resided. He angled in response and I flattened against him, braid flopping against my shoulder as he increased his speed. I loved this feeling: the swooshing of my stomach, the thrill of peering down at the world from above, the hint of trepidation of riding an arrow's edge between necessary risk and pure folly.

All too soon, he banked and landed, talons clattering on the hardened tile of the roof. I slid off and adjusted my clothing, checking for tears while Soren transformed back into his human self. There wasn't anything he could do to soften the edges of his scales, but I had thrown a blanket over part of his back, which had protected my arms and legs from the worst of the damage.

"No wolven on the castle grounds," he observed, tucking his shirt into his pants. Though the wind ripped at us, he didn't so much as shiver in his thin black shirt. "And while I wouldn't put it past them to ransack the castle, it doesn't look like your rioters are trying to burn it down."

He said it affectionately. Proudly.

My rioters.

Snorting, I unstrapped his sword from its spot between my shoulder blades, flat against my spine, and handed it over, careful to keep our hands from touching. Now that my relief at finding him alive had faded, I wasn't sure how to act around him. Everything we'd gone through felt too fresh, and I wasn't sure how to balance my new relationship with Viv with the intimacy he and I had shared.

"It's possible Aleksi is keeping the most rambunctious hot-heads cool." I slid down the tiles to the overhang of the window that opened just below the edge of the roof. "Or it could be they realize it's still your home—just with a bunch of strangers living in it. No point in destroying it."

Soren rubbed his scar, skeptical, and joined me. "Explain to me again why we're looking for a Fiorian prince and why I should care about his welfare."

"Let's get inside first." I swung so my back was to the open air and slid down the side of the castle, searching for the windowsill with my toes. Soren snagged my wrist, holding me steady, and I dropped to the platform with ease. The window opened without a squeak of complaint, and I slipped inside. Soren followed in short order, silent on the plush carpet.

We'd entered some sort of sitting room. A settee embroidered with pink thread and three hard-backed chairs ringed a golden coffee table on one side of the room, opposite a wall of glasses and plates that looked far too breakable. A map of Idilea engulfed another wall, cleverly worked around the closed door, while portraits of people with straight faces and hawkish eyes adorned another.

"We're outside my parent's chambers." Soren nodded to a door tucked between the bar and the wall. His expression was hooded. "This was where they met their most personal guests. Friends. People they trusted implicitly. Eero and I were only allowed in here on rare occasions. We had our own rooms on the other side of the spire."

I took in the delicate patterns painted onto the chairs, the china plates stacked on a tri-legged table, and understood why children wouldn't have been allowed in here much. I couldn't imagine the pain he must be feeling being back in here, so close to the place where he'd been with his family the most, yet so far from them in reality. Even Zos couldn't bring back the dead.

I plucked a crystal goblet off the serving station, needing something in my hands. "We are searching for Crown Prince Dominik Zeit, his best friend, who you probably met in jail—Colonel Julian Kohl—and any people of Fior he might be protecting. I know he was escorted here, but I'm not sure what happened after that."

"And what exactly did this *prince*—" Soren spat the word like poison—"do to endear himself to us? His father ordered this invasion. His mother sustained it. And he came here to watch me die. Why do I care what happens to him, again?"

"Soren, you can't keep thinking like that." Patterns painted on the chilled metal dented the skin of my hands. "The sins of the parents aren't the sins of the child, and he's working to rectify that blight on his record. It's because of his help we were able to stage this rescue at all. He risked the life of his best friend to find us—and took a huge risk by meeting with us in person. He helped us break into the prison, and while our plan didn't work, he also gave us the drakkentorre that spurred so much hope. The stone I gave to you came from him, too."

Soren's brow lifted, and he pulled the stone from his pocket once more, examining it as if it was a bug that might bite.

"That was a stone your father gave him when he was a boy. He's returned it to you," I explained.

The shifter closed his hand around the rock. "I sense there's more to your worry."

I put the goblet down and crossed to the door built into the wall with the map. It swung wide on silent hinges. "Lenore was your rat. She fed Brandt information about the attack on the mines and details about our plan to break you out. She was there when we met with the prince and he sold us his treasonous soul. There's no way the duke didn't know he was involved."

"Good to know." Soren felt for a torch on the wall and flicked his flint and steel over the top. "I get all that. But what makes you think he's still alive? Or that we can even find him in this mess? The castle is bigger than it looks."

I hovered several feet behind him as he walked, flashing the torch into various rooms as we passed. "Soren, do you really not get it? If we find him and we keep word of his involvement from getting out, we can end this war. He wants to surrender. He wants to give up his country's illegitimate claim on our territory. We find him—"

The torch swung my way, revealing the triumphant look on Soren's face, the stern set of his jaw. "We end this here and now."

I nodded, the motion pulling on my partially healed wound. That seemed to be enough for the prince, who I still had a difficult time viewing as a king, who moved at a faster clip, apparently satisfied we were alone when no wolven jumped out and attacked. The rioters must have not made it up this high, likely distracted by the riches in the guest rooms one floor down as well as the various servant's rooms on the first and second levels.

My theory was proven correct when we finally emerged at the base of the tower. Dozens of people lingered in the halls, limbs twitchy, eyes bright with lust as they shoved their pockets full of bits of gold and items they found in the rooms. They paid us little heed, distracted by the triumph of having breached their target. However, something must have seemed off to Soren, who took my hand in his and pulled me to his side, eyes shifting from side to side.

I felt a little better for it.

We left no room untouched, carefully picking our way through the third floor before descending to the second, finding even more people scattered about. I knew we were getting closer to our target when the crowd thickened, their grumbling growing louder at the far end of one long hall. Soren abandoned his torch and shouldered his way through the crowd, his grip firm around my hand. When we finally hit a point in the masses where he couldn't walk any farther, he snapped.

"Your prince is here," he shouted into the fray. Someone else seemed to be having trouble with titles. "Given you're in my home, I would think you'd have more respect."

A few people threw us wild looks and the tenor of conversations changed. More than a few stared skeptically, and one man finally said what everyone was thinking. "I heard Prince Tristan died. Who's to say you're not an imposter?"

Soren held up his arm and tugged back his sleeve, revealing the shimmering red tattoo of his family's crest on his bicep: a pair of crossed swords with a shadowy dragon flying overhead. Red ink was so rare only royalty could afford it. "Do you want me to transform, too?" Soren asked icily.

That was enough proof for everyone in our vicinity, who shuffled aside, clearing a path. Some dropped to their knees, and most bowed their heads. The rest of the crowd picked up on the cue and stepped out of the way, leaving a long path clear to the end.

When we finally reached the massive set of double doors marking the largest of the keep's ballrooms, I nearly froze in shock when I realized who was causing all the commotion. "Archer? You're here?"

I pushed Soren aside and flung myself at the silvery figure swathed in light and coated in blood. He swept me up, pressing his face into my shoulder. "I've been hearing a lot about you," he said, setting me down before clasping Soren's hand. "And you're the reason for this mess, highness. Are you pleased with our efforts?"

"I'm actually not sure if enough blood was shed today," Soren quipped.

The two murmured too low for me to hear, and I eyed the rest of the group standing before the doors, weapons drawn. Tugs shouted my name in his booming voice. Crude and crusty bandages were wrapped around his head, obscuring one eye, but he grinned despite it. Several other faces seemed familiar, though I couldn't place their names—other members of the Requiem who must have come to Archer's aid.

The fact they were barricading this room meant something.

"Is Prince Zeit in there?" I asked Tugs under my breath. "Is that who you're protecting?"

"One in the same."

Archer rapped the door with his knuckle. "The prince gathered those who arrived with him and squirreled them away in there. Smart, really. The windows in that one have inner shutters. Not as easy for a drakken to crash through them. I thought it would take us forever to find 'em, but Aleksi figured it out pretty quick."

I scanned the faces. "Where is Aleksi, anyway?"

"Went to protect the crown jewels, or what remains of them." Archer gripped the pommel of the sword sheathed at his hip when one of the watchers got a little too close for comfort. "We hunkered down here, hoped you would show up at some point. Honestly, weren't sure if we were wasting our time." He paused. "I hate to ask, but did Lukas and Viv find you guys?"

Soren nodded. "They're cleaning up the city with Zos and Vey."

Archer blinked. "Excuse me?"

"Details, details. We're getting off track and this crowd is getting rowdy." I nudged Tugs aside. "We need to resolve this situation before we can't hold them back anymore."

Soren sighed, clearly not liking where this was going, despite the case I'd laid out before him.

"Do you trust me?" I finally asked, hands on my hips. He'd wanted me to be an advisor, one who didn't always advocate for bloodshed. Consider this his first test.

He held my stare before dropping his shoulders. "I'll follow your lead, Telleree."

Archer pulled a key from his pocket and shoved it into the tiny hole. "The three of us?"

"Always."

He knocked three times on the door. "Open up. Crown Prince Tristan Ahlgren wishes to meet with you."

The door opened a crack. A single pale blue eye peered out at us. "Crown Prince Zeit wishes to know the context of your conversation."

Soren nudged me aside. "The terms of your surrender."

54

By My Side

O ne month later

I shoved a sheaf of documents into the overflowing pouch of paperwork hanging from the corner of my desk and dropped my head in my hands, rubbing my smarting eyes. I needed a break. Reviewing the latest batch of reports from the four mines and our efforts to aid those we'd liberated from them had a way of draining me dry. Those in hospitals represented roughly a quarter of our population, and only a fraction of the drakken who'd embraced their abilities before the invasion had made it out alive.

Talons scratched on my desk and I turned my head so my cheek pressed against my folded arms. Pip chirped, pecking at the quill I'd shoved into a damp sponge on my desk. A shadowy figure sliced through the sunshine pouring through the wide array of windows overhead, and the snowy owl settled in the rafters among the other owls. Carrier pigeons cooed from their nests across the room, wary of the birds of prey. I'd instructed the owls to not harm our messengers, but instincts were instincts.

I'd called dibs on the aviary before the dust settled in the aftermath of the fighting, and no one protested when I took over my father's old offices. Given my newfound stature as the girl who'd roused the gods, it wasn't safe for me to hide in the comfort of the woods that surrounded Aeros, and I needed my birds around me somehow. Soren had offered me the guest room with the widest balcony, one right below his, but I'd declined. This tower and its distance from the main castle felt most like home to me.

I stroked Pip's head, and she nipped at my fingernail.

Things moved quickly after Prince Dominik agreed to the terms of his people's surrender. His mother had apparently sent him to the execution as a representative of the crown, with all the authority that came with it.

Soren had asked for a lot, more than I expected, and the Fiorian prince signed off on nearly every point: Fior withdrew its claim on Idilea's territory, all wolven were removed from Idilean borders, all drakkentorre that had been mined and stolen from our lands would be returned, and a lump payment of one million fifes, a number that made my jaw drop, would help us rebuild our lands.

Dominik hadn't batted an eye. His only amendment was to pay the sum over a period of ten years with a promise to reexamine trade opportunities in the future.

In the weeks that followed, Dominik made good on his promises. Most of the surviving wolven were sent back to Fior in droves. I asked Soren if he wanted any of them to stay, to try them in court and seek justice. He'd given me a look and said if they didn't leave now, he would run them through with his sword. That was all the justice he could stomach.

It was an answer I didn't like, but could accept.

I hoped he wouldn't regret that decision one day.

The Crown Prince of Fior still had yet to leave. He was overseeing the stragglers we kept uncovering in the forests and deep in the mines, making sure they were properly escorted to the border.

"I'm in deep enough trouble back home as it is," he told me as we watched the last round of wolven depart the capital four days ago. "I'm in no hurry to face the wrath of my mother. I deserve it. I'm prepared for it. But hurrying back now does me little good." He flashed that too-white smile, one tinged with deep sadness. "It might even come across as suspicious."

Now, I straightened the three piles of paperwork crowding the far side of my desk.

The people of Idilea were proving as resilient as ever. I thought more might protest Soren's decision to cast the wolven from the country without trial, but they showed a surprising lack of interest in the matter. I believed most wanted to move on from the horrors forced upon our country rather than hold trials that would only extend the healing process and potentially open new wounds.

Part of me was glad. We didn't have much of a justice system in place, and creating one would have been a nightvision on top of everything else demanded of the crown. From protection from looters to requests for more supplies, our work was never done. The mountain just kept growing.

One of our primary efforts was rebuilding the battered parts of Aeros—the neighborhoods ruined by fires and riots. The other three major cities also required a significant amount of work. On top of monitoring our situation with the mines, I helped Lukas navigate much of that effort. If I thought the paperwork on my desk was bad, there wasn't an inch of space left on any of his seven desks or his bed.

Aleksi returned to Dowhurst to oversee matters there, and Archer was helping with redevelopment issues in Stavanger—taking a temporary reprieve from his role as Soren's Chief Advisor. Tugs was gallivanting all over the country, too, managing the small, yet fierce band of warriors he hoped to transition into our first official army in seventeen years. Right now, they were focused on catching robbers and thieves.

"Look at you." I perked up at the voice coming from the doorway. "Right where I left you."

Viv leaned against the doorjamb, hand on her hip, knife in its sheath on her thigh, inches away. Sticks and straw were matted in her hair, her tunic dark with sweat around her neck and chest, and the gray trousers she'd left in this morning were almost black with mud. To me, she had never looked so beautiful.

"The work never ends," I replied, rising on knees gone stiff with disuse. I lifted my legs experimentally, wincing at the pinpricks as my blood started flowing again. "If I don't hold up my end of the bargain, you know Lukas will throw a tantrum."

"We wouldn't want Lukas to get angry." Viv sauntered closer.

I pulled her into a tight embrace, pressing my nose to the curve between her neck and shoulder, inhaling her lemonseed scent. "Never." She shivered when my lips grazed her skin.

"You know." Her voice hitched as I ran the tip of my nose up the line of her neck. "You're still perfectly clean. Pristine. And I'm all muddy and sweaty and worked up." I hid the smile that wanted to burst from me like sunshine. Her hand swept up my spine. "It wouldn't take much for you to come down to my level. It might be fun, even."

My shoulders shook with the effort it took to not burst out laughing. But she knew my tells and thrust me away, eyes hooded playfully, offsetting the stern expression on her face.

"You'll need more than that to get me to join you out there, teaching the castle guard defensive maneuvers." My laughter subsided. "But that was a pretty good try." I hoisted myself onto the edge of my desk and crossed my legs at the ankle. "How is training going, anyway?"

Viv covered her yawn with the back of her hand and reached for the mug of lukewarm tea on my desk. I enjoyed the floral scent while I worked, but I rarely remembered to drink more than a few sips. "They're eager. Many of them are battered and bruised, but they want to learn. I can work with that." Viv launched into the story of our youngest recruit, describing in detail a take-down she performed on a man four times bigger than she was.

I spun a quill between my fingers, appreciating the roughness of her voice, the excitement that danced in her eyes when she mimicked a complicated move. Viv had worked nonstop just like the rest of us these past few weeks, toiling alongside carpenters and farmers and whoever else needed assistance, refusing to let her injury hold her back. Last week, Soren had asked her to put together a group of elite fighters who would serve as the castle guard. He wanted her to train them to the best of her ability—which we both knew was substantial.

"He asked me to be captain of the guard."

My mind went blank. "What?"

"Soren. He wants me to stay here, in the capital." She tugged the tie from the end of her mangled braid and wiggled the loops apart. "He's impressed with the work I'm doing and asked me to head the guard. He says it's a perfect fit and I can join the army for exercises whenever I want, so I won't feel too strapped down."

Clever. He claimed he would make a terrible king because he knew absolutely nothing about politics or decorum, but I had to hand it to him: Soren was a born tactician. The beautiful flower that was his offer also came with its share of thorns.

"What did you say?" I asked, fiddling with a spare quill.

She fought a particularly tough tangle of hair. "I told him I wouldn't give an answer until you made your decision." She winked. "You know I always give as good as I get."

My belly swooped, tingles sparking low against my spine. Did I ever. Soren may have handed her a barbed rose, but Viv came packing knives.

"Have you decided?" she asked.

I had. And I hadn't. She read the indecision on my face. "He wants to see you in the throne room. Something about sending that 'Good-for-Nothing-Waste-of-Space-Pompous-Asshole-Prince' off once and for all?"

That sounded like Soren. Tugs had returned this morning, so I figured he would likely escort the last dozen wolven to the border. Prince Dominik would be among them.

"I'll go now. I need a break before my eyes start bleeding." With a sigh, I hefted my heavy bag of paperwork over my shoulder. It all needed to go to the main castle with me. "The throne room, you said?"

Preparations for his upcoming coronation were well underway, and Soren typically avoided that part of the castle.

Viv tugged on the strap across my chest before I got too far. "Think about your answer to him on your walk. You know his patience only stretches so far."

I did. Just like I knew the location of this meeting served a dual purpose.

"I will," I promised.

She dipped, and when our lips brushed, my heart fluttered wildly. I slanted my head, finding the perfect fit of the bow of our lips, savoring her taste. This evolution to our relationship was still shiny as freshly polished silver and just as vulnerable to dents and damage. We'd had our share of fights, but we were finding our footing.

"Get cleaned up," I ordered her. "I can tell the mud is making you twitchy."

She saluted as I slipped out the door.

* * *

The sun shone warmly upon my face as I crossed the castle grounds, meandering through the wildflowers rather than the stone path they lined. I hooked my fingers around the strap of my bag, hugging it tightly against me. In the distance, swords clanged and hammers banged, the sounds of training and reconstruction still lively despite it being past noon, assuming I'd counted the latest round of bells correctly.

Soren had asked me to stay on as his personal advisor, a position of equal weight to Lukas and Archer, who both served on the cabinet. He claimed he needed me by his side to offer the advice he feared no one else would be brave enough voice. I argued Lukas always had the best vision for the country in mind, but Soren reminded me of how easily Lukas got lost in his experiments and translations. He wanted the pair of us together, offering dueling perspectives, one rooted in a moral compass and the other in brutal reality, just like we had on the road to Stavanger.

That offer had come two weeks ago, and I still had yet to make a decision.

On one hand, I was flattered the future king wanted me to stand by his side and guide Idilea through this critical time of reconstruction. The position came with stability, authority, and an opportunity to do good for the nation. I rubbed my face. On the other hand, things were still strained between us as we navigated the waters of our friendship. Choosing to stay by his side also meant forever giving up the last vestiges of the freedom I'd enjoyed so much in the Owl Wood.

It was more than that, too.

My name was one that people knew. They referred to me as the Right Hand of Zos after word of her claiming me as her champion got out. Plenty of people had seen me in my cloak of feathers riding across the country, shouting hostilities to the wolven, climbing the walls of the castle, even standing before the goddess of death herself the day of our Requiem. I was keenly aware of the stares in the marketplace and the quivering voices of children who asked if they could touch my cloak or tattoo. Many came to me hoping for an answer or miracle.

To stay by Soren's side meant embracing that role and using it responsibly. I never wanted to wield it like a weapon, even though I already had: inciting the riot hadn't come without its costs.

I stepped into the shadow of the main castle doors, flung wide to allow the warmth of the changing seasons in. As expected, the great hall was bustling. Women carrying armfuls of blue and yellow ribbons fluttered across the room, their soft voices drowned out by the hammering and sawing of carpenters working on the walls and windows and doors. One woman lay on her back on the scaffolding, paintbrush in hand, working on a design of Qet that would engulf the ceiling. A boy pulling a handcart of potted plants nearly crashed into me when I entered the mayhem, and I swung to the right where I would find the throne room at the end of the hall.

The tall, wide door with the Idilean crest painted upon its surface was closed. I adjusted my bag, so it stopped cutting into my shoulder, knocked twice, and pulled the door wide. Someone had pulled back the heavy blue drapes that traditionally obscured the floor-to-ceiling windows, illuminating the pattern of scales cleverly worked into the floor tile. Carefully, I set my bag beside the door and walked down the center of the room, in the middle of those arching scales, fixed on the figure lounging in a tall, wooden-backed throne at the far end of the room. Soren's dark clothing nearly blended in with the walnut wood and black velvet cushions. His leg thrown over one arm was the only thing that gave him away as his foot bobbed in time to some inner tune.

"You look comfortable for a man who insists thrones were made for discomfort," I said, stopping a few yards away from the dais upon which the throne sat. "I thought you said something about avoiding this room as much as realistically possible."

Soren surveyed me for a long moment. "Can you hear the din? Everyone's so loud and cheery it's impossible to think. Figured if they were doing what they could to get ready for this damned coronation, then I might as well make my peace with the space where I'll live out the rest of my days."

He sounded so forlorn I wanted to laugh. "Poor baby prince. Do you need someone to hold your hand?"

He removed his leg from the arm of the chair, straightening. "Eero would have made a far better king than me; I was never meant for all this fuss and muss." He ran a hand down his face, concealing the grief he admitted hit him on the best of days. "But I'll do my best to serve the way he would have."

I sensed what was coming next. Braced for it.

"I need you by my side, Telleree." He leaned forward, elbows braced on his knees. I never could look away from him when his eyes were this intense. "My father and brother both had morals I'll never possess. I live for blood, breathe in battle. I don't know how to be fair or manage justice. I never learned how to manipulate people to do my will, especially when I need them to do things I don't want them to do."

I mounted the first step. "Lukas can help you with all that. He's the most elegant person I've ever met, and surely he's read enough books to help you navigate your way through diplomacy."

Soren was already shaking his head. "I need Lukas like I need my left lung. He's a necessity in my life and one I'll be forever grateful to have by my side. He and I understand one another. We get how the other thinks. We adapt to our strengths and weaknesses, and we also give each other leeway because we know each other so well. I need someone who isn't afraid to speak their mind, who won't hesitate to call either of us out and force us to consider our actions a different way." He rose fluidly, the gold embroidery of his tunic catching the afternoon light in such a way that he practically glowed.

"You've never hesitated to put your foot down. You regularly go head to head with Lukas, and you disagree with me all the time." He toyed with a golden button on his sleeve. "You believe in this world in a way I'll never be able to: both in the goodness of people and in your faith in the gods."

We still butted heads over our viewpoints on religion, though I held my tongue this time, unwilling to reignite the fight.

Despite seeing the gods with his own eyes and hearing Qet's rumbling voice with his own ears, Soren still lacked faith in their abilities. He no longer doubted their presence, but he did not believe they always acted in the betterment of our country. He claimed Idilea had gone too long without their support and he would never give them his endorsement—no matter how many bowed their heads before him.

Zos. What a mess.

"Soren—"

"Archer says I need a pacifist on my team." He took two steps down, less than three yards from me now. "He says it's good for me to think less about fighting and more about the spoken word." His lips quirked in that smile I couldn't quite resist. "You fit that mold perfectly."

I rolled my eyes. "I'm not a pacifist. I believe in the necessity of violence as much as you do. I'm just more willing to try other routes first."

"Exactly." He hopped down the final step. "Archer, Lukas, Tugs, even Viveca—we all think with the sword first and our tongues last. I need you to counter that, to give us the perspective we all desperately need."

If I had any resolve to not take this job, it would have crumbled into a pile of smoking rubble at my feet.

"Please, Telleree," he whispered. "Don't leave us. Don't leave me. You're meant to be here, helping me rule this country." He reached for my hand but stopped short, remembering the distance I always put between us. "Help me be the king Eero would want me to be."

My voice was trapped in my chest, caught behind a bundle of feathers in my throat.

I knew what I wanted to say. I'd come to my decision before he'd asked Viv to join as the captain of his guard. I had my doubts, but I felt it was right. Aeros had become the place where I belonged. I'd said to Viv once that my peace now resided alongside the will of the nation, that my purpose had expanded far beyond the reaches of the Copper Mountains and the Owl Wood.

Purpose that hadn't ended with the war.

The feathers floated away.

"Yes." I drew up straight. "I'll stand by your side. I'll provide your counterpoint. I'll be what you need me to be—to an extent—until the end of our days."

Soren stood so still I thought I might have spoken a spell that turned him to stone. Then his arms twitched as if to reach for me, to pull me against him, blinking back emotion that filled his eyes to the brim. Yet he respected our boundary. That thick, dark line that ran between us.

My heart thumped.

I'd made my decision. I knew who I would love for the rest of my life, but part of me would always yearn for the impossibility of him. Soren deserved someone as good for him as Viv was good for me.

Someone who would help this country heal and provide the support he desired.

"I feel like I need to call a ceremony or order a banquet." The prince slumped on the stairs, legs flung out in front of him, relief softening his features, making him appear the twenty-two winters he was.

"Let's not get carried away." I quirked my thumb over my shoulder. Coincidentally, we had dressed similarly today: black on black with hits of gold, not a cloak in sight. "I just ran the numbers, and our coffers are depressingly low."

He laughed, the sound easy and relaxed. "Alright. How about you and Viveca join me and Lukas for a meal tonight, something small and simple? It's not every day I finish filling my cabinet."

I wondered how many moments like this we would have in the years ahead, him sharing this surprisingly light side to his soul. It called to me the same way his darkness drew me in.

"I think that sounds wonderful."

A trio of bells trilled outside, and his smile slipped into a scowl. "But first, let's cast that Fiorian rabble from our borders. I can't wait to get that poor excuse for a prince out of my home."

I hitched my bag over my shoulder. "Let me remind you for the dozenth time that prince saved your life and sacrificed his pride and possibly his throne to set our country free. Without his help, we might still be on the run today. Or dead."

Soren matched my stride. "I know, I know."

"He's going to be a powerful ally one day. I can feel it."

Before he pushed the door wide, the prince hesitated, palm braced flat on the wood. "See what I mean about faith? It isn't just belief in those gods of yours, either. It's in people and the goodness of which you think they're capable. I can't think like that, but I'll believe you. Always."

Together, we pushed the door wide and stepped out into a world. One bright and beautiful and full of potential.

I'd love to hear your input about my latest universe. From ratings to reviews, I want to know what you think, how Of Dragons of Defiance made you feel.

The part of my brain that loves spinning stories never quits, so I'm always tinkering with some project or another. Stay up-to-date with my work by signing up for my newsletter. In those, you'll discover book updates and free, exclusive content related to The Three Kingdoms trilogy and my other work.

To find out more, head to www.septemberthomas.com.

Author's Note

This book flowed from me like a sigh of relief. After diving deeply into a previous universe, it was truly wonderful exploring this new world and the kingdoms within it. I never thought I'd write about shifters. Many books I read feature shifters, but as an author, they never appealed to me. Until now.

Every element of this book came easily. Surprisingly easily. I pictured the opening scene while hiking up a mountain on the outskirts of Denver, Colorado. Tell's fall from the cliff - also inspired by that same climb. I clearly remember picturing the dragons swooping below the cliff I stood upon, could feel Tell's relief when she realized she was safe.

I also had an intense desire to write a female character who didn't want to fight. Who wasn't good at it—and knew it, too. Tell encompasses so much of what I appreciate in strong women: fierce resolve, unwavering loyalty, a curious mind. Though afraid to leave the familiar behind, she rallied her introvert spirit and faced her fate. She's subtly feminine without being too masculine. She loves and heals and believes and is that person I think we all need in our lives: the one who sees the stars not as big balls of gas burning in the skies, but as the dreams we aspire to reach.

I have to mention Soren here, too. My favorite drakken is an amalgamation of a popular anime character I adore and the desire to see "short men" in literary fiction accomplish fantastical things, who risk losing themselves in their mission if they aren't careful. His straightforward attitude calls to me.

Tell and Soren were such opposites, yet their story came to me so naturally. Cohesion at its finest.

Speaking of cohesion, this story wouldn't be as beautiful without the attentive efforts of my favorite editor, Fiona McLaren. To my family, who has always stood beside me in my pursuit of my dreams - and especially my Mom, who I recognize in this dedication. To Anna and Amsley, who are the epitome of supportive, the kind of friends every writer needs in their life. And to Josh, who gave me the space I needed to get all these words down on a page.

Finally - to Sydney. Who laid for too many long hours behind my chair in the office, waiting patiently for the passing pat and occasional comment of how wonderful she truly is. She heard every click of the keyboard and every frustrated rambling. She knows this book start to finish like no one else ever could.

About the Author

September Thomas is the author of The Three Kingdoms trilogy and The Elemental Gods series. She lives in Nebraska with her boyfriend and rescued Australian Cattle Dog. She also boasts a large collection of owls that some consider amusingly ridiculous.

You can connect with me on:

- https://www.septemberthomas.com
- https://www.facebook.com/SeptemberThomasAuthor
- https://www.instagram.com/september.thomas
- https://www.pinterest.com/september_thomas

Subscribe to my newsletter:

- https://www.septemberthomas.com

Also by September Thomas

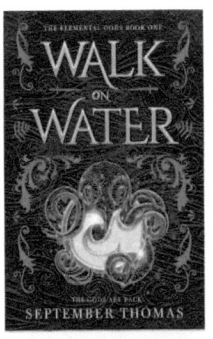

Walk on Water
After 2,000 years, magic is finally back. 17-year-old Zara Ramone wants none of it. Too bad a dark force bent on destruction won't let her stay on the sidelines.

Fan the Flame
My name is Zara Ramone.
I should have died several times now.
But the fates aren't ready to let me go.

Wind and Reign
When the magic turns against its maker, is she ready?
Zara Ramone set out to get stronger.
She didn't expect to uncover a sinister plot to destroy magic forever.

War of Earth
Reincarnated God of Water Zara Ramone finally understands who she is and what she stands for, but will she have the fortitude to overcome her greatest challenge yet?

Rise from Ruin
Zara Ramone sacrificed her magic, body, and soul to save the world from annihilation, only to release a far greater evil.